Code Red

Reclaiming Wonderland #1

Taila Cantrell

Contents

To Grammy, who always supported my dreams, and believed in me when I didn't believe in myself. I miss you every day.

And to all the people who left and the bridges that were burned.

Oh 'tis love, 'tis love that make the world go 'round.
    -Lewis Carroll

The Sectors of Wonderland

Sector One: The Red Party's base (formerly the White King's home), home and offices of the high-ranking members of the Red Party.

Sector Two: The business quarter, offices, banks, etc.

Sector Three: The Grove, theaters, museums, galleries, etc.

Sector Four: Department store, electricity hub, etc.

Sector Five: Middle class apartments and jobs.

Sector Six: Uninhabitable due to the destruction during the final days.

Sector Seven: The Hearts Club and other night life.

Sector Eight: Inhabited by animals, avoided by most citizens of Wonderland.

Sector Nine: Suit barracks and training center.

Sector Ten: The mental hospital and other doctors' offices. Many buildings in this sector were destroyed before The Dome was in place.

Sector Eleven: Dodo's store, the bistro, as well as other shopping and fast food.

Sector Twelve: Hatter and Dina's apartments. Lower class living area and jobs, heavily policed but not well maintained.

Prologue

Recovered from the dream diaries of Eumonia Lyon 2157

Panting breaths echoed off the bare concrete walls of the tiny cell. No one in the house above would concern themselves with the older woman chained to the floor, even if they knew she was there. Too afraid of the woman's captor to save her from the years of torture she'd already endured. Once bright golden hair hung lank and tangled around her head. Sweat dripped off her pale forehead onto the floor. The heat of the cell was crushing, another way to torture her. She could hardly remember her own name. Only the memory of her daughters' smiling faces stopped her from giving in to the pain that wreaked havoc on her body. She shook the thoughts of them from her head, always careful to keep them at a distance. Heels clicking on the stone floor caused her eyes to well with tears, but they never fell. So, it began again. Another day trapped in a hell of her own choosing. Sudden pain forced a scream from her dry throat before the figure even appeared in the doorway. When it stopped, the first thing she saw were red eyes glaring down at her. The anger in those eyes filled her with a numb, cold feeling. What mistakes had led her here? She couldn't remember exactly how long it had been. Her days were filled with pain, but staring into the eyes of her older sister, seeing the hatred that dwelled there. That was one of the worst pains of all.

"So, Cindy, are you ready to tell me where I can find your precious daughter?"

She had been resolute for years; no words would leave her lips. Her sister would never get a single piece of information from her. Anything to protect her city, to protect them.

A sigh of disappointment left the woman looming over her. "You can't protect her forever. If she is so powerful, she'll never be able to avoid me."

Ignoring the words, her mind wandered again to her family. Their golden hair that shone in sunlight, a trait that she had passed to her daughters. Lily was a protector of those around her, just like her father. Pain shot through her heart at the thought of Charles. The father of her girls had saved her in more ways than one, but they were alone, with no parents to guide them through the confusion of young adulthood. She'd already missed so much of their lives, years locked in a dungeon. It didn't matter. She would always protect them. That was a mother's love. When another wave of agony rushed through her, she couldn't tell if just the thought of them caused it, or if once again her sister was torturing her. Few things haunted her, but the lack of time she had with them would always be her biggest regret.

"Really, this is getting quite boring." Fingers dug into her scalp, fire spread down to her limbs, she couldn't even scream as it clawed at her voice box. Sweat dripped down her nose, but she stared steadily into her sister's red eyes.

"Pen…" A hesitant male voice cut off the pain suddenly, and she collapsed onto the stone floor with a sob of relief.

"I told you to never interrupt me, Frederick." Her sister snapped at him.

"Knave just brought me the records you've been hunting for," He rushed to say.

Her ears perked up, a sick feeling forming in the pit of her stomach had her dragging her tired body off the floor. The manila envelope held aloft in the air seemed to float there for a moment. Time stopped, as a toothy, evil grin spread across her sister's face. Long nails ripped through the paper, red eyes widening as they frantically scanned the pages.

"Lilian Young?" She cackled, "Named after our cunt mother, and you really believed I'd never figure it out."

Horror filled her at the sound of her oldest daughter's name leaving that hateful mouth. The sick glee in her sister's eyes forced the small amount of food she was allowed each day from her stomach.

"I have her now, Cindy." She took a few steps, bending to eye level, "You suffered for nothing. I'll rend the flesh from her bones slowly, forcing you to watch as I kill the only hope for your little Resistance. Your daughter will die."

"No," A voice that hadn't been used in twelve years rasped from her. She reached up, raking her nails down the perfect pale skin of her sister's face. "You'll never win."

Her sister's shriek made her ears ring, before a hard slap caused her to fly back, and slam her head into the wall. Her vision was hazy as a heeled shoe pressed into her fingers, breaking them. "Just like your pathetic father. Completely delusional."

Tears finally slipped down her face as Penthea turned and left, leaving her in the darkness. She had failed, but a spark of hope still existed. They only knew of Lily. Reserved, protective Lily.

Alice was safe. For now.

Chapter 1

July 25th, 2157

My feet had become sore forty-five minutes ago, but the line had barely inched forward. Out of boredom I had become entranced by the propaganda lining the concrete walls of the building. The beady eyes of the King of Hearts promised wealth to every young man and woman who joined the Suits. Some nonsense about the greater good of Wonderland; I couldn't help rolling my eyes. The Red Party only cared to drain everything from the citizens of the last city in the world. The line began moving forward as I listened to the pop music pumping through the speakers at the door. I avoided going out whenever possible, but it was Dina's birthday. Otherwise, I wouldn't be standing in this miserable heat, sweating through the thin dress Dina had insisted I wear for her night on the town.

"Snap out of it, Alice," Dina said, catching my attention. "We're up next. Put on a smile, you don't have to look like I'm torturing you."

I bared my teeth at her, causing us both to burst into a fit of giggles. I tried to shake off my negativity, it was Dina's twenty-fifth birthday; I could leave my comfort zone for one night. I watched my friend's excited face for a moment. She had accented her cheeks with golden glitter which complimented her dark skin beautifully. She'd twisted her long black hair into an intricate braid on her head. Dina was the most striking women I'd ever seen, which would have meant nothing if she wasn't also one of the most empathic people to ever exist.

"IDs, ladies." The bouncer demanded as we approached the open door. Dina showed her inner wrist, where the tattoo preferred by the Red Party for identification purposes shone a sickly green on her dark skin. The bouncer scanned the tattoo as I sifted through the tiny clutch I carried and produced my own identification, a small plastic card.

He sneered down at me when I handed it to him but allowed us through without comment. I was unphased by his reaction; I refused to bend to the strange customs the King of Hearts had introduced. It had become custom for eighteen-year-olds to get their private information tattooed for easy identification. Before my parents died, they had insisted that I never participate. I had tried to convince Dina not to get the tattoo, but her mother had given her no choice. Dina shook her head at my stubborn refusal to conform, before she dragged me further into the club. The Hearts Club was unremarkable on the outside, but once you walked through the doors loud music and pink-and-white flashing lights greeted you. Writhing, drunk bodies crowded the dance floor. Mirrors lined the walls, reflecting the lights, giving the club an eerie red glow.

"Quit thinking and just dance, Ali," Dina said, pulling me into the sweaty bodies in front of us.

I moved my body to the music, focusing on the drumline that vibrated through my chest. The feeling of strange bodies brushing against me began to make me feel nauseous. It was the price of the magick I held. My mother taught me to keep my powers hidden at a young age. Back then I felt special, but now I knew that while I had been blessed with these abilities, they weren't always glamourous.

"I think I'm going to get something to drink Di," I shouted, wincing as a short man without a shirt brushed against me.

"Hell yeah! Live a little," she yelled over the music before disappearing.

I heaved a sigh and made my way to the bar. Staring at the menu, I tried to decide what type of drink would appeal to me. I finally settled and turned to call to the bartender, an older man with a full grey beard.

"A rose petal delight, please," I asked as he approached.

"Anything for you, darlin'," he replied with a wink.

I nodded in thanks when he set my drink down. I immediately chugged it, trying to ignore the buzzing on my skin from all the energy coming off the club's patrons. I wished for a moment that I could shut the intuitive magick off, as it distracted me. Ultimately, I appreciated how useful it was in dangerous situations. For now, I ignored it because I knew it was reacting to my anxiety at being crowded.

"Seems you aren't very happy to be here," a man said to my left.

I chose not to acknowledge his comment, hopeful he would take the hint and leave me alone.

"Most of the women here are looking for a good time," He paused as I made eye contact, "I get the feeling you aren't."

"No, it's my friend's birthday," I stated.

"And where is she?" He asked.

I finally took the time to really look at the man speaking to me. He was not unattractive, but nothing about him appealed to me. He was unimpressive with dull brown hair and unremarkable brown eyes. He could be anywhere from twenty to forty; nothing about him stood out. Put simply, he was an uninteresting oaf who clearly couldn't take a hint.

"Dance floor," I responded after several moments of awkward silence.

"My name is Greg, by the way," he offered me his hand, holding it out until I had no choice but to take it.

I noticed that the bartender had placed another drink in front of me. The buzzing had intensified to an almost unbearable level; I chugged the rest of my drink hoping it would numb the feeling.

"You might want to slow down, sweetheart," a deep voice said to my right.

I turned to find a stunning man watching me. I couldn't help tilting my head as I appreciated his height. He had long black hair, or least it seemed long. I couldn't entirely tell because an orange beanie covered most of his head. His bright green eyes filled with mirth as he stared back at me; his dimples stood out as his grin widened. I rolled my eyes and turned away.

"I'm a grown woman," I quipped.

He chuckled, "Trust me, I can tell."

"You heard the lady, move along," Greg chimed in, irritating me.

"I didn't ask for your help," I snapped. I knew there was no reason to be rude, but I didn't like the feeling I got from him.

The bartender came over with another drink in hand. "These boys bothering you darlin'?"

After a moment's thought, I replied, "Everyone bothers me."

He roared with laughter, "Love me a girl who knows what she wants."

I chugged the rest of my drink before standing. I needed the liquid courage before I started looking for Dina. I wanted to leave in hopes that we could get an early start on girls' night with Lily. As I walked around the club, my head began to pound, and strange colors floated in front of my eyes forcing me to rush out the backdoor. My heart raced in my chest. As my lungs began to constrict a choked sound left me. When I tried to reenter the club for help, a voice spoke. "That worked quickly,"

I looked up, through my hazy vision I saw Greg's outline standing before me. I knew without a doubt that whatever was wrong with me now was his doing. I tried to summon my magick to protect me, but whatever they'd given me had made it impossible for me to access the well of power inside of me. I slid down the wall closest to me, unable to hold myself up anymore.

"I told you it did, now where is my money?" a new male voice answered.

"Wha...what is happening to me?" I choked out.

"Oh, that'll be the drugs I slipped into your drink while you were distracted by that asshat at the bar." Greg replied, grabbing my face.

"I might be hurt by that. Name calling isn't very nice, even for Red Party goons," A voice said. I looked up, blinking my eyes until the orange beanie of my savior came into view.

"Fuck off dude. She's ours fair and square," the unknown voice chimed in again. I turned my head trying to catch a glimpse of the person. While my vision was still badly blurry, I could see a tall, blonde man in a red suit.

"You can't own a human being. Besides, I don't think you can call drugging someone fair." My savior spoke again, looking down at me as he removed his beanie to run his fingers through his hair.

As the three men towered over me, arguing loudly, I could only groan and clutch at my head. I blinked my eyes open, taking in the kaleidoscope of colors that swam in my vision.

"Leave or die asshat," Greg said, grabbing something out of his pocket.

"Can I see what's behind door number three?" my savior asked, chuckling.

"This isn't a fucking game," the unknown voice said.

A gunshot rang out. The sound of my own scream was the last thing I heard before I passed out.

The feeling of being moved brought me back to consciousness. "Well, damn," I heard, "Hatter, what the f-fuck? We can't just take her with us. Are you crazy?" a new voice asked.

"Well, they do call me Mad, so I guess I must be a little crazy," the guy from the bar said.

I wanted to speak, but I couldn't make my mouth move. I heard myself groan.

"Oh Creator. C-Ca-Caterpillar is gonna be so pissed. We can't bring a civilian back to our base," the newest voice said, growing more panicked.

"Calm down, March. We'll take her to my apartment until she wakes up. Cheshire is supposed to meet us there, we can take her home once she wakes up." The man, whose name was apparently Hatter, said.

I was laid gently onto supple leather seats. I tried to bring my body to do anything, I couldn't simply trust strangers even if they might have saved my life.

"I think she's choking," Hatter said, lifting me up again, "You're okay, sweetheart. We're going to get you somewhere safe until you're back on your feet."

At the soothing tone of his voice, I found myself feeling calmer. With the pounding behind my eyes still intense I allowed myself to fall back into darkness.

"Damn it, Hatter, what are we going to do with a girl here?" a voice yelled, waking me up from the drug-induced stupor.

I laid perfectly still, listening, assessing my situation. Panic clawed at my throat, but I refused to allow it to win. If I was going to die, I would do so on my feet, fighting.

"I don't know, but I couldn't exactly leave her in the alley defenseless," Hatter yelled back. I could tell this was the same guy who'd saved me from the Hearts Club. My concern eased a little, it was unlikely he would save my life just to kill me himself.

"Why the fuck not? One girl is not worth Caterpillar handing us our asses." The unfamiliar voice bellowed, somehow louder than before.

"Caterpillar can go fuck himself, I was not leaving a pretty woman who had been drugged in an alleyway. Also, this is my fucking apartment;

you can leave if you don't agree with my choices." Hatter seethed. Silence followed his declaration; no buzz lit across my skin, so I laid there taking deep breaths.

Eventually, I decided it was safe enough to move. I needed to get home. Dina and Lily would be worried sick at my disappearance. The room was dark, but I could make out the outline of a door. I stood, and immediately sat back down when my head started to spin. Once my body had acclimated to sitting up, I stood and stumbled toward the door. In a moment of stupid bravery, I swung it open, to reveal three men standing in a brightly lit room.

I immediately recognized the orange beanie of my rescuer, Hatter. Slightly behind him stood another man with dirty blond hair. He was a couple of inches shorter than Hatter, and skinnier. I glanced toward the other man who scoffed and walked out of the room. I was left staring at the first two men, when the taller one said, "Hi."

I could feel the last of the drugs slowly working their way out of my system. Whatever Greg had slipped into my drink wasn't very strong. "So," I began, leaning against the doorway, "it sounds like you need me to get out of here before your boss gets pissed off. I'm cool with that. Just drop me off at the nearest bus station and I'm gone."

"Fuck. I like her Hatter. C-Can we keep her?" The man with dirty blonde hair said. I recognized his voice from the alley. I studied him for a moment longer, deciding he was likely the less threatening of the two, and I moved closer to him. Though some part of me found it strange that I took a liking to the stranger so quickly, I pushed it aside. Some people just had a way about them.

"No March. We don't know anything about her," the man who had been yelling said, as he poked his head in from another room.

I finally got a good look at the third man. My eyes drifted to his pink and purple hair, and I smiled.

"Got a problem with my hair, blondie?" he asked, narrowing his eyes.

"Not at all! I love it. Can I touch it?" I asked, bouncing on my toes. I slapped my hand over my mouth, surprised by my brazen statement. Apparently, the drugs had lowered my already terrible filter. All three men froze and stared at me. The one with the pink and purple hair looked stunned. A few beats of awkward silence passed before Hatter started laughing.

"Can I ask a question?" I inquired.

"Pretty sure you just did," the guy with the cool hair said.

"What are your names?" I asked, ignoring his snark.

"I am the Mad Hatter, although everyone just calls me Hatter." The guy from the bar said, sweeping that hat off his head and bowing.

I giggled a bit at the move but found myself a tad worried that he was using a codename. It had become more and more common that people refused to give their real names as fear of the Red Party mounted. Most people took them from old books that had been found in dusty libraries. I refused to hide who I was.

"I'm the March Hare, but you can call me M-March," the quieter guy said, giving me a small smile.

"Cheshire Cat," the guy with the pink and purple hair said. His deep blue eyes were cold, but I could see curiosity inside them. He wasn't as threatening as he was pretending to be.

"My name is Alice," I deadpanned.

"Oh, you've got to be fucking kidding me." Cheshire threw his hands in the air and flopped on one of the leather couches that took up most of the living room. "Hatter, I have no idea why you wanted to bring a Red Party spy home, but this is so not my problem."

I furrowed my eyebrows at the comment. I certainly didn't understand why they would think I had anything to do with that political mess. Or why anyone would be spying on these three men anyway.

"I need to head back to the club; I'm sure Dina is getting worried about me." I changed the subject; the energy of the room had shifted to be far more awkward.

"Is that your real name?" Hatter asked, ignoring me.

I nodded instead of answering. He grabbed my left wrist, flipping it over. The intake of breath when they didn't find what they expected surprised me even more. I grabbed his arm in return, the unmarked tan skin stared back at me. "Who are you?" I asked, stepping away.

"Alice, I need you to stay calm. I can explain some of this, but you should probably sit down," Hatter did his best to seem unthreatening.

"Listen, I don't really want to get involved in whatever you've got going on." I said carefully.

"I understand that. Here's the thing, we had information that led us to saving you," He paused, taking me in, waiting for me to react.

I took a deep breath, seeking the place where my magick slumbered inside me. I imagined a cage forming around it. If I panicked and accidentally revealed my biggest secret to these strangers. I might not survive the night. "What kind of information?"

"It was just word that the Red Party was making some kind of deal tonight. We had no idea there would be any civilians involved." Hatter explained.

"So, it's a coincidence you stepped in when that man was bothering me?" I found that highly unlikely.

A light pink suffused Hatter's cheeks, "I just saw a beautiful woman being harassed."

I scoffed, "Right. So let me guess, you're the Resistance?"

Three sets of eyes widened as the words left my mouth. Maybe it was a bit too nonchalant, but I didn't want to continue to ignore the elephant in the room. It wasn't as if they were being particularly subtle.

"She's dangerous." Cheshire said, staring at me darkly, "Any secrets you tell her I'm not responsible for. Maybe tell her I'm wearing a blue bra and pray she'll leave."

"Are you?" I asked, unable to keep from smiling, despite his tone.

"Wouldn't you like to know," he said, wiggling his eyebrows.

I was surprised at the lightness of the banter but continued. "I might be into it,"

I got the satisfaction of seeing his mouth hang open for a minute before he snapped it closed.

"Oh, my Creator, Hatter, she shut up Ch-Ches, we have to keep her. Please?" March begged. Mischief was alight in his honey brown eyes. I cocked my head at him, he was adorable, with his puppy like personality.

"Oh, shut up Hare," Cheshire said.

"Maybe we should focus on the fact she knows about the Resistance," Hatter said, watching me. I saw the suspicion in his eyes and knew I couldn't get away without giving some kind of answer. I realized they were all staring at me, probably waiting for an explanation of some sort. I wondered how little I could manage to tell them without giving everything away.

"My mom told me about your cause before she died," I muttered.

"What was her name?" Cheshire asked.

"Alcinda Young," I answered.

It wasn't a lie, necessarily. I didn't have to tell them the whole truth; at least, not yet.

"She could have been anyone. There's a reason we use code names," Hatter said, watching Ches.

"It doesn't matter, she's just some random girl," Cheshire said.

"A random girl, whose mother told her about the Resistance?" Hatter shot back. "Who was being actively attacked by a Red Party thug? Cheshire, please pull your head out of your ass for a minute."

"Lots of people know about the Resistance." Ches countered, "Or she could be a part of the Red Party planning to infiltrate us. We don't even know that her name is really Alice," he pointed out, gesturing to me.

I rolled my eyes. It was like he forgot that I was brought here after being drugged at a bar. I hadn't asked for help and certainly didn't want to stay here. Maybe I could convince them to let me go since March was the only one who seemed to want me to stick around. I sighed and reached into the front pocket of my dress pulling out my wallet.

"Here's my ID," I said, handing it to him, "I don't have any love for the Red Party, and I sure as hell don't work for them. All I want to do is go home."

"This doesn't prove anything," he scoffed, throwing the card back at me before exiting the room. I watched him storm off, wondering why he was so defensive.

"Why don't I drive you home, sweetheart," Hatter offered. "Ches is right about one thing, Caterpillar would not be happy to find out I brought you here. You made it out of the Hearts Club safely, that's all that matters."

"Caterpillar is your boss?" I asked, curious.

"I don't have a boss," Hatter said.

"Whatever. Just take me home," I said, rolling my eyes.

"Why can't you st-stay. It's very late," March spoke up. "I'm sure the d-drugs are still in your system."

I just shook my head and followed the Mad Hatter out. I sent a pray to the Creator that my life wasn't going to turn into the nonsensical story of the original tales. March grinned at me, waving as we left. I wiggled my fingers at him, a smile forming at the slight disappointment on his face.

Chapter 2

I was a bit shocked to find the huge, bright yellow Ford Hummer sitting right outside Hatter's apartment building. It was an attention grabber. It was stupid of them to drive this around the city. Especially considering how few private vehicles there were. Motorcycles were the most popular form of transportation. They didn't require as much energy to keep running, and they were small enough to hide.

"Alice, I wouldn't go back to that place. A lot of the patrons are members of the Red Party," Hatter said after we had settled into his Hummer. The plush seats cradled my body, lulling me into a bit of a daze, this was an extreme amount of luxury. I wondered again how they had managed to hold onto this vehicle. The Red Party often repossessed any luxury items. The greed that infiltrated Wonderland made me sick.

"Yeah, I don't really want to be drugged again," I finally said, watching as the city flew by. Even a hundred and fifty years hadn't changed the crumbling architecture. Buildings were wrapped in vines as if Mother Earth herself was choking the life out of the parasites that had nearly destroyed her. I didn't entirely understand what had happened to our world that caused such devastation. There were several versions of the story. My mother believed that someone with magick protected Wonderland from the destruction the rest of Earth faced.

Three am in Wonderland was eerily quiet, not even the homeless milled the streets. The only sound to be heard was the quiet engine driving me closer and closer to home. I lived in one of the few suburban areas outside of the city, I didn't often venture as deep as Dina had taken me tonight.

"I'm sorry about Cheshire," Hatter said, trying to make conversation, "He's not usually such an asshole."

"Excuse you— ".

A scream ripped out of me as a pink and purple mop of hair popped out of the back seat and Hatter nearly went off the road.

"I was not being an asshole," Ches continued as Hatter regained control of the massive vehicle.

"Fuck, Ches, are you trying to kill us all? Don't sneak up on someone driving," Hatter yelled, trying to slap Cheshire and drive.

"Sneaking is my specialty, Maddie," Cheshire said innocently.

"Don't call me Maddie," Hatter growled, "I'm not a woman." I made an indignant sound and Hatter smiled at me apologetically.

"I had to make sure you actually got rid of her," Cheshire said, ignoring my glare.

I rolled my eyes, but neither of them were truly annoying me. I was just anxious to make sure Dina had made it home safely from that horrible place.

"I'm sure you understand," Ches finished.

"Of course," I stared at him, levelly, "You're scared of a little girl." I let a grin spread across my face as he turned pink.

He scoffed, "You don't scare me."

"Apparently, your boss does." I shot back. They both went still, and I watched them with triumph on my face.

"You haven't met Caterpillar," Cheshire finally said, giving me a fake shiver, "He's a scary motherfucker."

I watched Hatter roll his eyes; I could tell Cheshire's fear of their mysterious leader annoyed him. He didn't seem to be afraid of much of anything, which I appreciated. Most people let their fear control them. Everyone was afraid of something, but to stop it from letting you live was the worst type of existence. I took a moment to take Hatter in. He was muscular, even with the loose grey button up he was wearing, you could see the outline of the muscle in his arms. He had a powerful body, and for a split second I imagined him thrusting into me. He caught me watching and sent me a wink, as if he had heard my thoughts. I winked back and considered a world where we had met under different circumstances.

We made the rest of the drive to my home in silence. Flashing lights greeted us as we turned onto my street. I was unbuckling my seatbelt and reaching for the door handle before Hatter had even stopped the car. Cheshire was the one who grabbed my arm before I stormed towards the Suit standing outside my house.

"Let us go in first, Alice. Something is wrong," Cheshire said. I ignored him, stomping toward the Suit. His blood red suit emblazoned with a spade caused my fists to curl. I had never let myself show any outward hatred of the Red Party. It was too dangerous, but the panic in my chest was winning out over my better judgement.

"Sorry ma'am, you'll need to find another way through this neighborhood. This area is coordained off." He explained.

"I live here." I replied, emotions warring inside of me.

"Ah," He stood for several minutes, looking at some papers he was holding. The confusion on his face sent chills through me. I could feel an all-too-familiar buzz building along my skin. "Lilian Young and Dina Carroll have been arrested for inciting insurrection." he said, handing me a white envelope, "These are the dates of their executions. As I'm sure you know, treason is punishable by death, without trial. You may have a few moments to gather your things; we will be repossessing the house."

I felt Hatter at my back, I knew he had heard what the man had said. I turned, staring up into his bright green eyes. I was holding back tears and fury. The mental cage I had placed around my magick earlier was bursting, at any moment I would explode with it. "Get me out of here before I kill them all," I whispered.

"What about—" he started.

"Now Hatter," I insisted, "I'll kill them all and I won't be able to save my sister or my best friend,"

"Cheshire and I will go see if we can gather some of your things," he said gruffly, opening the car door. I made a noncommittal sound but decided to climb back into the car. I waited in the passenger seat, seething with absolute rage, while Ches and Hatter went into the house to gather my things. I couldn't think clearly. My nails were dug so deep into my palms I expected they would be bleeding when I could uncurl my fists. I stared at each person milling around the house cataloging each of the Suits' faces. I would find a way to punish them all.

Hatter and Cheshire climbed into the car, one of Lily's purple duffle bags was overflowing with things they'd clearly found in my room. I didn't take any time to consider what they would have grabbed. It would be easy enough for me to get anything I needed once I had a clear head. As I stared into the flashing lights on top of the Suit's black van, I quietly said, "Drive out of the city. There's a field about twenty minutes from here, just drive straight."

"Alice?" Hatter asked, "I know you must be in shock."

I said nothing.

"Hatter, just do what she says," Ches said, shocking me. Considering how defensive Cheshire had acted with me so far, I couldn't fathom why he would change now. It didn't matter, I would forever be thankful for it. Hatter followed my directions and drove away from my home without another word. I watched my childhood home disappear in the rearview mirror; I couldn't describe the feeling in my chest. Some part of me knew this would be the last time I would see the home my parents had created for me and Lily.

The energy building against my skin almost burned as I fought hard to keep control of it. Thoughts raced through my head. What had Lily and Dina done? Why didn't I know? They were hardly ever alone. How could they possibly have committed treason without me knowing? This was insanity, I didn't believe it for a second. So why were they taken? And on the same night I encountered the Resistance after being drugged. The three incidents had to be related, but I couldn't understand why the Red Party would come after us. Lily and I had always been very careful to keep our heads down. While Dina would occasionally express her dislike of the Red Party, I couldn't imagine her doing anything to actually harm anyone.

After half an hour of driving, we were parked in my field. The purple and yellow spots of color brought some peace to my chaotic thoughts. I always came to the fields of wildflowers when I was overwhelmed or upset. My father had brought me here as a child, it made me feel closer to him. Tears welled in my eyes as memories of my family rushed to the surface.

"I would suggest you leave me here so that you aren't injured," I said, no hint of emotion in my voice.

"I'm not leaving you," Hatter said, crossing his arms over his chest.

Instead of answering, I simply exited the car and walked into the field. I could feel the tall grass on my bare legs where my stockings were torn. The hem of my dress started getting wet with the early morning dew. I let a scream rip from my mouth, releasing the seal on my magick. Electricity crackled through the air, snapping against my skin. It was intense enough that sparks lit the air around me. I heard Cheshire curse, but I didn't care. I screamed until I could no longer feel the buzz against my skin, then I collapsed to my knees and my vision darkened. Tears ran down my face, unchecked, and I heard someone approach.

"Alice?" Hatter checked on me, placing a hand on my shoulder.

I expected him to fall to the ground in pain, but my magick was spent for now.

"I can't be alone," I whispered, "They can't take the last of my family."

"We'll get your family back for you, sweetheart," he vowed.

"Don't make promises you can't keep," I snarled back.

"How do you have magick?" Cheshire asked, approaching us slowly, "Caterpillar told us the last magick user died."

"My mother taught me how to keep my powers hidden," I said weakly. I was surprised Cheshire even knew magick existed. Most people in Wonderland ignored the obvious signs that something different existed in the city. Though neither of them were as shocked by my outburst as I would have expected. Though many aspects of the city ran because of magick users, they were no better than slaves. Forced to use what powers they could maintain to keep the city running. The few people I had told were always a bit shaken after even a small amount of exposure to what I could do. I tried standing. I swayed and both men rushed to catch me before I fell. Their hands steadied me, and I took a deep breath, trying to recover from the overload. Hatter kept a hand at the small of my back and Ches held on to my arm to make sure I was stable. They both seemed to be in awe, but I was too exhausted to care.

"The last known magick user–" Hatter started to say.

"–was the White Queen," I finished, "I know. She was my mother."

They stared at me for a moment before I started walking back to the car, leaving them to follow me.

"You mean to tell me that the White Queen had two daughters that she never told anyone about?" Cheshire asked as Hatter drove us back into the city.

"Yes, Lily was born first, and I followed five years later. My father took care of us most of the time, so my mother could help the Resistance," I explained. My emotions had settled and now I had a mission. I had to save

Lily and Dina, little else mattered to me, but I knew I had to have the help of the Resistance. The Red Party was at least four hundred members strong, and they held the majority of the wealth and power within the city. No one person could take down a government alone.

"How do you have magick?" Hatter inquired.

"Sleep," was all I said in response. Explaining the inner workings of magick would be far more complicated and time consuming than I felt like dealing with right then.

"Sleep? We all sleep, and I sure don't have magick," Cheshire snorted.

"How much sleep do you get every day," I asked, turning to face him.

"Well, probably five or six hours," he said, looking confused.

"Your brain is so busy trying to keep your body functioning on so little sleep, it cannot access its natural abilities. That's assuming you even have some magickal talent. To my knowledge most people don't." I explained. "Do you have any weird talents?"

"I can sneak up on pretty much anybody, and sometimes people don't notice me even if I sit in front of them." Cheshire looked puzzled as he responded.

I thought for a moment. That had to be a very useful ability in the Resistance. I hadn't personally encountered anyone outside of my family with magickal gifts. Though my mother had said that there were others in Wonderland. She had tried to liberate some of the magick users being abused by the Red Party. I didn't know exactly what happened, but apparently it was a huge failure.

"If you slept ten hours each day you would begin to feel the power buzzing beneath your skin." I explained, "My mother believed that is why the Red Party makes people work such long days. If they are too tired, their bodies have to heal instead of building their magick."

"Fucking hell. I always knew the Red Party was evil, but..." Hatter trailed off, a haunted look in his eyes.

"We have to take her to Caterpillar, she's the answer to our problems," Cheshire said, looking at me in wonder.

"I will not follow anyone's rules. The only thing I care about is saving my sister and Dina," I said.

"Caterpillar isn't going to like this," Hatter warned, glaring at Ches.

"We need to pick up March if we're going to the base," Ches said, ignoring him.

"I already sent him a message," Hatter said.

Silence filled the car, and I could feel my magick returning. It creeped toward the two men in the car feeling them out for threats. When it deemed them friendly, it settled against my chest, warming the coldness there. I rubbed at the warmth, feeling tears threaten to fall again.

"Are you okay?" Cheshire asked, genuine concern shining in his eyes.

"What do you think, Ches?" Hatter asked angrily. "She's just been told her last living family member, and her best friend are going to be publicly executed."

"I'm okay. I... thank you guys for helping me. I know you didn't want me here," I said, looking down at my torn black and white stockings.

Cheshire coughed uncomfortably, but Hatter laid his hand on my thigh and said, "We will help you."

"I told you not to make promises you can't keep," I said, though I didn't flinch away from his warm touch.

"I never do," he said, quietly.

After we picked up March, we left the city again. As the early dawn light swept across the city, I watched the buildings get smaller and more spread out as we drove further away from the city. Eventually I closed my eyes and kept quiet. I listened to the men speak quietly, bickering occasionally. Something about it comforted me, reminding me of Lily.

"Alice, we should probably prepare you. Caterpillar is a bit... grumpy at times," Hatter said.

"Cheshire said he was a scary motherfucker," I replied, turning to face him.

Cheshire groaned, "I would prefer you didn't repeat that to him."

"He's just a burly guy, with a hard time trusting people," Hatter said, ignoring our banter.

"Too bad, I'm gonna tell him," I replied, sticking my tongue out at him in defiance.

"Stick that thing out again and I might put it to use," Ches threatened.

"Will you be wearing that blue bra while you do? Because, if so, I would be willing to risk it," I joked.

March and Hatter laughed, but Cheshire only glared. I shouldn't have felt like laughing considering the circumstances. Ignoring my guilt, I was thankful for the distraction they were providing me. I could only hope Caterpillar would be able to help me. "Oh, how I regret saying that." He whined.

"We're here," Hatter announced, putting an end to any more jokes.

"Alice, I think Hatter has a point. Caterpillar barely trusts us. I don't know how he's going to react to everything we've learned tonight. Maybe you should stay in the car," Ches suggested.

"Absolutely not," I said, immediately jumping out of the car once it was parked.

"She is as stubborn as he is," Cheshire said, rolling his eyes, "Let her go head-to-head with him. Maybe we can escape before the inevitable blowup."

"I think she might be sc-scarier," March said, giving a fake shiver. He sent a small smile my way and I grinned in return.

"You should have seen her when her magick exploded." Hatter agreed, "It was... well, if I was anyone else, I might have pissed myself."

Cheshire led the way into a depleted-looking warehouse. No signs of life could be seen from the outside. The factories that had existed before the world changed mostly stood empty now. Only six were still in use. The workers were abused and underpaid, but they kept Wonderland running. Most were closer to the city than this one and heavily guarded. As we entered I found a surprisingly cozy home. Several black leather couches were pushed against the wall. A fireplace was crackling in the living area despite the heat outside. I could tell there was no woman involved in the simple but comfortable design of the large room.

Cheshire gave me a final warning, "Listen, you need to be quiet while I talk to Caterpillar. He's not going to like—"

"What am I not going to like, Cheshire?" a huge man said, stepping in front of Ches, who paled. Cheshire was only a couple of inches taller than me, and this man, who I could only assume was Caterpillar, dwarfed us both. A few moments of silence allowed me to take the man's appearance in. His shirt looked too tight across his chest as his muscles bulged in anger. The scowl on his face did nothing to take away from the masculine beauty of his jawline. What surprised me was how put together, and almost... fashionable he was. His hair was shaved on the sides, but long on top. I finally made eye contact with him; my breath stopped in my chest as his swirling grey eyes pulled me in. The buzzing against my skin had started again, lighter than usual but it put me on edge. I stared at Caterpillar, trying to puzzle out why my magick was reacting to him. He seemed almost... familiar. I shook my head, zoning back into the conversation. "Might it be the fact that you three should have been here hours ago? Or maybe that you brought a civilian to our home? Perhaps it's that you didn't even have the decency to call?" Caterpillar did not yell, but he might as well have with the way Ches, Hatter, and March looked. I would have laughed at the fact he sounded like a mother hen if not for the tone of his voice. I didn't like it at all, so I stepped forward, ready to defend the men who had helped me through this terrible night.

"I'm sorry, sir. They were helping me after I was drugged and nearly kidnapped. When they took me home, the Suits were there. They've taken my sister and friend for insurrection," I explained quickly. "They offered the Resistance's help,"

Caterpillar snorted, "They are as good as dead. I suggest you find someone who will take you in and pray that they don't arrest you too."

"Caterpillar–" Hatter started.

"I don't want to hear from you three," he said, halting Hatter.

Energy cracked against my skin as his voice raised. "Now listen up asshole, you don't get to dismiss me." I said, poking my finger into his chest as I spoke, "They may put up with your imposing bullshit, but I don't have time for this. They will execute Lily and Dina in the next month. Help me or don't, I don't give a fuck, but don't talk to them like that."

Caterpillar had the gall to laugh in my face. I could feel a different kind of rage racing through my veins. Electricity cracked just under my skin; I hated bullies.

"Caterpillar, you pr-pr-probably shouldn't..." Before March could finish his sentence, I punched the man in the jaw, putting as much magick into the blow as possible. He flew back a couple of feet and I glared at him, my hands shaking with anger. An angry red mark had already bloomed against his skin.

"I am Alice Young, daughter of the White Queen. Do not fuck with me," I hissed at him

I saw something pass across his face that I didn't understand before he growled, "Get her out."

Cheshire reached for me, but I slid by him with ease and marched toward Caterpillar.

"This isn't the Resistance," I growled at him, "You're as much of a bully as the Red Party."

"Get. Her. Out!" he bellowed.

I was so tired of being pushed around by bullies, and Caterpillar was the very last straw tonight. If this is what the Resistance had turned into, I was probably better off on my own.

"Alice," Hatter begged.

"Never mind, I don't want your help anyway," I said, stomping out of the warehouse.

I was dimly aware of Hatter and March trying to follow me, but I pretended not to hear their pleas. I grabbed my bag out of the Hummer, strapped it to my back, and noticed a motorcycle a few feet away. Lucky for me, the keys were in the ignition. I jumped on, revved the engine to life, and headed back into the city, ignoring the tears that fell down my face. After I thought through my options, I decided to ditch the bike, just in case they came looking for it. I made my way to Dina's apartment on foot. I knew I couldn't do anything until I had slept. I pulled the key out of my bra and quickly unlocked the door. I was lucky that Dina did not advertise that she had her own home. The dingy apartment was under an assumed name, so no one would come here looking for me. I dropped my bag and stripped off my clothes before falling into her bed. Her scent, vanilla with a spicy undertone, clung to the sheets. I sighed deeply and held back the emotions that threatened my sleep. We were supposed to still be celebrating her twenty-fifth birthday. Lily had planned to make a cake and stay up watching movies with us. I bit my tongue to hold in the whimper that was building in the back of my throat. I wondered if they were okay... how scared Dina must be... I knew Lily would take care of her if they were together. Finally, after an hour of holding back my emotions, I fell into a fitful sleep.

Chapter 3

July 27th, 2157

The sunlight streaming through the window woke me from the fitful sleep I had been trapped in. Two days had passed since I'd run from the Resistance. Guilt ate at my insides; I should already have had a plan on how I was going to save Lily and Dina from execution. I was alone, with very little time before they would be executed. The problem was even if I could manage to break them out of wherever they were being held by the Red Party. Where would we go? Most people in Wonderland believed that the air wasn't breathable outside the edges of the city. I couldn't be certain this was true, but it wasn't willing to risk all of our lives. The help of the Resistance could have made a huge difference. I shook my head, unwilling to think too much into the events that had occurred that night. I stretched, catching a whiff of my unwashed body, and nearly gagging. I had laid around and moped for too long. I pulled myself out of Dina's bed. There were many reasons we kept clothes and important items spread across the few safe places we had in Wonderland. There was always a chance we would need to run and hide. I peeled my clothes off, and stood naked in the bathroom listening to the pipes rattle as they tried to push lukewarm water out of the showerhead. When it finally heated to a temperature that was safe for the human body I stepped in. I imagined the water washing away all the hopelessness I felt. I scrubbed my skin until it was bright pink. Ripping the knots from my hair was the worst part but I felt entirely refreshed when I stepped out of the now freezing water. I wrapped myself in a plush purple towel letting my hair drip down my back. As I opened the bathroom door, I heard male voices just outside the bedroom door. I started to panic when I recognized Cheshire's voice.

"We tracked her here but... Caterpillar, you should leave her alone if we aren't going to help her." Cheshire said, sounding defeated.

"First, she turned you all against me, then she had the audacity to punch me and steal my bike. I think I have the right to at least talk to her," Caterpillar replied.

I rolled my eyes at the idea that I had done anything to turn anyone against him. It wasn't my fault if Hatter, March, or Cheshire took issue with his boorish ways. I grabbed the handgun Dina kept hidden in her nightstand. I busted through the bedroom door into the tiny living area, aiming the gun at Caterpillar. I held my towel up with my other hand, and said, "Hey boys."

"Put down the gun, Alice," Cheshire said, stepping toward me.

"I really don't want to shoot you. But considering you've broken in while I was showering, I think everyone would understand if I did." I replied. There was an audible gulp as he moved away from me.

"Leave," I demanded, turning my attention to Caterpillar. I locked eyes with him. My eyebrows scrunched when once again a memory niggled in the back of my mind. It distracted me from the four men who had just broken into Dina's apartment while I was showering.

"How ya d-doin', Alice?" March greeted from behind Hatter.

I shook my head; Caterpillar probably just reminded me of all the assholes I've met living in Wonderland. I had never met any of the Resistance. My mother shielded Lily and I from her work at all costs. "Oh, you know, four men just broke into my apartment while I was showering, so things are just about normal." I told him amiably.

"Only after you punched me and stole my bike," Caterpillar said, coming toward me.

"I really wouldn't hesitate to put a bullet in you, buddy. I don't like bullies, and I've had a real bad couple of days." I said, although the smile on my face probably didn't help him take me seriously. "Also, if you want your bike back, it's parked on 21st street," I added to be nice.

"I know. We already picked it up." Caterpillar shot back, crossing his arms, "I came here to prove to these dumbasses that you are not who you say you are."

"You can believe what you want, but please leave me out of your bullshit," I said, lowering my weapon.

"I think I know what I'm doing," he said with a smirk.

"Alice, show him your magick," Hatter spoke up for the first time.

Caterpillar rolled his eyes, looking toward me. Their stormy grey color was so striking I could have fallen into their depths. If only they weren't attached to him. "Hatter, no one has magick anymore; she tricked you." He said, his tone that of an adult trying to explain something to a toddler. "It's not as if we're really living in a fairy tale where a girl named Alice has come to save us from the wretched Queen." There was so much bitterness in Caterpillar's statement, I wondered for a moment if at some point he had believed in fairy tales. My heart squeezed; I had believed in fairy tales until my mother was ripped from me.

I set the gun down and dropped my towel, drawing all four men's attention. I had no shame; I knew exactly how hot men thought I was, I used it against them when it was necessary. I snapped my fingers for show and made everything, including the four of them, float up to the ceiling. I had learned how to manipulate my gifts past their basic abilities. Electricity was present everywhere but especially in the human body. Learning to use that to levitate and paralyze people was something I was especially proud of. I walked from the room to find clothes. After I was dressed, with my hair in a bun on the top of my head, I stepped back into the room.

"I think you made your point, sweetheart. Can you please let us down?" Hatter asked, looking a bit green.

With a thought, I made everything fall back down, not bothering to cushion their landing. "For the record, there are no real Queens in our Wonderland," I said with a smile.

Caterpillar glared at me, opening his mouth to speak but Cheshire interrupted him. "I think I'm going to be sick,"

I pointed him toward the tiny bathroom just inside the bedroom. When he went running in, I followed.

"Sorry Cheshire, I didn't mean to make you sick," I said, rubbing his back as he puked.

"Call me Ches, everyone else does," he said. He trailed off for a few moments to take a gulp of water from the sink. "I should apologize for Caterpillar; it's been hard since the White...your mom disappeared. We didn't know exactly what happened to her. I was only fourteen when she went missing, and things have been falling apart ever since." Cheshire explained, sitting on the bathroom floor.

"I was thirteen when she died," I said as I sat next to him, "How did you end up with the Resistance?"

"The Red Party killed my parents. They were caught planning to kill the King of Hearts." He explained, emotionless, "I was with Caterpillar when they were executed. He was already an adult at the time, so he took me in," he added, still looking sick.

"I'm sorry. My dad died a few years before my mom; had a heart attack," I said, trying to comfort him.

"Your sister is lucky to have you, especially if you're willing to risk getting killed to save her," Cheshire said, standing.

We looked into each other's eyes for a moment, after he used some of Dina's mouthwash. I took in his straight nose and full lips. Cheshire was a beautiful man, and when he smiled showing his perfect, white teeth, I had no doubt he'd used that smile against a few women. No words passed between us, but I realized we understood each other. I knew the conversation was over, but I quietly said, "I should have stopped them from taking her in the first place."

"Why didn't your mother explain to us how to access our magick?" Caterpillar asked, the minute we exited the bathroom.

"How the hell would I know?" I shot back, annoyed.

"Guess," he demanded.

Trying to guess my mother's reasoning was impossible. She never gave me any information about the Resistance if she didn't absolutely have to. I only knew what I did, because I had a journal, she had left for me. It dawned on me that it hadn't made it into the bag that they packed me for the night everything happened. I wouldn't worry about it now, there were more important things to handle. "Fine," I huffed, "I would say she didn't want you to draw attention to yourselves. It's hard to control and difficult to keep if you can't get enough sleep. On top of that, not everyone has magick; those who don't often become obsessed. If you were focused on it, then how could you help the Resistance?"

"She didn't have the right," he said, curling his fists. I could see the muscle in his jaw pumping.

"Let me ask you something. Have you ever made decisions for your men that were hard to make, maybe one that hurt or killed them? My mother did the best she could with what she had," I exploded, stomping up to him.

"I thought you didn't know anything," he shot back.

"I don't, but if I was her, that is exactly what I would have done to protect the people I loved. You didn't know my mother like I did. She died to save someone. She died never telling anyone about me or my sister. I didn't get to spend hardly any time with my own mother because she was too busy trying to save us *all*." I finished, breathing heavy. "So, fuck you for trying to blame her for doing her best to save Wonderland," I added, before leaving the apartment.

"Do not walk away from me," Caterpillar said, yanking me back through the open doorway.

"Don't touch me," I growled.

I watched as Hatter, March, and Ches stepped back. Caterpillar and I stared at each other, fighting for something I didn't understand. Electricity snapped out at his hand, but he didn't even flinch as it connected. I raised my eyebrows at him surprised.

"I don't trust you," he finally admitted.

"Good, the feeling is mutual." I said, stepping away from him and grabbing the bag I dropped by the door two nights before. "Now if we're done here, I have things to do."

"Like what?" Caterpillar asked.

"None of your damn business, bitch," I said, walking away. I heard March huff a laugh and Cheshire coughed.

"Did that tiny woman just call me a bitch?" he asked, looking at Hatter.

"I think so," Hatter replied, mirth in his voice.

I glanced back and noticed the grin on his face, and I had to stop myself from smiling, too.

"Where are you going?" Hatter asked, falling into step beside me.

"I already said it was none of your business," I pointed out.

"I did save your life. It's not like I plan to hurt you now; we'll leave you alone if you tell us what you're doing," he offered.

"Like hell we will," Caterpillar said, catching up with us.

"Shut up, man. She's a grown woman, and it really isn't any of our business what she does," Hatter said.

"I'm making it my business," he growled back, grabbing me again. I was prepared for it this time and I turned my body, causing him to slam into the brick wall of the apartment building. He groaned loudly, and I laughed.

"Why are you letting the 'tiny woman' beat up on you again, Caterpillar?" Hatter teased, laughing along with me.

"Shut the fuck up, Maddie," Cheshire said, glaring at Hatter as he went to help his friend. "Do not encourage them." He snapped at me.

"I'm going to… my boyfriend's house," I lied. I couldn't fathom why I felt the need to lie to them, other than I wanted them off my back. I had finally formulated a plan, and the last thing I needed was them getting in my way. All four men looked at me, silent. I hoped they wouldn't see through my fib.

"We'll take you there," Caterpillar said, leaving no room for argument, "So you aren't walking the streets alone."

Wonderland was not the safest place for young women since the Red Party had come into power. The Suits took what they wanted, and seemed to enjoy inflicting pain and suffering when they had the opportunity. Even the ones who didn't take an active role in the abuse were complicit.

"Fine," I said, with a sigh.

I let them lead me to the Hummer, parked behind the apartment building. The ride was silent, even Hatter and March refrained from bickering in the back seat. I didn't intend to make this detour, but it was for the best.

"Thanks for the ride," I said, climbing out of the car.

"We'll escort you inside," Caterpillar offered, and I knew he didn't believe me.

"That's not necessary," I objected.

"I think it is. Wouldn't want you to get hurt. I'm sure your boyfriend would be very upset if you did," he said, motioning for me to lead the way.

I silently cursed him as we climbed the stairs. I knocked quietly, hoping that my friend was not home.

"Just a second," a muffled voice said, before the door was thrown open.

"Alice? What are you—" Griffin started, but I interrupted him, throwing my arms around his neck and kissing him.

"Sorry," I whispered, before pulling away. I grinned at the shocked faces of the men standing before me.

"Well," Cheshire coughed, looking confused, "we'll leave you in your boyfriend's… capable hands." He finished, raising his eyebrows at me.

"I guess we will be going," Caterpillar said, narrowing his eyes at Griffin.

"Nice to meet you too," I murmured, not listening to him. I realized I didn't want them to go, but I choked down those feelings and waved at them as they left. Something about them drew me in. Maybe I enjoyed the bickering. Or maybe it was something else. I didn't want to think on it anymore, they were leaving.

"Boyfriend?" Griffin mouthed, as the Resistance disappeared down the stairs.

I shook my head, pushing him into his apartment. "I'm sorry about that Griff, but I had to get rid of them. Did you hear about Lily and Dina?" I asked, sitting on his couch.

He nodded but said nothing.

"Okay, well, let me give you a quick rundown." I explained, talking quickly, "The guy in the orange beanie saved me after a dude drugged me at the Hearts Club. When he and his friends went to take me home, Lily and Dina had been taken for 'inciting an insurrection.' I had a bit of a problem with my magick, met their leader—the really tall one—and punched him, and then I stole his bike." I paused long enough to make sure he was following along. "They broke into Dina's apartment this morning, but I had to get rid of them so I can go back to the Hearts Club."

Griffin sat in silence for a minute staring at me. I wondered if I went too fast, but then he spoke. "First of all, you don't have to apologize for kissing me, since I chased after you for years." I laughed, remembering our childhood, we had spent many happy days together. Even as he chased after me. "Second, those dudes were all super into you. Why ruin your chances with them by making out with me?" he asked.

It was my turn to stare at him in shock. "No, they aren't," I sputtered.

"The one with the pink and purple hair looked like he wanted to punch me after you kissed me," he said, smiling at me.

I shook my head furiously and he laughed. "Oh, my god, Ali. You're into all four of them," he accused, pointing at me.

"Absolutely not! They're all assholes, who I never want to see again," I claimed, ignoring the heat that rushed into my cheeks.

"Fine, I'll let you continue to lie to yourself, if you tell me why the hell you want to go back to the Hearts Club," Griffin conceded.

I sighed, "Are you going to try and stop me?"

"Of course not. I just want to be able to explain when those guys come back here for you," he said, hiding a smile.

"Assuming they even come back here, which I highly doubt." I rolled my eyes when Griffin smirked at me, "Please don't tell them my plan."

"Which is what exactly?" He asked.

"I am going to go and get arrested. They'll take me to the same place they're holding Lily and Dina, then I can use my magick to escape." I explained.

He stared at me for a moment. "That's... not the worst plan I've ever hard, but it does rely on you being able to use your magick. It's very dangerous, you know how the Suits treat people."

"I can defend myself, just promise me if any of the Resistance group comes back you won't tell them where I've gone."

"I'm not promising you that," he said, crossing his arms over his chest.

"Okay, fine. At least stall them long enough for me to get arrested, assuming they come back, which I don't believe," I added, quickly.

"Now that I will do," he said, "Need help getting ready?" he asked.

"Yeah, can you do my makeup?" I asked, "I need to draw as much attention as possible,"

"Only for you, Ali." Griffin had a talent for makeup. Of course, he was always hanging out with me and Dina when we were kids and we practiced on him a lot. We went into his small dining room, and he started my makeover. It took him over an hour, and I was starting to get restless.

"Stop fidgeting, I'm almost done," He snapped, he took art very seriously. In a different world Griffin would have been a great artist. His makeup skills barely scratched the surface of his talent. I'd seen the paintings he'd been able to create from the few art supplies he'd been able to scrounge up. They were amazing. I wish I could give him the life he deserved. Instead I had to focus on saving our best friend and my sister from certain death. My stomach rolled just thinking about the situation I was in.

"Done," Griffin said, interrupting my thoughts, and holding up a mirror.

Black liner complimented my blue eyes along with smoky eyeshadow and long, false lashes. My cheeks were rosy, pink, and my full lips were bright red, a color that I would have never worn otherwise. I jogged to Griffin's spare room, knowing that he had some of my clothes stashed away for when Dina and I stayed over. I picked a silver dress that hugged my body somewhat uncomfortably and six-inch heels.

"I'm not sure this is a good idea." Griffin said, starting on my hair.

"I'll be fine," I said, watching his hands work my hair into a long braid.

"I'm sure of it," he said, smiling, "Bring Lily and Dina here, and we'll run together," he added seriously.

"Can you go to Dina's apartment and pack what we'll need?" I asked, "Lily should have some clothes there, too."

"Sure," he said.

I pressed the key into his palm before giving him a kiss on the cheek.

"Careful Alice, I may start thinking you actually like me," he said, joking.

"I may not have wanted to date you, Griffin, but I've always loved you," I said.

"Don't talk like that Ali, makes me feel like you're saying goodbye," he said, escorting me to the door.

"I am," I whispered, giving him a sad smile. I was confident in my abilities, but there was always a chance things could go wrong. I couldn't account for everything, and I wasn't a seasoned soldier.

"Please don't, you're one of my best friends, I don't want to lose you," he said, pressing a kiss to my forehead.

"Lily and Dina deserve to live," I tried to brush him off.

"So do you," he replied, opening the door for me, "We'd all be completely lost without you."

I went out the back door, just in case anyone was watching the apartment. As I stepped outside, I wondered if I would ever see him again. I looked back at Griffin standing in the doorway. "Be careful," he yelled after me.

A slight shiver crept up my spine, almost as if I was being watched. I glanced around but didn't see anyone. I took a deep breath, preparing myself, if my plan went wrong, I wouldn't end up in jail with my sister, I'd end up dead.

Chapter 4

Griffin apartment was in sector five of the city. Unfortunately, the Hearts Club was in sector seven. It could have been worse, but the heels I was wearing were killing my feet. When I arrived and saw the line stretching around the building I groaned. An hour later, I was finally entering the club. The bouncer from the night before looked at me with disgust, but let me in. I took a deep breath, preparing myself for the buzz that accompanied large crowds. I made my way to the bar and the bartender grinned at me.

"Rose petal delight, right?" he asked.

I raised my eyebrows, surprised.

"I don't often forget pretty ladies," he said, answering my unasked question.

"I'm not here to drink tonight," I said, ignoring his flirting.

He leaned in close to me and whispered, "I'm glad you got away from the Red Party last night." He patted my hand and I glared at him.

"Why didn't you tell me my drink was drugged?" I hissed.

"This whole bar belongs to the Red Party. I couldn't have told you without being executed." He whispered before making his way to a new customer at the other end of the bar.

I almost felt bad for the old man, but I didn't have time to think about it. I watched the patrons, trying to decide how I was going to go about my plan. Getting arrested wouldn't be that difficult once I found a Suit. I spotted a tall man with dark hair looking my way. I immediately recognized the pin on his lapel. I hesitated for a moment, my mind running through the plan that began to hatch. Finally, I sauntered toward him, running through my options. He locked eyes with me, and I tried to give him a sultry smile. He rolled his eyes but continued to look me up and down.

"I didn't know the infamous Jabberwocky was going to be here tonight," I whispered, saddling up to him. He grunted but did not reply.

"If I had, I might have worn something more appealing," I said, as I ran my fingers along his bicep. I'd found men that hated women didn't like for a woman to seem confident in herself. I felt sick but continued the game I was playing. He looked down at me, a mean smile curling across his face, and making me feel like prey. Energy crackled against me when his eyes finally met mine. I could almost feel the coldness of his heart, but I repressed the shiver. His eyes left my face, falling to my breasts, which were on display thanks to the silver dress.

"A fragile thing like you might get hurt if you don't learn your place," he muttered into my ear.

I had the urge to puke on his expensive shoes, but instead I whispered, "And I might like it." I had no doubt wouldn't, but I had to lead him to believe I would. I had heard from neighbors that the Jabberwocky was cruel. Especially to his lovers. How they knew? I had never asked. A ruckus on the other side of the bar drew his attention away from my breasts. I cursed quietly under my breath when I saw an angry Cheshire storming toward me.

"Why don't we get out of here," I offered, running a hand over his chest. He nodded, gripping my bicep and dragging me out. When we made out into the cool night air, another hand wrapped around my wrist, stopping us.

"Sir, my wife is very drunk. Would you mind unhanding her?" Caterpillar said, glaring down at me. My mouth went dry. I hadn't expected them to actually show up, the look on his face as he met my eyes sent shivers down my spine.

"You should keep the bitch on a leash so she doesn't stray if you don't want her to whore herself out." Jabberwocky growled, yanking on my arm, "Since she made the offer, I think I will take her up on it."

"You may be right about the leash," Caterpillar said through his teeth, his eyes never leaving mine. I gulped, the intensity of his eyes made me regret coming her.

A few moments of tense silence followed, before a cruel smile split Jabberwocky's lips. It was an eerie look, as if the man was incapable of happiness. "You'll take care of her far better than I could." I shivered at what he was implying and tried to pull away from Caterpillar.

"But–" I tried to protest.

Caterpillar put his other hand over my mouth before I could go after Jabberwocky. Something about the way he held me against his body caused my nipples to harden. I could feel the heat of him through my dress, the hardness of his chest pressed against my back.

"You're lucky Griffin told us what you were up to, and we were able to get here before he could take you." Caterpillar growled into my ear.

I spun away from him and tried to kick him in the balls, ignoring the way my body responded to his tone of voice. "How dare you?" I seethed.

"Hush, before he comes back. If he figures out you are not a subservient little wife, he will be suspicious," Caterpillar said, having caught my foot.

"I cannot believe you implied I would marry you," I hissed, yanking away from him.

"I can't believe you thought trying to have sex with Jabberwocky was a clever idea," he shot back.

"I wasn't going to have sex with him. I was going to get arrested by him," I started, "Which I do not have to explain to you," I said, stomping away.

"Oh, no you don't." Cheshire said, appearing out of nowhere and grabbing me. "You'll explain it to me or I will actually put a leash on you." Ches said, grinning. Cheshire must have been close by if he had heard Jabberwocky's comment. I wondered for a moment why I hadn't noticed him sooner. I checked in with my magick to ensure it wasn't depleted. When I realized everything was normal I glared at Cheshire, and tried to yank away from him. He held on tight, surprising me with his strength.

"I'd like to see you try," I hissed, before biting him.

He yelped but did not let go of my arm.

"Miss is there a problem?" a man in a red suit asked, staring at the two men.

"Ye—" I started, before Cheshire slapped a hand over my mouth.

"No sir, our wife is just very drunk," Caterpillar explained, and I glared at him.

The man laughed and moved along.

"Our wife. Our wife!" I hissed, sending electric magick into Cheshire making him let me go. "I would never... How dare you imply that I would not only date both of you, but also marry you," I ranted.

"Well, I sure as hell wouldn't marry you," Caterpillar said, "However, it is a good excuse. I couldn't exactly let you go with that maniac."

I ignored the part of me that was hurt that he wouldn't marry me. The venom in his voice felt far more personal than what I had said. It was ridiculous, I could barely stand to be around this man. Why the hell did a twinge of hurt squeeze my heart from his disdain. "It isn't up to you," I said shrilly.

"It's my job to make sure my team is safe," he shouted at me, causing me to go silent.

"I'm... I'm not a part of your team," I whispered.

"You were the minute you walked into the warehouse, as much as I detest it. You are reckless and you don't think of anyone but yourself. Unfortunately, my men are fascinated by you for some reason," Caterpillar said. Tears pricked my eyes. I looked back and forth between Caterpillar and Cheshire. They had come back for me, just as Griff predicted. Even though they completely ruined my plan to save Lily and Dina, they were saving me once again.

"I just want to save my sister," I said, my voice thick with emotion.

Cheshire wrapped his arms around me and said, "It's okay Alice. We'll help, but manipulating the Jabberwocky isn't the way." He rubbed my back while I cried. I felt ashamed to be crying in the arms of a man I barely knew. I hated to show any kind of weakness.

"We'll do what we can," Caterpillar said, when I pulled away from Ches. "I can't make you any promises."

"I'm sorry," I said, wiping my face.

"It's okay," Cater replied, looking uncomfortable.

"This is nothing in comparison to the time Hatter tried to infiltrate the Red Party by sleeping with Duchess." Cheshire said.

I blinked several times before I started laughing. "You're kidding! He slept with the King of Hearts daughter?"

"Yeah, she was pissed when he ended it. He still avoids anything to do with her," Cheshire grinned.

"Can we please continue this elsewhere?" Caterpillar asked, frustrated.

"Why don't we go back to Alice's boyfriend's apartment?" Cheshire suggested, looking at me, "Liar," he added.

"She's committed," Caterpillar pointed out, trying not to smile.

"Creator you really planted one on him," Ches said.

"I was trying to get rid of you," I said, sliding into the Hummer.

"It didn't work," Caterpillar said, taking the driver's seat.

"It almost did," Cheshire countered, surprising me.

"What changed your minds?" I asked.

"Griffin didn't seem like your type," Caterpillar answered.

"What do you mean?" I asked, curious where I had gone wrong.

"While there was obvious familiarity, you didn't exactly behave as if you were dating. Hatter pointed out that he didn't seem jealous to find you with four random men," he explained.

"I'm sure he wasn't. Griff had a crush on me when we were younger, but I shut him down because Dina was interested in him. He's used to me having partners around," I said.

"Plural?" Cheshire asked.

I furrowed my eyebrows, and he clarified, "More than one lover."

"I'm not exactly an ugly woman," I replied, offended.

"You also don't seem like a slut," he shot back.

"How would you know?" I asked, and then added, "Also, a woman having sex doesn't make her a slut."

"You haven't tried to sleep with any of us," he pointed out, "I didn't say it did, but only sluts sleep with Jabberwocky."

"When would I have had time?" I wondered.

"Touché. Do you intend to sleep with any of us?" he asked, wiggling his eyebrows.

I rolled my eyes and willed the heat to leave my cheeks.

"Who she sleeps with is irrelevant," Caterpillar snapped.

I glanced up at him, his jaw was tense as he drove. I hadn't even noticed when he grabbed my arm and began pulling me down the alley. Cheshire was a distraction.

"To you maybe," Cheshire muttered.

"If that was the case, you would have let me leave with Jabberwocky," I said, ignoring Ches.

"That wasn't about sex, and you know it," Caterpillar shut down the argument. I sighed, Caterpillar was difficult to read. I stayed quiet for the rest of the ride. When we got to Griff's apartment, I knocked on the door before letting myself in. The sight before me made me laugh. Hatter and March were sipping out of dainty teacups, Griffin was pacing behind them.

"What's so funny?" Hatter asked, handing his teacup to March, who accidentally dropped his phone into it.

"Damn it March, you've ruined another one," Caterpillar chastised, "We don't have endless supplies."

March hung his head, looking too much like a kicked puppy. I slapped Caterpillar in the chest and hissed, "Be nice. He didn't do it on purpose." I patted March on the head as I took a seat in one of the mismatched wingback chairs in Griffin's small living room.

"She hits him like he isn't a foot taller than her," Cheshire muttered.

"Imagine what I would do to you, since you're only a few inches taller than me," I said, pointing at him.

"Yeah, Ches, she might take you across her knee." Hatter joked, pulling me into a hug, "I'm glad you're okay sweetheart," he whispered before releasing me.

"She was going to have sex with the Jabberwocky, and she gets a hug," Cheshire complained.

"You what?" Hatter asked, eerie calm filling his voice.

"Now, Cheshire. She was never going to have sex with him. I expect the dagger strapped to her left leg was meant for him." Caterpillar explained.

My eyes went wide. He had seen directly through my plan with no problem. Caterpillar had the potential to be a great ally in saving Lily and Dina. A spark of hope filled my chest, together I might have a chance to save the people I loved.

"How did you figure that out?" I asked.

"Well, I felt the knife when you tried to kick me. Plus, I don't believe you would actually try to fuck the Jabberwocky. It wasn't that difficult to figure out. I've seen more well thought out plans though," he smirked at me. I had the sudden urge to electrocute him. I knew he didn't care if I got hurt, it was just about his male pride. Egotistical bastard.

"You didn't consider that he might take the knife as an invitation to slit your throat? Or that he might consider it foreplay since he seems devious that way? You couldn't overpower him. He would have raped you, not arrested you. It was incredibly stupid," Hatter said, looking pissed.

"You've both forgotten one very important thing," I said, trying to defuse the situation, "I have magick."

"How much did you sleep last night?" Cheshire asked, crossing his arms, "Are you at full power?"

"Around eight hours," I replied, sheepishly.

"And you told us you had to have ten, so you obviously aren't at full power," he said.

"Well, missing two hours for one day won't drop my power level much," I defended.

"Prove it," Caterpillar said.

"What do you mean?" I asked, furrowing my eyebrows.

"Fight me off. If you win, we'll admit that your plan was stupid, but doable. If you're wrong, you defer your plans to me in the future," he said.

I felt the challenge against my skin, Caterpillar smirked knowing I wouldn't admit defeat.

"Fine," I said, crossing my arms.

"Guys, I'm not sure this is the b-best idea," March said, looking between us.

"No, let them have this out now. It's like letting dogs fight for dominance." Hatter said, helping us move furniture against the walls of the tiny apartment. I snorted at his comment.

Once all the furniture was moved Hatter, March, Cheshire, and Griffin stood against the empty wall. All four of them displaying varying degrees of nervousness. I smiled, thinking it was cute that they would be nervous on my behalf. Just because Caterpillar was a foot taller than me and probably a solid hundred and twenty pounds heavier didn't mean I wouldn't win.

"Let's pretend this is as close to the situation earlier tonight as possible," I suggested, facing off with him.

He grunted before slamming my back into the wall behind me, effectively trapping me. He grinned at the shocked look on my face, "Whenever you're ready, princess."

I took a deep breath, causing the oak and vanilla scent of Caterpillar's cologne fill my nostrills. I met his eyes, holding my breath when I found his intense gaze focused entirely on me. I pulled the knife from under my dress. I rolled it over my knuckles several times, trying to decide what my next move should be.

"Quit stalling," Caterpillar growled in my ear, causing shivers to run down my spine. If this man knew how he affected my body he'd be insufferable. I moved my dagger to his neck digging the tip gently into his throat. A small drop of blood ran from the pinprick. It distracted me, trailing sensually down his neck to his collarbone, before disappearing below his shirt. I shook off the urge to lick him, disgusted with myself for even considering licking blood off this brooding asshole.

I ducked under one of his arms, but before I could complete my escape he grabbed my wrist, he'd fallen into my trap. I wasn't terrible at hand-to-hand combat though I was far less practiced than I'd like to admit. I reached into my well of power, conjuring an exact copy of myself. Illusion was my weakest ability, and while I knew it wouldn't hold for long. I hoped that it would be long enough to take care of a few things. I stepped away, hoping the cloak I'd used in my illusion would hold. I appreciated the accuracy of my copy for a moment. She whined as Caterpillar grabbed her, playing a damsel in distress. Her wide, pale, blue eyes, and blonde hair flying as my copy beat pale fists against him. It sent an embarrassing thrill to my core to see Caterpillar pressing my double into the wall. While he was distracted, I slipped a hand into his pocket, snatching the motorcycle key I'd seen earlier. I saw Cheshire track my true movements, but no one else noticed, so I winked at him. A grin, much like his namesakes, spread across his face.

I snuck to Griffin's bedroom climbing down the fire escape and making my way to Caterpillar's bike. I shoved the key in the ignition and drove away as quickly as possible. I knew Cheshire would tell them of my deception when he realized I wasn't coming back. I had very little time to handle all of the racing thoughts in my head. I couldn't place all of my hopes on the Resistance. When I finally made it to Dina's apartment, I poured myself a drink. I settled in to ensure that if the Resistance failed me, I still had a chance to save the people I loved.

Chapter 5

It was well over an hour before I heard voices outside Dina's door. Caterpillar burst in, looking pissed. I remained seated on Dina's couch, raising an eyebrow at his dramatic entrance. I noticed Cheshire hovering in the doorway and gave him a wink. He sent a worried glance towards Caterpillar, but smiled when he realized he was not in Cater's periphery.

"What the fuck was that, Alice," Caterpillar yelled, yanking me up from my seat.

"I knew I couldn't physically fight you, so I tricked you instead," I explained, calmly.

"Your illusion fought him until he pinned her to the floor, and then she said, 'I win,' before disappearing." Cheshire said, looking awed.

"And you saw her leave and said nothing." Caterpillar growled at Ches, but kept his eyes locked on mine, "I don't want to hear from you."

"You aren't prepared to fight magick. You didn't even feel my body slip away, all you would have had to do is say my name for the illusion to disappear," I explained, feeling victorious.

"I was worried that you went back to the Hearts Club," he whispered, before turning away from me. I didn't understand why he was so concerned, it seemed genuine, but I had to make him understand.

"I considered it, but I needed to prove my point first. You're too cocky. All I had to do was cast a simple illusion to get around you. I am not the only person with magick in this city." I said, laying a hand on his shoulder,

"It wasn't my intention to worry you, but you need to understand magick. I desperately need your help," I added, knowing I had to make peace with the infuriating man.

"Magick isn't the answer to every fight," he grumbled, his shoulder tense under my touch.

"I never claimed it was, which is exactly why I need your help. Magick is what I'm good at—not strategy, not hiding, or finding intel. All I can do is storm the proverbial castle, which isn't going to work." I admitted, "I need to sneak. I need information to save Lily and Dina, and, ultimately, I will need someone to save my ass when I fuck all of this up."

"I still don't trust you," Caterpillar said, a tick in his jaw, "and if the choice comes down to you or my men, I will not help you."

"I respect that. I will save my family before you, as well." I answered, although the more time I spent with them, the more I wondered if I could choose. I was curious about these men, something about them made me want to get to know them better. No one deserved to die because Wonderland was full of corruption.

"If you take a risk and it kills someone I love, I will put a bullet in your head," He said, coldly.

"I expect nothing less but understand that if that bullet will stop me from saving Lily or Dina... I will fight you and I won't lose. You can kill me after they are safe," I offered.

"I would prefer if no one to died," he said, his honesty surprising me.

"Me too," I answered, and just like that we had come to an understanding.

"As heartwarming as this discussion has been, we have one problem." Cheshire chimed in, "She is completely unprepared. We're going to have to take her to Dodo."

"We can't take the risk. He would readily give her over to the Red Party for money," Caterpillar barked, and I regretted using Ches in my game.

"She can't be running around with only a knife and magick to defend herself." Cheshire argued, crossing his arms.

I kept my mouth shut, watching the conversation. There was no need to reveal more about my life than was necessary. I couldn't trust them entirely. Not yet. Anything that would help me know more about how they operated was important for me to know.

"Fine, but if this gets her in trouble it's your fault," Caterpillar said, dragging me out of the apartment. I allowed him to continue dragging me along. There was no reason to continue to make unnecessary waves with the Resistance leader. Some part of me admired that Caterpillar had managed to keep my mother's work going.

"What about your motorcycle?" I asked, as he started to walk away from the building.

"Leave it, it will be safe in the garage here, and if one of us needs it we know where it is." Caterpillar responded, continuing to drag me along.

"So, Al, do you not have something to do every day, most of Wonderland works?" Cheshire asked, filling the silence. I considered how I should answer the question, but instead chose to change the subject.

"You called me Al," I pointed out, emotion swelling in my chest.

"So?" He stared at me as I avoided his question.

"The only person who has ever called me that was my dad," I explained, a sense of longing filling me. No amount of time would heal my grief. Losing both my parents had changed something in me I couldn't begin to explain. Especially my father.

"Oh," he looked at me, pink filling his cheeks, and he quickly added, "I won't do it again."

"No, it's fine," I said, patting his arm. Caterpillar seemed to be ignoring us both, even though his grip on my arm did not loosen.

"What was he like?" Ches asked.

"Wonderful. My parents were complete opposites, my mother was a bit like Caterpillar." I cringed as the words left my mouth, realizing they were true, "Far too serious for her own good. She took on everything for everyone. She would have given someone her last dime and the shirt off her back. It literally killed her, but I wish I was more like her in some ways. Dad was funny and carefree; he spent more time laughing than anyone else I've ever known. He thought magick was fascinating, even though he had no gift." I said, smiling at the memories, "We used to run every morning. It shocked all of us when he died, he was so happy and healthy."

"They sound great," Cheshire said. The pained look on his face reflected the way I felt thinking of my parents. I remember that he lost his parents, too, and wondered if he had fond memories of them as well.

"Did you punch your mom, too?" Caterpillar asked, and for a moment I was shocked, until I saw the small smile on his face.

"Of course not, even when I was mad at her, I knew her intentions were good," I said, seriously. "Plus, that woman was terrifying. She would've kicked my ass."

"And, yet, you damn near broke my jaw," he pointed out.

"You have a stick up your ass, Mom never did," I shot back. He stopped walking and stared at me.

"Shit," Ches murmured.

"A stick up my ass?" he repeated, "You've got to be fucking kidding me." he muttered to himself, looking up at the night sky, "Why did the Creator do this to me? I never did anything to deserve this." He continued to walk but turned to look at me. "Do you get off on insulting me?" he asked, watching my face.

"If I said, 'Yes,' what would you do?" I asked, cheekily.

"Find a better way to get you off," he stated, looking serious.

I looked at Ches, who honestly looked as surprised as me. I gaped for a minute, unable to come up with a response. "Did he just offer to get me off?" I asked Cheshire, trying to comprehend the flirtation. He nodded, but said nothing, staring at Caterpillar. I tried to push away the heat that had rushed to my face. I saw a small smile on his face and started to laugh.

"Oh, my god, he does have a sense of humor. Shocking." I roared, taking the lead after I finally pulled my arm away from him. Caterpillar and Cheshire both stared at me for a moment before following me.

"So, who is Dodo?" I asked as we got closer to Griffin's apartment.

"Dodo is an arms dealer who sells to both sides. He also has other things, such as drugs, Kevlar, and phones. Hatter got the Hummer from him." Ches explained, although he looked uncomfortable, "He's also March's grandfather." he added in a whisper.

"Oh, I bet March will be glad to see him," I said. Cheshire shook his head but didn't explain. I wondered why March wouldn't be happy to see his grandfather, I would have loved to meet any of grandparents. My father's parents had been killed in a building collapse just outside the city when he was very young. They left a large inheritance; he'd been taken in my family friends until he was of age. My mother had never said anything about anyone in her family.

We walked through Griffin's apartment door without bothering to knock.

"Alice, will you please tell Hatter that I'm not dating you," Griffin groaned, as we walked in.

"We're not dating," I said simply.

"I told you so," Griff said, waving his hands toward me.

"She kissed you," Hatter pointed out, narrowing his eyes.

"Exactly, she kissed me, I didn't kiss her," he groaned, rubbing his forehead. I patted Griffin's shoulder and smiled.

"You didn't object." Hatter said, standing and turning his attention to me. "I don't think I've ever seen Caterpillar look more shocked than when you disappeared out from under him." he said, kissing the top of my head. My face reddened at the action, but I didn't move away from him. Not everyone in Wonderland was very loving. The Red Party used anything they could find against people; love could easily be used against you. Hatter's easy affection was refreshing. I found that in the worst of times love was the only thing we could lean on.

"We're going to Dodo's," Caterpillar announced.

March had just entered the room, and immediately paled. I could see him struggling to get out any words. A strangled sound left his throat just before the teacup in March's hands flew at Caterpillar, who ducked gracefully, as if he was used to flying teacups.

"Hey," Griffin exclaimed, "Those were my grandma's."

"Alice needs supplies. You don't have to come with us," I could tell Caterpillar was trying to reason with him, but it was obvious he was failing.

"She d-doesn't need anything that bad. He will h-h-hurt her," His face was red as he struggled with his emotions making his stutter much worse.

"We don't have any other choice," Caterpillar said, crossing his arms.

"No, she can't go," March said, holding his ground.

My heart squeezed, but I had to see this through, I needed to know every detail about these men as I could figure out.

"She'll have to be fitted, he'll want to see her to pick a few good weapons," Ches said, trying to defuse March.

"Fuck you, Ch-Cheshire," he replied, before storming out of the room. I noticed that Hatter remained silent, although he was tense against my back.

"Why doesn't March want me to go to see Dodo?" I asked. The tension in the room rocketed even higher at my question. I glanced at Griffin for support. Instead, he shrugged his shoulders and began cleaning up the broken glass from the teacup.

"Sit," Hatter commanded, "I'll go calm him down and Caterpillar can explain."

"It's not my story to tell," Caterpillar said, stiff.

"Fine, let me go get him and I'll explain. We aren't going to Dodo's tonight, anyway. Ches, go call and make an appointment for tomorrow," Hatter said, leaving the room.

"It's bad, isn't it?" I stated, looking at Caterpillar, "It's why he stutters, right?"

"We all have our sob stories, but I would say March's is the worst," he replied, settling down across from me. I sat down, chewing my lip. I imagined all the horrible things that could have happened to the sweet man who had just stormed out of the room. Caterpillar was right, we all had sob stories, life took something from us all, but some suffered much more than others.

An hour passed before Hatter and March came back. March looked awful, his dark blond hair was standing up like he had been running his fingers through it and his eyes were bloodshot. I smiled and patted the seat next to mine, signaling him to sit with me. He took up my offer and Hatter sat on the other side of me. I waited patiently as March tried to find words to explain why he was insistent we couldn't go to Dodo's. When he finally turned pleading eyes to me, words lost to him, Hatter began to speak. "March and I met when we were kids. Our parents lived in the same neighborhood. When I was six my mom died, I don't remember how or why, but she'd been sick for a while. Dad started working more, so I spent as much time running around outside as I could. I think March did the same thing," Hatter stopped and I looked at March who was nodding in silent agreement.

"Anyway, I always noticed that March was a beat up, but I just assumed he was clumsy." Hatter continued, "My dad may not have been around much, but he was good to me, so I had no idea some parents weren't. One day—I guess I was probably eleven or twelve—March knocked on my door, crying, and I just let him in, no questions asked. At that point, we'd been friends for several years. My dad was a doctor, he'd focused on psychology. You know they have to do all the training with how few people go into the medical field, so he started bandaging the cuts and bruises. March went home the next day, and Dad didn't go to work. I should have known something serious was going on then. When I was about to leave for school the next day, he asked me about how my friend got hurt. I told him I had no idea. That's when he told me that someone was hurting him. I was so pissed; I just assumed it was some kid on the street. I was naïve back then," he stopped, shaking his head.

"It wa-wasn't your fault, Hatter," March spoke up.

"It doesn't matter. I should have realized what was going on sooner. No ten-year-old runs into that many doors or falls that much," Hatter hissed, before adding, "Sorry. I still feel stupid for not knowing. You were my friend, and I didn't do anything to help you."

March just shook his head and leaned across me to grip Hatter's shoulder. When he sat back in his seat, I held his hand, wanting to comfort him. He smiled at me and nodded for Hatter to continue.

Hatter resumed his story, "I skipped school and went to March's house. I had never been there before, and I guess that should have struck me as odd, but I was a stupid kid." March huffed but didn't interrupt. "His mom opened the door, and I knew immediately something was wrong. She had similar bruises to March and smelled like whiskey—I still can't drink that shit." He confessed, shaking his head in disgust, "Anyway, I asked her to see March and she told me he wasn't home. I left and went looking for him. I spent six hours hunting across our neighborhood for him before I went back to his house. This time when I knocked, March's stepdad answered the door, He told me March had run off. I was shocked, but I didn't question him. Dad taught me to never question an adult." Hatter stopped again and turned to Griffin, "Hey, Griff, do you have any of the hard stuff?" he asked, rubbing his hand across his face.

"Yeah, hold on a second," Griff replied, dragging himself off the floor. He came back a few minutes later with a bottle and a new teacup. He pointed a finger at March and said, "Try not to break this one." The smile on Griffin's face was the only thing that stopped me from punching him for the comment.

Hatter sat the teacup aside and drank straight from the bottle before handing it to me. When I started to shake my head, he whispered, "You'll want it." I settled the bottle between my thighs and motioned for him to continue.

With a sigh, Hatter started talking once more. "I went home that night, dejected, March was my only friend, and I believed he had run away. Dad told me he didn't believe March would leave without telling me, and that only made me feel worse. I spent a week locked in my room, depressed. The week after that, I searched around town for March; it simply didn't occur to me that his stepdad was lying. I was about to give up when I decided to sneak into March's house late one night and look for clues. It's important to note that I am not sneaky, that's all Cheshire."

I wondered why Hatter's Dad hadn't checked on March's living situation himself, but I chose not to ask any questions. "Thank g-god you did." March interrupted, grabbing the bottle from between my thighs and taking a large swig, before handing it back to me. I decided I needed liquid courage and took a large gulp myself. It burned all the way down my throat, and I found myself glad for the warmth as I heard the next part of the story.

Hatter's voice shook as he agreed with March, "Yeah, thank the Creator. I found March, naked, lying in bed sobbing. I froze, I didn't exactly expect to find my missing friend in his home, considering I had been told he ran off. Luckily my dad had given me a phone just in case I needed it. I called him, sent him pictures, and hid. I knew I couldn't do anything for March if I didn't have help. It felt like hours before the Suits showed up. They arrested March's mom and stepdad for prostitution and child abuse. Probably the only good thing those assholes have ever done." Hatter finished, leaving us all to sit in silence, breathing heavily.

"Prostitution?" I asked, not able to look up from my feet.

"My stepdad s-sold me," March confirmed. "I d-don't want to go into detail, but he sold my body to fuel their addictions."

My head snapped toward him, and I felt like I was going to throw up. Instead, tears welled in my eyes, and fell down my face. I grabbed March and hugged him.

"Oh Creator, I'm so sorry," I cried, holding him.

"It's okay, Ali. I w-went to l-live with Hatter and his d-dad," March explained, tears falling from his eyes, too.

"It is not okay," I yelled, standing, "Why didn't your grandad do anything? I'll kill him myself!" I exclaimed, looking for my shoes.

"Alice, it's okay," March said, surprising me, "Please don't murder anyone for m-me. Dodo didn't w-want me because I stutter," he added, laying a hand on my shoulder.

A feeling of calm settled over me, and I nodded, sitting back down next to March who pulled me into his chest. "I'd still like to rip him into tiny pieces with my bare hands," I whispered, and March laughed quietly.

"I'm used t-to it," he said, "I j-just don't want him to hurt you."

"He'll be lucky if I don't hurt him. Why didn't he do anything to help you?" I asked, then cringed, "Sorry that was insensitive of me. You don't have to answer."

"It's fine. H-He wasn't around, and by the time he came b-back I was living with H-Hatter," he explained.

"Why do you do business with this sleaze ball?" I asked, turning on Caterpillar. He'd been silent through the entire story. It was cruel to subject March to a grandfather who would reject him after all he'd been through.

"We don't always have a choice, and I always try to leave March at home, although he refuses to stay. Stubborn ass," Caterpillar defended.

"I'm a hare, not an ass." March said, at the same time I chimed in, "I'm pretty sure you're the ass."

"Whatever you have to tell yourself to sleep at night," Caterpillar said.

March crossed his arms and raised his eyebrows. Caterpillar sighed but did not continue the argument.

I looked out the window, noticing that it had grown completely dark in the time we'd been talking. Not even the moon hung in the sky tonight, as if it wanted to hide from the horror of March's past.

"Is it okay if we sleep here?" I asked, turning to Griffin.

"Of course, but I only have two bedrooms and the couch. Everyone will have to double up... well, someone will have to triple up," he responded.

"I'll sleep on the couch," Caterpillar offered.

"I'll come sleep with you Griff," I said, walking toward his bedroom.

"I think I'll sleep with him," Cheshire said, beating me to Griffin's room, "You can suffer with March and Hatter. Hatter talks in his sleep and March kicks." I wondered how Cheshire knew that information, but decided not to broach the subject as a yawn took me over.

"Well, don't seem too excited about it. Griff is bisexual, and you never know who he might be attracted to," I said, grinning.

"Jealous that your boyfriend will think I'm cute?" Ches shot back, throwing an arm over Griffin's shoulder.

"Nope," I said, popping the p, before sauntering to the guest room.

Hatter was already in bed when I got in there. I walked into the adjoining bathroom and stripped out of my silver dress. I groaned when I couldn't find one and walked back down the hall to Griffin's room in my underwear. Caterpillar was sprawled across the couch, already asleep. He looked almost peaceful, and I smiled at his quiet snore.

I opened the door and asked, "Hey, Griff can I borrow—"

"Woman, what is it with you and being undressed?" Cheshire squawked. He didn't look away as he said the words taking in my bare chest, my tiny, nude colored thong. I stood straighter enjoying the attention. I had never felt any shame at my naked body, as much as the Red Party tried to shame the natural human experiences.

"I don't have anything to sleep in," I said, ignoring his behavior.

"You can have one of my t-shirts, it'll be a bit big, but comfortable." Griffin replied, but I could see that he was trying not to laugh at Ches.

"Night Cheshire," I said, slipping the black shirt over my head.

"Goodnight, Al," he said, quietly.

I was surprised to find March and Hatter snuggling when I entered the room, "Do I need to go sleep with Ches and Griff? So, you can," I waved my hand, instead of finishing my sentence.

"We aren't a couple Alice, and even if we were we wouldn't have sex here. It would be disrespectful. March is just very cuddly," Hatter said, smiling.

"Okay then, I want to be in the middle," I said, wiggling between them.

Once I was comfortable. March tucked his head against my shoulder and Hatter wrapped an arm around my waist.

"Would it have bothered you if we were a couple?" Hatter whispered into my ear.

I ran my fingers through March's hair, marveling at the softness. "Hm, not really. I wasn't kidding when I said Griffin is bi; he's had both male and female partners, and it never bothered me. Also, I'm almost positive that my sister is gay. She mentioned something about liking girls to my mother when I was ten. I didn't understand what that meant back then, but she hasn't had any that I know of," I explained.

I turned to face Hatter so I could run my fingers through his hair. He let out a sound that went straight to my core, but I tried to ignore it.

"That wasn't what I meant, and you know it," he whispered back and I was suddenly glad the room was dark.

"Maybe I would have been a bit disappointed, but I've only known you guys for a couple of days," I admitted.

"Don't let Caterpillar run you off," Hatter said.

"I won't," I whispered back, and I felt myself drifting off to sleep, content.

My dreams that night were filled with knights coming to save the princess from the evil queen. Lily and Dina's faces appeared in my mind's eye, unharmed and happy. I only hope that when I woke, we would make that dream come true.

Chapter 6

Cheshire

There was no way to even begin to process the last few days of my life. Alice had come into the Resistance like a whirlwind, a golden headed tornado. She'd even managed to put Caterpillar in his place. I was obsessed, afraid, and yet utterly besotted. I should've been focused on the intel that Hatter had picked up at the Hearts Club that I hadn't had a chance to look at. Instead, I was laying on my back, listening to Griffin tell stories about him and Alice when they were growing up.

"So, then she walked in on him with another woman. I don't think I've ever seen her more furious." He was laughing, as he reminisced.

"What did she do?" I asked, turning onto my side to face him.

"Kicked him in the balls and slept with his best friend."

I could tell that Griffin had been obsessed with Alice as well. I couldn't blame him; she was everything a man could want and more. "So, she's always been—" I trailed off, looking for the right words.

"Strong willed? Violent? A pain in the ass?" He offered.

"I was going to say impulsive... but all those works as well." I chuckled.

"Alice is led by her emotions, has been as long as I've known her." Griffin said, interrupting my thoughts.

"How do you think she's really handling Lily and Dina being arrested?" I asked.

"When I didn't hear from her right away, I knew something was wrong. Alice may keep things to herself, but she cares more about the people she loves than her own feelings." He explained, before adding, "It's her blessing, and her curse."

"That doesn't answer my question." I said.

"Having the four of you around is a good distraction for her." My heart skipped a beat at his words, "She may never admit this, but she's attracted to all of you. I've never seen her click with anyone as quickly. She's letting you four into parts of her life even Dina and I have been kept in the dark about."

"So, are we going to be nothing more than a distraction, so she doesn't have to deal with her feelings?" I asked, ignoring my own disappointment at the idea. Alice was everything I'd ever looked for in a woman. Pretty, intelligent, sassy, and selfless. I could see the way March worshipped the ground she walked on; the way Hatter wanted to treat her like a girl who needed his protection. Even Caterpillar stared at her with lust and something else I couldn't quite put my finger on. I couldn't compete with them, I'd always been the goofy, geeky friend. Not to say I hadn't ever been with a woman, but I couldn't offer anyone the things my friends could. I admired them all, they'd stood by my side in the worst of times. I wanted nothing more than to stand with them during the best of times. We'd spent years working toward the that. The more I got to know Alice the more I envisioned her with us in the best of times. Wonderland deserved to be free if for no other reason than Alice Young would smile more.

"Cheshire?" Griffin asked, reminding me that I'd asked a question.

"Sorry." I mumbled.

"Anyway. It isn't my place to tell you how she feels, because I don't know for sure," He began, "Alice doesn't deal well with grief. When her dad died, she didn't talk to anyone for weeks. Lily finally snapped her out of it."

"How?" I asked, when he didn't continue.

"Started a fight." He refused to explain more so I changed the subject. "What about her mom?"

"Alice has a lot of guilt about her mother's death, because she was there when her mom was killed. She went off the rails, she partied hard, she threw herself at any man who showed interest, she drank. Until Dina, Lily, and I had an intervention." He said, and I found myself with more questions than answers. "If I were you, Cat, I would trust that Alice will do anything for the people she cares about. I have a feeling you and your friends are quickly becoming a part of that. I'm not as violent as Alice, but if any of you mistreat my best friend, I will find a way to end you." Griffin added, before turning over to go to sleep.

I appreciated Griffin's threat even if it was unnecessary. Everyone deserved to have people that would protect them no matter what. I had no idea what to think about everything I had just learned about the beautiful, violent girl sleeping next door, cuddled up with two of my best friends, but I wasn't going to ignore the way I was already starting to feel for her. Curiosity might have killed the cat, but satisfaction brought it back. I needed to know everything about Alice, every inconsequential detail, but I couldn't scare her away. It wasn't fair of me to be feeling this way while she was trying to save people she loved. I would do anything to help her save her sister and friend, then I would worry about how to make her mine.

Chapter 7

❧ ⚜ ☙

July 28th, 2157

"Alice. Alice?"

A voice pierced my dreamless sleep, and I fluttered my eyes open to find Hatter smiling at me. "Good morning," he said, "Can I ask you a question?"

"Sure," I replied, not quite awake.

"Do you glow after sex, too?" he asked, grinning.

I looked down at myself to find that I was covered in a silvery glow, heat rushed to my cheeks, and I tried to extinguish it. I yanked at the sleeping core of my magick, dropping a heavy cage over it.

"It's b-beautiful, ignore him, Ali," March said, rubbing my arm. The glow returned to its vibrant color when he touched me.

"Shit. Shit. Shit," I cursed, sitting up. I pinched myself hoping to dim it slightly. When that didn't work I climbed out of bed. I ignored March's stares. "Damn it all straight to hell," I continued, as I stomped into the kitchen.

"Woah, what the fuck have you been doing?" Cheshire asked. I looked up to find him shirtless and staring at me. Cheshire wasn't as muscular as Hatter or Caterpillar, but it was obvious he worked out. His body was packed with lean muscle. I glanced down to see that the light happy trail leading into his jeans was the same pink and purple as his hair. I felt heat rush to my cheeks as I imagined what lay past the black leather belt. I shook myself to clear my heated thoughts. Cheshire smirked at me as I stomped past, my face must have shown exactly what I had been thinking about.

I heard a quiet groan from the living room and then Caterpillar shouted, "Can you assholes please shut up? I'm trying to sleep."

"Damn. This is a bad time to have to explain that," Griffin said, rubbing his head and staring at me.

"No shit," I replied, frustrated. I barely knew these men, as much as I might like them so far, having to explain this aspect of my magick wasn't ideal.

"What the fuck is wrong with your skin?" Caterpillar asked, entering the room, rubbing his eyes. Embarrassment flooded me as he stared at me speechless. I pulled one of Griffin's sweatshirts over my head hiding as much of my skin as possible.

"Goddamn it," I muttered, "Fuck." I groaned as Hatter and March entered the kitchen. They started ransacking the cabinets for Griff's supply of tea. They were all throwing glances my way clearly wanting answers about the strange glow. I snatched his loose leaf tea he'd chosen, and began making tea.

"I woke up, and she was glowing like the moon," Hatter said. He tipped his head quizzically.

It happens when she's satisfied," Griffin explained, pouring himself some orange juice. I sent him a death glare, that was an assumption we had made when I was a teenager and it had first started happening. My mother had seemed a bit shaken by how vivid the glow was. It would happen at the most inopportune times, after an orgasm or in the middle of a family dinner. Lily only showed signs of a glow when she was actively using her magick, and it was never as bright as mine.

"Which one of you assholes satisfied her?" Cheshire said, pointing at March and Hatter.

"Not satisfied like that dumbass. Well, at least not all the time, although the first time she masturbated—" Griffin began.

"You better stop right there, Griffin Alexander or I will remove your tongue," I said between sips of my tea.

"Oh, no, Glowworm, I have got to hear this," Ches said, waving me away.

I growled at him but said nothing. Everyone was looking at me expectantly and it was clear they were not going to drop it. "Okay, fine. I'll explain, but can we please go sit down?" I said, giving up. Ches clapped his hands and led us all into the living room. I watched as they all took seats, before turning to stare at me expectantly. "As Griffin already said, when I am satisfied— sexually or not—my magick floats to my skin and causes it to glow. Obviously, this is awkward when you first have sex with someone who doesn't know about your magick. Two people screaming immediately after you have an orgasm is a big turn-off."

"You take afterglow to a whole new level," Ches said, and I came out of my seat, grabbing him by the arm.

"How would you like it if every time you're content your skin glows, I have no control over it. I fucking hate it," I growled, before stomping out of the room. I was so frustrated; I was close to crying. I heard footsteps behind me as I slammed the bedroom door and crawled underneath the covers. I loved my magick, it was a huge part of who I was, but it set me apart from others. I was so lucky to have Griffin and Dinah. As my mind drifted to Dinah I cringed, I was ashamed to be caught up in my emotions when she was in danger.

"Did someone really r-run away from you?" March asked, closing the bedroom door behind him. I nodded, unable to bring myself to speak. "Th-They were stupid, Ali. I think it's cool that your skin glows. I don't do anything interesting like that," March said, sitting down next to me.

"You're amazing. Your skin glowing wouldn't make you any better," I said, looking up at him.

"It might help p-people ignore my stutter," he said, pulling me into his lap.

I shook my head and said, "I bet people don't scream after you have an orgasm—and I don't mean in an enjoyable way. Terrified is not the kind of scream you want to hear from someone you're sleeping with."

"No, they usually scream be-beforehand," March said, and I immediately felt bad.

"I'm sorry, I swear I would never scream before having sex with you," I promised, "Maybe during though." I wiggled my eyebrows and March chuckled in response.

"Thank you," he whispered, rubbing my back. I crawled out of his lap and offered him my hand. We walked back into the living room where everyone was still sitting quietly.

"Apologize," Caterpillar snarled at Cheshire. His arms were crossed over his chest as he glared at Cheshire from his spot at the counter. I had no idea why he would care if they had offended me, but I appreciated the gesture. I'm sure everyone getting along made Caterpillar's life a little easier.

"I'm sorry, Al. I didn't mean to offend you; I just thought it was fucking amazing," Ches said, looking at his feet.

"It's fine, I'm just sensitive about it," I said, patting his arm.

"I'm not asking this to be rude, but when will your glow diminish? We can't go to Dodo's like this," Caterpillar explained, sipping his drink.

"Uh, it depends..." I trailed off, heat rushing to my cheeks.

"On what?" he pressed.

"If I had to use my magick it was stay longer. Or if I felt... satisfied again," I said, looking at Griffin, who gave me a smile.

"This is gonna sound rude, but does it get brighter?" Hatter asked.

"Yeah, it can," I stated simply, hoping the conversation would end.

"So, if you're already glowing, and you were to have an orgasm, you would brighten?" he asked. I groaned and put my head in my hands.

"Hatter," Cheshire scolded, "She obviously is embarrassed by her glow. Which is ridiculous, because if I could glow after sex, I would glow as often as possible and gloat about it."

I found myself laughing at his rambling. "It would only prove that you masturbate," I choked out. It was his turn to blush, and it caused me to laugh harder.

"It's starting to fade already," Griffin pointed out, stopping my laughter. I looked down at my arms to find that they had, indeed, dimmed. I suppressed a shiver, I'd managed to avoid most of my former partners from ever seeing my weird glow. Only two people outside of my family and friends had ever seen it. They'd both been so terrified it wasn't hard to convince them to keep it to themselves. Few people in Wonderland still believed in magick users. Even though it was clear to me that several magick users worked to keep the city running. Thankfully, I had managed to avoid any Suits showing up at my door asking questions about a glowing girl.

"Okay, we need to leave in about two hours. Why don't we get ready and have some breakfast? By then, maybe Alice's glow won't be as obvious," Caterpillar said.

"I only have one shower." Griffin said, "But I can make breakfast," he added, quickly when Caterpillar glared at him.

"I'll go get our clothes out of the Hummer," Ches offered, exiting the room.

"Why don't you take the first shower?" Caterpillar said to me. I nodded instead of replying.

Griffin's bathroom was much larger than Dina's. While he had plenty of hot water, I opted for freezing cold in hopes it would help diminish the glow. I tried to be quick, scrubbing my skin with a rough cloth and basic soap I'd found in Griffin's cabinets. After a very cold shower, the glow on my skin was barely noticeable. I threw on some ripped jeans and a light blue blouse. I took a few deep breaths before I joined the guys in the living room.

"Good," Caterpillar said, startling me, "it's almost gone."

"I took a cold shower," I explained, playing with the bottom of my shirt, "I hate them, so I knew it would help."

"I'm sorry about Cheshire and Hatter. They both think everyone is comfortable with their teasing." he said, awkwardly patting my shoulder, "It shouldn't embarrass you, by the way, it's... very pretty," he added, not looking at me. He left before I could respond. My heart warmed a little at his effort to make me feel better.

"Do you need help?" I asked when I found Griffin trying, and failing, to crack eggs.

"How do people avoid eating the shells?" he muttered angrily.

I gently took the eggs from him. "How do you feed yourself when Dina and I aren't around?" I joked, hip-checking him.

"I hate eggs. I just assumed your men wouldn't just want to eat bread and bacon," he replied. "How much do you think Hatter and Caterpillar have to eat to keep those muscles?"

"They aren't my anything," I said, rolling my eyes.

"Have you told them that?" he snorted, handing me a spatula. I took it and slapped him with it, irritated. There was no reason to focus on my not-relationship with the rag-tag Resistance group. The only thing that mattered was saving Lily and Dina.

"I don't think I have to. I mean, sure, they're all conventionally attractive, but that isn't everything," I defended.

"They also think you hung the moon, or at least three of them do. I'm pretty sure Caterpillar wants to protect you, but he's a hard man to read. You didn't him rush out of here when your illusion disappeared. You also didn't see them when I told them you went to the Hearts Club; they panicked," Griffin said, stopping me.

"It doesn't matter anyway, whether I like them or not, I can't date all four of them. I don't even know their real names," I said, trying to hide my disappointment.

"Why can't you date all four of them? What about Lacie and her five husbands? No one objected to her relationship. Last I heard, they have two children," Griffin shot back, ending my argument.

"Lacie is a badass; even if someone objected, she would have done it anyway," I said, stirring my eggs.

"Her sister, Tillie, has two husbands and she's as meek as a mouse. Plus, you're pretty badass yourself. You tricked the leader of the Resistance," Griffin reminded me.

"Only because I have magick... They would never agree to such a thing," I muttered.

"You'll never know until you ask," he said, patting my back.

"Ask what?" Hatter asked, snatching a piece of bacon.

"Nothing," I snapped, glaring at Griffin.

Hatter stiffened but did not say anything else and I felt bad for snapping at him. "Who's Lacie?" I glared at him for eavesdropping. Cheshire entered the kitchen, grabbing himself a piece of bacon as well.

"Lacie is an old friend of Lily's. She has multiple partners." Griffin explained, before I could stop him, "Her sister Tillie does too," he added, stepping away from me.

"Why were you talking about that?" Ches asked, tilting his head.

"Just reminiscing." I said, before muttering, "So that Griff will remember why I almost smothered him with a pillow when we were nine."

"Dina was the one who told your mom, not me," he defended, holding his hands up in surrender.

"Back to the woman with multiple partners," Hatter said, "At the same time? Isn't that polyandry?" he asked, shocking me.

I nodded, before asking, "How do you know that?"

Hatter's cheeks turned pink, and I was suddenly very curious. "Well, I was very interested in history and law as a child. As I got older, I wondered more about what was illegal—in a more sexual sense—before the world started to fall apart. The entirety of America saw marrying multiple partners as a criminal offense. I always thought that was ridiculous. Love is love," he explained, "Plus, I've shared partners before, it's... nice," he added, flushed.

"With who?" Ches asked, although I already knew the answer. Hatter looked at me, immediately saw the recognition in my eyes, and shook his head. It was clear to me that March and Hatter were involved, I couldn't see how Cheshire could miss that.

"Cheshire you shouldn't ask that. It's none of your business," I said, saving Hatter from giving an explanation.

"None of my business? Come on, sharing your lady with another dude? That's... fun. Why can't I ask questions about it?" Ches whined, "Maybe I would enjoy it," he added, wiggling his eyebrows at me and I turned beet red.

"It's a threesome, Cat. I'm sure you've heard of threesomes," I said.

"Actually, polyandry is not just a threesome. It is a committed relationship with one woman and two or more men," Hatter said, although we both ignored him.

"You ever had one, Glowworm? Double the opportunity to turn silver," Cheshire shot back.

"I'm not gonna tell you if I've had a threesome or not," I said, rolling my eyes. Cheshire was nosey, and I wanted to change the topic sooner rather than later.

"Because you haven't," he said, sticking out his tongue.

I grabbed him by his shirt and whispered in his ear. "It's one of the most amazing things a person can experience—two people worshipping your body. Their sole focus on your pleasure, even above their own. It is as if the three souls intertwine, dancing along your skin. While you move closer and closer to your own release, knowing that when you get there it'll be as close to Heaven on Earth as any of us will ever get."

Ches was breathing heavily when I released him, and I smirked. "Fuck," he groaned, watching me closely. I could see the pupils had widened, and I had to force myself not to check if he had become hard from my words. Griffin and Hatter were looking between the two of us like they were watching a sports match.

"Why aren't you ready to go yet? We have to be at Dodo's in an hour," Caterpillar said, breaking the tension. He had only a towel wrapped around his waist, and my mouth was suddenly dry. His wet chest was glistening, and I had to turn away to stop myself from staring like an idiot. For the first time, I noticed the tattoo that led from his chest down his bicep. I couldn't quite make out the details from so far away, but I was curious to see more. The tattoos along his fingers and hands elicited thoughts I refused to entertain about him.

"Did you get our stuff, Ches?" Hatter asked. '

He nodded and motioned toward the living room, and then grumbled, "I'm going to take a cold shower,"

"I don't think we should leave Griffin here," Caterpillar declared.

"Why not?" Griffin asked, putting down his toast.

"I was thinking about how odd it was that, right after Alice was drugged, her sister and friend were taken into custody. I think the Suits knew exactly who they were taking, and, when they didn't get her, they took the people closest to her. They're trying to lure her to them," Caterpillar explained. I suddenly felt dizzy, so I slid to the floor, my stomach sinking. I hadn't even considered that the two events were connected. I felt like an idiot, there were no coincidences.

"Why didn't they take me when I went back to my house?" I asked, looking up at Caterpillar. I saw the pity in his eyes, and it ignited my rage.

"I don't think they could. Maybe they didn't want to push their authority. I don't have all the answers." he replied, taking a step away from me when he looked into my eyes, "If they know about Griffin, they'll take him next. I don't know what their intention is. I...I've never seen them do something like this," he admitted. Caterpillar went silent, clearly trying to puzzle out my situation, nothing made sense. Lily and Dina were completely innocent, they both worked and kept their head down. I did my best, but I had made the choice to enjoy the money our parents had left us instead of falling into the Red Party's trap of working my life away for them. "The Red Queen," Caterpillar said, snapping me out of thoughts. My breath hitched, horror filling my entire body.

"Who?" Hatter asked.

"My mom once mentioned someone who went by the name of the Red Queen. She runs the Red Party and controls the King of Hearts. She told my dad that if I ever found myself in trouble that he couldn't explain, the Red Queen was behind it." I ranted, searching through my bag. I stared at Caterpillar wondering how he knew about her. I trailed off when I couldn't find what I was looking for and I went running into the bathroom.

"I don't know anyone by that name," Hatter replied from the other room.

"You wouldn't, Mom said she couldn't tell anyone, yet. I don't know why..." I shouted back. "Cheshire, when you gathered the stuff in my room, did you find a leather-bound journal? I need it," I asked, grabbing the shower curtain, and yanking it back.

"Creator, Alice. I'm showering here," he yelled, grabbing the shower curtain from my hands, to cover himself.

"I don't care. Leather-bound journal. Quickly, Cat," I said.

"I didn't see anything like that," he answered.

"Fuck," I muttered, "It would have been sitting in plain sight, on top of my dresser. Are you sure that you didn't see it?" I asked again.

"Yeah, I'm sure," he said, furrowing his eyebrows, "What's going on?" he asked.

"Finish your shower. Hurry. I'll explain when you're done," I said. Exiting the bathroom, I ran into March who was pulling on jeans.

"Wh-What's wrong, Ali?" he asked, trying to chase after me.

I shook my head and went back to the living room to find Caterpillar, dressed and looking through my bag. "They aren't in there," I snapped, yanking my bag away from him. I didn't need him looking at my unmentionables.

"Tell me what else do you know about the Red Queen," he demanded.

"I already did—leader of the Red Party, she's the puppet master. Mom seemed concerned about her," I said, yanking on my boots. "Scared even."

"Why did you need the journal?" he asked.

"They were my mom's. If the Red Party has it, they know everything about my family." I said, trying to control the shaking that had started in my hands, "I never read it in detail, just skimmed it. I couldn't bring myself to after Mom died. I never told Lily about the journal, I didn't want her to worry about a threat I had no information about."

"What is everything, Alice? I need details," he begged, trying to make me focus.

"The first half started when she and my dad got married. It ended suddenly, but the last entry was about the Resistance. She talked about someone, a young man, who would take her place," I explained, running my finger through my hair.

"Who was the young man?" he asked.

I sat in silence, thinking, so I could choose my next words carefully. "She never mentioned him by name, although she talked at length about his parents. How much she respected them, how they died defending her. I think she wanted to adopt the boy, but he refused her help." Everyone went silent, staring at Caterpillar, who had paled. Once again, I found myself really studying the brooding man before me. Something stirred in my mind that I couldn't quite place. There was no way he knew my mother. Why would he hide it from me for this long? I wondered who the boy was. I doubted he was still alive since Caterpillar was the leader. "The last line was 'I must stop these entries I've given Alice enough information to find them.' I don't know who she meant. I finally gave up trying to figure it out," I confessed. "She wanted me to find someone, I think she wanted me to take her place in the Resistance, but I don't know why. Lily is far more suited to leading. I was only thirteen when she died, I couldn't lead anyone," I admitted, tears running down my cheeks, "I failed her. I was selfish for not reading more of what she had written for me. I can't believe I chose to leave myself in the dark."

I cried. Arms wrapped around me, picking me up. At first, I was not sure who held me, but then Caterpillar's voice rumbled near my ear. "You have to calm down. We don't know for sure what your mother meant. If she wanted you to find the Resistance, then you've done it. You haven't failed. You may just be a bit behind schedule." Caterpillar said, trying to soothe me, "We need to go, Dodo will not wait for us." he added, setting me on my feet, I nodded, wiping my tears away.

"Pack a bag, Griff. You've just joined the Resistance," Cheshire said, trying to lighten the mood.

"I packed one the minute Alice left for the Hearts Club," he replied, disappearing into his room.

"Let's do this," Hatter said, throwing his arm around my shoulders. I nodded, trying to smile.

Chapter 8

The City of Wonderland had twelve sectors. Griffin's apartment was in sector five, while Dodo's shop was in sector eleven. The storefronts in sector eleven were not colorful and exciting the way one would expect. They didn't draw the eye, or beg you to buy products. Storeowners knew business would come. There were tons of people roaming in and out of stores, the smell of fried food hung heavy in the air. The vendors lining the streets were different, desperate for a sale. Their pleas to buy their products a dull roar. A few Suits milled around ensuring no one got out of line. Dodo worked out of a smaller shop than most shop owners. Caterpillar had explained on the way here that several ranges existed in the basement for practice. The entire store was soundproofed for privacy. It was smart that Dodo laid low considering his line of work. I was surprised the Red Party hadn't shut him down, that was enough for me to know Dodo was up to no good. No one was in the store as we entered. I was shocked to find that the inside was far more welcoming than the bleak, grey bricks outside.

"It's yellow." I said. The walls were lined with a number of weapons, everything from rifles to crossbows was on display. Clear cases held various daggers, swords, and other small weapons I didn't know the names of.

"I've always found it a bit disconcerting," Ches said, fingering a large knife that had been left on the counter.

"I can understand why. It looks like dolls should line the walls, not guns," I replied, keeping my distance from the weapons. I didn't feel uncomfortable here because of the weapons. My parents had ensured I felt safe with guns at a very young age. My magick buzzing insistently under my skin had me on edge.

A man with gray hair and shining brown eyes appeared from behind a curtain and went to embrace Caterpillar. Caterpillar stiffened and slapped the older man's back just a little too hard. "It's been far too long my friend. What can I do for you today?" Dodo asked.

"I need some weapons for the girl," he grunted, gesturing toward me.

"Of course." Dodo said, clapping his hands together, "What is your poison, my dear? Do you prefer guns, knives, axes, swords. Maybe a bow and arrow?" he asked, circling me, tapping his chin, "No, you seem like a dagger woman. Prefer to slice open the enemy's throat don't ya?"

I felt energy crackling up my arms. I dug my nails into my palms to stop myself from grabbing the man and pumping him full of electricity. He had guessed correctly that I preferred daggers which made me extremely uncomfortable. I watched him carefully as Caterpillar drew his attention away from me. "She'll need Kevlar, a pair of boots, at least two guns. Probably... ten knives will do." Caterpillar continued to list off supplies before finally saying, "and we'll need a few new phones."

He glanced at March, who was standing between Hatter and me. This drew Dodo's attention to him, and I saw the immediate change in his demeanor. March tensed beside me, and I had the sudden urge to punch the little, old man. Dodo was shorter than his grandson, and his hair had greyed, but I could see the family resemblance. "I told you last time you brought him in here, I would not sell you more phones, if you kept destroying them." Dodo replied, sweeping past us to pick up a few weapons.

"I c-c-can leave," March said, hanging his head.

"I see you still haven't gotten that horrible impediment under control." Dodo snarled, "Disgusting," he muttered, and I had had enough.

"Listen to me, you douche canoe." I said, grabbing him by his shirt, "You will sell us everything boss man over there just asked for. Then you will apologize to my friend or you may find one of these nice weapons shoved in some very uncomfortable places." I growled, before letting him go.

He straightened his shirt, and nodded, "Of course, Miss. I'll have your things ready immediately." he said, and I saw a bit of fear in his eyes, "I apologize for my unprofessional behavior," he added, looking past March. I decided to leave well enough alone, though my magick had pushed to the surface with my surge of emotions. I took a deep breath trying to control the electricity that raced under my skin begging to be released.

"Boss Man?" Caterpillar asked, with a small smirk.

"Seemed appropriate," I said, shrugging.

"You d-didn't have to do that," March whispered into my ear.

"Yeah, I did," I smiled, wrapping an arm around him.

We stood in uncomfortable silence for what felt like hours before Dodo reappeared. "Here are your things. That'll be a thousand even." Dodo said, holding up several large bags.

"A thousand?" Cheshire said, mouth hanging open, "We've never paid more than eight hundred before," he argued, and I felt bad.

"I got it," I said, sweeping my wallet out of my bag.

"Alice, you don't have to—" Hatter started.

I held a hand up to stop him. "I have the money, and it's for me," I said, stopping all arguments, "The phones are in here?" I asked, handing him a thousand dollars in cash.

"As I told your boss…" Dodo began, shaking his head.

I pulled out an extra thousand dollars. I saw the greed alight in his eyes when he saw the wad of cash. I had learned to always carry extra cash. Money spoke louder than anything else for most of the citizens of Wonderland. Even a small amount could go a long way. "For the phones… and your silence," I said, handing him the money. I heard several sharp intakes of breath, but no one stopped me.

Dodo smiled, before sweeping six cell phones into a bag and handing them to Hatter.

"Of course, miss, pleasure doing business with you," he said, escorting us to the door.

"How the fuck do you have two thousand dollars in cash?" Caterpillar asked once we were back in the Hummer.

"Mom had a ton of money saved up in case something happened to her. I always carry cash, just in case I need it," I said, stuffing my wallet back into my bag.

"You shouldn't have done that we can't pay him two thousand dollars every time we need something." Caterpillar said, exasperated.

"Oh, we're not going back there," I said, crossing my arms.

"We don't have a choice, unless you know of another place in Wonderland that has a weapons cache," he shot back.

"If I had known that's all he was getting us, we wouldn't have had to go there in the first place," I muttered.

"Then where do you suggest we go, Princess?" Caterpillar snarled. I frowned at the nickname, he had called me that once before, but I found it almost cute. I just wasn't certain if it was an insult.

"My house... or at least my old house. We'll have to sneak in, but I don't think that should be too big a problem for you big Resistance boys," I snarked.

"They could be watching your house," Hatter pointed out.

"Even if they are, we need to go there. Maybe Lily hid mom's journal," I said.

"Fine, but if this goes bad, I'm letting them arrest you," Caterpillar said, turning the car around.

"We'll be fine," I said, confidently.

"We most definitely are not fine." Ches said, as we all stood behind the Hummer, watching the two Suits sitting outside my house.

"We can get around them," I said, tapping my chin trying to think of a plan.

"Can you turn invisible?" he asked.

"No, but you said people don't notice you. Maybe you can get around them," I said.

"Not with this many people, someone is bound to notice me," he said, looking defeated.

I could tell that Cheshire had some amount of magick ability, but without time I couldn't train him to utilize it. I watched as two Suits chatted casually on the front porch of my childhood home. My heart squeezed as memories flooded me. My parents would be horrified that Suits had taken the home they had built for their daughters. I felt sick watching, anger soon following the nausea. I wanted to unleash my magick, pull the electricity straight from their hearts and watch as they fell to the ground helpless. No one would hurt my family like this and get away with it. I cringed at my vicious thoughts, tuning back into the conversation when I heard Griffin speak. "I have an idea."

"Oh great, now I know we're all going to die," Cheshire said, throwing his hands in the air.

"Don't be rude," I said, smacking his arm.

He grumbled but did not say anything else. I thought it was cute how well Griffin seemed to fit in with the other guys. I'd never seen Griffin have any other male friends, he'd spent most of our childhood following Dina and I around.

"What if we acted like we wanted to buy the house? Alice can sneak around back with March and Hatter." Griffin suggested, "But I'm not sure three people can get around them."

"That's not a bad plan," Caterpillar said, "I'll stay in the car, so we can get away quickly. Cheshire, I want you to go with Griffin. Play up a couple angle; most people aren't affectionate in public, so you may take them by surprise. If all else fails, have a fight," he commanded.

We began taking our places, Ches and Griffin walked hand-in-hand to the men sitting on the front porch, talking to them excitedly. They swung their arms back and forth slightly to draw attention to it. Even from a distance I could see the discomfort the Suits were feeling. As Griffin spoke, Cheshire would lean his head on his shoulder, looking up at him adoringly.

Hatter grabbed my hand and led me into the backyard. "We have to hurry," he whispered.

I took the lead, slipping around the house to the basement entrance. We could still hear Griff. "Oh my, this is a beautiful house. Why would anyone move out?" I heard Griffin say, and I had to hold back a laugh at his flamboyant accent.

"He's really laying it on thick," Hatter muttered, shaking his head.

"Through here," I motioned for them to follow me. I ignored the things that had been strewn around the house from the search the Suits had done. Ignored the scratches on the hardwood floors, and the strange smell that wafted through the house. I especially ignored the pictures of my family hanging on the hallway walls, in the darkened house our smiling faces were eerie. We descended the stairs to the basement, and I felt my way along the wall. It was dark, light only coming in through small windows at the top of the walls. However, it wasn't difficult for me to feel my way to the secret switch, hiding between the fuse box and a metal shelf. I punched it, watching as the wall spilt in half. "Damn," March breathed, staring at the wall that had moved to allow us through. They stared at the space beyond the wall as I moved forward. There was not much to see in the darkness, but they were both in awe.

"Who did this?" Hatter asked.

"My dad. He was certain it would be a necessary evil at some point," I said, searching for the light switch. I flipped the light on, causing Hatter and March to gasp again. Three of the walls were lined with shelves full of weapons, food, and other supplies, while the final wall had four cots stacked against it.

"This isn't a bunker, it's a fucking bomb shelter," Hatter replied.

I ignored him, and looked around for something to carry the things we needed in. When I found what I was looking for, I handed the thick, black duffel bags to March. He immediately began putting the weapons in them. "You weren't k-kidding when you said we wouldn't have to go back," he said, gracing me with a bright smile.

"No, I wasn't," I replied quietly, "And you won't have to worry about phones anymore. Mom always kept at least twenty down here." March blushed a bit but nodded. "And if Caterpillar ever says anything about it again, tell me, I'll beat him up," I joked, bumping him.

"Why pay Dodo at all?" Hatter asked, helping me gather supplies.

"I knew we needed to give him something so he wouldn't sell us out. Plus, it never hurts to have extra... To be honest I didn't want to come back here..." I trailed off.

I found a picture of my parents tucked behind some supplies. Mom was pregnant with Lily and Dad had his arm wrapped protectively around her shoulders. I sat down, staring at their smiling faces. My Dad's chestnut hair was shining in the sun, as he glanced down at my mother, a hand on her pregnant belly. Mom's curly golden hair was a braided halo around her head, beaming at the camera, their newly bought home in the background.

"You l-look like your mom," March said, sitting down next to me.

"I guess... Lily and I both inherited Dad's blue eyes. God, I miss them," I said, laying my head on his shoulder.

"You know, I would never tell H-Hatter this, but I miss my mom," March admitted in a whisper.

"Why wouldn't you tell him that?" I inquired, curiosity winning out.

"He's still angry with her for not protecting me, I..." March trailed off, watching Hatter packing things up on the other side of the room. "I love him," he whispered, looking at me, "He's my b-best friend. He never complains when I stutter. He... he takes care of me, he always has," he continued.

"I can tell he feels the same way," I said.

"He really likes you, Ali. P-please don't hurt him. I wouldn't know what to do for him," March said, "Of course, he's n-not the only one."

"I like you guys, too," I admitted, trying to hide the color in my face. March grinned before standing and offering me his hand. I tucked the picture I had been staring at into the pocket of my jeans, glad to have something to remind me of my parents. I lifted two of the bags, finding that they were surprisingly heavy. I heard a scuffle upstairs, and I knew we had run out of time. "Take the stuff, and go," I said, pushing the bags I had just picked up into Hatter's arms.

"What are you going to do?" Hatter whisper-yelled after me.

"Go," I hissed at him, running up the stairs. I made eye contact with Cheshire who was holding his cheek. I assumed Griffin had smacked him, and I almost wished I had seen that, but I didn't have time. I kept tight to the wall, avoiding the creaky wooden floors, and slid into my room.

"I can't believe I ever agreed to marry you." Griffin yelled, putting on a beautiful show, "Especially after I caught you with that slut."

"I wasn't doing anything with her," Ches shot back, but I could hear the humor in his voice.

I searched frantically through my room, hoping to find the journal. Griff and Ches were buying me time, but it sounded like they were about to be shut down.

"Sirs, I'm going to have to ask you to leave. If you decided you want the house you can return... after you've resolved your argument," the Suit said.

I silently cursed when I didn't find my mother's journal. I rushed out of my room and down the hallway. I could only hope Hatter and March were already in the car. I ran out the back door, hoping to make it back to the vehicle before any of the Suits saw me. "What the fuck, Alice? I told you to stay together," Caterpillar said, yanking me into the Hummer.

"I couldn't risk all three of us getting caught in the house, plus no one saw me," I said, after catching my breath. Caterpillar glared at me but didn't say anything else. Griffin and Cheshire approached us, careful to be out of sight of the Suits before they began speaking. "I can't believe you actually slapped me. You could have at least pulled your punch," Ches grumbled at Griffin, who was smiling.

"I had to make it look realistic," he replied, winking at me. Griffin had thoroughly enjoyed the act he and Cheshire had just put on, even under the circumstances.

"Did you get everything?" Ches asked, settling into his seat, interrupting my train of thought.

"You should have seen that basement; it was amazing—wall-to-wall supplies and more guns than we could carry. We made a big dent, but there was still stuff left down there," Hatter said.

"We can't risk coming back," Caterpillar and I said at the same time. I glanced at him, only to find him glaring at me.

"That was just creepy," Ches said, "Please don't start doing that all the time, I can't handle two fun suckers," he begged.

"I have never sucked in my life," I said,. Hatter raised his eyebrows suggestively, but I chose to ignore him. "And I wouldn't consider what we just did fun," I added, with a huff.

"I enjoyed myself," Griffin said, lightly.

"Only because you got to hit Cheshire," I shot back.

"Touché," he said, not trying to hide his smile.

"Ugh, we should have left him at his apartment," Cheshire pouted.

"Children please," Caterpillar groaned.

"We're not that much younger than you, Caterpillar," Hatter replied.

"You act like teenagers. Horny teenagers at that," Caterpillar grimaced, "The fact that Alice is more mature than all four of you is just embarrassing."

"I feel like I should be offended," I muttered, crossing my arms over my chest.

"You're the youngest," he replied.

"Women mature faster than men," I shot back.

"Then what's your excuse?" he snarked, meeting my eyes in the rearview mirror.

I tried to come up with a witty response, but I found myself unable to, so, instead, I rolled my eyes and asked. "Where are we going?"

"Back to base," was the only response he gave.

I sighed and settled back into my seat. I thought more about the journal, I regretted not reading more of what my mother had written for me. Obviously, she wanted me to know more about the Resistance than I did. If that was true, why did she hide so much from me when she was alive?

"What are you thinking about, Alice?" Caterpillar asked.

"My mom..." I trailed off for a moment before saying, "She taught me so much, but I always felt like she was hiding something. I know she started the Resistance. I know she learned how to keep in touch with her magic from her father, but at the same time I know so little."

"Parents always do what they think is best for their children, even if it leaves them in the dark." He responded, his tone was almost comforting, and I wondered for a moment about where his parents were.

"Why didn't I read the damn journal more carefully!" I cried in frustration, smacking the back of the seat.

"Hey, Ali, calm down, it'll be okay. We will help you figure this out." Hatter said, patting my leg.

I leaned onto his shoulder, letting him comfort me as we drove away from my childhood home. I had a feeling this would be the last time I would see it.

Chapter 9

There was a black truck sitting in front of the warehouse when we pulled up. When Caterpillar spotted it, he slammed the Hummer into park and jumped out. "Who's that?" I asked, pointing to a man who had just exited the vehicle.

"White Rabbit," Cheshire said, as I slid out of the car.

"Hello, I'm Alice," I introduced myself to the new man who smiled at me warmly. I noticed Hatter and March saunter into the warehouse, followed closely by Cheshire and Griffin.

"Codename?" he asked, looking me up and down.

"No," Caterpillar answered for me, glaring at my interruption.

"Curious," White Rabbit said, titling his head.

A glance passed between the two men that I couldn't read, but I had a feeling they knew something that I didn't. "Ignore her, she's the newest pain in my ass," Caterpillar replied, annoyed, "What do you have for me?"

"You shouldn't be rude to pretty women," White Rabbit chided, "I taught you better than that. You can call me Rab, dear," he said, waving Caterpillar off.

I immediately liked him. His salt and pepper hair was slicked back in an attractive style. His grey eyes were filled with warmth as he smiled at me. "You didn't teach me anything," Caterpillar snapped back, and I frowned at him.

"Do you know why he's so grumpy?" I asked, smiling at Rab.

"I don't have a clue," he replied, returning my smile, "He was a delightful child."

I heard Caterpillar huff, and I noticed a slight pink to his cheeks. "Should I repeat myself? What do you have for me?" he asked, glaring at both of us.

"I have some intelligence about the King of Hearts," Rab replied, and I was suddenly feeling serious.

"Let's go inside," Caterpillar said, rushing us in the door.

I was curious what Rab found, hoping it might get me one step closer to saving Lily and Dina. I paused though, taking a moment to appreciate the outside of the warehouse. While at first glance it looked a bit dingy, it had a vintage quality to it that made me smile. I hadn't been able to see the mismatched bricks in the dark when I'd been here before. I ran my fingers over some grey dust that settled between the bricks. "Come on, Alice." Caterpillar snapped at me.

Ches was standing just inside the doorway, apparently waiting for us, "I have the phones set up." He announced.

I raised my eyebrows, "That didn't take long."

"I did most of it on the way here." He said, before winking.

He slapped the phone into my hand and said. "I programmed all of our numbers into it and added the contacts from your other phone."

"Thanks." I said, scrolling through them. "What did you do with my phone?"

"I deactivated it before we left Griffin's apartment. We couldn't take the risk that someone could have been tracking your whereabouts." I nodded scrolling through the new phone. When I came across the names Boss Man, Sexy Cat, Bun Bun, and Maddie, I laughed.

"Cheshire," Caterpillar said, grumpily, "Can you find a room for Griffin?"

"What about Al?" Ches asked, putting an arm around my shoulders.

"Give her the room between Hatter and March. Have them help you drag the desk out," Caterpillar commanded, before dismissing Cheshire. I watched Cheshire walk out, glancing around at the room Caterpillar had ushered us into. The walls were painted a dim blue but paired with the dark furniture it almost looked grey. A fireplace was set into the left wall, while a huge oak desk took up most of the rest of the space in the room. "King of Hearts, go," Caterpillar added, eyes trained on Rab.

"He will at The Grove tomorrow at ten o'clock, and it just so happens that I booked a five-person table," Rab explained.

"You're going with us?" Caterpillar asked, leaning back in his chair.

"That was my original plan, until I met a cute blonde," White Rabbit said, wiggling his fingers my way.

"Absolutely not," Caterpillar demanded, smacking his hand on his desk.

"It's a perfect cover, why would five men be sitting around watching the King? Unless four men took a pretty woman that they are trying to impress somewhere our dear leader is known to frequent. If she just so happens to beg to speak to him... well, that's not your fault, is it?" Rab offered, grinning.

"Creator damn it, fine, but I don't like this," Caterpillar said, before pointing to me, "You better do everything I say."

"This is a good plan, Caterpillar. I won't mess it up," I said, holding up my hands. I chose not to be offended by his tone. He didn't know anything about me. I would prove that I could be a useful part of his team.

"It was very nice meeting you, Alice, but if you would excuse us, I would like to speak with my nephew alone," Rab said.

"Nephew?" I asked, raising my eyebrows.

"Oh yes. Can't you see the family resemblance," he said, waving between them.

I took a moment to really study Caterpillar, before turning back to look at Rab. They had the same grey eyes and height. However, Rab's eyes were filled with mirth and his posture relaxed. I'm surprised I hadn't noticed the resemblance sooner. "It's the attitude," I pointed out, waving at him.

Rab laughed before Caterpillar grumbled, "I think he asked you to leave."

I left without saying anything else, thinking about all I knew about my four companions. While I knew quite a bit about March's young life, I only knew a few details about Caterpillar, Cheshire, and Hatter. I wanted to learn more about each of them, but I had to be careful. I had secrets of my own, I still wasn't certain I could trust the Resistance. "Hey Ali, come check out my room," Griffin yelled, interrupting my thoughts.

I walked toward him and found myself standing under several skylights. The ceiling was at least twenty feet high; you could see more sky than ceiling. "Woah," I muttered.

"Right? Can you imagine this at night?" Griffin replied, staring at the sky with me.

"How did we end up in this mess?" I asked, taking a seat on the bed, shoved in the corner.

"Don't ask me. I was about to go grocery shopping when you showed up on myid. doorstep and kissed me," he said, sitting down next to me.

"I'm sorry, Griff. I shouldn't have dragged you into this," I sa

"It's fine, I didn't really want to go anyway." he joked, bumping our shoulders together, before seriously adding. "As much as I like Ches, Hatter, and March, you shouldn't handle all of this alone."

"I'm used to it," I said, shrugging.

"You shouldn't be. Dina and I have always been there for you. We spent more time with your family than our own, but you've never let us take anything on for you," Griffin said. "Not to mention I knew the moment I heard about Dina and Lily that I'd have to protect you from yourself."

I stood and began pacing, "It isn't fair to burden you guys with my problems. And it's not fair that you have to deal with any of this." I was so tired of not being like the normal people who went about their life in blissful ignorance of the atrocities within our city. No one here had it easy, but at least not everyone had the burden of knowledge. Ignorance would have been bliss.

"Life's not fair, Alice," he shot back, "You have the chance to do the right thing, take it. Your mom died believing in the Resistance."

"I am not my mother," I growled, electricity crackled around my fists, "I'm tired of living in the White Queen's shadow. I loved her, I even agreed with what she was working for, but all I've ever wanted was to settle down and be happy. I don't want to be a leader."

"Then don't be. Save Lily and Dina and leave Wonderland. There must be somewhere else to live outside of this city." Griffin said, sounding reasonable.

"Wonderland is my home," I whined, sliding down the wall.

"Then make shit right and settle down. Lily can take over the government if she wants to, or maybe someone else can. I know you; you aren't going to leave until things are right. You may not be your mom, but you will always do what you feel is best for others," Griffin said, and I knew he was right.

"I'm going to the Grove with the guys tomorrow." I offered, hoping to change the subject, "The King of Hearts is going to be there."

"What are you going to wear?" he asked, grinning.

"I don't know, a dress probably. I've never been to the Grove, but I know they have a dress code," I replied, picking at my jeans.

"You're going with four of the hottest men I have ever laid eyes on." Griffin said, "Wear that red dress Dina bought you for your birthday."

I rolled my eyes and asked. "Why are you so interested in my love life?"

"Because you ignore your feelings, and people who are right in front of you, waiting," he replied. I felt bad that I had ignored his feelings for so many years. "Don't look at me like that. By the time you realized I had a crush on you, it was over," he said, looking at my face.

"I'm sorry, Griff." I worried my lip.

I loved Griffin, but not the way he would have liked. "Stop it, Alice Evangeline Young. It's been ten years; I was never upset with you," he said, holding his hands up, "Now, back to the subject of your four men."

"I definitely don't have four men." I argued, "I have two, maybe three, if you count Cheshire." I said, before adding, "I don't have them, anyway, I just kind of like them." I nearly choked on the lie. They were a distraction I couldn't afford; my feelings didn't matter when Lily and Dina were in the Red Party's dungeons.

"Bullshit." Griff called my bluff, "Cheshire kept me up half the night asking questions about you, and Caterpillar watches you with this weird look in his eye."

Watching Griffin try to imitate Caterpillar made me laugh until tears ran down my face. Griffin could never pull off the broody look of Caterpillar. "That weird look is called disdain," I said.

"It is not. I am a dude, so I know," he shot back, crossing his arms.

"You've never hated anyone," I pointed out.

"That's not true, that one guy you dated... remember, the one with the pinup leg tattoo. I hated him; he was a douchebag," Griffin said.

"He really was," I admitted.

"I'll never know what you saw in him," he replied, shaking his head.

"He had a nice ass," I said, completely serious.

"That is not a good enough reason," Griffin sighed.

I shrugged, and then groaned. "I really like them all, even Caterpillar which is just...embarrassing."

"Spend time with them, talk to them about it. If it works it works, and if not, at least you tried," he said, patting my shoulder. "You need a little distraction."

I sighed, before saying, "I guess, but I don't want to be rejected."

"No one does, trust me," he replied, looking at me pointedly.

"Okay fine, if the opportunity arises, I will talk to them." I conceded, knowing I wouldn't win this argument with Griffin.

I looked back up at the skylight to find a purple and orange sunset staring back at me. "I think we should get something to eat,"

"I'm starving," he agreed.

We made our way back down to Caterpillar who was sitting at his desk, reading a file. Other papers were strewn around him, and I raised an eyebrow, surprised by his messiness. It was obvious he was deep in thought. His hair looked like he'd been running his hand through it obsessively, sticking up all over the place. "What are we doing for dinner?" I asked.

"The kitchen is through there." he said, pointing down a hallway, "Help yourself," he offered, without looking up.

I rolled my eyes, grabbed Griffin, and went to find food. We found March and Hatter, who were both covered in flour, sitting at a large metal table, eating some disfigured bread.

"Hey, I was about to come find you guys," Hatter greeted us, "Want some?" he offered, pointing to a basket with more oddly shaped bread.

"Do I want to know what happened?" I asked, motioning to their messy clothes.

"We were arguing about our bread recipe, and, in retaliation to me being right, March tossed flour at me." When Hatter finished explaining, March grinned at me.

"Caterpillar was wrong, you aren't teenagers. You are actual children," I joked, taking some bread.

"You wound me," Hatter said, clutching his heart.

"I would never," I replied, before adding, "This bread is actually really good."

"See March, I know what I'm doing," Hatter said, pointing at me.

"She has to s-say that, she likes you," March pouted.

"I like you, too, but this bread is delicious," I said, winking at him.

"Alice always has wanted to open a bakery, so if she says it's good, I believe her." Griffin chimed in, snatching some of the bread up. March smiled back, before patting the seat next to him, I sat down, and he wound our fingers together under the table. It was an easy gesture of affection, and it eased some of the anxiety I was hiding. Hatter went back to cooking over the stove while Griffin, March, and I chatted.

Hatter cooked a delicious meal of rice and beans. It was cheap, which made me wonder how much the Resistance was struggling to stay afloat. I would have to find time to get some more cash out so I could help them more. I found myself laughing, eating, and playing with March and Hatter late into the night.

"Alright, it's as late as I can stand to be up." Griffin said, throwing his cards down on the table, sending me a wink that caused a blush to break out on my face as he left the room.

We continued playing cards, betting with chocolate covered pretzels, trying not to eat too much of our winnings. After another hour of fun, Caterpillar came into the kitchen and tried to break up the party. "You three should go to bed, we have to be up early in the morning for a mission,"

I pulled a card from the deck, ignoring Caterpillar's comment. I had to suppress a grin, when I saw the card was exactly what I needed to win the game. "Read it and weep boys," I said, laying my cards on the table proudly.

"Take your loot." Hatter said, helping me rake in the pile of chocolate laying in the center of the table. I noticed him steal one but didn't say anything. "Join us?" Hatter asked, turning to Caterpillar, who was leaning against the doorway, watching us.

"Absolutely not," Caterpillar replied, going to the fridge for a beer.

"Come on, we could play strip poker," Hatter wiggled his eyebrows.

"No," Caterpillar said.

"Take the stick out of your ass for an hour and have a little fun." I said, popping a piece of chocolate into my mouth, "Unless you're afraid I'll beat you," I taunted. He shook his head, rolling his eyes at my challenge.

"Come on, C-Cater, it'll be fun," March said, smiling. Caterpillar was silent for a minute before he took a seat. He took the cards from Hatter and began shuffling them. I was surprised he had put up so little fight against March but chose to just enjoy the game.

"Fine. One game of strip poker. You're going to bed naked," he poked back, a rare smile lighting up his features.

"I think I'd like to see you run to your room nude," I said, picking up the cards he dealt me.

An hour later, Hatter and March were stripped down to their underwear. When Hatter had taken his shirt off, revealing the words 'non desistas non exieris' along his ribs I'd been entranced. Hatter explained their meaning, 'never give up, never surrender', and I liked him a little bit more. All three of the men were avoiding looking at my naked chest, careful to make eye contact when they spoke to me. Caterpillar was shirtless and smug, chugging another beer. It was interesting seeing him let loose a little, it made him seem much younger. "I think that's another layer for you three," he said, laying down four of a kind. I yanked my jeans off and threw them at him, happy that I had put underwear on that morning.

"Sore loser." he taunted, laying my pants with the pile of clothes sitting next to him, "You can give up now, and at least go to bed with something on." he added, staring unabashedly at my bare chest, although I was doing the same thing to him. Caterpillar was covered in tattoos; I definitely had a thing for them. I'd stared at the words over his knuckles, 'rise' on his right hand, 'fall' on his left. I wondered what had inspired them but hadn't been brave enough to ask.

He flexed the muscles in his chest as I stared, heat rising in my face and other places. "Fuck off, Caterpillar," I growled.

Hatter and March both took off their underwear, and I had the hardest time not staring at their bodies. Hatter met my eyes, a smirk on his face as I struggled not to let my eyes wander past the narrowing of his hips. "That's not nice," Caterpillar responded, shaking me out of my lustful thoughts. I realized that he was drunk and laughed quietly at his pouting face.

"What the fuck are you four doing," Cheshire said, rubbing his eyes.

"Playing cards, Cat," I said, glaring at Caterpillar, who was grinning at his new hand.

"I can see that. It's two o'clock in the morning," he replied, shuffling toward the fridge, "You woke me up," he added, glaring at the four of us. "Fucking naked as always,"

"Damn, it's late. How did I let you people convince me this was a good idea?" Caterpillar swore, grabbing his shirt and leaving the room.

"That means you forfeit, and I win, asshole," I yelled after him.

"How did you convince him to play strip poker at all?" Ches asked.

"I'm not sure, I think March used puppy dog eyes," I said, watching as March pulled on his sweatpants.

"He's a damn card shark, you shouldn't have let him trick you." Ches replied, grinning, "Although the view is nice for the rest of us," he added, slapping my ass.

"Try that again, Cheshire, and you'll lose that hand," I threatened.

"Worth it," he said, running back to his room. I tried to chase after him, but nearly tripped over my clothes.

"N-Night, Ali," March said, kissing my cheek. I stood watching him leave, and turned to find Hatter stretching, naked. He caught me watching him and grinned. He had his clothes thrown over his shoulder, not bothering to replace them.

"Ready for bed?" he asked.

"Ready for something" I muttered.

"Like what?" he replied, and I was surprised that he heard me.

"Bed," I said, blushing.

"Of course," he replied, with a smile, throwing his arm around my shoulder.

I could feel the heat coming off his naked body, and I found my mind wandering toward the gutter. When we arrived at the door to my room, he said, "Night, Alice."

I waited for a second before saying, "Hatter, would you like to come in?"

"For a night cap? I doubt there's alcohol in your room," he joked.

I laughed, my plan solidifying in my mind. "Something like that," I replied, biting my lip.

"You're drunk." he said, watching me carefully.

"I had less than half a beer, I'm not even buzzed." I shot back, crossing my hands over my breasts, drawing his attention lower. I let my eyes trail down his body, appreciating every muscle, line, and curve leading down past the v in his hips. His member was thick, and it looked like a comfortable length, I shifted as my pussy flooded with heat.

We stood, looking at each other for another moment, before he came toward me and pressed his lips to mine. I wrapped my arms around his neck, dropping my clothes on the floor. His lips were warm against mine. The usual awkwardness of first kisses was nowhere to be found, as his tongue mingled with mine. "Probably shouldn't leave those out here," he said, letting me go and picking up my clothes. I opened my bedroom door, and he threw them on the floor, before pouncing on me once again. I bit his lip, wrapping my fingers in his long, dark hair.

He pulled away, "Are you sure about this, Alice? We've only known each other for a couple days; you've got so many—"

I cut him off, pressing my lips to his once again, "I need you, Hatter. I want to feel you inside me; I want to experience everything you have to offer."

"I've wanted you from the moment I saw you in that little blue dress in the Hearts Club, but once I met you... Alice, I like you. You're strong, you're bringing back hope in my best friends, you're so kind."

"I like you too." I said, as he picked me up, and we started kissing again. I pulled away, panting, and asked, "Bed?"

He nodded into my mouth and walked me backwards. I squeaked, as my knees hit the bed, causing me to fall backwards. Hatter laughed, and then climbed on top of me, kissing my neck, moving ever so slowly closer to my breasts. His hands began to explore lower, brushing the insides of my thighs. I spread my legs, whining for him to touch me. When he finally did my back arched off the bed. His fingers well practiced as they played with my most intimate parts. "Hatter, please," I moaned, wanting him inside me.

"What do you want, sweetheart?" He whispered in my ear, his hot breath fanning across my face adding to the sensations.

"Fuck me." I begged.

"All you had to do was ask," he said, sitting up to move between my thighs.

I saw stars as he entered me, his pace painfully slow as every inch of him slid into me. I held onto his shoulder as his rhythm became faster, my nails digging into his skin. My orgasm built slowly at first, the tingles spreading from my toes into my hips, until finally I let out a guttural moan as Hatter slammed into my g-spot. His pace slowed, and I opened my eyes to see him staring down at me, something strange in his eyes.

"We're not done yet, sweetheart I'm going to need to feel your pussy tighten around my cock like that at least a couple more times." he said, as he rubbed a thumb against my nipple.

I moaned, my body still so sensitive from my orgasm, "Yes, sir."

He smiled, and commenced making me feel things I hadn't felt ever before.

"I like that you glow, lets a man know that he's doing something right," Hatter said, I laughed, and snuggled into his chest.

"You're probably the first one to ever say that to me," I admitted.

"Then everyone you've ever slept with is fucking stupid," he said, surprising me.

"Can I ask you a personal question? You don't have to answer if you don't want to," I rambled.

"Sure," he said, rubbing my back.

"What's your real name?"

"You'll think this is ironic, but my real name is Hayden O'Hare," he said, and I smiled.

"Why aren't you the March Hare?" I asked, laughing.

"The kids I went to school with used to call me Mad Hatter, because I always wore a hat." he admitted, and I could see the slight blush on his face. "I actually have a huge collection of hats."

"I think it fits," I said.

After a moment he said, "I know this might sound weird and clingy, but what are we now? This... this was nice Alice. I've liked you since the moment I laid eyes on you in that bar."

I chewed on my lip, and thought for a moment before asking. "You remember when you heard Griffin and I talking about Lacie in his kitchen?"

When he nodded, I continued. "He was telling me that I should act on my feelings if I liked you, because it was obvious that we had a connection... I argued with him, but I knew he was right. I've never been great with relationships, but this was wonderful, and I don't want it to end." I admitted, looking across the dark room.

"That was when you realized March and I have a unique...situation." he stated, and I knew he was nervous about admitting it out loud.

"Not quite, I knew you were close, maybe even together, the night before, but I wasn't going to pry, because it's not any of my business." I said.

"March and I spent all of our time together, even before he moved in with us. Most nights he would end up in bed with me, so his nightmares weren't so bad. It didn't occur to me that it wasn't normal, until my dad asked if I was dating him. He warned me that I shouldn't sleep with March, because he might feel like that's how he was repaying me for helping him. I sat him down, and told him that we could never have sex, because it wasn't fair to him. He told me he loved me, and I'll be honest there've been a few times I've been tempted to just date March, but I can't bring myself to do it. We've done a lot of partner sharing, but I don't even know if March has sex if we don't do that. His fucking stepfather..." Hatter trailed off, and I wiped the tears that had gathered in my eyes away.

"I would be fine if March wanted to join us, I think you already know I'm interested in him. And Ches," I said.

Hatter kissed me, and said, "We already talked about it. He said that if you want him, he would be happy to do something like that, but that if you didn't, he was okay with me being with you." he added, "You probably shouldn't leave Caterpillar out I see the way you two look at each other."

"Ugh, don't get me started." Caterpillar's bipolar treatment was a huge turn off. If he ever gave a single sign that he was interested in me, it was always followed by a clear rejection. I had no desire to force myself on him. A quiet knock on my door interrupted me and I said, "Come in."

March appeared in the doorway, and Hatter immediately went to him, "C-Can I come sleep with you guys?" March asked, looking at me, nervously.

"Of course," I said, patting the bed beside me.

"Nightmare?" Hatter asked, running his fingers, through March's hair. He nodded but said nothing. March settled in between us, and I felt like everything was as it was supposed to be. I drifted off into a peaceful sleep cuddled against March. Hatter had his arm thrown over March gripping my hip as he too fell asleep.

Chapter 10

July 29th, 2157

"You do realize you have your own beds, right?" Cheshire said, causing me to sit up suddenly, smacking my forehead into his. Hatter groaned and rolled out of bed.

I rubbed my forehead, and replied, "Yes."

"So, why are all three of you..." he asked, gesturing wildly while wiggling his eyebrows.

"Wouldn't you l-like to know?" March said, rubbing sleep from his eyes.

Ches looked at me with a raised eyebrow. "We all had crazy monkey sex and you missed out," I deadpanned, and I saw Hatter turn bright red, before leaving the room.

"Next time, maybe?" Ches asked, with a grin.

"Only if you bring that blue bra," I said, winking at him.

Cheshire groaned, "I don't think I've regretted being sarcastic more in my life," he rolled his eyes, and left the room, leaving March and me alone.

I watched as he stood and stretched showing off a bit of midriff that should not have excited me as much as it did. He turned and caught me staring, I smirked, and wiggled my fingers at him in greeting. He smiled back, and said, "Your glow is almost gone this m-morning."

I ignored the heat the flushed my face. "It doesn't always last long." I took him in for another moment and noticed the slightly purple bags under his eyes and asked. "Do you want to talk about it?"

"The glow?" March said, looking away from me.

"No, your nightmares," I replied, walking toward my bag to pull out my dress for brunch.

"I...I never have before," he admitted.

"You can tell me. You shouldn't hold things in," I said, taking a seat on the bed, and motioning for him to join me. "Pain will eat you alive if you don't let it out."

"They always start off the same, y'know..." He trailed off, and I nodded to encourage him to continue. "Usually I'm b-back at the house I used to live in, I can hear my mom screaming, and then Martin bursts in. I always feel so helpless," he admits. "I couldn't do anything to he-help my own mother, and here comes Hatter, but it all goes to shit. Martin usually kills Hatter, sometimes not, sometimes he makes me watch him..." March trailed off again, and I could see the distant look in his eyes. I waited for him to go on, allowing him the time he needed to continue. After a moment, he finished the story. "I never cared what Martin did to me or who he s-sold me too, but I was always scared for Mom and Hatter. He once told me he thought Hatter would make him a lot of money, because he was so p-p-pretty."

"Oh March..." I said, reaching for him. He flinched when I laid my hand on his arm, and I immediately jerked away. "Have you ever told Hatter?" I asked softly.

March started shaking his head viciously, before turning a pleading gaze on me, "You can't tell him, Ali. It's only been in the last ye-year or s-so that he quit being careful when he touched me. I'm not a fragile piece of glass just because of what happened to me. I'm sure Hatter told you about our relationship. You should have heard him when we were teenagers. His dad mentioned something about sex once, and he quit t-touching me entirely. I've had other lovers, men and women, I can distinguish the past from the present. Sex is natural and as long as it's between consenting parties there is n-nothing wrong with it."

I opened my arms, offering him comfort if he wanted it. He hesitated for a moment before stepping into the embrace. "I'm sorry. I didn't mean to upset you." I said as I ran my fingers through his hair. "I am not going to push you, because it isn't any of my business, but you should tell Hatter what you just told me. He would be relieved."

March sighed and rubbed his face against my palm, it was an almost a cat-like move and I enjoyed the sensation. "Maybe..." he said.

"What are you doing loitering around out here, Hatter? Get ready." I heard Caterpillar bark from the hallway, before he busted my door open.

"Get ready," Caterpillar said, causing March to jump, and I sent a glare toward the hulking man.

"Please don't tell Hatter," March begged, after Caterpillar left.

"I won't," I said, kissing him on the cheek. He pulled me into another hug, and I nearly melted.

"Go," I told him, "Caterpillar seems especially grumpy this morning."

"It could be because we k-kept him up until two in the morning," March said, as he left the room.

Before I could close my door, Hatter appeared, and gave me an odd look. "I forgot my phone," he muttered, slipping past me, "What were you and March talking about?" he asked, staring me down.

"Nothing much," I said, not wanting to betray March's trust.

He stared me down for several moments, an indecipherable look on his face. Eventually, Hatter huffed and stormed out of the room. I furrowed my eyebrows, before following after him, "Hatter, wait."

"We don't want to be late." He said, slamming his bedroom door closed. I pushed away the emotions that started to circulate through my body. I felt a slight buzz against my skin, and furrowed my eyebrows, noticing that it was not as strong as usual. Unfortunately, I didn't have time to worry about either problem. I ignored the sting of rejection as I walked slowly into my own room and took a fast shower. I threw on the red dress Griffin had mentioned the day before. I carefully did my makeup, knowing we were going to have to sell a specific image. As a finishing touch, I swept deep red lipstick over my lips, trying not to think about March and Hatter.

"Alice, we need to go," Cheshire said, standing in the doorway. His eyes took in my dress, before quickly settling on my face. "You look nice,"

"Thank you. You do too," I said, motioning toward his dark violet suit. While his hair was still pink and purple, he had tamed it a bit. When he grinned at me, I noticed the small silver ball on his tongue. "You have a tongue piercing?" I asked, raising my eyebrows.

"You just now noticed?" he shot back, offering me his arm.

"How did I manage to miss that?" I muttered, walking carefully in the four-inch black heeled boots I was sporting. They reached up to my thighs, nicely complimenting the short dress.

"No idea. I've been wearing it," he smiled at me again. He gave me a cheeky wink and I narrowed my eyes at him.

"I've seen you with your mouth open, it wasn't there. Is it fake?" I grabbed his chin. We were the same height with my heels on and I tried to take advantage. "Open up," I said, "I wanna see."

"You have to buy me dinner first," he said, smacking my hands away.

"I spent two thousand dollars yesterday on weapons, and we're about to go to brunch," I protested, "Now, let me see!" I struggled with him, but despite our now-equal height, he was still stronger than me.

"With three other men, you gonna have to do better than that, baby," he taunted, dancing away from me.

"Must you two act like children? I have a headache," Caterpillar grumbled, rubbing his temples.

"I didn't know you were an old man," I said, still trying to wrestle with Ches. I kicked my foot into Cheshire's chest, causing him to fall to the ground.

"I am too old for this, I can tell you that," he said, rolling his eyes, as I straddled Ches on the ground.

"Now open up, Buttercup, I wanna see this supposed tongue ring up close," I said, tapping his nose. Cheshire shook his head and smashed his lips together. "Oh, come on, I just want to see it. They've always fascinated me. They have so many different purposes," I whispered into his ear, causing his breath to hitch.

"Alice, good to see you in such a good mood today. Why I might even say you're practically glowing." White Rabbit said, causing me to lean away from Cheshire, although I was still sitting on him.

"Of course, Rab, never better, and I have to say, a good night's sleep really does something for a person," I replied, smirking.

"Would you get off me? For such a small woman, you sure are heavy," Ches complained, trying to wiggle out from under me. I had an idea and quickly smashed my mouth into him, kissing him. He groaned, sat up, and wrapped fingers into my hair. I felt the metal ball slip into my mouth, and I nearly moaned at the feeling. I jerked back, suddenly aware that we had an audience. "Really Al, all you had to do was ask," he said with a grin.

I quickly stood up and kicked him in the thigh for good measure. Rab looked positively tickled, and Caterpillar was glaring at me. "I'm sorry Rab," I said, with a slight blush, tucking some hair behind my ear.

"Nothing I haven't seen or done before, dear. I've known these boys for a long time, and I am a married man after all," he replied.

My eyebrows shot up at that confession. "Really?" Most people in Wonderland chose not to marry, although the rich did to show off. The only other people who married did so for love, like my parents. Marriage had gone out of style soon after the Red Party took over. I didn't understand why, and if I was being honest with myself, I didn't want to know. I'm sure it had to do with controlling the general population.

He nodded and turned toward Caterpillar. "I stopped by this morning to tell you that Dormouse will also be that restaurant."

"You could have called," Caterpillar replied, looking suspicious.

"I was in the area," Rab shot back, "I must be going, I'm late for a meeting," he added, before rushing out of the warehouse.

"Your uncle is a bit weird," I said, straightening my dress, "Nice though."

"You have no right to call anyone weird with the... the display I was just forced to watch." Caterpillar said, snarling his nose.

I rolled my eyes before saying, "You act like a nun. Have you ever seen a naked woman before, Cater baby?"

"Well, since I've seen you nude... twice now," He trailed off and I thought back to that day in the apartment. It seemed like so long ago, when in reality it had only been a few days.

"Fine, I can't help your sexless existence," I said, turning back toward Cheshire.

"You would do well to keep your nose out of my existence, sexless or otherwise." he replied, "And, for the record, I have had sex before."

"Oh, that makes me believe you," I shot back, finally catching a glance at his outfit as he stood from his desk. He was sporting an all-black suit that hugged his body sinfully.

"It's none of your business anyway." he said, before shaking his head, "We have to be going," he added, before yelling for March and Hatter.

They came down together, and I noticed that March looked upset. "What's wrong?" I whispered, looping our arms together.

"Hatter is really pissed off, and I'm not entirely sure w-why." March replied, watching Hatter talk to Caterpillar.

It seemed that he was purposefully avoiding us. If I had the time to talk it out, I would have, but getting any information from the King of Hearts was far more important.

"Let's go," Caterpillar bellowed, waving at us.

Chapter 11

The Grove was a large metal building surrounded by a six-foot-tall wrought iron fence. It could only be described as swanky. Past the fences, the industrial-looking building was gleaming silver in the early morning sun. Large bay windows allowed the guests inside to see the people gawking at them. Most of the people who spent time here were high-up members of the Red Party and their supporters. I didn't consider the wealthiest citizens of Wonderland anything but members of the Red Party. They rubbed elbows with a government that abused its people without a second thought. Even though it was ten o'clock, the tables were occupied by busty women and older, bald-headed men, all dressed in the finest clothes they had. In comparison, our group looked a bit out of place among the patrons. Several people looked our way as we stepped in the building, a few sneered, but most of them were throwing appreciative glances our way. I took a moment to look over our group. I stood in the center, Caterpillar, Cheshire, March, and Hatter flanking me. Caterpillar was an imposing presence, nobody dared make contact with the stormy eyes that glared back at them. Dressed in his all-black suit that accentuated his wide shoulders, he was the definition of mouthwatering. Hatter was wearing a classic suit, with a deep, red tie. His long, black hair loose, no hat gracing his head, green eyes took stock of the exits clearly planning an escape if it was needed. March was looking a bit uncomfortable in his grey suit. His honey brown eyes met mine as I took them in and my breath stopped for a moment.

While March wasn't as toned as Caterpillar and Hatter, he held his own compared to them. We all looked our very best, but we were also quite a bit younger than the average patron. "It's...pretty," I said, glancing around the dark, wooden interior.

The smell of roasting meat permeated the air, making my mouth water a bit. I couldn't remember the last time I had a full meal. Meat was harder to find, the few farms that raised animals had exorbitant prices to afford the animals' upkeep. Caterpillar threw arm around my waist, "Sure it is, and it would be much nicer if all the meals weren't forty bucks a pop. You don't even get that much food."

"Your names, please," a host asked, glancing at the five of us with disdain.

"Ainsworth, party of five," Caterpillar replied, haughtily. He sounded as snobby as the man behind the podium, and I had to bite my tongue to stop from laughing. The host was a thin man, in his early forties with his mousey brown hair, slicked away from his face. A permanent sneer was etched into his face.

"Right this way," the host said, motioning for us to follow him.

A woman with short, curly blonde hair suddenly shoulder-checked me, causing me to stumble. Arms wrapped around my middle to keep me from falling, I glanced back and mouthed a quick 'thank you' to Cheshire.

"Excuse you," she screeched. I watched as she did a double take and made a beeline for us.

"Maddie, is that you?" the woman squealed, throwing her arms around Hatter's neck, "It's been forever!"

A growl rumbled through my chest. I started to step toward them, when March pulled me to a stop, and whispered. "Ali, that's the King of Hearts' d-daughter, Duchess."

A knot formed in my stomach as I recalled Hatter's past ties to her. Duchess was drop- dead gorgeous. Red leather boots wrapped around long tan legs, a white mini dress decorated in red hearts hugged her curves in an obscene way. Her brown eyes were wide as she threw her arms around Hatter. I felt March tense at my back, Cheshire was wearing a look of disinterest, but I could see the way he watched the tables around us carefully. Caterpillar wasn't paying any attention, as he quietly argued with the host about our table.

"Duchess, how have you been?" Hatter asked, looking perfectly at ease.

"Wonderful, Daddy just got me a Corvette, you must come visit so we can take it for a drive." she said, clapping her hands together.

I could barely hide how obnoxious I found her display. It was clearly an act, intelligence shown in her eyes as she finally glanced toward the rest of our group. "Hello, I'm..." I paused and glanced at Caterpillar, before quickly saying, "Annabeth Ainsworth. It's so nice to meet a friend of Hatter's."

Duchess took a moment to look me over from head to toe, keeping her expression neutral until her eyes met mine. She glared at me but stuck her hand out. "Duchess. It's a pleasure. How do you know each other?" she asked. Her voice had a sickly-sweet pitch, and I found that it grated on my nerves.

"Work—" he said.

"School—" I replied.

Our simultaneous and contradictory answers made Duchess look at us quizzically, but I intervened. "Hatter teaches at my daughter's school," I lied.

I saw Caterpillar's mouth drop open, but he quickly added, "Yes, Nyla just loves Mr. Hatter, but you know how The Grove feels about children." I took a moment to breathe and thank the Creator that Caterpillar not only played along with my spontaneous cover story.

"I didn't know you were a teacher, Maddie," Duchess said, wrapping her hand around his bicep.

"It's a new thing," he muttered, glaring at Caterpillar and me. I rolled my eyes at his petulance.

"Come eat with Daddy and me," she paused looking at the rest of us distastefully, "your friends can join us, of course,"

"When can I punch her?" I whispered, falling behind to loop my arm through Cheshire's.

"Another day, possibly. She's the best way to get close to the King of Hearts," he replied, with a chuckle.

"I can't believe he's just letting her hang all over him," I whispered in disgust.

"Jealous, are we?" Cheshire taunted.

"Creator forbid. I think he's showing off because he's angry at March and I," I replied, rolling my eyes again.

I was afraid that my eyes might get stuck that way by the end of this shit show. We took the stairs that curved into the private dining area. It was empty save for the King of Hearts, who was hunched over his computer typing like mad.

"Daddy, I brought some friends back with me," Duchess announced.

He was a man in his fifties, with thinning, grey hair, and a pot belly. A small golden crown sat atop his head, and I nearly laughed when I realized just how crooked it was. I doubted that it was real gold, more likely a costume piece, just like the King of Hearts himself. "Alright, sweetie. Just let me finish my business, and then I will meet them," he said, eyes glued to the computer screen in front of him.

Large windows lined the room, giving us a magnificent view of the city. The sun set high in the sky, gleaming off many of the metal buildings. I stared for a moment, wishing I could save the city from the man sitting just a few feet away. When I went to sit between Cheshire and March, Caterpillar pulled me down beside him, and whispered. "You're supposed to be my wife. Don't forget."

"Maybe, I'm cheating on you," I whispered back.

He snorted, drawing Duchess's attention again. "How long have you two been married? Oh, you must tell me about the wedding! I can't wait to get married!" she squealed, looking between us.

I could not tell if her enthusiasm was fake or not, but the way she glanced at Hatter when she said the words gave me a better idea about her intentions. I tried to ignore the jealousy that was rising in me, I hadn't known him for long. Just because I had sex with him didn't mean I owned him. "We've been married for five and a half years," he replied.

I gave him an incredulous look, hoping he realized how unbelievable that sounded considering he was ten years my senior. I hadn't taken the time to really do the math, I would have been nineteen and he would have been twenty-nine. The age difference between us didn't seem that large now that I was twenty-five, but it would have been much weirder if I was any younger. I realized I had zoned out, and Duchess was looking at me expectantly. "Our wedding was... huge. I think we invited everyone we knew," I grinned, faking a giggle.

"How old is your daughter?" she asked.

"Four," we said at the same time. I took a deep breath, happy that we were on the same page.

"I'm surprised you get to have any fun. Children just ruin most people. Of course, you two seem... um... happy," she said, moving her attention away from us. I could feel her condescending tone cascade over my body. I fought the urge to dive across the table and cut her tongue out.

"We are," Caterpillar spoke up, nudging my leg under the table.

I watched as Duchess sat in Hatter's lap and flirted with him. I glanced at March and noticed he looked as uncomfortable as I felt. Hatter was laughing and drinking the alcohol she offered him. Cheshire was sitting across from me in silence, staring into his glass. I found myself wondering what he was thinking about. He looked up, meeting my eyes, a half-smile forming on his plump lips. I could tell he wanted to get out of here just as much as I did. I cut my eyes toward the door, and he gave a subtle nod.

Duchess giggled loudly, drawing all of eyes back to her and Hatter. She was whispering in his ear, and I watched as he put one hand on her rib cage. "I have to use the restroom," I said, standing from the table suddenly. Everyone glanced at me with comically large eyes. Duchess glared for a moment, before Hatter said something I didn't quite hear. I glanced toward the King of Hearts whose eyes were still glued to his laptop.

"I'll join you," Cheshire said, grabbing my hand, and dragging me out of the room.

Once we were well out of ear shot, I said. "I would rather have my retinas burned out, than go back into that room and be witness to Hatter's disgusting behavior."

"He's really bad today. You mentioned earlier that he was upset with you and March, could that be why?" Ches asked.

"If it is, I'm not going to put up with it. Whatever he's pissed off about, it's just a misunderstanding." I fumed, "I get that this is a mission, but fuck, I don't believe for a second he's this dedicated to his role." I pushed my fingers, through my hair and took a few deep breaths.

"Alice? Is that you?" a quiet, female voice said, shocking me.

I turned to find Tillie Dodgson standing behind me, her two husbands flanking her. She was completely dwarfed by the mocha skinned twins she had married just a year prior. Jackson and Cahir were some of the kindest men I had ever met. I couldn't have been happier when she'd announced their marriage. "Tillie? What on earth are you doing here?" I asked, pulling her into a hug.

Her eyes strayed to Cheshire, and she said, "Please tell me you aren't here with this alley cat. I've seen you date some dumbasses, but he takes the cake."

"Lovely as ever, Dormouse," Ches shot back, crossing his arms.

I furrowed my eyebrows at his angry tone before I comprehended his words. "Wait, Dormouse, as in the Dormouse we're supposed to meet up with. Tillie is Dormouse?" I said, looking between the two of them.

"I sure am," she said proudly, putting her fists on her slim hips. "What are you doing here? Have you joined us? Well, of course you have. Why else would you be with Cheshire? You don't even have to use a codename within the Resistance," she rambled, twisting her fingers a bit.

"Jackson, Cahir, how are you?" I asked.

"Fine," they both responded, and then grinned at each other.

"Still doing the creepy twin thing, I see," I said with a smile.

"Oh yeah," Tillie replied, looking at the two men in awe, "But, I keep them around anyway."

"We wouldn't let you get rid of us. Don't lie," Cahir said, leaning down to kiss her cheek. My chest tightened at the easy show of affection. I always wished to have someone who was as good to me as Jackson and Cahir were to Tillie. I shook my head to dispel my thoughts. I knew that road would take me back to Hatter and I simply could not go there right now. Maybe he hadn't meant what he'd said last night, sex could cloud feelings. I'd learned that lesson the hard way many times.

"But seriously how did you end up with the Resistance?" Tillie asked.

"It's a long story for another day. How is Lacie?" I asked.

"Doing fine, you know the triplets will be three in a few months." She replied.

"Oh my god, really? Time flies." I said.

"How is Lily?" Tillie asked, and I immediately became somber.

"You haven't heard?" I said, glancing to the people around me, leaning in closer as I lowered my voice, "The Red Party has her and Dina."

Tillie's eyes widened in horror, tears filling her eyes. She had always been a sensitive person. When she started to open her mouth to say something, I shook my head, knowing here wasn't the place to have any discussion about it. I hoped we'd get somewhere in getting Lily and Dina away from the Red Party soon.

She nodded and continued chatting, keeping the subject light. It was nice to talk to a girl for the first time in several days, but it made me realize how much I missed Dina. Tears almost filled my eyes, but I pushed them away. I felt my phone vibrate in my bag and yanked it out. Caterpillar had sent me seven texts and called me twice. We'd been out of the room for nearly ten minutes. I checked the last message sent.

Boss Man: Get back here, now, or I'm coming to get you. Maybe that leash Jabberwocky mentioned would be a good idea after all.

I rolled my eyes but grabbed Cheshire. "We have to go back up," I told him, "Pray for us," I added, over my shoulder.

Tillie giggled but did not respond. I could see the haunted look in her eyes. I wondered for a moment what had made Cheshire silent during our conversation, but I didn't have a chance to ask him with Caterpillar's urgency. Cheshire opened the door, revealing chaos. March was standing in the middle of the room, eyes wide but glassy. Hatter was leaning over Duchess, holding a cloth napkin to her head. Caterpillar looked furious, as he stormed toward us.

"So nice of you two to rejoin us," he growled.

I glanced around the room and found that the King of Hearts was missing. I hadn't seen him come down the stairs, and I wondered for a moment where he disappeared to. It was obvious he had left before this mishap. "Sorry, Cheshire was taking forever," I said. "What happened?" I asked, hoping to avoid this day getting any worse.

Caterpillar pulled me into a corner of the room so we would not be overheard "To be perfectly honest, I'm not even sure. I was trying to speak to the King. I heard glass breaking," he paused to take a deep breath, "March threw a teacup at Hatter, who was smart enough to duck. Duchess, on the other hand, didn't see it coming. Probably because she was straddling Hatter and running her fingers through his hair." he explained, exasperated, "Can you please help?" He gritted his teeth, and I knew he hated asking for my help. I took a moment to assess the commotion around the room, before deciding it was time to leave. I walked toward March and laid a hand on his arm.

"Hey, baby," I cooed, "Go to the car with Cheshire. We're going to wrap up in here." His eyes immediately cleared, and I realized that this had been part of his show. March was not unhinged in the least; well, not as much as he led some people to believe. I was impressed at his ability to appear entirely broken.

"Alright," he said, quietly. He wrapped arms around me, and whispered, "I h-hope it leaves a f-fucking scar."

I agreed but made no move to tell him that. Caterpillar was still standing in the corner watching the room. I could tell he was trying to figure something out. I left him to his thoughts, as I walked toward Hatter and Duchess. "Are you okay?" I asked, fake concern coating my voice.

"He should be locked up," Duchess said, in a shrill voice.

Hatter flinched slightly, but I couldn't bring myself to care about his feelings. "I'm so sorry. He's a bit...delicate. You must have offended him," I said, unable to hold back the bite in my voice.

Hatter sent me a nasty glare and said, "You can't possibly blame Duchess for this, can you... Annabeth?"

"Oh, of course not," I said, pitching my voice just as high as hers.

I blamed him, but it wasn't the time and place to tell him that.

"I am so sorry, darling, please let me make it up to you," Hatter said, turning away from me.

I turned toward Caterpillar, tears burning in my eyes, and snarled "Why don't we go, honey? Maddie can take it from here."

Caterpillar said nothing in response; he simply followed me out. I ground my teeth in anger, feeling my magick buzzing angrily against my skin in response to my emotions. I could almost understand Hatter being rude to me, considering that our relationship was new. However, his treatment of March had nearly sent me over the edge. It wasn't the time or place to lose control, so leaving was my only option.

Once we were out of sight of the building, Caterpillar finally spoke, "You know we can't just leave him here, right? The Hummer is his car after all."

"Is your bike still parked over by Dina's apartment?" I asked, "That's about a block away, think you can find the time to drop me off? I need to pick up some more of my clothes anyway," I added.

"Sure. Do you want to… talk about it?" he asked, looking away from me awkwardly.

"No, I'm too pissed off right now. Maybe later," I said, jumping into the car.

March was sitting in the back seat and scooted closer to me when I settled in behind the driver's seat. My fingers were shaking in anger, and he took my hand, holding it in both of his.

It took less than five minutes to get to Dina's apartment and I had never been so glad to see any building in my entire life.

"I assume you'll be back to base later," Caterpillar said.

I nodded, in lieu of response, and simply took the keys from his palm. I ran up the stairs and unlocked the apartment door. I changed out of the red dress, leaving it lying in a crumpled mess on the floor. Ripped jeans, and a black tank top replaced it, I owned plenty of dresses, but I was always more comfortable in casual clothes. I packed a backpack full of clothes, and a photo of Dina, Griffin, and I at our high school graduation. I shouldered the bag, glancing around the apartment to make sure I didn't need anything else, and headed out to the community garage, swinging the keys around my finger. The bike was easy to find as it was the only thing parked on the second level. I straddled the bike, popped the key into the ignition, and brought the engine to life, letting its pleasant rumble take away the stress of the last few hours.

The first time I had ridden a motorcycle flooded my mind, my father hadn't been much of a daredevil, but he did prefer a bike that didn't require as much fuel. When I'd turned fifteen and been interested in driving, he'd convinced me that learning to ride his old, beat-up motorcycle was the way to go. I'd had a few falls, but he'd ensured I was well padded, so I walked away with very few injuries. Mom had begged me to not drive anything, she was always the worrier, but somehow Dad had managed to convince her I needed independence. Thinking of them caused tears to roll down my face behind the helmet I had put on. I swung out of the parking lot, revving the engine, desperately wanting to run from all the feelings I was having.

Memories flooded me as I flew past buildings, parks, and shops that I had been to a million times. The sun was high in the sky, making everything seem far brighter than I felt. I thought of my mom, and all the things she had taught me, the hours she spent telling me of the Wonderland she dreamed of, where everyone was free and could pursue all the dreams they had, where magick was common to anyone who had the talent, she believed magick could improve the lives of everyone in Wonderland, even the non-magickal. The anger I had felt for years welled up inside me, why had I never been enough for her? Not me, or Dad, or Lily could convince her that she was going to die if she didn't stop trying to destroy the Red Party. And now? Now I was following in her footsteps, just like she had always wanted.

Eventually, I found myself sitting in the meadow of yellow flowers, thinking back to the night this journey had begun. When I had left the house to celebrate Dina's birthday, I never imagined I would find myself working with the Resistance. Dark clouds passed overhead, promising another storm soon, the damp grass soaked through my jeans, causing me to shiver slightly.

"I should just leave," I muttered to myself, staring off into the distance. Defeat tasted sour in my mouth, but I was no closer to a plan to get Dina and Lily away from the Red Party. Even if I managed to get them out of the dungeon how long could they really hide before they would find us.

It didn't make sense to stay; there was no way I could beat the Red Party and I was tired of feeling defeated. If I couldn't handle Duchess, there was no way I could put an end to the Red Party. Mom was dead, so I couldn't disappoint her like I would Caterpillar, Cheshire, Hatter, and March.

I stood, walking toward the bike. I could hear my phone going off and I tried to ignore it.

Ultimately, annoyance won out. I snatched the phone as it began to ring for the third time, I answered the call.

"What?" I demanded.

"Al, come back to the warehouse," Cheshire pleaded.

I could hear other voices talking, demanding the phone.

"I told Caterpillar I would be back," I replied, "Just give me some time."

I heard a scuffle on the other end of the line, including a muffled protest from Ches.

As the noises on the other end quieted, Hatter said, "Alice, come home."

I gritted my teeth. Of all the people who could convince me to come back to the base, Hatter was on the very bottom of the list.

"My home is currently occupied by Suits, who've taken my sister and best friend. Or did you forget that little fact, while you were busying canoodling with Duchess?" I retorted, venom dripping from my voice.

"Duchess was our way in, and you know it. Quit being such a bitch and get back here," he demanded.

My mouth dropped open and I was silent for several seconds. How dare he.

I finally said, "I think it would be best for the both of us if you give someone else the phone. Otherwise, I'm going to say some things I won't regret." I paused, rage causing tiny sparks to light the air around me, "You're just like everyone else."

When the words came out of my mouth, I knew I had hurt Hatter, but it was true. He'd made promises he'd managed to break in a matter of hours. I didn't care what had caused his change in behavior so suddenly.

"Alice..." Hatter trailed off, before sighing, "Whatever. Come back or don't, I don't even care at this point. March wants to talk to you."

Tears gathered in my eyes, but I pushed them away. I could not believe Hatter; Maybe my taste in men really had not changed. I thought back to my most recent ex, a man named, Bobby, who had a predilection for young girls. When I realized this, I'd made sure he couldn't touch another person again.

"Ali? Did you h-hear me," March said, stopping my train of thought.

"No, what's up?" I asked.

"Ignore Hatter and p-please come back," he begged, making my heart ache.

March had not done anything wrong. In fact, Hatter was being almost as much of a dick to him as he was to me.

"What the fuck is wrong with him anyway? If he overheard part of our conversation, why not just ask about it?" I wondered out loud. "He's being a real dickhead."

Several beats of silence followed, before March said, "It's my fault."

I had no response to that. It wasn't entirely his fault, neither one of them was honest nor open with the other. It wasn't fair for Hatter to take out his bottled-up emotions on me, I couldn't ignore the immaturity of that.

"I... I don't think it's a great idea for me to come back right now, love," I finally said, more confused than before.

"Okay," he replied, quietly. "I'll l-let you go."

I hung up the phone and started crying. For the first time since that night at the Heart's Club I finally let out all my pent-up emotions. I was so terrified for Lily and Dina, but I was powerless to stop the Red Party. If my mother couldn't do it, how was I supposed to manage? Add that to the fact that Hatter had hurt my feelings, and proved he didn't trust me, and I was a mess. I had let these men comfort me, but it was a distraction from what was important. Saving Lily and Dina should have been the only thing that mattered not pointless bullshit with useless men. I was deeply ashamed of myself.

I sat for two hours, watching as the sun moved across the sky. I cried off and on until I ran out of tears. It couldn't bring myself to get up and drive further out of the city. Wonderland had been my home all my life and leaving it behind was impossible. I heard the rumble of a car coming toward me, but I couldn't bring myself to turn around and look. Within seconds I heard the engine cut off and a car door slam. I wrapped my arms around my legs and rested my head on my knees. I closed my eyes as heavy footsteps walked toward me. Someone sat down beside me, and I recognized the energy immediately.

"How long have you known I was here?" I asked, opening my eyes to look at Caterpillar.

His features were softer than I had ever seen them; I found myself wondering what he would be like without the stress of the Resistance.

"Within the first three minutes of the phone call," he replied, his eyes examining the field of flowers.

"Thank you for holding them off," I offered.

He gave a quick nod and I turned to look back. No one was waiting in the Hummer.

"And leaving them at the base," I added, smiling for the first time since leaving the Grove.

"Are you going to leave?" he asked, finally meeting my eyes.

"I've been sitting here, trying to decide that very thing. Wonderland may be my home, but it isn't safe. If I stay, then more than likely, not only will I witness Dina and Lily's execution and I'll be captured. If I leave, they'll die for sure. Their deaths are inevitable, no matter what I do. I have no idea what the outside world is like. Mom once told me there wasn't a city or house for hundreds of miles. I'll be completely alone out there, and I'll probably die anyway," I stopped, wiping tears away, "I'm fucked regardless of the path I take," I added, standing up.

"I probably shouldn't let my fake wife run off all on her lonesome," Caterpillar joked, trying to lighten the mood.

I stared at him, a feeling of familiarity filling me. From the moment I laid eyes on him something about him had always niggled at my brain. I closed my eyes trying to remember what I had so obviously forgotten. Suddenly it hit me, "You're the boy my mother talked about in her journal. The one who refused her help."

He looked away from me and I knew I was right.

"Why didn't you tell me? You knew she had two daughters. Why didn't you believe me when we first met?" I demanded.

My eyes widened, as my memories flashed back to my younger self. I was staring up at a teenager Caterpillar, less muscular, and with a happier glint in his eyes, but no less my Caterpillar.

"Hell, we've even met before. I remember it... I was four!" I shouted causing him to flinch.

"I didn't think you'd remember," Caterpillar admitted.

"You gave me a piggyback ride and played with me. Mom was having a meeting," I said, my voice softening as I stared at him, "You should have told me."

"Why, Alice? So, what if we knew each other? We only met once," He looked away, and I wondered if he was lying, "and you were so young,"

He stood up, clenching his fist, and I immediately followed.

"Why do you hate me?" I asked, dejected.

"Hatter told me you slept with him," he said, ignoring my question, "I assume that's why you two are fighting."

"It's none of your goddamm business," I shouted, stomping away from him.

"The hell it's not, this is my family" I was shocked he considered the guys his family, "you've caused a problem. Leave or fix it." he said, grabbing my arm and pulling me to a stop.

"Tell me why you lied, I deserve to know." I begged.

"I don't owe you an explanation, Alice." He said, "You need to grow up, running off because of Hatter and Duchess is ridiculous." He took a deep breath, staring at me, "What about Lily and Dina. The White Queen would be ashamed of you."

My mind was racing as I ripped my arm from his grip and jumped onto the motorcycle. I brought the engine to life and drove away. There was no point in going back to Wonderland. No point in watching as everyone I cared about died, when I couldn't stop it. No point in continuing to live in this world of lies.

Chapter 12

Caterpillar

August 5th, 2157

I was trying to read Rab's latest report on the King of Hearts movements. Ever since he disappeared from the Grove without hardly a word to his daughter. I had an itching feeling something was going on. The clicking of keys from the other side of the room grated against my nerves as I read the same line again.

"It's been over a week. Why hasn't she come back?" Cheshire asked, irritating me.

He was hunched over his computer, dark circles under his eyes. I was never quite sure was he was up to when he sat in here staring at the screen, typing frantically. He always got results, so I didn't ask questions. "Quit asking. I told you she left. She isn't coming back," I responded.

When he didn't respond, I read further down the page. No movements had changed with the Suits, but Jabberwocky and the Knave hadn't been spotted in several days. The creaking of my couch forced me to look. I found Cheshire had moved and was now reclining with his shoes on propped up on my table, throwing a ball into the air. "Why don't you get to work, I'm fairly certain I gave you a mission today," I added, glaring at him.

"Don't want to," he said, staring at the ceiling.

I wondered for the umpteenth time why he came in here. I'd already told him that Alice wasn't coming back, there was no point in irritating me about it. I ignored the slight guilt I felt at not explaining to them why Alice had actually run off. It was better they believed she was so immature she ran off because of a spat with Hatter. "It wasn't a suggestion, Cheshire. Go," I said, sternly. "You've spent enough time on the computer for today."

"Hatter's been running around this place like a rabid dog and you're picking on me," he whined. "Why do you always take his side?"

I had never seen Cheshire act so childishly and considering that I'd known him since he was nine. That was really saying something. I really wasn't taking Hatter's side. In all honesty I was pissed that he'd even slept with Alice, but I tried to ignore that feeling. My opinion on who she chose to sleep with didn't matter, even if I needed it to. Hatter, on the other hand, had been a surly son of a bitch since the morning we went to the Grove. I tried to get to the bottom of it, but he'd brushed me off. I sent him into the city to work on some leads with a couple of members of the Red Party who had expressed some dissatisfaction. I had hope they would give Hatter some information on why Alice's sister and friend had been arrested in the first place. We were in the dark on the situation, with no time to truly decipher it. "Because when I tell him to do something, he does it." I put down the file I was reading and rested my head in my hands, "I am not your parent, and I'm not going to act like it. Go do your work."

"You know, March doesn't seem to be all that upset that she's gone. Maybe, I read the situation wrong, but I got the idea she was going to pick him next," he continued. I rolled my eyes at his insistence that Alice had the intention to date all of us; he claimed it was polyandry. I knew a couple of women who had these kinds of arrangements, Dormouse being the first to come to mind. I crushed the feeling of hope that welled in my heart. Even if Alice wanted that kind of relationship, she wouldn't want it with me. I had betrayed her by not revealing who I was, but I was just trying to protect her. It was a ridiculous idea, but I took note that he was trying to tell me something. I felt a pull I couldn't explain and tensed at the sensation.

"Explain," I demanded.

"No. Figure it out. I want her back," he said, jumping up from the couch and leaving.

I stared after him for a moment, and finally decided it might be a good idea to talk to March.

"March," I barked, lengthening my stride to catch up with him. I noticed him tense, and I immediately knew he was up to something. More than likely Cheshire's instinct was right. "Well shit." I muttered under my breath. I hated when the Cat was right.

"Wh-What's up, Caterpillar?" he asked.

"Cut the shit, Hare. Where is she?" I said, cutting to the chase.

He looked down at his phone and hesitated, before finally asking, "If I t-tell you, will you bring her home?"

I made an impulsive decision; I was tired of avoiding Alice. She had something I wanted, and she would give it to me. "Yes," I responded. There was no I was letting her stay away any longer. If Cheshire's crazy rantings about polyandry were right. She needed to be with us, even if they weren't... I had to protect her. I had promises to keep.

I stood in front of the dingy building, staring down at my phone and contemplating whether or not I should leave her alone. Maybe I was wrong. She was a grown woman, but I couldn't forget that her mother, a woman I looked up to, had told me to protect her. The White Queen's death had haunted me for many years, but Alice's appearance scared me. I was fourteen when I first met Alice. I had watched her for the White Queen and my parents while they had a meeting. It shouldn't have been fun, but she had been a talkative, bright child. Now she was a sassy, beautiful woman, and I found myself drawn to her even as she drove me crazy. I should have felt guitly that was attracted to her, but I wasn't. We hadn't had a relationship when she was a child. I could never admit I felt something for her. She was ten years younger than me, and already interested in my team, it would never work. I took a moment to inspect the building I was about to enter, it sat on the outskirts of Wonderland, where a few vagrants and outlaws chose to stay. No one in the Red Party was willing to come this far from the safety of their precious homes.

"Go in," A voice said, startling me. I looked down to see a white-haired woman looking at me seriously. Her bright blue eyes stared at me as she repeated, "Go in."

"I—"I started to respond to her, confused on why she was pushing me. She didn't look familiar to me; I rarely came this far outside the city.

"Whatever reasons you've come up are stupid at best," She sighed, leaning against the Hummer, "Stay with Alice." My eyebrows rose in shock, and I opened my mouth to respond when we were interrupted.

"Hey, Sugar, what can I do for you?" a large breasted woman asked, rubbing against me.

"Nothing," I barked. I looked down to where the old woman had been standing only to find she had disappeared. I stood in shock for a moment, my head spinning.

When I realized the woman who interrupted the weird interaction was walking away, I asked. "Actually, have you seen this girl?"

I took out my phone and pulled up a candid picture of Alice that Cheshire had taken without her knowledge. Her head was thrown back in laughter, cards held aloft in her hands.

"Annabeth?" the woman confirmed, "Yeah, she's up on the tenth floor, haven't heard from her in a day or two. Her and Sammy are.... Oh, never mind, I'm sure you don't want to hear about that." I furrowed my eyebrows, wondering what Alice had been up to, but let it go. The woman examined me head to toe, causing me to shift in discomfort. "You're an awfully fine man, why would you want a twig of a girl like her?" she asked.

"She's my wife." I responded, without a second thought. It was a story we'd been using since Jabberwocky, and it just seemed a natural answer now. That concerned me more than I wanted to admit.

She rolled her eyes and walked away, leaving me to look for Alice. I made my way to the tenth floor, skirting around drunks and prostitutes on nearly every floor. The smell of paint and stale alcohol permeated the building causing me to cough slightly.

"I ain't seen you around here before," a small man said, squinting his eyes at me, "Who are ya?"

"Have you seen this woman?" I asked, holding up the picture of Alice and ignoring his question.

"Annabeth," he exclaimed, a smile lighting up his face. "She's a sweet lass. A bit sad though. She's just down the hall."

He pointed me in her direction. The inside of the building was no better than the outside. Many of the doors hung off their hinges, the paint was chipping in some places, showing layers of yellowing. Smoke hung heavy in the air, likely from cigarettes but I couldn't be certain that a fire wasn't burning somewhere on the floor. "Be nice to her sonny, or I'll have to take care of you," he called back. I paid his threat no mind, the only thing that mattered was getting Alice out of here as quickly as possible.

There were only two doors in the direction the old man had pointed. One door was charred black and standing wide open. The aged smell of burnt wood and fabric still faintly recognizable. The other was a green door, the paint chipped and peeling in places. I pushed it open with my foot.

"Not now, Sammy," Alice slurred, "I'm far too drunk to play cards with you." She had an arm thrown across her eyes and a cobalt glass bottle in the other hand. She was wearing a simple white tank top, and black shorts, and her hair was in disarray around her head.

"You got time for me?" I asked, leaning a shoulder against the doorway.

"I wondered when March would give me up," she sighed, sitting up, "How you been, Cater baby?" The dark purple circles under her eyes almost made me flinch, but I pushed those feelings away. I couldn't let my protective nature take over now. First, I had to convince her to come with me.

"I hate when you call me that," I complained.

"And I hate that you can't seem to leave me alone, but we don't always get what we want," Alice said, struggling to her feet. She sat her drink down on the table with a hard clink before turning to face me again.

Suddenly I was pissed, I couldn't believe she'd spent a week getting drunk, and then had such a bad attitude with me. Where had the girl that cared about her family gone? This wasn't Alice. "What happened to leaving Wonderland?" I snarled, stalking toward her.

"I would call this the boondocks. Not exactly the lap of luxury in Wonderland," she shot back, standing her ground. "Wouldn't you agree?"

I got in her face, which was difficult considering her head was below my chest. She swayed slightly, and I immediately noticed just how bad she looked. Up close I could see past the deep circles under her eyes. Her skin was pale, her normally bright eyes were dimmed, but defiant as always. "Why even talk to March if you're going to leave?" I shouted, "Huh? I told you to fix it, running away isn't fixing it," I shouted.

"You told me to leave," she hiccupped, and I watched in horror as tears dropped from her eyes, "Why even come here?" She dropped to the floral couch and held her head.

"Hatter and Cheshire are unbearable," I said, in lieu of response.

"Fuck Hatter," she muttered, glaring at me.

"You already did," I shot back. She flinched at the comment, but I refused to feel bad. She needed to hear what I had to say. "It's only a week and a half until they're executing Dina and Lily. Are you going to stay here and mope, or come save them?" I asked.

"Oh, fuck you, Caterpillar." she yelled, a surprising burst of energy coming from her, "When I met you, you didn't even believe that I was who I said I was. You told me then to run and never look back. That's what I'm trying to do. Instead of letting me, you're being a selfish prick, rubbing it in my face that I can't do anything right." I stood, staring down at her in shock. Without thought I pulled her into my chest, holding her against me. I wanted to soothe her, but I knew that the best I could do was light the fire inside her that she had lost. "I don't want to be tough anymore." She whispered, tears filling her eyes, as she looked up at me. For the first time since she punched me in the face, I saw her bravado drop.

"Come back. I'm sure you can work out your problem with Hatter. I've never seen him act this way before. It's none of my business what you do with him," I said, although I wanted to take it back the moment, I said it. I wanted it to be my business, but I knew it wasn't the time to have that conversation.

She tried to step away from me but stumbled. So, I stepped forward to catch her. It was easy to sweep her off her feet. I cradled her in my arms for a moment before, settling her back down on the couch. As her warmth left my arms, I felt empty. Unfortunately, I'd been used to the empty feeling since my mother had died. My father had followed shortly after, her death making him reckless.

"How many times did we meet?" she asked as I took a seat beside her.

"Just the once." I lied, if she didn't remember the other time, we met it was for the best. "But I spent a lot of time with your mom, and I've met Lily a few times, as well."

"I wonder why I didn't realize it was you the second we met. You haven't changed that much..." She trailed off.

"You were young," I looked away from her open gaze.

"We're orphans now, and you collected the other orphans too. Like a matched set," she rambled, her head dropping to my shoulder.

"Technically, Hatter and March aren't orphans." I said, trying to lighten her mood.

She looked up at me, entrancing me with her blue eyes, I hated the tears I could see forming in them. I didn't know how to fix how she felt, causing my anger to flare I was helpless to fix her problems. "Mom would be so disappointed." She whispered.

"I don't think she would, and I'm sorry I said that. She wanted you to be her successor. I heard her tell my dad that you were exactly what Wonderland needed. I've tried to fight it but.... Alice, I agree," I said.

"Why are you being nice to me? You hate me." she said, pulling away from me.

"I have never hated you," I admitted.

We sat in silence for several minutes, before I heard a soft snore. I smiled, seeing how peaceful she was now. I got up, and went around the small room, grabbing her things and stuffing them into her bag. I threw it over my shoulder and leaned down to pick up her sleeping form. She stirred slightly, and asked, "Home?"

"Home," I responded, and carried her out of the building.

I settled her into the backseat, making sure her head was in a comfortable position, before climbing into the driver's seat. Once I was back on the road, I picked up my phone, calling the only person I trusted to vent to. "Hello, Nephew," Rab said, his deep timber echoing through the car speakers, "What can I do for you?"

"I'm bringing Alice back." I started, drumming my fingers on the wheel in thought.

"Ah... I take it you have worked things out?"

"I hope so..." I had never felt insecure before now, always in charge of my emotions and the things going on around me.

"Roman, I know you have feelings for the girl. Maybe all of you boys do, that isn't my business. However, you should always trust your instincts. My only advice, try not to smother her, she's an independent young woman who has been through a lot." My uncle never failed to be wise, "So much like her mother." The pain in his voice stopped my thoughts of Alice for a moment.

"I know you miss her, but there was nothing either of us could have done." I didn't know if comforting him would work, but it was all I could do.

"Take care of Alice. Her mother always believed she would be our savior." He hung up, without another word.

I knew Rab was right, Alice was the key to saving Wonderland. I made a choice as I sped back into the city limits, I would stop trying to push her away. I had made the wrong choices, letting my fear and ego lead the way. I couldn't anymore. Because I loved Alice.

Chapter 13

Alice

August 6th, 2157

"Al. Al, wake up," I cracked open an eye, and found Cheshire standing over me. Groaning, I flipped over, and covered my head with the blanket.

I had vague memories of Caterpillar showing up at Sammy's bunker while I was drunk. The pounding in my head kept me from even trying to figure out how I'd ended up back here. He shook me, until I finally sat up. "What do you want?" I growled.

"Since you've been nice enough to return to our lowly hovel, Princess. I thought I would let you know lunch is ready," he said, mock bowing.

"Missed you too, Cat," I grumbled, getting out of bed. I gripped my head, groaning from the hangover.

"As a warning, Hatter's on the warpath, and Caterpillar is in a particularly foul mood. If we're smart, we'll run away," Cheshire said, winking at me.

"Ches, I tried that once, and look where I'm at. Boss Man dragged me back." I said, smiling. A sharp pain in my head made me wince, but I swung my legs over the bed. "This should be fun," I muttered, walking toward the shower, stripping my shirt off on the way.

"What is it with you, and not having clothes on in my presence," Ches yelped, from behind me.

"Why can't I take my clothes off around you?" I shouted back.

"You haven't even taken me on a date, and I've seen you naked," He replied. "Multiple times."

"Why do I have to take you on a date, why can't you take me?" I asked, turning on the shower.

"Gender equality, love. Treat me like a gentleman, make an honest man of me, all that jazz." Cheshire said.

"If you're pregnant it's not mine," I said, barely containing laughter. It felt good to be back here.

"How dare you deny our child. You used me," he cried. I turned to find him clutching his chest. We both started cracking up, until I saw tears run down his cheeks.

"It's good to have you back, Al," Cheshire said, he placed a hand on my cheek. "I don't know exactly what happened that caused you to leave, but next time, will you tell me where you're going so, I can join you?" he added.

"I shouldn't have left in the first place, it was childish and stupid," I admitted, embarrassed.

"We all have our stupid moments, learning from them is what's important. Running away never solved anything." Cheshire said, surprising me with his wisdom. It was easy to forget that Ches was incredibly intelligent, he hid it so well behind his humor.

"I know, I let my emotions get the better of me," I said, finally stepping out of the shower. He handed me a towel, respectfully looking away from me. I found it endearing that he tried to protect my modesty. I didn't have any, but it was cute anyway.

Instead of responding he patted my shoulder and left me to get dressed. I searched around the room for my clothes, and finally noticed a small dresser, pushed against the far wall. It hadn't been there last time I'd been in the room, so I assumed one of the guys brought it in here for me to put my clothes in. I opened the top drawer to find my bras and panties, folded carefully and neatly. I found that the rest of the drawers were much the same way. I'd have to thank them for being nice enough to organize my stuff, even if they did rifle through my unmentionables. I grabbed a pair of leggings and an oversized, blue sweater, and left the room, my wet hair soaking into my top. I found Caterpillar, Cheshire, and March sitting around the dining room table, talking. Caterpillar went silent as I took a seat. We all sat awkwardly, until I finally broke the silence, "So, who put my clothes up?"

March broke out into a grin, and said, "Me."

I smiled back, and said, "Thank you, you didn't have to."

"It w-wasn't a problem...," he trailed off for a minute, his smile dropping, before adding, "I haven't had much to do lately."

"What do you do March?" I slapped a hand over my mouth, "I'm sorry that sounded rude."

"Hatter's dad taught me a lot about medicine while I lived with them, so I take care of any b-bumps and bruises." He explained, taking the rude question in stride.

Caterpillar cleared his throat and said. "I think we need some new ground rules, but I don't want to start until Hatter comes down."

I furrowed my eyebrows in confusion, but chose not to say anything, nodding my head instead. March stood up and walked behind me. I turned my head to raise an eyebrow at him, but he didn't answer my silent question. I felt fingers comb through my hair, slowly massaging my scalp, and I groaned in happiness. "Do you have hair ties?" he asked, I slipped one off of my wrist and held it up to him.

March took several minutes braiding my hair, and I found myself asking, "Where did you learn to do this?"

"My friend, Idalia, taught me," he replied.

"Where's Griffin?" I asked, glancing toward Cheshire.

"When you left, he went to hang out with Rab. His exact words were 'I would rather be shot in my left testicle than stay with you guys, without Alice'."

"Sounds like Griff." I said, glancing at Cheshire. I heard footsteps, and Hatter appeared in the doorway. He seemed to be in disarray, his hair was messily thrown into a bun, and he was not wearing a shirt.

"Done." March said, proudly patting my head. I reached up and found that he had braided my hair into a crown around my head.

"Appropriate." Cheshire said, with a wink.

"Sit, we have to talk." Caterpillar directed, and Hatter pulled out a chair.

I started to fidget as we sat in silence. Caterpillar looking between Hatter, March, Cheshire, and me. I felt like I was a little kid who got caught with their hand in the cookie jar. I could tell Cheshire was feeling similarly, and I winked at him out of boredom.

"I assume at this point we're all aware that Hatter and Alice slept together the night before we went to the Grove?" I winced, but nodded, looking at my hands. "Good... Creator I never expected I would be having this conversation. I knew the White Queen before she died, and through her I met Alice," he admitted, locking eyes with me.

"What does that have to do with me fucking—" I started.

Caterpillar raised his hand to stop me. "Please, for all of our sakes don't finish that sentence. I wanted to be totally honest here, and I think it's important we all do the same thing." he gave me a pointed glance, but I didn't understand what he wanted me to say.

Cheshire was the one who answered my unspoken question, "Are you interested in being with all of us?"

"I mean, we are all together," I laughed, nervously.

I couldn't believe Cheshire had actually asked me that question. I had to be dreaming, the pounding in my head had eased, so I pinched myself to ensure I was awake.

"Cut the shit, Alice." Hatter snarled, and I was taken aback at his tone of voice.

"Fine. Yes, I've found myself attracted to all of you." I admitted, heat rushing to my cheeks, "But, saving Lily and Dina is still my priority," I demanded.

"That is a given." Caterpillar said, and I found myself sending him a thankful smile. "We need to discuss boundaries, and such, if we're doing this."

"You want to date me?" I asked, somewhat shocked he was so willing to admit it, when only a week ago he told me to leave. "You all want to be with me?"

"It won't be easy, because you're such a pain the ass, but yes, I think we would be good together. And I'm not going to deny you your happiness," he said.

"Well-uh- I'm going to take that as a compliment," I said, eyes wide.

"First of all, you three," Caterpillar pointed between, Hatter, March, and I, "need to figure your shit out. I don't have time for drama, and neither do Lily and Dina. I don't think sleeping schedules or planned dates are genuine. We'll let things happen naturally, and at Alice's pace," he watched me closely before asking, "Is that okay with you?"

"I...uh... I have to be honest, I've never been in a relationship with more than one person, so I don't know the rules." I said.

"It's new for all of us." Cheshire said, placing a hand on my arm.

"If we have a problem, we'll talk about it." Caterpillar reassured me. I found myself wondering what had changed his attitude. I knew I would have to ask him the next time we were alone.

"I'm so confused, we barely know each other. I can't deny I've felt something for all of you, but to just start dating... in the middle of all of this... it seems selfish." I said, rubbing my arms.

"Is it what you want?" Cater asked, staring at me with his gorgeous grey eyes. They always captured me before, but now I thought I saw a warmth in them I hadn't noticed before. I don't know what changed his mind, but I wanted to be close to him. Close to all of them.

"I'm tired of not allowing myself to feel things, so yes. I think we can do this." I said, a smile spreading across my face. Cheshire and March high fived, and I thought I noticed Ches slip March some cash.

"I have some work to do. I will see you all at dinner." Caterpillar said, before leaving.

We sat in awkward silence for a moment. Hatter had been silent through the conversation, and was now glaring at March and me. "I'll be in... my room." Cheshire said, awkwardly pointing toward the ceiling.

After he was gone, we sat in silence for several more minutes, before March said. "Hatter, I don't know why you're u-upset, but if you'll j-j-just talk to us we can fix it."

"Why would we? You two are keeping things from me, obviously you don't want me to know whatever is going on." Hatter snarled, but I could finally see the hurt beneath the anger. It didn't excuse his behavior, but I understood it.

"First, you need to calm the fuck down. If you can't be civil, we aren't having this conversation. Second, I'm not entirely sure why you think we're keeping things from you, so you'll have to enlighten me." I said, smacking a hand on the table.

"I heard you talking the morning we went to Grove. March begged you not to tell me something, and you agreed. End of story. When I asked if everything was okay, you lied to me. I can almost excuse that you don't trust me, but for him not to. What's the fucking point?" he ranted, throwing his hands in the air.

I looked at March, whose mouth was hanging open, "I-I-I," he started, unable to start his sentence. I patted his hand in encouragement, and he finally spit out, "I wasn't trying to keep things from you. I was telling Alice about my nightmares. I don't want you to treat me the way you used to." March spoke so quickly I barely understood what he was saying, but apparently Hatter got the gist.

"Why not? I've always supported you." Hatter asked, looking confused.

"I'm going to let you guys' hash this out," I said, standing to leave.

"Th-Thanks." March said, but quickly dropped his eyes to the floor in discomfort.

"Be nice," I told Hatter, who ignored me.

I walked upstairs and found myself standing in the doorway of Cheshire's room watching him hunch over a desk. "What's up, pussycat?" I asked. He nearly jumped out of his seat in fright.

"Shit, you scared me," he said, clutching his chest. "Everything worked out?" he asked. I shrugged my shoulders in response and leaned over him to see what he was doing. Two matching guns sat on the desk, surrounded by cleaning supplies. "Admiring my babies?" Cheshire asked, as I rested my chin against his shoulder.

"They are pretty," I said, stroking the floral detail that was etched into the black barrel.

He scoffed, "Pretty? Please, they are masterpieces. Beautiful, perfect masterpieces."

I rolled my eyes at him, and stood, glancing around his room. The walls were a deep purple color, nearly black. A queen-sized bed was covered in a black comforter, and I soon found myself flopping down on it. I sighed and curled myself around a pillow. I glanced over at Cheshire who was giving me an odd look but turned back toward his desk without comment. I don't know how long I laid there in comfy bliss, before Cheshire plopped down beside me. "Move over, you're hogging the bed," he said, pushing me.

"Can't you see I'm trying to rest?" I asked, cracking open one eye. "Why is it that you keep waking me up?" I glared at him.

"The hardest jobs always fall to me," he said, before pushing me onto the floor.

"You're a meanie," I fake pouted, crawling in beside him.

"I've been called worse," he joked. "Hand me the remote, if we're gonna relax I want to watch a movie," I groaned, but rolled over to grab it.

As the projector displayed a large logo over Earth. I cuddled further into Ches' side finding myself completely at peace.

I jerked awake, confused. Cheshire sat up beside me, his hair was sticking up everywhere, and rubbed his eyes.

"What's goin' on?" he asked, sleepily.

"I don't know," I responded, straining my ears. Shouts sounded again, and I was up and jogging down the stairs, before Cheshire could even react. I found Hatter and March standing in the middle of the living area, screaming.

"It's n-none of your Creator damned business." March yelled, pushing past Hatter.

Hatter grabbed his wrist, and shouted back, "The hell it isn't, I cannot believe you've kept this from me for years."

"I knew you were going to fr-freak out. I don't want to have this conversation." March said, jerking away.

"That's the problem, isn't it? I'm not going to do everything you want. I won't let you do this." Hatter said, walking after March.

"It isn't up to you! I'm twenty-six years old Hatter, we aren't little kids anymore. I can protect myself." March ranted.

"You're making a dumbass decision, and I'm not letting you." Hatter said, towering over March. They weren't that different in height, but March had a far more submissive body language, making him seem smaller.

My protective instinct kicked in and I stepped further into the room speaking up. "What's going on?" I asked, resting a hand on Hatter's shoulder.

"Thank the Creator, Alice. Tell him he doesn't need to get his mother out of the mental institution." Hatter said, waving his hands all over the place.

I furrowed my eyebrows, "Why do you want to do that?" I asked, looking at March.

"None of it was her fault, she was a victim as well, and she's been clean for tw-twelve years," he explained.

"She's been locked up; she hasn't exactly had a choice about being clean." Hatter pointed out.

"I can see why Hatter might think that's a bad idea. If she's somewhere that is helping her, where she can't access drugs and other things. Why wouldn't you want her to stay where she is safe?" I asked.

March's sighed, "She's been sending me letters, she says she hates it there. I just want to get her out. She's my mom."

"Who let you be horribly abused." Hatter chimed in; arms crossed.

"I don't want you to be manipulated, baby. Most people like that just want out so they can go back to their old habits." I said, Hatter made a sound of agreement, but I ignored him. "However, I think you should go visit her, so you can make that opinion for yourself," I added.

"What? No, he shouldn't. She's obviously dangerous!" Hatter exclaimed. "You know what, fuck it. Do whatever the hell you want, but I'm out," he said, leaving the room.

I watched as Hatter stormed upstairs, before turning back to March. I saw the defeated look on his face and found my heart breaking for him. I noticed Caterpillar standing shirtless in the doorway of his office. I nodded to him, before turning to March.

"Why don't you go relax," I said, grabbing his hand.

"Will you go with me to see her? I was going to have H-Hatter go... but you can see how that worked for me." He asked.

"Sure, when?" I asked.

"Tomorrow?" He offered.

"Alright, let's go early, so we can get back," I said, "I'm going to go talk to Caterpillar for a minute, you can wait for me if you want to."

I stepped into Caterpillar's office, leaving March to decide what he wanted to do. I watched him standing with his back to me. I couldn't tell exactly what he was doing, but the muscles in his back flexed alluringly. "I know you're there," he said.

"We need to talk," I flopped down on one of his couches, "A lot has been left unsaid." He stayed silent, pulling a chair to sit across from me. I bit my lip trying to figure out what I wanted to say. "I need to know why you didn't tell me when you realized who I was." I said carefully.

He sighed, "I'm not sure. We had already gotten off to a bad start, I genuinely didn't recognize you at first..." He trailed off. "You could have just as easily been a Red Party plant, I had no idea what happened to you after... everything." I said nothing, waiting for him to continue. When we sat in silence for several moments, my mind wandered. I worried over the time I had left to find and save Lily and Dina. I knew where they were being held, I needed a layout of the Red Party base. It was a huge building; without a plan I couldn't exactly storm the castle. Caterpillar finally spoke, "I'm sorry."

"I want to believe you, but I feel hurt," Tears welled in my eyes, "I have so few connections to my mother. If you had just told me..."

"I know. I made the wrong decision. You're a grown woman, and I treated you like a child who had to kept in the dark. I promise it won't happen again." My heart stuttered at his words.

I threw myself across the space, slamming my lips into his impulsively. I felt a moment of embarrassment when he didn't immediately return the kiss. Within seconds he'd wound his fingers into my hair, pulling me properly into his lap. I moaned into his mouth when I felt the heat of him pressed into me. He growled, standing with me in his arms. When he sat me down on his desk, pushing the papers away without breaking the kiss, I nearly wept as feeling welled inside of me.

"I want you," I whimpered pulling just far enough away to speak.

He stopped moving, I wasn't sure he was even breathing as he stared down at me, "I... Not yet, Alice." I was stunned, until he said, "I haven't treated you the way you deserve. When I take you there won't be doubt in your mind about how I feel about you." He stepped further away regaining his composure, "I didn't lie when I said I had work to do." I must have looked upset because he grabbed my chin, "You need time, so do I."

I nodded, sliding off his desk, taking in the mess he'd made. "You're going to have a hard time working like this."

"I'll take care of it." He dismissed me, "Did you work things out with Hatter and March?"

"March asked me to join him to go visit his mother tomorrow." Caterpillar's eyebrows rose comically, and I had to stifle a giggle.

"Cheshire and I are supposed to go have a meeting with Rab. I'm hoping we can find a mole within the Red Party base who may be able to smuggle Lily and Dina out." Caterpillar changed the subject.

"Really?" I couldn't believe he'd continued working on saving them while I'd been away.

"Don't look so surprised," He growled, "I'm not going to let innocent women suffer, no matter what happened with you."

"Thank you," I whispered as I walked out the door, knowing our conversation was over. March was sitting crossed legged on the floor, elbows propped on his thighs staring off into the distance. When I closed the door to Caterpillar office, he looked up at me and I could tell he'd been crying.

"I was going to go back to Cheshire's room, he's got to have the most comfortable bed I've ever slept in, would you like to join me." I offered him a hand to stand.

He said nothing as he took my hand, using it to pull me into a hug, "Thank you for t-taking care of me, Alice. I know it isn't e-e-easy."

"Yes, it is." I dismissed him as I pulled him toward Cheshire's bedroom, pushing the door open with my foot before I flopped down on his bed.

Cheshire opened his bathroom door and started. "I... What are you guys doing in here?" he asked, glancing between us.

"I'll g-go." March said, red flushing across his face.

"No, it's fine. I just wasn't expecting Alice to come back." Ches said.

"I'm going to sleep in here every night, your bed is comfy." I laughed, trying to lighten the somewhat dark mood that hung over us all.

"Caterpillar has the king size version." He replied, nervously.

"What's wrong?" I asked, confused.

"No one has slept in my bed with me before." He admitted, shocking me. "Until earlier."

I glanced at March, who was staring down at his phone, not paying any attention. "You've had sex before, right?" I asked, quietly.

"What- I- Why would you ask- Of course." Cheshire stumbled, turning red.

"It's okay if you haven't," I said, watching him closely.

"I have had sex before, Alice." He said, looking a bit offended. "It's just... I haven't exactly invited them into my home, much less into my bed." He admitted, looking away from me.

"Oh..." I said, finally understanding. "We're just going to sleep, and if that makes you uncomfortable, we can go to my room," I offer, hoping to assuage his fears.

"No, it's fine. I want you in my bed." He said, smiling at me.

I climbed in first, followed immediately by March. Even though he was the tallest one, he curled up in between Cheshire and me. It wasn't long before his breath evened out, and he was asleep. "What's going on, anyway?" Ches asked, quietly.

"Hatter is mad that March wants to go sign his mother out of the mental institution she's in," I explained. "We're going to go visit her tomorrow," I added.

"Damn, that's going to be rough on him. I'm glad he's taking someone with him, but I hope he decides to leave her to rot." He replied.

"Cheshire," I chided.

"That woman is evil to her soul, and the fact she's manipulating him again only proves it." Venom dripped from his voice as he continued, "I met her once when he asked me to go with him to visit when we were younger."

I was surprised Cheshire and March had managed to keep that a secret from Hatter, but it wasn't my business. I sighed praying he was wrong. March groaned in his sleep, and flipped over, kicking Cheshire out of the bed.

"Ow, shit." Ches said, catching his fall, right before he would have face planted. March continued to groan, and writhe around, but I had no idea what to do.

"Can you wake someone up from a nightmare?" I asked, and then realized what I needed to do. "Watch him for a minute make sure he doesn't hurt himself," I ordered, leaving the room.

I slammed open Hatter's door, only to find him, standing in the middle of room. "Nightmare?" he asked. I wondered for a moment how he knew, I certainly couldn't hear March's quiet groans from in here. I nodded, and he immediately went to Cheshire's room. I followed closely on his heels and watched in silence as he kneeled beside the bed.

"March, March, Marchie. It's time to wake up, you scared Ali and Ches." He whispered, barely loud enough for me to make it out.

March bolted up, breathing heavily, eyes glassy. He glanced at Hatter, and immediately fell into his arms, shaking. I walked over, and kneeled beside them, laying my head on Hatter's shoulder, and reaching to tangle my fingers into March's hair. I could feel his body shaking, and I found my heart weeping for him. I couldn't imagine being haunted so strongly by the demons of the past. Sleep was one of the few peaceful escapes I had in life. Hatter muttered nonsense things, and I found myself joining in. I watched as Cheshire sat on the bed and motioned for us to move from the floor. I sat down in Cheshire's lap, and pulled March into me, Hatter joined us, leaving the four of us tangled and hot.

I don't know how long we sat there together, but eventually I heard quiet snores from Cheshire and March. I looked at Hatter, noticing the bags under his eyes. I wondered how often he found himself up in the middle of the night, tending to March. "I'm sorry for the way I treated you, sweetheart. I should have just come out and asked what was going on. I can't forgive that he's going to put himself back into a horrible situation with his mother." Hatter said, staring off into the distance. "Not even accounting for that fact he's lied about it for years."

"I'm going with him tomorrow. I won't let him get hurt," I offered.

"He shouldn't drag you into this either. It's selfish, but I'm glad he's taking someone. Maybe he will listen to you," He sighed, and then removed himself from the bed. "I need space to think. We can… talk tomorrow after you guys get back." I nodded, wiggling my fingers at him.

I laid in bed, with so many thoughts circling through my brain. I had to protect March, partially from himself, I had to save Lily and Dina, and save Wonderland from the Red Party. I knew it would eventually become too much. I suppressed the panic that welled in my chest. I knew it was my duty to protect the people I loved; nothing would stop me from doing that, especially not my own petty emotions. Not anymore.

Chapter 14

August 7th, 2157

I had a hot cup of tea in one hand, and a bagel in the other, as I sat at the large kitchen table, trying desperately to wake up. Caterpillar and Cheshire had already left to see Rab. I had gotten ready quickly and was waiting for March to go see his mother. I hoped they would find some information, we only had six days to get Lily and Dina to safety. What we would do after the fact didn't matter until they were safely home.

"March should be ready in a minute." Hatter startled me as he padded into the kitchen, only wearing a pair of grey sweatpants. I nodded, still feeling a bit awkward around him, we hadn't had an actual conversation since our foray. I watched as he poured himself a cup of tea and settled across from me. I shoved the rest of my bagel into my mouth to avoid having to speak first. "I meant what I said that night." Hatter said, staring into his cup. I chewed faster trying to respond, but he continued, "I felt something for you the moment I saw you. I know how ridiculous that is Alice. I don't believe in love at first sight, but I've always been interested in more than your body… though that is absolutely… never mind I'm rambling."

"You should have just talked to me, Hatter," I didn't know what else to say.

"I don't want to excuse my behavior, but March is a sensitive subject for me." He took a deep breath. "Alice, I love him, but he's been keeping things from me for years. Proven by this absolutely asinine trip the two of you are taking today."

"Your relationship really isn't any of my business. I care about you both. While I do see where you're coming from... sometimes we have to let people we love do things for themselves even when we know they shouldn't."

"I just don't know if I can," He ran his fingers through his hair, fidgeting restlessly. I felt bad he was so worried about us going to see March's mother.

"You don't have a choice," March said, standing in the doorway.

"March..." Hatter sighed. "I can't convince you not to do this, but I'm not going to pick up your broken pieces this time." Hatter stormed out of the room, not giving March a chance to respond.

The more I thought about what Hatter was really saying I understood where he was coming from. I hadn't been taking care of March's trauma for years. I certainly hadn't witnessed it firsthand; I couldn't judge him for being biased. I looked to March expecting him to be upset, but he was staring at me stony faced, I gave him a small smile. "Caterpillar gave me the keys to the bike back, do you want to drive?"

"I d-don't actually know how," He admitted, his cheeks turning pink.

"Well, I guess you'll have to wrap your arms around me," I winked as I grabbed his hand leading him outside.

We both put helmets on, I swung my leg over the bike holding it steady as March climbed on as well. Once his arms were wrapped firmly around my waist. I zoomed away from the warehouse, trying to ignore a sinking feeling in my stomach.

I parked the bike in a spot between an armored vehicle and a junky looking green car. The hospital was the only medical building in Wonderland, so plenty of people were milling around outside. We weaved through the crowd, making our way into the multistory brick building. March led me through the glass revolving doors, towards an elevator. I gritted my teeth as we entered the death trap machine, hating the smallness of the metal box. "You okay, Ali?" he asked, furrowing his eyebrows.

"I hate elevators," I said, gripping the metal railing until it bit into my skin.

"I'm s-sorry." March said, grabbing my other hand. "Are you claustrophobic?"

"No, Lily and I got stuck in one when I was six and I've hated them ever since. I almost always use the stairs." I forced myself not to remember that day, one of the few times we had visited the city when my parents were both alive. The bell dinged, and I breathed a sigh of relief as I rushed out of the tiny, metal box. A bored, young woman sat behind a desk; paper strewn in front of her. She glanced up at us, her face lighting up. I smiled back, calmed in her presence. I glanced around, seeing no one else roaming the halls, but distant, distressed voices reminded me where we were.

"Hello, I'm h-h-here to see, Claudia Danara." March said.

"Of course, honey. You and your friend here will have to sign in," The woman said. Her name badge said Denice in block letters. She handed the pen to me first, and I quickly jotted my name into the log. March did the same, and we took the shiny orange visitor stickers she gave us.

A bulky orderly appeared out of nowhere, and lead us further into the bright, sterile building. "Visiting hours end at 2pm, don't forget to sign out." he said, before opening the door.

I don't know exactly what I was expecting March's mother to be like, but a petite woman, dressed entirely in a lavender jumpsuit wasn't it. She had the same honey brown eyes as her son, her grey hair was pulled into a tight bun. "Maxie! I wasn't expecting you," she said, standing from her chair to wrap him in a hug. I raised my eyebrows at the nickname and made a mental note to ask about it later.

"I thought I would c-come visit, since you want me to ch-check you out soon." He said, moving away from her.

"Of course, dear. Have you tried all the things I sent you to get rid of that horrible stutter? I know some of them are a bit unconventional, but I'm sure they would work," she asked. I realized instantly her kind appearance was deceiving. She was a conniving little woman, and she had wrapped her son around her finger. I knew March wanted to have a good relationship with her even with all the things she had put him through. I decided I would do my best to make this visit easier for him. The glint in her eyes as she stared up at her set me on edge.

I cleared my throat and stepped around March, "Nice to meet you, Ms. Danara. I'm Alice Young," I said, offering my hand.

She looked me up and down, before plastering a smile on her face, "Please call me, Claudia. It's a pleasure to meet a friend of my son's," she said. "How do you know each other?" she asked, glancing at March.

"She's my girlfriend." He answered, I looked at him in surprise, but a smile lit up my face.

"Oh! How wonderful." She wrapped her arms around me, trapping my arms against my body in an awkward pseudo-hug.

"Tell him to listen to his mother and do the exercises to fix his stutter. It's shameful and unattractive," she said, as she released me.

My mouth dropped open in shock, but I recovered quickly when I saw the redness in March's face, "Why would I do that?" I asked, my voice unfamiliar to my own ears, "It's a part of who he is. He's perfect to me," I added, wrapping an arm around his waist.

"Of course, dear," she said, her lips pinched. "I'm just happy to know he's found someone that's not the O'Hare boy. I was dreading the day my boy came to me to tell me they were together," she added, patting my arm.

I hated the look in her eyes as she mentioned Hatter, "Hayden? Yes, he's a good friend of mine, in fact he lives with us. I'm excited for you to move in so we can be one big, happy family," I bit out. I kept my tone sweet, but it was all I could do not to punch her. Hatter had absolutely been correct. Coming here was a waste of time, over my dead body would this woman ever see the light of day free again.

"Of course, there's nothing wrong with Hayden liking men, just not my boy." Claudia said, but her disgust was evident. "May I just say so many girls your age are worried about their appearance, I'm so glad you're not." The topic change and snide remark caught me a bit off guard. I felt March tense beside me, and I knew exactly how uncomfortable he was.

"Sit, sit. Tell me all about how you met," she said, waving us into seats.

I groaned internally as we began constructing a lie.

We had been visiting Claudia for three hours when my phone began to ring, "Excuse me," I said, standing to leave the room.

"What's up?" I asked.

"How's it going?" Cheshire asked.

I groaned, "She's awful. If I hear one more backhanded comment about March's stutter or his relationship with Hatter. I'm going to lose it," I said, quietly to make sure they couldn't hear me.

"I don't see how he stands her." He replied.

"Me neither. This woman sure as hell isn't moving in with us," I said, leaning my head against the wall. "Did you get finished with your business?" I asked, needing a break from Claudia.

"Yup, all set for some fun hacking." Ches joked.

A few beats of silence followed the comment. I found myself wondering what exactly Cheshire did for the Resistance. I glanced at the clock; I didn't want to leave March alone with his mother for very long. "Did you get any information that's going to help get Lily and Dina?" I asked.

"Caterpillar is going to look over the paper we were given, he seemed hesitant to believe the man we met," He paused. My heart plummeted in my chest, losing even more hope we'd save them. "But I think there's some valuable information, Alice. We'll save them."

"I'm going to go back in, pray for me," I said, rubbing my forehead. I couldn't find the words to respond to his reassurance.

"You got it, Al," he said, before we said our goodbyes.

I took a deep breath, before opening the door, "Sorry, just a friend checking up on me." I said, returning to my sit.

"Doesn't your friend know you're with your boyfriend?" Claudia asked.

"He does." I said, shortly.

"Hm, you should set boundaries with your friends, so they don't bother you while your spending time with Maxie." she offered.

I nodded, because I didn't have anything nice to say. I looked at March, trying to silently communicate that it was time to go.

"We're going to h-have to go, Mom." March said, twining our fingers together.

"Oh, okay, it was nice of you to visit. I don't often get visitors, not since Martin was executed." Tears welled in her eyes, and my magick reacted to my anger, tiny sparks lit across my hand that was in March's. "I just know he was innocent, that stupid whore probably robbed him."

March's eyes grew wide, and his grip tightened. "Bye." he said, yanking me out of the room.

I was confused, I had assumed that Martin had been executed for his crimes against March. I didn't have time to think more about it as I looked at March. I could see the panic in his eyes, so I pushed him down on a bench once we had cleared the reception desk. "Look at me." I demanded.

His eyes met mine, "Breath with me." I took several calming deep breaths; I kept my hand wrapped around his wrist so I could feel his heartbeat. March's eyes slipped closed, as he followed my instructions my heart ached for him. No one should live with the kind of pain he did, but there was nothing I could do about his past. After a few moments his heartbeat slowed, and he opened his eyes.

"We aren't coming back here." I said, sternly. I watched as his eyes widened at my command.

"But- "He started.

My body tensed, and a slight buzz began against my skin. I locked eyes with March, the determination in his eyes surprised me after the panic attack I had just witnessed. I took a deep breath, stealing myself against the feeling of magick.

"No. I came here completely open minded, willing to believe that Hatter and Cheshire were wrong. However, I sat in that room with you, as she manipulated and berated you under the guise of a loving mother. I will not let you put yourself through that abuse." I said, firmly.

"She's my mother." He whimpered, and I saw the tears begin to fill his eyes. I felt my resolve breaking. I had the realization that he was, whether intentionally or not, manipulating me. As the buzz became more intense, I wondered if March knew what he was capable of. I had never heard of a magick that was emotionally driven, but nothing could surprise me anymore.

"So? Just because someone gives birth to you, doesn't mean they deserve your love and respect." I said, and decided he needed to hear one more hard truth, "She doesn't think what he did to you is wrong. She doesn't hold any guilt for what you were put through. I'm sorry, March, but she doesn't love you the way she should."

March stared at me with wide eyes for a moment, before breaking down. I held him as he cried uncontrollably. All the while whispering how much

Hatter, Cheshire, Caterpillar, and I loved and respected him. Eventually he stopped crying, and he returned to his calmer self.

"Th-Thank you for your honesty about my mother," he said, but I could tell he was embarrassed. I just didn't know why. "Hatter wouldn't have said that to me." he added, continuing to look away from me. "He always dances around the harder topics. Until last night at least." He admitted.

"Guess I'm here to tell you no." I joked, and then added, "I... I think the reason he gives you what he wants is because of your magick."

"I don't have m-magick." March said, looking confused.

"I think you do," I explained, "but it isn't like mine. I think yours is always on. It is your only defense when you feel attacked. It's protecting you."

"Wh-Why do you think that?" He asked.

"Because after your panic attack was over, and I was telling you no. I felt the buzz that happens against my skin when I need to defend myself. My resolve weakened..." I glanced around us, "it's the only thing that makes sense." I said, pulling him up from the bench.

"I'm s-sorry." he said, blushing.

"It's okay, magick is instinctual, and with all that you've gone through I'm not surprised it wants to protect you. If my mom was still around, she could help you recognize when you're using it." I said, walking toward the bike.

He stopped, obviously thinking through something, "Why can Hatter say no to me at all then?" He asked.

I thought for a moment, "I think if his instincts lead him to believe that giving you what you want will hurt you, then he's able to tell you no. I'm just spit balling all of this. I don't know for sure." I replied.

"Is it b-bad?" He asked, looking a bit panicked again.

"No, of course not. Magick can be manipulative, but that doesn't make it bad, at least not if you use it correctly. You're not a bad person, and more than likely your magick has protected you from more than you know." I explain, straddling the bike.

March got on behind me, and changed the subject, "I'm hungry."

"Let's go to the little bistro over on seventh." I said.

"Wait.... Alice..." I could tell March was struggling to say something, so I turned the bike back off and asked. "What's going on?"

"Alice... I love you." He said, leaning in close to my ear.

My breath caught in my throat; a tear ran down my cheek. I felt those words in my chest, and without hesitation, "I love you too, March."

"I know it's p-probably too soon to be saying that, but it's how I feel. In the short time I've known you I've felt more at home and safe than I ever did before." He said, resting his chin on my shoulder, "I love Hatter too, but I doubt I'll ever convince him to change."

"Oh, March..." I trailed off, unable to find the words.

"It's okay, I know how you feel." I turned the bike back on, still at a loss for words, "Let's go to that bistro now."

"Sounds delicious." I murmured back.

"Oh my god, this baked mac and cheese is the best." I moaned, shoveling another fork full into my mouth. "Heaven."

"I love the f-food here, but we don't actually come to this part of the city, unless we're staying at Hatter's apartment." March said.

Remembering Claudia's nickname for March I put my fork down, and said, "What's Maxie short for?"

March turned pink, but replied, "Maxton."

"That's cute." I said, smiling.

"Th-Thanks." He said, still blushing.

Getting to sit and eat a quiet meal with March was a dream come true after the last couple of days. Our meal was delicious, and having a moment of true peace was a special thing. I felt extremely guilty for a moment before realizing I was doing what I could today. It's not like I wanted to sit on my ass while they were murdered, but a girl needed a break on occasion.

"We better get b-back. They'll be worried." March said, adding a couple dollars to the tip jar as we walked out the door.

I nodded, savoring one last moment, before taking his proffered hand. We made it out of the restaurant, and were walking to the bike, when I heard a feminine scream. I turned without thinking and headed toward the source of the noise. I could hear March close on my heels as I ran into an alley behind the bistro. I saw the small, brown-haired girl first. Her shirt ripped open, revealing her naked chest, cowering against a wall. My eyes then zeroed in on the man who was towering over her. His blond hair was perfectly coiffed, as he fondled under the girl's skirt. "Hey jackass, why don't you pick on someone your own size?" I shouted, letting my magick out to play. The girl's wide green eyes turned to me first, tears ran down her face, but there was a look there I recognized, determination and a touch of hatred. She would do anything to get away from him and I respected her instantly.

"I'm not a fan of blondes, but you'll do too." He said, leering at me.

March scoffed in disgust, "In your dreams."

"Go." I told the girl, pulling my leather jacket off, and handing it to her, leaving me in a thin white tank top.

"Thanks." She whispered, running away.

"You're about to wish you hadn't done that." The man said. As he turned fully toward me, I noticed the pin on his chest.

Fuck, okay I could still deal with this. "Knave, I'm not even surprised." I said, trying to keep my cool.

"You have me at a disadvantage," He grinned down at me, "I don't know you."

"Alice." I offered. I realized his lie when my name hung in the air between us. The Red Party knew exactly who I was, I had made a big mistake stepping in, but it was the right thing to do. I had confidence I still had the advantage. We circled each other, almost dancing as I tried to read what he was thinking.

"Hm, interesting." He smirked. He suddenly lunged at me, and I sent shock waves into him, but not before he slammed my head into the brick wall behind me. He grunted, gripping his head, just as I held my own. "You're under arrest. If you back down now, you may be given a lighter sentence." He said, coming toward me.

"How bout, no?" I asked, grinning. The Knave couldn't really believe I was that stupid, if he took me away from here it was a death sentence. I'd be swinging right next to Lily and Dina. As the thought entered my mind, I knew what I had to do. I turned hoping I could clue March in. As Knave came closer, I noticed a man creeping up on March, "Watch out," I yelled.

Knave grabbed my hair as I tried to dodge around him to reach March. I watched in horror as the suit knocked March out. Panic filled me as he crumped to the ground, I had to get to him, no one knew we would be here.

"I think the Queen will be very interested in this one." The Knave said, clapping cuffs around my wrists. I tried to cast an illusion but found myself totally drained of magick. The shock I gave the Knave shouldn't have depleted my energy that quickly. The Red Party must have more tricks up their sleeves than I realized.

"What about him?" The other Suit asked, motioning toward March.

"Leave him," Knave said, dragging me away. "He's useless anyway."

I started shouting, praying that somebody would notice, and call for help. I'd failed, even if I made it to Lily and Dina there was no way I could

escape without my magick. A sharp pain shot through my head before I
blacked out.

*Mom and I were walking down main street, carrying several shopping bags.
I talked excitedly about something going on at school. She suddenly stopped,
handing me the bags she was holding, and quickly said "Stay here, Ali. I'll
be right back."*

*I watched as she ran into the road, dodging through traffic and around
other pedestrians. Several Suits were milling around, but no one seemed to
notice as my mother grabbed a small boy out of the road. She grabbed him
moments before a car would have hit him. I saw her hand him to a crying
woman. I could tell that there were words exchanged, but couldn't hear them
over the loudness of the city.*

*I smiled at her as she turned around to walk back toward me. Only to
watch in horror as a van pulled up into the sidewalk, nearly mowing a group
of teenagers down, and hit her. I screamed trying to rush toward her, but
strong arms grabbed me, and pulled me away.*

*"No, no, that's my momma, let me go to her. I gotta make sure she's okay."
I said, fighting the man who gripped me.*

*"She's dead, kid. Don't look." He whispered, turning me into his chest. I
stared up at the statue of Wonderland's founder as the man carried me away.
The stone woman was holding a large sword pointed toward the sky, almost
as if she could take on the world by herself.*

Chapter 15

March

I awoke to a throbbing in my head and the smell of rotting food permeating the air around me. I opened my eyes, gripping my head when the world spun around me. Images flashed through my mind. Being at the hospital to see my mother, my panic attack, Alice telling me I have magick, the bistro, the young woman yelling, the Knave. I groaned as my head pounded harder, stopping me from standing. I could tell I likely had a concussion, but I didn't have time to worry about that. I glanced around when my vision stopped spinning. I was lying near a large green dumpster in the same alley Alice had run into to save the girl from the Knave. As I continued looking around, I felt panic bubble in my chest; Alice was nowhere to be seen. I took a deep breath, counting to ten trying to calm down.

"Are you okay, Mister?" A small voice asked me, drawing my attention to the opening of the alley. A small blonde girl stood before me, wearing a pink dress, her hair in pigtails. She couldn't have been older than six, the baby fat still hadn't left her rosy cheeks.

"I...I," I swallowed hard struggling to get my words out, "I'm f-f-fine...Did you see a girl leave this area?" I could remember the moments before I heard Alice scream my name, I guess I had been knocked out. I didn't believe for a moment she would leave me here if she had had a choice. The horror set in when I realized she must have been taken by the Red Party.

"No." The little girl rocked back and forth on her toes, "Are you one of them drunks my daddy is always complaining about?" she asked, watching me carefully. I shook my head unable to respond to her. I didn't want to have a panic attack in front of the little girl, so I stayed quiet. I stood from the ground, brushing myself off. "Are you sure? Normal people don't lay in trash." She pointed out, her bright green eyes never leaving me. "I think something must be wrong with you."

"You're not wrong... I-I-I have l-lost my friend. Do you know what time it is?" I asked.

The little girl opened her mouth, but was interrupted by a masculine voice. "Slyvie, Slyvie, where have you gone little pixie?"

"Over here, daddy! Did you find Bruno yet?" The little girl turned away from me, the man she was talking to coming into view. He was taller than me, muscular, but his eyes were soft toward the little girl in front of him.

"Slyvie, I thought we talked about not playing hide and seek in the city. It's far too danger—" The man's sentence was cut off as his eyes shifted to me. "Slyvie you shouldn't be talking to strangers."

"Daddy, this is.... Uh I guess I never asked his name. He said he's not one of those drunks you're always complaining about, he seems nice." She rambled on a bit as her father picked her up off the ground, eyes never leaving me.

"What's your name, son?" He asked.

"M-Maxton, sir." I responded, shifting back and forth on my feet. I didn't often interact with normal civilians so I hoped giving my real name would be for the best.

"I'm Arthur. Is there anything I can do to help you? I know my daughter can be a little much." he said, offering his hand for me to shake. I took it, trying to find words to explain my position to him, but coming up empty for far too long. The man coughed and said, "I should probably try to find my son as well, he's a master at hiding in plain sight."

"I have a friend who can do the same thing," I chuckled thinking of Cheshire. "Do you... sorry... Do you happen to know how to start and ride a motorcycle?" I hated talking to new people, hating constantly stuttering over my words in new situations.

"I do actually," The man gave me a warm smile, and moved out of my way so I could lead him to the bike.

"You'll upshift with the pedal, while also maneuvering the clutch into the correct gear. You really should have more protective gear if you are going to be riding. Hopefully, you aren't going too far," He explained as I stood with the keys in my hand, staring at him like an idiot. I shook my head, opening the seat and pulling out my helmet and jacket.

"Not too far. Th-Thank you for all your help." I said.

"I don't want to ask too many questions, and I really should be going, but... Look out for yourself. This city is dangerous for anyone who doesn't conform." Arthur said, patting my shoulder.

"My friends and I are trying to fix that for everyone." I murmured as he walked away from me. I watched him walk off; his daughter's hand held tight in his as he began calling for his missing son.

I dreaded going home without Alice. Tears sprung to my eyes as I swung my leg over the bike and shoved the key in the ignition. How was I going to explain to Hatter that in the midst of doing something he told me not to I had been knocked unconscious and left Alice to fend for herself against the Knave? That's all, the Red Party really were the villains in our story. I had never met a single Suit or member of the Red Party that was worth redeeming. They were the wealthy elite, they didn't care what happened to the lowly citizens of Wonderland. Only what would gain them more money and power. Hatter, Cheshire, and Caterpillar would never forgive me for letting anything happen to our girl. If Hatter didn't kill me, Caterpillar probably would. I'd heard their interaction in his office the day before, I'd never heard him express so much emotion. I reversed away from the parking lot, still lost in thought and fighting tears. Thoughts of magick stood out the most, why couldn't I tell I had magick? How could I control it if I couldn't even feel it? What would Hatter say when he found out I had manipulated him for years? The bike swerved underneath me. I gripped the handles trying to correct my course away from the stone barricade in the middle of the road. The bike tilted underneath me, causing me to lose control and skid across the pavement. A car swerved around as I finally came to a stop. My body hurt as I tried to stand, I felt something rush out of my nose underneath the helmet. I chose to ignore it, picking the bike off the road and checking it over. I climbed back on, starting the ignition again, ignoring all the zaps of pain shooting through my body. I had to get home, we needed to save Alice before they killed her. I could not live with myself if anything happened to her because I was so weak. In the few weeks since I had met Alice, she had changed everything. Alice Young was a force to be reckoned with and I was already in love with her.

Chapter 16

Hatter

I glanced at my watch again, the time read 4:03pm, less than five minutes since the last time I checked. Alice and March had been gone for well over six hours, and I was worried something horrible had happened. I was laying in the middle of my bed, listening to Cheshire drone on about some hacking he was having trouble with. I fixed him with a glare hoping that he would shut up. "They'll be back soon enough. I'm sure March just needed some time to calm down." Cheshire said, his feet propped up on my desk.

"Neither of them are answering their phones. Doesn't that bother you?" I asked, standing up to begin pacing again, "You said visiting hours ended at two. What could possibly take them two additional hours to do?

"I'm sure they're fine, getting into some mischief in the city to blow off stream." Cheshire said, dismissing me.

I heard the rumble of the motorcycle coming up the road. I sprinted down the stairs, bowling over Caterpillar as he opened the door to his office. I heard his grunt of dismay, but didn't care, I had to know what happened with March and his mother. I had barely made it out of the warehouse when March came stumbling toward me, blood running from his nose. I reached for him, barely catching him before he fell. "What the hell happened?" I demanded, steadying him.

"A-A-Alice, fight, Red P-Party, Kn-Knave." He said between hard breaths, "I'm sorry, Hatter, I swear I tried to help."

March continued to pant, eyes looking panicked. My heart squeezed at the blood droplets that were landing on the ground around him. I knew he needed medical attention immediately, but I wasn't sure what to do. "Alice had a fight with the Knave?" I asked, "Is she okay?" I added, fearing his answer.

"They a-a-a-arrested her." March said.

"Fuck." I said, running into the warehouse after handing March off to Cheshire. March's injuries became secondary to getting Alice out of the hands of the Red Party as I rushed toward Caterpillar office. I wondered for a moment why he hadn't come outside, but I didn't have time to think about it as I slammed his office door open.

"Caterpillar! Alice has been arrested by the Knave of Hearts." I panted.

"What?" he asked, jumping up.

"We have to get her, they'll execute her." Cheshire said, startling me.

"Woah wait a minute. We can't just storm into the Red Party's base; you'll get us all killed." Caterpillar said, causing the room to go silent. "We aren't ready yet. We need at least two more days to arrange an extraction."

"What would you have us do then? Pick our suits to attend her execution?" I said, anger and panic warring inside me.

"We don't know that they will execute her at all." he said, glancing down at the paper strewn across his desk.

I could tell that he didn't believe what he was saying but chose not to mention it. I would get Alice away from the Red Party whether Caterpillar liked it or not.

"We can't leave her in a prison cell." Cheshire demanded.

"We don't have a choice right now." Caterpillar replied, slamming his hands on the desk, "I forbid you three from going after her. Am I clear?" He asked.

"Crystal." I gritted out. I turned to find March standing in the doorway, nose still dripping blood. I was suddenly pissed off at him, "If you hadn't demanded to go see your damn abusive mother, she would be safe." I chastised him, unable to keep my cool. His mouth dropped open, but he quickly closed it to avoid getting blood in his mouth. "Come with me." I snarled, grabbing his wrist on my way out the door.

I dragged him up the stairs, through my bedroom, and into the bathroom. I bent down to retrieve the first aid kit from under the sink, pausing to take a deep breath. He kept silent, probably aware of just how mad I was. "Wash your face." I ordered, smacking the kit down on the counter. March did as he was told, but I couldn't seem to calm the agitation I was feeling. I needed to go out and find Alice, but all I could do was stand there and patch March up; frustration boiled inside of me. Alice was the queen of taking unnecessary risks. I didn't know if I could let it go that March had allowed her to take one this extreme.

When he finished, I immediately grabbed some tissue to stop the blood. "Lean you head forward." I instructed, before adding, "I'll be right back, don't move." I walked into his room, and grabbed him a green hoodie and sweatpants, before going out to the linen closet for a towel. I stomped back into the bathroom, sat the things I was carrying on the counter, and pulled the tissue away from his face. "It's not broken..." I said, surprised, "What happened?"

"I w-wrecked Caterpillar's bike." He explained.

I rubbed my temples trying not to snap at him, "You shouldn't have been riding it in the first place. Why didn't you call me?"

"I couldn't find my phone after the Suits knocked me out." He murmured, before adding, "I think I need st-st-stiches." he said, quietly.

"You should have told me sooner." I growled, before adding, "Where?"

He turned, and pulled the hood off his head, revealing a nasty gash at the back of his head. My stomach turned at the sight. I'd always been a bit squeamish. It's why I avoided anything to do with the injuries that occasionally happened here, but I had no choice. I sighed, and grabbed some antiseptic, bandages, and needle and thread. "This is going to hurt." I said as I poured antiseptic on his head. He didn't respond, but I saw him fidgeting with the strings of his blood-soaked hoodie. I led him into my bedroom and sat on my bed. "Sit on the floor." I commanded. Once again, he did as he was told, without comment, and I worried that my anger may have scared him. I quickly shook the thoughts from my head, knowing I had every right to be upset with him. "How did your visit go?" I asked, trying to distract him from the pain I could tell he was feeling.

He let out a hiss, but didn't move, before responding. "Ali t-told me I couldn't go back."

I raised my eyebrows in surprise, "Are you going to listen to her?" March shrugged.

I slowly began stitching his wound. When he didn't respond I knew I had my answer. If Alice could convince him to stay away from that monster of a woman. I would get her home and make sure she glowed as bright as she ever had.

"What did Claudia do that pissed Alice off, Maxton?" I asked.

He turned toward me, his eyes widened, "I-I..." He stopped talking, and just looked up at me.

I didn't often use his real name, and especially not in anger. I rolled my eyes, and said, "Turn back around, I'm not finished."

"Mom told Alice my st-stutter was shameful, and that she was glad that I wasn't d-dating you." March eventually admitted.

I started laughing my ass off, before saying. "And Alice didn't slam your mother's head into a brick wall," I asked in amazement, "She has more self-control than I thought."

"I'm done," I finished the final stitch and placed a big of gauze and tape over the wound to keep it clean.

"She...uh...a-also told me I have magick." He said, standing up.

I sat quietly for several minutes, waiting for him to continue, but he just stared at me. "What can you do?" I asked.

"Well...its... Promise you won't get mad?" He asked, and I nodded, worried about what he was going to tell me. "She said I have magick that m-manipulates those around me into protecting me." He said it so fast I barely understood.

My mouth dropped open, as my mind raced through all the times. I had protected him, deciding whether I had done it out of my own will or if I was being manipulated. "Okay... do you use it on me?" I asked, watching him carefully.

I had always known March so well; he was an easy read for me. When he flinched at my question, I knew the answer. Intentionally or not, he had been manipulating me with magick, possibly our entire lives. I stood, needing space.

"Wait, Hatter. I sw-swear I've never done it on purpose. I wouldn't do that to you!" March shouted after me, I turned to find that he was crying. My anger and frustration warred with my love for Maxton. A few seconds passed as I tried to process my emotions. I took a series of deep breaths.

"Go take a shower. I left your clothes on the counter. We can talk when you're done." I said, patting him on the back. He tried to wrap his arms around me, but I stepped away from him before he could. I saw the devastation on his face but ignored the way it made my heart hurt.

"Okay." He whimpered, leaving the room.

Thirty minutes later I knocked on the door, worried that March hadn't exited the shower. When he didn't respond I opened the door. "Are you okay?" I asked, opening the glass sliding door.

March was sitting in the bottom of the shower, eyes red, and blood coating his fingers. It took me several moments to realize that his nose was pouring blood again, "I don't feel g-good." he said, looking up at me with unfocused eyes.

"Fuck." I muttered, grabbing the towel, and wrapping it around him. He was shivering and swaying so much that I decided to carry him into my room. Even though he was only a couple of inches shorter than me he was much lighter. He had always been lean to the point of fragility, but he could hold his own when it was necessary. I sat him gently on my bed, and then went back to the bathroom to get his clothes. I returned to find him curled up, starting to fall asleep. "Nope, get up. You might have a concussion. You're going to have to stay awake." I said, pushing his shoulder.

"Don't wanna." March said sleepily, ignoring me.

"I don't care, sit up." I said, pulling him up. "Arms up." I commanded, pulling the hoodie over his head. "Put your pants on, while I go get you something to drink." I added, handing them to him.

I tossed the sweatpants on the bed beside him and went to the kitchen to grab two bottles of water. "We need to talk." Cheshire said, causing me to jump.

"Please announce yourself." I chided, embarrassed that he'd been able sneak up on me.

"Whatever. We have to get Alice out of there." He replied, slapping his phone against the palm of his hand.

"Caterpillar said not to." I pointed out. I didn't actually give a fuck what Caterpillar had to say. If he actually loved her, he wouldn't have forbidden us from going after her.

"When do you ever pay attention to him? Are you going to leave our girlfriend to fend for herself against the Red Party?" he asked, angrily.

"Come upstairs, after he's gone to bed, and tell me your plan. I've got to go back and take care of March." I demanded, leaving without his reply.

March had curled up under my covers by the time I got back to the room.

"Get up. I told you that you can't sleep right now." I said, trying to pull him up.

"I don't have a concussion." He muttered into the pillow. The uncertainty in his voice didn't ease my nerves, but I didn't feel like continuing a losing fight.

"Then move over." I said, rolling my eyes. Instead of moving, he sat up, stood, and started walking toward the door. "Where are you going?"

"To my own b-bed." He replied, shortly.

"Why the hell do you sound pissed off?" I asked, crossing my arms over my chest.

"Because for the l-last several days I've dealt with your bad attitude. As if everything that is happening around you is my fault," He ranted, "I'm t-tired of it. Alice wanted to know what my nightmare was about. So, I told her, I can't tell you anything because you freak out at every mention of my past. All because of some bullshit your father said to you years ago. I wasn't the one who acted like a jackass at the Gr-Grove, and upset Alice enough for her to run off, and yet you still blamed me." He said, fists clenched at his sides. "Honestly, Hayden, do you really think it doesn't bother me that my own mother doesn't give a fuck about me? You think I don't know I f-fuck everything up? Go to hell, Hayden!" he yelled, swiping his sleeve across his face.

"Max, I..." I began.

"No, I don't even want to h-hear it." He said, stomping out of the room.

I stared after him for several minutes before a smile broke out across my face. I went slamming into his room, and pulled him into a hug, before he could say anything. Years of walking on eggshells around March lifted off my shoulders. I'd been waiting for the day he would finally be completely honest with me.

"Never thought I'd see the day you stood up for yourself." I whispered.

He heaved a quiet sigh and sunk into me. "Sorry." He replied.

"Don't be. You're right after all. I shouldn't be such a dick when someone hurts my feelings, especially if it's you or Alice." I admitted. March twined his fingers with mine in a silent acceptance of my long overdue apology. I squeezed his hand and started back toward my room. "Come on, after Caterpillar goes to sleep Ches is going to come plan how we're breaking Ali out of the Red Party's base." I explained.

I studied March's profile as we walked back to my room, he'd always been pretty. I knew he'd probably be offended if I said that. He had a perfect smattering of freckles across his nose and cheeks. In the right light his brown eyes turned golden. Love and dread filled me, if we couldn't save Alice, he would be devastated. I'd never be able to help him control whatever magick Alice had noticed.

"Can I ask you a qu-question?" March asked, once we had settled into my bed.

"Sure," I said, running finger through his hair, careful to avoid the cut.

"Since Ali is okay with it, are we gonna...do st-stuff?" he asked, turning red.

"We do stuff all the time. Can you be more specific?" I teased.

"Don't b-be an asshole," he said, rolling his eyes.

I turned serious. "I don't know, there's a lot of feelings for us both to work through before we broach... that but now doesn't seem like the time." I replied.

"True," he agreed, looking up at me. "Everything is gonna be okay, right?"

"I don't know if it will or not." I admitted rubbing a hand over my face.

"Wake up, Maddie. Al doesn't have time for you to be sleeping." I heard, through the fog of my dreams. I sat up, and rubbed my eyes, only to find Cheshire standing next to my bed with his arms crossed. "Bout time you woke up. We have to come up with a plan." he said, taking a seat at my desk.

I glanced at March, who was still sleeping peacefully, and found that the last remaining dregs of my earlier anger had dissipated. I considered waking March up considering I was pretty sure he had a concussion, but I decided against it. We could clue him into the plan once we'd figured out what the hell we were doing. "Do we know where she's being held?" I asked, trying to get my mind to focus on Alice.

"Yes." Ches replied.

"Can we get in?" I asked, again.

"Probably." He replied, glancing down at some papers he was holding.

"How soon?" I was anxious to get her out of the hands of the Red Party. His phone buzzed, and he grabbed it. A moment passed, and I watched as his face paled.

"What's wrong?" I asked, bouncing my legs.

"The King of Hearts has announced an execution, in less than twenty-four hours." He replied.

"It might not be her." I said, hopefully.

"Are you willing to take that chance?" Cheshire asked.

"No." I trailed off for a moment thinking through our options. "We have to get her out."

"No shit, Sherlock. Get some more sleep, we leave in five hours." He said, before leaving my room.

I sat and stared down at March for a moment. I wondered how different our lives would be if his stepfather had never come into his life. It shouldn't matter, but the man lying next to me had been my first love, and now we had to save the girl we'd both fallen for.

Chapter 17

Alice

August 8th, 2157

I woke up gasping for air, drenched in freezing water. It took me a moment to get my bearings. I was laying on a lumpy mattress, in a dark room. As I looked at my surroundings my fingers grazed the stone floor beneath the mattress. Three of the four walls were rough cinder blocks, the fourth wall was filled with iron bars. I glanced toward the bars and found a Suit standing there watching me carefully. The bucket held in his hands explained my drenched clothes. He said nothing at first, so I continued to gather my thoughts. The cell had no lights aside from the glow of the corridor which outlined the Suit standing there silently. I quirked an eyebrow at him in confusion. "The Queen is coming." He informed me, before disappearing.

I don't know how much time passed before I heard the shouts of other prisoners. I strained my ears, praying that I would hear Lily or Dina. The only sound I heard was the deafening clicking of heels against the stone floors. A light buzzing started beneath my skin, softer than it should have been, but I was glad to feel my magick at all. A woman in a pale grey dress stopped in front of my cell. Her black hair was pulled into a severe bun. Her features were familiar in an uncomfortable way, all except her reddish colored eyes. The only eyes I'd ever seen with such an odd color was my mother's golden eyes. The sneer on her face as she stared me down, clearly assessing me, was nothing short of hatred. "Alice Young, do you know who I am?" she asked, her voice echoing against the stone walls.

"The Red Queen." I breathed out.

"Ah, very good. This makes our conversation so much easier." She paused for a moment, and turned to a Suit before commanding, "Bring them here." I furrowed my brow, but didn't move a muscle, trying to keep my wits about me. Several moments passed, before the Suits came dragging two women with them. I immediately recognized Lily, and panic seized my heart. I stood, tripping over my feet to get to her. She was covered in dirt, most of her exposed skin was covered in bruises, she'd clearly been tortured.

"Move back." The guard commanded, before opening the cell. He pushed the two women into the cell with me, and I rushed to Lily.

"Are you okay?" I asked, helping her to her feet.

"Alice, what are you doing here?" she asked, eyes skimming across me.

"It's not important." I said, my eyes moving to the Red Queen who had stepped in the cell with us.

"Leave us." She commanded her guards. They immediately did as she asked, and I found myself stepping in front of my sister.

"Oh, Cindy. I know you wanted to believe little Alice here could stop me. You worked so hard to hide her." The Red Queen said, directing her statement to the other woman in the room.

My eyes floated toward her, and I found myself rooted to the spot. Even with her golden hair turning white, and her face dirty I knew the woman standing before me. "Momma?" I asked, taking a step toward her. I shook my head, turning angry eyes to The Red Queen. "What have you done? What is going on?" I asked, venom dripping from my words. When I glanced back, my mother was still standing there.

The evil woman before me trilled a laugh as I began screaming, "Alcinda Young, White Queen, Alcinda, Mom." I gripped my hair in frustration as the illusion refused to disappear.

"Alice, it's really her." Lily whispered.

My mouth dropped open, and I was breathing heavily. "How?" I asked, staring at her.

"Well, I couldn't very well kill my own sister, especially not when her brats were still running around my city." The Red Queen replied.

"Sister?" I asked, finally moving my body.

"Of course. Can't you see the family resemblance." she asked, grabbing my mother and putting their faces next to each other. All I could see at first was the way her long, red nails dug into my mother's sunken cheeks. As I inspected them more closely, I was struck by how similar they looked. Aside from their different coloring they could have been twins. I was dumbfounded by the idea that the horrible creature standing in front of me could be related to me. "We aren't full blooded siblings of course; our whore mother couldn't resist sleeping with a man of power." She ranted, pushing my mom away from her.

"Your father beat her, Penny, what did you expect her to do?" My mother asked.

"Don't talk to me like that." The Red Queen snarled, slapping my mom.

"Don't you dare do that again." I said, jumping between them.

My aunt began to laugh, before she said, "So much like my sentimental sister, willing to save anyone in need. I'll enjoy making her watch as I have you executed." she said, getting right in my face. "Ta-ta. Enjoy your final hours together." She added, before exiting.

I followed behind her and slammed my hands against the bars in anger. I knew it was unlikely I would be able to escape with my lack of magick. I couldn't figure out why she'd leave the three of us together, unless she was just that confident that she was in control. My stomach felt sick as I turned back toward what was left of my family.

"How did you end up here?" Lily asked, coming to stand beside me.

"When I found out you and Dina had been taken, I ended up with some of the Resistance. We've been working on a plan to break you out." I explained, taking a seat on the cold floor, shivering as the water soaked through my clothes.

"Who?" My mother asked, easing herself onto the ground across from me. Her bright nearly golden eyes bore into me, almost as if I would disappear if she blinked. The time locked away hadn't treated her well. Her hair was streaked with white now, crows' feet and laugh lines were beginning to make themselves known on her beautiful face. She had lost a lot of weight, looking nearly emaciated. Her skin was ashen, deep scars littered her arms, she'd been tortured for over a decade. Why had the Red Queen kept her alive?

"Caterpillar, Cheshire Cat, Mad Hatter, and March Hare." I replied, snapping out of my thoughts.

She looked confused for a moment, "The original Caterpillar died... no, it can't be." She said, mostly to herself. "Is White Rabbit still around?" She asked.

"Yeah, I've met Rab a time or two. Caterpillar is his nephew." I explained. "I remember him..." I trailed off trying not to think about the guys too much.

"Oh, he was always a good boy. How is Rab doing? I assume he's leading." She said.

I shook my head, "I think technically Caterpillar is the leader."

No one said anything for several minutes. As we sat in silence, I could hear water dripping in the distance, and groans from the other prisoners. Lily had taken a seat next to me and was leaning her head on my shoulder. "We have to find a way out of here." I declared, standing up.

"Alice..." Lily trailed off.

"I tried to escape the first couple of years, without magick we'll never make it past the Suits." Mom said, staring at me with pity. "Penny has learned how to dampen magick with something she found within the vaults of my father's home."

"So, we should sit here and accept our fates? I don't think so." I said, pacing.

"I didn't say that." Mom snapped.

I considered what she had revealed, and questions swirled through my head. My mother had hidden so many things from me, soon I'd get my answers. I took a moment to study her. My mother was never a meek woman. She stood tall no matter what the situation. The pale creature sitting before me barely resembled the woman who had raised me. I couldn't imagine what she had gone through to make her so dejected. "I'm dating four men." I blurted out, discomfort making me honest. I had to change the topic while I formulated a plan. My mother and Lily clearly weren't able to help me think. I couldn't blame them; I don't know if I'd be capable of even sitting up after the prolonged torture they'd been through. Lily and Mom stared at me for several seconds in shocked silence, before Lily burst out laughing.

"You...you... I've been in prison for nearly three weeks. In that time, you've started dating four men, joined the Resistance, and been arrested." Lily said, struggling to breathe through her laughter.

"I've been busy." I said, rubbing the back of my neck.

"Understatement of the year, Al." She replied.

I glanced at my mother, awaiting her response. "As long as you're happy." she said, a small smile alighting her face.

I grinned and pulled them both into a hug. Something about their easy acceptance wiped away the darkness of our situation for a moment.

"Tell us about them." Lily said, excitedly. We sat in a small circle, and I began to relive the last few weeks.

We had talked for what felt like hours. Lily and Mom carefully skirted around what had happened to them during their time with the Red Queen. I couldn't decide if I was thankful for their protection or offended by it. It was silent in the dungeon aside from our hushed voice that still somehow echoed through the halls. The other prisoners gave no sign they were even alive, it was entirely unnatural. "So, then I punched him," I explained, giggling quietly.

Lily laughed quietly, leaning her head against the stone wall. "I can't believe you punched him."

"It was great." A familiar voice said, causing me to twirl around.

"Cheshire!" I whisper-yelled, running to the bars. "What are you doing here?" I asked, gripping his hands, nervously.

March's face appeared through the bars as well, stopping my heart. They had come for me; it couldn't have been an entire day since March, and I had encountered the Knave. I tried to imagine how they had been able to formulate a plan to get in so quickly, but Caterpillar and Cheshire had been working on it anyway. I shook my head, the how didn't matter right now, I could get my family out of here. "We c-came to get you." March chimed in, jamming a key into the lock on our cell.

"Are these two of your boyfriends?" Lily asked, hands in her pockets.

"Cheshire, March, meet my sister, Lily Young, and my newly not dead mother, Alcinda Young, also known as the White Queen." I introduced them as I helped my mother up.

"It's nice to meet you boys." Mom said, although she was inspecting Ches carefully. "You look an awful lot like Ruth Malone's boy." she finally said, as we exited the cell.

"Ruth was my mom." He replied, a slight blush across his cheeks.

"I'm so sorry about your parents. I always wondered what happened to you." She said, laying a hand on his shoulder.

"Thank you, but we can catch up after we get away from the Red Party. I really don't want to be on the other side of these bars." Cheshire said, looking uncomfortable.

"Of course, dear." Mom said, quietly.

"Where are Hatter and Caterpillar?" I asked, glancing around us.

"Caterpillar technically forbade us from coming to save you." I nodded, knowing he was right to try and protect them. I thought back to his promise to shoot me if I ever put them in danger and wondered if it was still in place. "Hatter was being accosted by Duchess last I checked." Ches added.

"I hate that bitch." I growled, then paused adding, "Dina, we can't leave her here." Finding out my mother was alive nearly made me forget about my best friend.

"I haven't seen her since they threw me in a cell." Lily said.

"We have to find her." I demanded, I started walking down the line of cells, glancing inside each one. Some were empty, while others held downtrodden people who barely spared us a look. "We can't just leave all these people here." I said, glancing at a young woman who cowered in the back of her cell, staring at us through her tangled, black locks.

"I think I can help with that, if you can give me a little boost?" Lily said, reaching for my hand.

"You know I haven't..." I trailed off, glancing at Cheshire and March, not wanting to reveal this facet of myself to them just yet. "I don't have nearly enough anyway." I waved her off.

"I know how to pick locks." Cheshire spoke up, sliding a small leather case out of his pockets. I stepped out of his way, fascinated as he used two small tools and worked the lock open with no problem. The girl bolted for the unguarded exit with a surprising amount of energy, considering how she looked. Cheshire had already made his way toward several other cells, unlocking them with speed and accuracy. People in varying degrees of exhaustion and fear flooded the small hallway, rushing toward the exit without hesitation. I could hear sounds of commotion, and knew we needed to move quickly. "This is the last one," Cheshire said, turning toward me as he pockets his tools again.

A man exited the cell, carrying a small boy, "Protect my son." He begged, shoving the child into my arms.

I furrowed my brows in confusion "How did you end up in here?" I asked.

"The Suits arrested my wife for prostitution, but then threw me and my son in here." He explained, tears forming in his eyes.

"You're free to go, take your son and run." I said, trying to hand him the boy back.

"No, no, they won't miss him, but if I go missing, they'll look for me. Take him." he said, pushing the child in my arms. He reentered his cell, taking a seat.

"Sir, I- "I began.

"I'm begging you." He said.

I considered continuing to argue. We had no way to care for a child properly, but as I took the man's determined face in, I knew there was no arguing with him. Leaving a child in this dungeon wasn't an option, so I conceded. "What's his name?" I asked, looking down at the small boy.

"Lewis, Lewis Liddell." He said, tears forming in his eyes, as he glanced lovingly at his son. "Thank you."

"I will do everything in my power to protect him." I vowed, handing the child to my sister, as March placed a gun in my hand.

"Bless you." The man said, waving us away. I hesitated at the stairs, looking back at the man. His honey brown eyes stared after us. Even from a slight distance I could see the tears that had left a trail down his dirty face.

This was exactly why the Red Party had to end, no loving parent should be separated from their child.

"Alice, Dina wasn't down here." Lily pointed out, seeming unperturbed by the strange interaction we had just had.

"Let's find Hatter." I said, taking the stairs two at a time. "Actually, March take Lily, Mom, and Lewis out of here. Cheshire and I can retrieve Hatter and Dina." I added, kissing him on the cheek. I watched as they went in the opposite direction, I couldn't stop the worry that filled my chest. There was a chance they wouldn't be able to get out. My hope was that they would get lost in the commotion of the other prisoners.

"What are we going to do with a child, Al?" Cheshire asked, distracting me.

"I don't know, but I wasn't leaving that little boy down in that dungeon." I said, creeping along the wall, looking for Suits.

"Let's just hope we don't get him killed, trying to get away from here." He sighed.

"Be positive. We might not die today." I snarled, glancing into an empty room.

Cheshire scoffed, but we continued to creep down the hallway unnoticed. The Suits must have been completely distracted by the prison break. The lavishness of the Red Party's base was disgusting. I couldn't imagine why anyone would waste this much money on silver and gold laced wallpaper, lush velvet furniture at every turn turned my stomach. I pressed my ear against a door, and heard Hatter saying, "Duchess, I don't think this is appropriate."

I kicked the door open, anger riding me hard. Duchess started to scream, until I pointed my gun at her and said, "Make another noise, and you die." I glanced at Hatter, finding him tied to her pink bed with his shirt ripped open. I couldn't help the giggle that bubbled out of me. It could have been the cover of a bad romance novel, his black T-shirt ripped open revealing the muscles that lie underneath. I glanced at Duchess, she had tears streaming down her face as she stood, wrapping her arms around herself. I almost felt about, but a glance back at Hatter had the feelings disappearing. "You really get yourself into some messes, don't you, Hatter?" I asked, moving to untie him.

"It's not funny." He grumbled, rubbing his wrists.

"Yeah, it kind of is." I argued.

"What do you want from me?" Duchess whimpered, causing me to roll my eyes.

"It's very simple," I snarled, "You are going to lead me to my friend Dina, and then I'm going to use you as a hostage to get out of here." I explained.

"I don't know your friend." she said, her voice higher in pitch than usual.

"Phone." I said, motioning to Cheshire. He put his cell phone in the palm of my hand, and I quickly pulled up Dina's picture. I had sent him several late one night, when we were reminiscing about our lives when we were younger. My heart throbbed at the memory. Dina had a big smile on her face, holding a large, orange tabby cat she had rescued from a storm drain. We'd named him after one of dumb old movies my father had in his collection. Gremlin had been our constant companion for seven years until he'd mysteriously disappeared. "Where is she?" I asked, shoving the phone in her face.

"A few doors down. They've been questioning her about something for a couple of days." She explained, her breath coming in quick pants. I almost felt sorry for her.

I exited the room, Cheshire and Hatter were dragging Duchess along behind me. She complied without any complaint, which I found surprising for the spoiled princess. "Is this it?" I asked, pointing toward a metal door, that was unlike the other décor in this hallway. She nodded, and I tested the door, finding it unlocked. "You go in first" I commanded, careful to ensure I remained in control of the situation.

Dina was slumped against one wall, her hair matted, and dress ripped. The same purple dress she had been wearing the night of her birthday. "Di,

Di." I shook her, "You've got to get up, we have to get out of here." I said, holding her face.

"Ali?" she asked, eyes unfocused.

"Yeah, Di, come on, help me get you out of here." I said, putting her arm around her neck.

"You shouldn't be here, they... they're looking for you." She said, pulling us to a stop, and looking panicked.

"It's okay, they already found me. We're escaping." I explained, dragging her.

"Oh, okay." she said, simply.

"Take us out of here," I commanded Duchess, Dina leaned heavily into my side, but I managed her weight without a problem.

Duchess followed my order and showed us to the front door. Unfortunately, several Suits were standing guard. As we approached, they reached for their weapons. "She dies if you stop us." Cheshire said, holding his gun to Duchess' head. She started to cry in earnest. I nearly asked him to stop, until I realized that she was the only reason they hadn't killed us already.

"Let them go." The Red Queen said, gliding toward us. I raised my eyebrows, surprised she cared for Duchess. There was no way the woman before me was capable of loving anyone. I was suspicious as she continued speaking. "Before you go, Alice. I should let you know that that is your cousin you're holding hostage." She explained, a look of glee spreading across her face, when she noted my shock. I saw Duchess study me for a moment, an equal look of shock, spreading across her features. It made perfect sense; Duchess was the King of Hearts daughter. The Red Queen was married to her father.

"It doesn't matter," I said, pointing my gun at the Queen, and backing away. "You will let us leave, and in return we won't kill your daughter." I added.

"Of course." She said, jaw clenched.

We made our way across the grass, toward the woods surrounding the Red Party's base. I took in as many details about the location as I could, knowing that one day I would be back to tear it down brick by brick. The Suits watched us with caution, letting us pass with a great amount of hesitation. Some snarled at us as we walked past. I could tell they were taking in every detail of our faces; it would never be safe for me in Wonderland until the Red Party was destroyed. When we finally disappeared into the woods, I breathed a sigh of relief.

A few moments later the forest opened to a clearing, true relief flooding me as I took in the Hummer and my sister. Lily came running toward us as we approached the Hummer, taking on some of Dina's weight, helping us move faster. Mom was sitting in the passenger seat, Lewis cradled against her chest. Once Dina was settled into the car, I turned to find Cheshire still holding Duchess. "What should we do with her?" He asked.

"Let her go," I said, looking over my cousin. "We aren't the Red Party."

"I'm sorry we took you hostage," I looked into her eyes, "I wish we weren't on opposite sides. Wonderland deserves better." She stared at me for a moment, before running off. I couldn't tell what had passed between us, but I hoped showing her mercy was the right choice. My heart pounded in my chest, adrenaline coursing through me. Too much had happened in such a short period of time I couldn't possibly process it.

"Alice," March said softly, gaining my attention. Everyone was piled into the Hummer. Only one seat remained. March signaled for me, sliding in, and helping me to sit on his lap.

"Step on the gas, Hatter." I said, praying that we would get away, before my aunt sent Suits after us.

It had been an almost entirely silent car ride. Dina fell asleep with her head leaned on March's shoulder. Lily had muttered soothing words to Lewis as he bounced in her lap. He was surprisingly happy for a child who'd been held in a dungeon for Creator only knew how long. Cheshire typed furiously on his phone. Hatter stared at the road, checking constantly if we were being followed. As the warehouse came into view tears filled my eyes, the stress of the last few hours hitting me. As soon as we parked Caterpillar, Rab, and Griffin came running outside. Before I could say anything, Caterpillar pulled me into a hug. "What happened to shooting me if I put them in danger?" I asked, my joke falling flat.

"March told me what you did. I want to tell you it was stupid, and that your empathy for others is going to get us all killed, but I'm happy you helped that girl in the alley." he said, ignoring my question.

"Roman Ainsworth?" I heard my mother say.

Caterpillar's eyes widened as he looked at my mother. "White Queen?" He said, looking at me, "Alice, wasn't your mother dead?"

"I thought she was too. Turns out, I have an evil aunt." I said, brushing it off in favor of saying, "Roman, huh. It's appropriate."

"That's what you got out of this conversation?" He asked.

"Yes, I'd like to know the names of my boyfriends." I said, glancing at Cheshire who winked.

"Dina, how are you?" Griffin asked, helping her out of the car.

"I don't know Griff; I've been held prisoner and interrogated for weeks." She snarked but immediately let him take on her body weight, leading her inside.

"Why do you have a kid?" Griffin asked, looking at Lily.

"Talk to Alice." She said, handing me the toddler, who was still sleeping.

Caterpillar was staring at me. "You definitely weren't gone long enough to have a two-year-old, so why on Earth do you have a baby?" He asked.

"It's not important right now." I responded, waving him off. I looked down at the young boy in my arms, something about him was so familiar. His light brown hair was mussed, and dirt marred his skin. I wanted to get him cleaned up, but I could feel myself fading fast. I started walking toward the warehouse, Caterpillar following close behind. I knew he must be worried if he wasn't helping get everyone settled back in. I turned to see Rab hugging my mother, before they began to talk quietly. "I'm going to lay down until my magick is recharged." I informed him, handing Lewis off to him. I took a moment to appreciate the way he looked cradling the child in his muscular arms. I didn't let myself begin to imagine him holding his own child. That possibility was nowhere near reality, not with the Red Queen still ruling the city. I couldn't even be certain children were something he'd want, I filed away the question for a more appropriate time.

"Rest, we can handle everything else." he said, quietly, almost as if he could read the thoughts in my head.

"Thank you." I said, standing on my tip toes to kiss his cheek.

A loud crash woke me from a deep sleep. I heard a feminine scream, and quickly jumped out of bed. Several more crashes had me rushing down the stairs. The building shook, nearly causing me to tumble over the rail. "Alice." March screamed, grabbing me off the stairs. Dust floated through the air; I assumed an earthquake had caused the shaking. They weren't uncommon in Wonderland, but they usually didn't cause much destruction.

"What's going on?" I yelled over the other shouts.

"The Red Queen." He shouted back. "Fi-," He growled with frustration trying to explain what happened.

Cheshire appeared covered in black soot, "The warehouse is on fire, we are trying to get everyone out."

"I'll deal with her." I whispered, ignoring their protests as I stepped out of the warehouse.

It was pitch black outside, I could barely make out anything. Only the glow of my recent home being on fire lit the way as I walked toward the Red Queen. She was standing a few feet from the warehouse. Her hands clasped casually behind her back, an almost peaceful smile gracing her face. The ground ceased shaking as her eyes met mine. "Hello, Alice. I was hoping you would join me." she said, calmly.

"I wouldn't miss it for the world." I retorted, trying to maintain my focus on her even as I worried about my family and friends inside.

"You are an unexpected problem." She replied.

"Damn, I was hoping to have made a bigger impression by now," I quipped, "I must not be trying hard enough."

"You are most definitely Alcinda's arrogant brat." She snarled.

Sounds of pounding feet interrupted my retort, but I didn't move from my place as I saw Hatter running toward me. "Ali, Caterpillar's been hurt." Hatter panted.

My aunt clicked her tongue and laughed. "I'll allow you to handle that."

I hesitated for a moment, wondering what her game was. I couldn't ignore the idea of Caterpillar being hurt, so I turned and ran into the warehouse, Hatter hot on my heels. I found March and Cheshire helping Lily with Lewis who was screaming at the top of his lungs. Everyone looked unharmed. "Get to a car and get out of here. Go anywhere you think might be safe." I commanded.

"We're not leaving you behind." Cheshire yelled back.

"I'll get away on the bike. Text me the meet up spot." I yelled. I could tell they all wanted to argue with me, but no one did. I rushed toward Hatter who was standing just outside Caterpillar's office. Only to find Cater prone on the ground, a large piece of rubble sitting next to his bloody head. "Go with March and Cheshire." I ordered, calling my magick to the surface.

"I—" He started.

"No, go." I demanded, pointing toward the door. I heard him grumble something unintelligible, but he obeyed. I let my magick wrap itself around Caterpillar. He levitated slightly, and I began making my way out of the warehouse, his body floating ahead of me. The ground continued to shake so I was forced to dodge around rubble falling from the ceiling. I could see the flames slowly eating away at the Resistance's base. I knew the men would be devasted by the loss, my anger riding me hard. I wanted the Red Queen's blood for all the damage she had done to the people I loved. Now more than ever I knew I had to be the one to end her. When we finally made it outside, I collapsed on the ground, dragging Caterpillar's head into my lap. I reached into the waistband of his jeans, gripping the gun I knew I would find there. I yanked it out, pointing it at my aunt as she approached.

"Aw, how sweet, you're trying to protect your little boyfriend. It would be almost endearing if it weren't useless." The Red Queen gloated, her hands beginning to glow red. "Neither of you will live through the night. Without the two of you, the Resistance crumbles. Alcinda will be crushed when I take her precious daughter." I leaned over Caterpillar, protecting him from the magick she was conjuring. The gun clattered to the ground as I felt the first wave of agonizing pain flow through me. It felt like an eternity before my body relaxed again. I could feel hot, wet liquid running down my back. All I could think of was how my mother must have suffered if this was her sister's power. I had no idea why the Red Queen hated my mother so much, but it was clear to me that she would do anything to destroy everything my mother had built.

I was completely drained; it had been too long since I'd had a chance to fully recharge. I summoned the final dregs of my magick, praying it would be enough to stun her. I placed my hands against the ground, noticing the blood running down my sleeves, and sent as much electricity as possible toward my aunt. I saw her three guards drop to the ground in pain and sighed a breath of relief. My head dropped back to Caterpillar's chest, and I could hear the strong beat of his heart. I glanced toward my aunt, seeing her building more magick into her skin, a red glow illuminated her. I'd always thought it was strange that I would glow when I wasn't calling large amounts of magick. Mom had said she'd seen a glow before, but never like mine. Soon pain overtook my body again, causing me to scream out. I noticed Lily walking toward me; a wave of peace caused me to relax. I watched in quiet horror as she faced off with our aunt. "You think you can hurt me little girl?" The Red Queen taunted.

"For Alice, anything." She said.

I watched Lily call her magick for the first time, a visible golden shield wrapping around her. Her thin body flew at our aunt, just before Lily's fist would have made contact with her the Red Queen side stepped. Her fist caught my sister in the midsection. I tried to move, to do anything to help my sister as she landed on the ground. Lily couldn't possibly have much strength after so long trapped in the Red Party's dungeon, but she shocked me as she stood again.

I heard the Red Queen laugh and felt the pain soak into my body again. Just before I passed out, I heard Lily say, "Not my little sister, you cunt."

Chapter 18

August 20th, 2157

I was floating, surrounded by darkness. Blissfully unaware of anything but the void around me. Every so often, panic would take over the peaceful darkness I existed in, pain would follow. If I had been able to scream, my throat would have been raw.

"It could be another full week before she wakes. I've never seen wounds like this. We're going to have to just wait and see what happens." A pleasant voice said, jogging me awake.

"She's strong, but she drained herself protecting Roman." A familiar voice replied. The voices were so muffled, almost as if I was under water, pressure in my head caused a lightshow in the darkness. I fought to do anything, to respond to the voices near me. "She'll wake up when it is her time. There is no point watching her." I could tell this was a woman's voice.

"We won't be able to keep them away from her much longer." Pain once again blinded me, "Roman can barely sit up, and he's begging to see her."

"No one needs to see her like this." I heard just before I fell back into unconsciousness.

"We should just leave Wonderland; we can't continue to let our loved ones be hurt because we want to be heroes." A warm voice said, causing shivers to run through my tired body.

"She will never agree to leave. She has found her purpose." I knew this last voice belonged to my mother, but I could not understand what she meant.

"Fuck her purpose, if she dies trying to protect these people, it isn't worth it." The warm voice argued. I finally recognized the voice as Caterpillar. I fought against the blackness, desperately wanting to comfort the pain in his voice.

"Let her make her own decisions, Roman. She will make the right ones." Mom said.

"And if those decisions lead to her death, am I supposed to accept that?" He shouted. I heard a door slam, and I spent a few moments trying desperately to wake up. I had so many questions, my memories blurred as my head pounded.

A quiet sigh was the last noise I heard before falling back to sleep. "I really wish you'd wake up, Alice. We n-need you here." March pleaded, I could feel him gripping my hand. I tried to flex my fingers but found that my body would not follow my commands. "I guess it's okay if you have to r-rest a bit longer, but I'm tired of Caterpillar arguing with everyone." He added, I felt him brush fingers through my hair.

"March, leave her alone to rest." Hatter said, and I felt March's presence leave.

"Creator fucking damn it, Alice. Wake up." Cheshire said. "I need you. This isn't worth doing without you anymore."

I blinked my eyes open, finding the room bright with sunlight. "Why are you always the one waking me up?" I croaked, trying to sit up. Pain shot down my spine and I fell back into my prone position, staring up at the white ceiling. Finally, I remembered the warehouse burning, the Red Queen's appearance, her glee at my pain.

"Holy shit, Al. I didn't think it would work." he said, rushing to my side.

"I need you too, Cat," I whispered, pressing my chapped lips to his knuckles, tears pricking my eyes.

"Let me get Mary Anne." he said, rushing out of the room.

"Who?" I asked, mostly to myself. I wondered if I had suffered from memory loss while I was out. The door swung open hard, revealing a short, brunette woman. A long length green floral dress hugged a soft body. Her hair was braided around her head, reminding me of the way my mother would wear her hair when she took Lily and I to the park when we were children. A beautiful smile lit up her face when she made eye contact with me, and I felt immediately at ease.

"Alice, it's so nice to finally meet you. I'm Mary Anne, Jonah is my husband." She said, coming to my bedside, noticing that I was struggling to sit up.

"Jonah?" I asked, watching her carefully.

"Oh, I forget about the code names. My husband is the White Rabbit," She explained.

"You're Caterpillar's aunt?" I was shocked by this information.

"I am." She confirmed, examining me, "It's amazing how quickly you have healed. Another few days, and you should be up and walking around without help." she finally said, patting my hand.

"I really have to pee." I blurted. I was nervous about meeting someone so important to Caterpillar. I hadn't exactly had a chance to make a good impression on her.

"I'm so sorry, I should have known after two weeks you would need the restroom."

"Two weeks?" I asked, dumbfounded.

"Yes, dear. You've been unconscious for fourteen days." She explained, helping me up.

"Is... is everyone okay?" I asked, hesitantly.

She gently put an arm behind my back, and another under my knees, lifting me without issue. She had to be at least five inches shorter than me. I would have expected any of the men to be able to lift me, but for this tiny woman to do so with ease was impressive. I could tell that her strength went far past her physical abilities. "Everyone is a bit banged up, but no worse for the wear." She said, a bright smile still on her face. "There are towels, right there, you can take a shower if you would like. I'll be right outside the door if you need help." She announced, helping me into the bathroom.

"Thanks." I said, awkwardly glancing around the bathroom. It was painted a light blue color, and the accent was a sandy yellow color. It was clear that the bathroom was meant to remind you of a beach. I'd heard stories about beaches, seen a few old teen movies that took place near the ocean. There were no oceans near Wonderland to anyone's knowledge, only the river that ran through the suburban areas. The water was crystal clear, swimming had been banned in it, for fear that the only fresh source of water would be contaminated.

After relieving myself, I stood, gripping the sink for support, and slowly peeled my pants the rest of the way off. I kicked them away, panting from the exertion. Next, I removed my shirt, a loud whimper leaving me as I raised my arms. I looked in the mirror, shocked by how I looked. My hair was in a messy bun, but not nearly as messy as it should have been given that it hadn't been washed for two weeks. I knew I could thank March for that. My face was pale, and deep purple circles lined my bloodshot eyes. My lips were chapped and cracked, something gray was smudged across my nose and cheeks. My eyes traveled to my shoulders where I could see several deep gashes that were only partially closed. I turned trying to get a good look at my back. It was in a similar state, deep gashes, and blisters, reaching down my back and around my stomach. None scattered the lower half of my body, but I knew I would have several scars. The Red Queen's power was horrific, to be able to cause this type of damage without ever touching anyone was completely unfamiliar to me.

A knock caused me to jump, "Alice are you okay?"

"I'm fine, just getting into the shower." I replied, leaning to turn on the warm water. I stepped in, and immediately hissed, as warm water hit the injuries on my body. Blood washed down the drain, and I watched it mesmerized. How had I survived this much damage to my body? I didn't know, but I sent a quiet thanks to the Creator. Washing my hair was difficult, as it caused the closed wounds on my body to stretch uncomfortably. The soap stung, but I powered through, careful not to make any noise. I heard voices talking just outside the door and decided I had holed up in the bathroom long enough. I grabbed a plush towel, and carefully wrapped it around my body. I gripped the door handle, finding that I was a bit dizzy, but threw the door open anyway. Everyone went silent as I stepped into the room. Caterpillar and Rab were standing near the bedroom door. Mary Anne was standing beside me like a guard. Cheshire was lounging on the bed, and Lily was sitting on the floor looking exhausted.

"How's your head, dear? Feeling dizzy?" Mary Anne asked. I didn't want to admit how much pain I was in after such a simple task, but I was using the doorjamb to hold myself up. I pursed my lips, staring at Caterpillar. It was bad enough I had been hurt so badly by the Red Queen; I didn't want any of my men to see me so weak. "Let me get you some clothes." Mary Anne said, shooing Rab and Caterpillar out of the room. I don't know if she didn't notice Cheshire, or if she just chose to ignore him. I carefully made my way to him, collapsing on my butt when I finally reached the bed.

"Even injured you can't seem to keep your clothes on around me." He joked, moving his legs so I could get comfortable.

"Excuse me?" Lily chimed in, glaring at Cheshire.

"I...uh... I think I hear Caterpillar calling." he said, rushing out of the room.

"You're a coward, Cat." I yelled after him, laughing.

I sighed after a moment and glanced at Lily who looked amused. "I can't believe you messed with him like that." I said to fill the awkward silence.

She snorted, "I don't know what I expected when you told me you were dating four men, but it definitely wasn't them."

We fell into a comfortable silence for several minutes, before I finally said, "Thank you for saving me, Lil. I wished you hadn't risked yourself like that."

"I would do anything for you Ali, you should know that by now." She replied, moving to sit next to me in bed.

"I'm sorry, we haven't been able to do much shopping." Mary Anne said, carrying a bundle of clothes.

"Thank you for taking care of me." I replied, taking the clothes.

"It's no problem at all dear." She said, before exiting the room again.

I didn't waste time pulling the black hoodie over my head and sliding into the leggings. I glanced down, noticing a small scrap of blue fabric caught in a t shirt. I yanked it out and started cracking up. "Okay, I finally know that you've lost it. What's so funny about a bra?" Lily asked, staring at me.

"It's... I don't even know how to explain. You should ask Cheshire." I replied.

The door slammed open, revealing Hatter, who took only a moment to look me over before rushing to hug me. I yelped as his arms wrapped around my back. "Sorry, sorry." he said, holding me more gently. "I've been so worried."

"I'm a bit banged up, but overall, I'm okay." I replied.

"Are you hungry?" Hatter asked.

"Starving." I replied. I hadn't really noticed it until he asked, but now I could feel the emptiness of my stomach.

"Your mom is making dinner, why don't we go join everyone else?" He offered.

I thought for a moment but nodded. I needed to see that everyone was okay. Hatter immediately came to my aid, gently helping me to my feet, a firm hand on my lower back as we made our way out of the room. Lily jumped up to join us, flanking my other side ready to jump in if I needed help. The house wasn't large by any means, in comparison to the warehouse it was tiny. Everyone I cared about was seated around the dining room table, and I found myself glad to be here.

"Good to see you up and moving around." Rab said, moving to give me his seat.

"You don't have to—" I started.

"Just sit. You nearly died protecting my nephew, let us spoil you just a little." he said, we both looked at Caterpillar at the same time, and I found him watching us.

He had a yellowing bruise on his forehead but looked fine otherwise. I gave him a half smile, glad to see him. "Don't praise her stupidity." Caterpillar bit out, surprising me.

"Well, it's good to be back to normal, Cater baby." I said, covering up my disappointment.

"Stop calling me that." He demanded.

"Has he been this grumpy the whole time I was unconscious?" I asked, looking at Rab.

"Worse. He paced around the house like an angry bear, snapping at everyone. It's almost endearing that he cares so much." He replied.

"It really is. If only he could be nice, when I'm awake." I said. I looked back at Caterpillar to find that a light blush had started to stain his cheek bones.

March stood up, and walked behind me, "Can I do your h-hair?"

"Sure." He brushed his fingers through my hair, careful not to pull. Within minutes he had it swept into a fluffy ponytail. "Thank you." I said, running my fingers down his arm.

"My pleasure." He replied, grinning at me.

Mary Anne appeared, Lewis on her hip, reminding me of the small boy I had taken under my wing. "Hi, Lewis." I said, reaching for him, "I don't know if you remember me, but I'm Alice." I said, settling him into my lap.

"Ali?" He asked, putting a chubby hand on my face. I felt my heart swell with love for the small boy, at the same time I cringed for the loss of his parents. I hoped his father was still alive, maybe we'd be able to reunite them at some point. He wrapped his arms around my neck, snuggling into me. I noticed that Hatter and Caterpillar were staring at me, with similar looks of awe. "What?" I asked, furrowing my eyebrows.

"That's one of the first times he's spoken." Hatter said, quietly.

My eyes widened in surprise, and I glanced down at the boy. "How old are you, Lewy?" I asked. He held up two fingers, before promptly beginning to chew on them. He bounced up and down on my knees, accidentally brushing against some of my injuries. I huffed a breath through my nose, careful not to let go of him.

"Come here, kiddo. Aunt Alice has some booboos, we don't want to hurt her." Rab said, taking him.

"Food's ready." Mom said from a door at the far end of the room, I assumed it led to the kitchen. She was wearing a blue apron that had been splattered with flour. Some part of me warmed seeing her looking like the person I had known before she'd been captured.

She walked over to me, placing a gentle hand on my shoulder, I tried not to flinch at the pain. I spent a moment looking at her. Her skin had returned to its normal tan color, her hair was lush, and her eyes were bright and happy. Just looking at her, I could barely tell she had been held prisoner for seven years. She squeezed me gently, everything that could have been said between us answered in a small form of affection. Years of anger melted away from me. Griffin and Dina entered the room. Their eyes fell on me, and for a spilt second, they both stood completely still, before Dina rushed toward me. "I've been so worried." She breathed, wrapping arms around my neck.

"I'm fine." I said, patting her back gently.

"You're such a fucking liar." Di said, hands on her hips. "I can't believe you risked your life saving all of us...No, no, wait I can believe that you're that much of a dumbass." She ranted.

Everyone was silent for a moment, looking between the two of us. "Love you too, Di." I said, smiling. Griffin patted my shoulder, before taking a seat next to Lily. Dina followed him, and soon everyone was chatting again.

Caterpillar slid a plate of food in front of me, causing a smile to curl across my face. He had never served me before, and I found it endearing that he would now. "Thanks, Cater baby." I said. He rolled his eyes at me but didn't say anything. Everyone began to dig into the delicious soup my mother had made. It was exactly what I needed to fill my belly.

The table was silent for several minutes as everyone dug in, until Lily said, "So, Cheshire, why did you give my sister a blue bra?" I nearly choked when I saw the look on his face. Rab patted my back, while he chuckled.

"It's.... I would never disrespect your sister in any way." Ches said, glancing at me.

"Of course not, she'd kick your ass, but that doesn't answer my question." She shot back, and I could tell she was enjoying torturing him.

"Lily, leave him alone, he made a sarcastic comment the first time they met, and it's been a joke ever since." Hatter explained, saving Cheshire from further explanation.

She narrowed her eyes at Ches, and said, "Sure, sure. I'll believe that for now."

The rest of our meal was uneventful. I found out that Mary Anne and Rab had been married since they were only eighteen. It gave me hope for the future, knowing that they had stayed together even when the Red Party became more influential. Mary Anne had never been involved with the Resistance before. Rab had been careful to keep his work with us away from her. It wasn't long before I was tired, once again, but I didn't want to go to bed yet, so I curled up on the couch with Hatter and March.

"You should go lay down." Caterpillar said, sitting on the end of the couch.

"I'm comfy right here." I whined.

"Hatter has things to do." He replied.

"Like what?" I asked, wiggling until my feet were in March's lap.

"That's not important, what's important is the fact that you need to go rest." He said, pointing toward the bedroom.

"If I didn't know better, I would almost think you were my father, but since you aren't quite that old…" I trailed off, grinning.

"Alice." My mother said, having been listening to the conversation, "Go lay down."

I noticed Caterpillar's gloating expression and kicked him in the shin on my way to my room, stopping halfway. "Wait just a minute, I'm a grown woman, why can't I stay in here?" I asked myself, turning around.

"I'm not trying to baby you, but you look terrible. For my sake, please go rest." Mom said, coming around the couch to hug me, "I don't want you to push yourself too hard."

"I'm fine, Mom." I said, laying my cheek on her shoulder.

"Thanks for saying it, but I know you aren't." she said, wrapping her fingers around my forearms. "You are my daughter, and I know you better than anyone." She added, "You've always had the bad habit of pushing yourself too far too fast."

"Fine, fine. You don't have to guilt me." I said, although it had no bite to it.

I waved to everyone who was lounging around the room and went to lay down. It wasn't long before I was fast asleep.

I woke up surrounded by darkness, sweat coating my body, panic clawed at my throat as I sat up. I dragged my sore body out of bed, desperately fumbling for a light. As light flooded the room, I tried to figure out what had caused me to wake up so suddenly. I strained my ears trying to hear anything that could have disturbed my slumber. Finally, I heard quiet voices, so I opened my door, moving toward the sounds. I found Caterpillar and Hatter huddled next to each other at the dining room table, papers spread in front of them.

"They managed to easily contain the chaos." Hatter flipped a page over, furiously writing, "There was no reason for them to let us get away."

"But they did," Caterpillar ran fingers through his hair.

"I can't figure out why, Roman, it makes no sense." I was surprised when Hatter used Caterpillar's real name. "My theory is that the Red Queen wanted to destroy the entire Resistance in one go. With the information Alice's mother has given us, it still doesn't make sense."

Caterpillar was silent for a moment, "There's something more, and it's driving me crazy. I can't protect Alice." I could hear the pain in his voice, and it no longer made sense to eavesdrop, so I stepped fully into view, and said, "It's a test of some kind."

They both jumped, turning toward me with wide eyes. "Sweetheart, you should be in bed." Hatter said, almost tripping over himself to come to my side. He led me to the table, forcing me to sit between him and Caterpillar.

"What do you mean by a test?" Caterpillar asked.

"I've been thinking through it since I woke up. You're right that letting us walk away easily made no sense. Unless it's exactly what she wanted to have happen..." I trailed off, it felt like the answer was so obvious, but I couldn't quite place my finger on it.

"It could have just been arrogance," Hatter offered.

"I've considered that, the Red Queen is clearly unstable, but I don't think she's stupid." A thought came to, and I gasped, "It has to do with magick. She needed to see what we're working with." They were both silent, waiting for me to elaborate, "My mother's gifts are passive. She occasionally has dreams and can heal minor wounds. My aunt clearly has a physical gift, she needed to figure out how much of a threat I was."

"But you were weakened..." Caterpillar acknowledged. "Lily was the one that forced her to retreat. She doesn't know how powerful you are."

"That's our advantage." I grinned. We still had hope.

"The rest of us can't fight magick, Alice." Hatter said.

"How did Lily get her to leave?" I asked.

"She's just kept punching her, it was all physical blows." Hatter confirmed my suspicions.

"Guys, she has no defense other than the Suits and her magick." If I hadn't still been in pain, I would have jumped for joy.

"Assuming you're right," Caterpillar started.

"She is." My mother's voice startled all of us, she appeared from the kitchen. "Penny has never had to defend herself against an attack like that. With Lily's shield she wouldn't have been able to use her magick."

"Is there any way to defend against magick?" Caterpillar asked.

"Not that I've ever found, somethings like Alice's illusions can be cast away..." My mother trailed off.

"March's manipulation..." Hatter tensed as the words came out of my mouth.

"Explain." Mom demanded.

"I haven't really had a chance to test it, but March has an innate ability to force others to feel the need to protect him... give him his way even." I explained, "The only time it seems that it fails is when someone truly feels that what he wants is a danger to himself."

"That is…" My mother stared into space, clearly trying to put pieces together, "I've never heard of an ability like that. We could use his abilities to our advantage. Cheshire also seems to have some untapped potential."

"Invisibility maybe?" I offered, a wave of dizziness came over me and I gripped the table to stay upright.

"Sweetheart, you need to go back to bed," Hatter insisted.

"We need to continue to make a plan," I whined, desperate to find a way to end the tyranny in Wonderland. It wasn't enough that Lily and Dina were safe anymore, my aunt was a threat to everyone in the city.

"No arguments," Caterpillar said, sweeping me off the bench in one smooth move. I squeaked not expecting the sudden movement. "You will rest, and we will continue this discussion later."

Hatter and Mom murmured their goodnight as Caterpillar carried me back to the room, I had been staying in. He laid me down in bed and turned to leave the room without a word.

"You've barely spoken to me, are you okay?" I asked, sitting back up.

He paused at the door; I could tell he was trying to find something to say. He kept his back turned to me as he responded, "You risked your life to get me out of the building. If I hadn't been hurt, you could have defeated her."

"You don't know that. My magick wasn't nearly at full power." I stood, walking to him, just as I was about to touch him, he turned around, gripping my biceps.

"Don't you ever choose my life over yours again." He demanded.

"I won't promise you that," I stood my ground, I was not afraid of Caterpillar.

His mouth crashed into mine; it was the first time since I woke up that I felt truly alive. As he claimed my mouth I moaned, needing to be closer to him. I bit his lip, reaching to wrap my arm around his neck. He lifted me by my thighs, walking us toward my bed and kicking the door closed as an afterthought. As my back hit the bed, pain shot through my body causing me to gasp. Caterpillar instantly pulled away his face stricken. "You're still hurt," He seemed to be saying it more to himself than me, "We will continue this another time."

Before he started to walk away, I whispered, "Stay." He hesitated, "Please, just... just hold me while I sleep."

I hated how weak I sounded as I nearly begged him, but I was desperate to feel something. The Red Queen had taken something from me that I couldn't process. I'd never felt so powerless, I had been able to rely on my gifts my entire life, and for the first time magick couldn't save me. Caterpillar crawling into bed next to me pulled me out of my thoughts. Once he was settled, he opened him arms, beckoning me to lay with him. I curled against him, resting my head on his chest. His arms cocooned me in safety, he pulled the blanket over us both and pressed a kiss into my hair. "Get some sleep, princess." I closed my eyes and within moments drifted into unconsciousness, completely at ease in Caterpillar's arms.

Chapter 19

August 27th, 2157

It took a week before I began to feel back to normal. I slept nearly twelve hours a day, slowly my magick returned, and my body healed. Mom had tried to heal some of the worst wounds on my back, which had made life much easier. I still had times where I would become so dizzy, I couldn't stand. Everyone tried to avoid the topic of the Red Party as I healed. Every conversation I tried to bring up was shut down in one way or another. Hatter, March, and Cheshire had been babying me, which I both enjoyed and loathed. Caterpillar, on the other hand, had started to drive me insane. He hovered like a mother hen, snapping orders at me constantly, and generally being overbearing. "You are not going with us." he demanded, bringing me back to the present conversation.

"I'm perfectly fine, and at the very least I would like to pick my own clothes." I said, standing my ground.

"We know that the Red Queen---" he began.

"Her name is Penthea, let's humanize her. She's not all powerful as much as she would like us to believe that." Mom interrupted.

"We all go by code names." He said, eyebrows furrowed. Watching Caterpillar face off with my mother was both hilarious and a bit scary. She's known him since he was a child. I could tell he viewed her as a mother figure, but when they were on opposite sides of an argument it was as if they couldn't stand each other.

"We do it for protection, she does it for power. When this fight is over, the code names disappear." She said, her quiet declaration quieting the room. Caterpillar eyed me angrily, as if my mother's opinion was somehow my fault. In all honesty I agreed with her, hiding behind code names makes us just as bad as the Red Party. "I agree with Mom on this one." I finally said, noticing that several people were staring at me. "I've never had a code name neither have Lily, Dina, Griffin, or Mary Anne. I will not hide behind fake names. It's just another way to separate us from our identities." I added.

"I'd like to point out that I prefer my codename," Cheshire pipped in.

"This is irrelevant to the topic at hand." Caterpillar ranted, pointing a finger at me, "She needs to stay here, and rest."

"You aren't going to force my daughter to do anything she doesn't want to; I gave up on that fight years ago. She nearly sacrificed her life to save us, I think she can make her own decisions." my mother said, causing a small smile to break out on my face.

I saw the frustration on Caterpillar's face, and almost felt bad. Not bad enough to stay home but I knew he was coming from a good place. "I'll be careful, and if I get to feeling bad, I'm sure Hatter can bring me back here." I said, laying a hand on his shoulder.

"Fine." He huffed; his arms crossed. "Let's go then." He said, grabbing my hand. Hatter, March, Dina, Lily, and Cheshire followed us. I watched as Dina, Cheshire, and Lily piled into Rab's black truck, before I jumped into the Hummer. Something told me this was going to be the most interesting trip to the store I'd ever taken.

The only department store in Wonderland was a three-story building, taking up nearly half a block. It sold everything imaginable, from clothes to food to home décor. I considered how close we were to Dodo's shop, hoping we wouldn't run into him. March had been quiet about his mother, but I'd heard him crying one night while talking to Hatter. I had been careful not to interrupt, they had things to work out and I wanted to respect their privacy. Hatter was still reeling from the revelation of March's magick. I knew March wanted to learn to control his powers, but he seemed to be ashamed of them. My mother had been slowly but surely warming him up to the idea of training. Caterpillar parked next to Rab's truck and insisted on helping me down from the Hummer. We entered the massive store as group, but it was clear we would have to split up. "Lily, I want you to do the grocery shopping. Take Hatter with you." Caterpillar directed, and they quickly left.

"Cheshire, you are going to stay with Alice and Dina to do the clothes shopping. March and I will get everything else. I assume you know everyone's sizes?" He asked. Ches nodded, and then Caterpillar turned to me. "If you start feeling tired, call me or Hatter and one of us will take you home." he demanded, locking eyes with me.

"I'm fine, Cater." I said, waving him away. He rolled his eyes, before motioning for March to follow him. I hated to see them go, but I loved to watch them walk away. I laughed at my own thoughts, before turning to Dina.

"We haven't been shopping in forever." Dina said, walking beside me.

"We went a few weeks before your birthday." I replied, glancing around the racks of clothes.

"And you bought that cute red lingerie set." She said, a grin spreading across her face as she glanced at Cheshire, who wasn't paying attention to our conversation.

"All of my clothes going up in flame is a good excuse to buy new stuff." I said, raising my eyebrows.

"We have to get some things for Lewis. Where is the kids section?" Cheshire chimed in. I was surprised Cheshire wasn't more aware of the layout of the store. Then I remembered that the Resistance wasn't well funded, and he had been an orphan for well over a decade. The thought hit me hard, for the first time I realized I was no longer an orphan. My eyes welled with tears that I had to push away, I'd never get over the fact that my mother was still alive. "Are you okay, Al?" Cheshire asked me, wrapping an arm around my waist as we walked.

"Just thankful that everyone I love is alive and well," I responded. He nodded, understanding everything I hadn't spoken aloud.

An hour later we were all laughing as Cheshire held up a bright orange button up. I could tell he'd been uncomfortable at first, unsure of himself when hanging out with Dina and I, but we'd all warmed up quickly. It was the most at peace I had felt in months. Even though soon enough we would have to return to our fight against the Red Party. At least for a little while I could laugh with people I cared about. "It would look great on Caterpillar." I said, "He needs more color in his wardrobe." Our cart was filled to the brim with clothing for everyone in our temporary home. We had bought Lewis more clothes than he would probably ever wear, but he deserved it. Poor kid. I had no idea how we were going to handle having a small child to care for during the war that was coming. I couldn't let the Red Party continue their reign; I was willing to risk everything I'd gained to save all of Wonderland.

"I still don't know about this white dress. I don't have anything to wear it to." Dina said, holding up the item in question.

"You never know when you might need a dress, get it." Cheshire said, surprising us both.

I noticed a deep purple shirt and ran to grab it. "You have to have this." I said, holding it up to Cheshire.

"It matches the purple in your hair." Dina said, nodding along.

"I don't know." He said, dropping some boots into the cart.

"Get it, and I'll finally take you out on that date." I joked, swinging the hanger gently.

"Bribery doesn't work on me." Ches said, barely containing a grin.

"Bullshit." I shot back.

"Okay, okay. You win, get the shirt, but you better take me on the nicest date ever." He laughed, wrapping an arm around my waist. I stared at him as we continued our shopping. Cheshire was still a bit of a mystery to me. I still didn't know his real name, I could definitely tell he was interested in me, but he'd made no moves to even kiss me. I never thought I'd feel more unsure of Cheshire than Caterpillar. I knew I needed to get some alone time with him soon. Just as I was formulating a plan Lily and Hatter appeared.

"Are you guys done?" Lily asked. I giggled when I noticed that Hatter was pushing the cart, looking exhausted. Lily was a slave driver. I had no doubt she'd run him ragged trying to get enough food to feed twelve people for as long as possible. We couldn't risk being in public too much, there was no doubt in my mind that the Red Queen was looking for us. She couldn't be certain any of us had died in the warehouse fire. I looked down at our haul, thinking through everything we might need.

"Underwear." I declared, motioning for everyone to follow me. As we approached the unmentionables, Cheshire's phone started ringing. He quickly excused himself and walked away. I wondered why he'd left to take the call, but I trusted he would tell us if it was important.

"Hatter can you—" I stopped motioning toward the men's section.

"Of course, sweetheart." He smiled, leaning to kiss me.

"Thanks." I said. We looked around the lingerie for a minute, throwing in a few items and chatting. It was almost normal if not for the nervous energy that had taken over our group. Cheshire's sudden departure and the worry we'd been spotted clearly haunted their eyes as well.

"So, Ali, what's it like to date four men?" Dina asked, suddenly.

"I... Well, we haven't got do too much dating yet." I admitted, fingering a lacy pink bra.

"What have you gotten to do?" she asked, wiggling her eyebrows.

"I've only slept with Hatter, and it was before we started dating." I said.

"Why the hell haven't you climbed Caterpillar yet?" Di asked, before adding, "Get it, because he's built like a tree."

I rolled my eyes, hiding a smile, "Caterpillar and I are... complicated."

"What's complicated about it? You want him, he obviously wants you, I don't see the issue," She responded, crossing her arms.

"I don't know, Cater... he's different than the others... with March, Hatter, and Cheshire it's easy. Caterpillar is bull headed and makes me want to scream.... And not in the good way." I explained. I didn't want to tell them that Caterpillar had outright rejected me twice, it was too embarrassing.

"It'll happen when it's meant to." Lily said.

I smiled, "I know."

"You're happy." Lily stated.

"I am." I confirmed.

"Promise me if that changes, you'll tell them." She said, laying a hand on my shoulder. I nodded, because I didn't have any words for her. It was ridiculous, but some part of me knew the happiness I felt with them would never change. In just a short time, they had become just as integral to my life as my sister and my best friend.

"I think we're finished." Dina said, clapping her hands.

Cheshire came jogging back over, a hurried look on his face. "We have to find Caterpillar."

"I'm right here." The man in question said, pushing a cart over.

"I just got a call from…" He glanced at me, before finishing. "The who isn't important. There is a Red Party caucus in an hour, we need to go. Apparently, there's going to be a big announcement." Ches finishes, seeming a bit out of breath.

"We can send Dina, Lily, and Alice home with our supplies. Let's go check it out." Caterpillar said, motioning for Hatter to join us.

"I'm going." I demanded.

"Absolutely not." He shot back, turning away from me.

"I. Am. Going." I said, jogging to keep up with him.

"No, you aren't at full strength, and you are easily recognizable." Caterpillar said, swinging around, causing me to crash into his chest. He steadied me, before continuing. "This is dangerous, these people will not hesitate to hurt you."

"I don't give a fuck, what your arguments are. If you, March, Hatter, and Cheshire are going. I'm going. End of story." I said, mimicking his angry pose.

"We can have this argument after we check out." He said, pushing toward the front of the store.

A perky brunette rushed us through check out. I noticed her gawking at the sheer amount of money we were spending, but I ignored it we were not short on funds by any means. My own savings from working part-time jobs I'd worked as a teenager. Plus, the money our parents had left us, left Lily and I more than comfortable. Lily had been working at a school in the city before she was arrested by the Red Party. So, she had never needed to dip into our parent's funds. I never understood why Wonderland had maintained currency after the rest of the world was destroyed. My best guess was that the leaders at that time wanted people to feel as normal as possible. "You must be very important to be spending so much money." The cashier said to Caterpillar as he handed her a large stack of bills. He grunted in his usual dismissive way. The money was mine, but I didn't like to carry a wallet or purse when I could avoid it, so I'd handed Caterpillar everything I had on me a few days ago. "We're not busy if you need help loading all of this into your vehicle. I'd be happy to help." she offered.

I realized she was trying to flirt with him, but he was too busy typing away on his phone to pay attention. I bumped my hip against his, and whispered, "She's flirting with you."

He looked up at me, glancing toward the checkout girl, and then leaned in, "No, I think she's flirting with your sister."

I furrowed my eyebrows, looking around for Lily. Only to find she was standing right behind Caterpillar, and her face was bright red. The cashier was staring at her awaiting a response. I chuckled quietly, and said, "I don't think she knows how to handle that."

Once we had all our arms loaded down with bags, we exited the store. The cashier pouted as she watched after us. I'd seen her write her number on the receipt before she'd handed it to Lily who had stuttered her goodbyes. As the guys packed everything into Rab's truck. I snuck my way into the Hummer, casting a simple illusion of me climbing into the other car. It felt good to be using my magick again, I hadn't touched it at all since that night. It almost purred as it wrapped around me, cloaking me. Cheshire slid in next to me, and winked, realizing what I had done. "You do realize Caterpillar is going to be pissed?" He whispered; his minty breath hot against my ear.

I nodded, staying quiet. A few moments later, Hatter and March climbed in the car. March took the seat next to me. I watched as the truck drove away, and breathed a sigh of relief that Lily didn't give away my trick. Caterpillar climbed into the driver's seat and started the Hummer. "It was stupid that you didn't let Alice come with us." Hatter said.

I silently cursed, dropping to the floorboard as my illusion broke. March's eyes widened, but he didn't give me away. I could tell Cheshire was barely containing laughter, so I bit his leg.

"Ow, fuck." He yelped, nearly kicking me.

I smirked, as Caterpillar asked, "What the fuck is wrong with you?"

"A little bug just bit me." Ches said, glaring down at me.

"Alice is injured, she doesn't need to put herself in danger by further exposing herself to the Red Party. Plus, she has exactly zero self-control." Caterpillar said, turning out of the parking lot.

"You're lucky she isn't here to hear you say that." Cheshire said, glancing down at me. March snorted, and I noticed Hatter give him a weird look, but he didn't notice me.

"She's probably smarter and more powerful than all four of us put together. As much as we may all hate it, she's the leader of the Resistance. Leaving her out of these types of things is a mistake." Hatter said, causing my heart to flutter slightly.

"Before she is the Resistance leader, she is our girlfriend. The fact that her safety is not your top concern, is bullshit," Caterpillar shot back.

"Don't even start with me. I care about her just as much as you do, but she's perfectly capable of protecting herself... and you if I remember correctly. Don't ask her to stand behind us. Alice is a lioness." Hatter replied.

"Just because she is able to take care of herself, doesn't mean she should have to." Caterpillar responded, with a sigh. The car was silent for the rest of our journey, so I contemplated what Caterpillar and Hatter had said. I could tell there was some tension between Hatter and Caterpillar. While I didn't need to be protected, I did need help. After all I was only one person, I couldn't protect everyone. Maybe coming had been mistake, but I couldn't let them walk into a dangerous situation alone. As soon as the car stopped, I sat up, waiting for March to move so I could get out. "You've got to be fucking kidding me." Caterpillar ranted, grabbing me by the arm. "Tell me you didn't use magick to make me think you were with Lily and Dina."

"You want me to lie?" I asked, not backing down from his anger.

He threw his hands in the air, "I can't believe you would use magick on us. Again."

"You weren't going to listen to me, so I did what I had to do." I said.

"So, help me Creator, if you get hurt, I don't know what I'll do." He replied, popping the trunk.

"I'll be fine." I said, leaning to grab a baseball cap, tucking my hair into it.

"Do you even have any weapons on you?" Caterpillar asked.

"Do you think I'm stupid?" I shot back, pulling out the gun that had been tucked into my boot all day. I looked around us, noticing the number of people milling around, heading into the convention center. A few Suits stood outside, checking bags and looking bored. I started toward the entrance, keeping my head down, but trying to behave normally. I glanced back to find all four of my men following closely on my heels. I wanted to smile at them, but I kept my face neutral as we approached the Suit at the door.

"Go on through." A tall, red-headed suit said, waving me through the line.

I breathed a sigh of relief, but stopped when I heard him say, "I'm going to need you to step off to the side." I looked back to find Caterpillar stepping off to the side. I clenched my fists knowing I couldn't leave him out here.

"Sir," I said, tapping the Suits shoulder, "Can you please let my husband through?"

"Miss, I have to do random checks to avoid any problems. You can wait inside the door." A line of people was starting to gather by the time he had finished his sentence. I saw some anxiety creep into his face.

"I promise neither of us are packing." I giggled quietly. I placed a hand on his bicep, leaning forward so my chest was more exposed.

I saw his glance drift down. Then he quickly glanced toward Caterpillar, who was standing a couple of feet away, watching us carefully. The suit leaned closer to me, and whispered, "I think your husband might not be happy that you're flirting with me."

"Trust me, he won't care." I said, letting my voice drop an octave.

He grinned, and winked, before waving to Caterpillar. "I'll be seeing you later." He whispered, as we walked through the door.

"That was disgusting." Caterpillar said, wrapping an arm around me.

"I think I need a shower." I agreed.

He chuckled quietly, and said, "I'm sure I could help you with that when we get back."

"Saucy." I replied, surprised he was being so forward.

He leaned down and whispered in my ear, "I am not happy you are here. I'm sure I can find some way to punish you when we get back." I could feel the heat flooding my cheeks and I pressed my thighs together trying to ignore the flood of sensation in my core. Caterpillar smirked at me knowing exactly how he'd affected me.

"We need to stay in the middle of the crowd, so we don't draw attention to ourselves." Cheshire said, grabbing my hand.

I spent a moment enjoying being sandwiched between Cheshire and Caterpillar. They were opposites in so many ways. Cheshire was relaxed and loose, while Caterpillar was tense, eyes darting all over the room. Hatter grabbed the back of my shirt, stopping us from moving forward. I turned, eyebrows furrowed, confused at his sudden movement. He nodded toward the stage, where the King of Hearts had just made an entrance. The entire convention center went silent as the portly man approached the microphone. A crown sat atop his balding head; a pencil thin mustache extended over thin lips. Even from my position so far away from the stage I could see the sweat dripping down his forehead. "Hello, friends," He began. "I know this meeting was called a bit last minute. I am sure you can understand how important this announcement is. Earlier this month, the Knave of Hearts arrested a young woman who attacked him in an alley." I snorted, causing a few people to glance my way. "She, with the help of other members of the Resistance, escaped. Taking my daughter, Duchess, hostage." He paused while several members of the audience gasped. "She is recovering from the shocking experience, but she wanted me to tell you this; The Resistance cannot win. They are bloodthirsty men and women who do not care for the peace we have in our great city."

People began to clap, and we followed suit, but I muttered, "Bastard."

"Please, allow me to continue." The King of Hearts continued, before pulling a phone from his pocket. "We need your help to apprehend these people."

I realized what was happening, and turned slowly, grabbing Cheshire's wrist. "This is Alice Young," I glanced back to find that my driver's license picture was on display for the entire crowd. "And Roman Ainsworth." A photo of Caterpillar popped up next. "They are the leaders of the Resistance. If they can be caught and tried, my daughter will be safe." Using Duchess's safety to manipulate all these people was genius, I had to give it up to Penthea for that move. People adored Duchess, she was a starlet in Wonderland, especially among the rich.

"Fuck." Hatter muttered, grabbing my wrist to pull me away.

"There they are!" A woman's voice shouted, and I glanced toward the noise, seeing the red tinted eyes of the Red Queen staring back at me. This had been a trap, she knew we'd hear about this, knew we couldn't resist a Red Party announcement. Someone ripped the hat off my head, letting my hair fall down shoulders. The people around us started to form a circle, forcing us to stop our advance. I felt hands wrap into my hair, and I was yanked back, falling into the screaming crowd. Someone spit in my face, as I hit the ground, and I felt boots kick me in the ribs and back.

"Bitch." Someone screamed.

"Down with the Resistance." Someone else cried.

I placed my hands flat on the ground, letting electricity skate across the sleek surface. The mob around me went down, and I stood, eyes roaming the crowd. I immediately found Caterpillar who was throwing punches and screaming my name. "Over here." I yelled, kneeing a man who came running toward me. I hesitated to pull any weapons out. These people were being manipulated by my aunt and her husband; they didn't deserve to die. That changed when a woman holding a crowbar came at me. She slammed it across my back, causing me to stumble. Pain shot through me as old wounds opened anew. I reached for the dagger tucked into the waist of my jeans and stabbed it into her thigh. She went down yelling, and I yanked it out, running toward Cater. Arms wrapped around my center as I made my way along the wall. I turned slamming the person who attacked me into the wall, dagger to their throat.

"Al, it's me." Cheshire breathed, glancing down.

"Sorry, sorry." I said, dropping my arms. I dropped my head against his chest, feeling dizzy. Pressure in my head caused lights to dance in front of my eyes. I stared at Cheshire, trying desperately not to lose consciousness from the pain in my back. We stood in silence for several moments, Cheshire's magick protecting us. I was surprised by how strong he was getting to be able to cloak us both.

"Sinclair Malone." he said, quietly.

"Huh?"

"That's my real name." Ches said, watching my face carefully. "I would prefer you didn't call me by it... I think my parents must have hated me." He added, a slight blush crawling up his cheeks.

"I like it." I said, smiling.

"Are you okay?" he asked, changing the subject.

I watched the mayhem around us. "Not really. We have to get out of here." I said, turning to look for Hatter, March, and Caterpillar.

"Alice, your shirt. It's soaked." Ches said, laying his fingers against it.

I hissed in pain, before saying, "Go get the car." I took off into the crowd, searching for March and Hatter. I dodged around people who were fighting, a couple of people tried to attack me, but I just shocked them. I found Hatter and March surrounded by several large men.

"Excuse me, sir." I said, tapping one of them on the shoulder. When he turned, I reared my fist back, and slammed it into his face. I shook my hand, knowing that my knuckles were going to be bruised. Two men came at me, but I danced away from them, careful to keep my back toward Hatter and March.

"Come quietly, little girl, and we won't have to hurt you." One said, his bald head shining under the harsh lighting.

"Ha-ha, no." I deadpanned. I held my hands out, letting electricity crackle between my fingers as the men came toward me.

One wrapped a hand around my forearm, but immediately dropped to the ground. I looked up and noticed a couple of men back away from us. I turned to Hatter and March and furrowed my eyebrows at their shocked looks. "Ali, you're glowing again. I thought that only happened during..." Hatter trailed off staring at me.

"It can happen, not often, but Lily was glowing when she saved me so I guess it can happen any time." I replied, quickly. I walked to March and grabbed the bottom of his hoodie pulling it up. He took it off and helped me pull it over my head.

"Thanks." I muttered, surprised by how warm it was, "Get to the car." Neither of them argued as I watched them run toward the exit. I turned searching for Caterpillar, but my vision was soon blocked by two women jogging toward me.

"Did you really take Duchess hostage?" One asked, a hand on her hip.

"Barely." I responded, keeping my magick coursing along my body.

"She's a friend of ours, but what her father said isn't true." The other one said, watching me closely.

"I know. If you aren't going to try and attack me, I really have other things to do." I said, trying to see past them.

"Be careful, Alice. I think you may have more enemies than you know." I ignored their final comment, and skirted around them, praying that Caterpillar was okay.

"Over here, Princess." He shouted. I ran to him, ignoring the way my vision blurred.

"Are you okay?" He asked, putting his hands on either side of my face.

"I'm fine. Careful though, I might begin to think you care." I said, laughing weakly. He rolled his eyes, and then tensed, causing me to look behind him. The King of Hearts, and a large group of people were approaching. I moved so that I was standing next to Caterpillar, wondering if I could throw an illusion of us both.

"Cuff them." The King of Hearts said, pointing toward us.

"Are you going to tell them that it's your wife that runs the show?" I asked, causing the crowd to pause and murmur, glancing at him quizzically.

"Do not let her confuse you, she's a master manipulator. Look at the way her skin is glowing, she's using magick on you." He replied, pointing to my face, which was the only part of my skin showing.

"Magick doesn't exist." A voice shouted from the back.

"Maybe she just has a condition." Someone else yelled.

"No, I do have magick." I said, stepping forward, "What he isn't telling you, his wife, who calls herself the Red Queen, also has magick." I started pulling my hoodie and shirt off, handing them to Caterpillar. "She attacked me in my home, after I stopped the Knave of Hearts from raping a young woman." I turned, allowing the crowd to see the marks covering my back. Gasps sounded, and I turned my head, noticing how several people flinched.

"The witch lies." The King said, spit flying everywhere.

"Those wounds aren't natural." A voice said.

"Why would she lie?" Someone asked.

"To save her own skin. She was with four men, maybe one of them did that to her." I growled at that comment but didn't respond.

"She's telling the truth." A young woman said. I recognized her from the alley, but I was surprised by her bold attitude. "I was the young woman the

Knave attacked. My name is Lory Newman. The Red Party does not care if we live or die, they only crave power." she explained, standing beside me.

I couldn't believe she was here, but I was glad to she had made it away from the Knave safely.

"Stop this. They are liars and murderers." The King of Hearts demanded.

Suddenly a loud crashing sound could be heard from behind the crowd, who screamed and parted in fear as Hatter's yellow Hummer, drove toward us. I grabbed Lory, stopping her from being hit by Cheshire's dangerous driving.

"Get in, bitches." Ches yelled over the crowd.

"Would you like to join us?" I asked, glancing at Lory. She nodded, although I could tell she was scared.

"Let's go." Caterpillar said, and I climbed into the backseat, pulling Lory along with me.

"Step on the gas, Cat." I said, watching as the crowd reassembled.

"At least I finally understand why we don't let Cheshire drive." I said, holding my stomach as soon as we parked outside Rab's house. Rab and Mom came rushing out of the house, and toward us.

"Are you okay?"

"What the hell happened?"

"Alice, you're pale."

I held up a hand to stop them. "The Caucus was a meeting to reveal mine and Caterpillar's identity and send the citizens of Wonderland on a witch hunt. Which worked when the Red Queen spotted us. It was a trap. Everyone but me is mostly unscathed." I explained, quickly gripping March's arm to keep myself standing.

"Oh fuck." Mom whispered, surprising me. I don't think I'd ever heard her curse before.

"Let's get all of you inside." Rab said, glancing toward our newest addition.

"Lory, meet my mother, Alcinda, also known as the White Queen, and Caterpillar's Uncle, White Rabbit." I mumbled right before I blacked out.

Chapter 20

September 1st, 2157

I had never been more thankful for my mother's minor healing magick than I was after waking up after the incident at the Caucus. It still took a couple of days, before I started to feel better. Mary Anne dressed the deeper wounds on my back so I wouldn't reopen them and restricted my activity. It was frustrating to be stuck in bed, but I wanted to heal fully. No one was willing for me to continue to take unnecessary risks, and I knew they were right. I listened as my mother, Rab, and Caterpillar discussed our options, I sat curled into Hatter's side, taking in the scene before me.

"How exactly do you plan to defeat the Red Queen?" Lory asked, hands on her hips. She had an attitude that occasionally irked me, but I chose to ignore it since she was only a teenager. She sort of reminded me of myself at that age. I still hadn't learned all of her story. I knew she was an orphan who'd been working at the bistro when the Knave grabbed her.

"I have no idea, but it has to be a one-on-one battle, between me and her." I declared. The room fell into chaos for several minutes, my mother was the only silent party, we made eye contact, and formed an unspoken understanding. I stood up, drawing everyone's attention, "I will fight the Red Queen. I will do it alone, because the rest of you, and anyone else we can gather to our side will be busy ending the Red Party's reign. My magick is the strongest, because I am trained, and I have a three-part gift. This is not a discussion." I could see Caterpillar's jaw clench at my words, but he couldn't argue with me. Even my mother knew ultimately the fight for Wonderland was between me and Penthea. Mom hadn't said anything specific, but I had a feeling she'd always known this was the case. Everyone sat in silence, varying degrees of worry and dread marking the faces of the people who had cared for me.

"Alice, you are still not healed enough for a confrontation with this woman," Mary Anne spoke up.

"No, I'm not. We need time to plan and train," I conceded. I had come to respect Mary Anne more than almost anyone sitting around the large dining room table. She was a quiet, reassuring presence, ensuring everyone was cared for. However, when she felt strongly about a subject, she didn't hesitate to speak her mind. The love that Rab showed her was something I could only hope the guys and I would grow into. It was clear they had been through hell together. Tears pricked my eyes when I looked at my mother. I knew she had to think of my father any time she watched the two of them together.

"I know some people who might be able to h-help." March said, pulling my eyes to him. He was sprawled across an armchair fidgeting with the strings of his hoodie.

"Get them on board. We need as many people as we can get. Cheshire, I want you to see if you can get ears at their base. I want to know their plans, so we don't have a repeat of the caucus." I commanded.

"I'll set up a meeting." March said, leaving the room.

"The problem with trying to get ears on the Red Queen is that no one believes she's the mastermind. The King of Hearts does nothing, from what I've been able to tell. He's exactly what we thought; a figurehead with no clue about the actual plan." Ches explained.

"Do what you can." I replied, "If you can't get anything, we can work around it."

"We have a meeting with the Tweedles in two hours." March announced, walking back into the room.

"Then I think we need to get ready." I said.

"They only w-want to meet with me and you." He informed me.

Hatter was the first to protest. "I'm not trying to an asshole, but the last time we sent the two of you alone somewhere Alice ended up arrested."

"I agree, you guys go, we all go," Caterpillar spoke next.

"If we want their help, the two of us g-go alone," March crossed his arms, standing his ground.

I'd noticed a very subtle change in March's behavior, he was slowly becoming more confident. My guess was that he was working with my mother, but neither of them had spoken about it, and I chose to keep my mouth closed. I was happy for him, he deserved to have the same quiet confidence that Hatter and Caterpillar exuded. "If March says we need to go alone, then we will." I held my hand up as everyone began to protest, "Do you really think risking allies is a good idea right now?" Silence answered my question, and I knew I had won the argument. "How long do we have before the meeting?" I asked.

"One hour," March responded.

"I'll be ready in ten," I walked out of the room, unsure what I needed to prepare for.

"Are you sure about this, March?" I asked, glancing around the darkened building. We had elected to take the motorcycle as it was faster and less recognizable than the Hummer or Rab's truck. The ride had given me plenty of time to think through every possible scenario we were walking into. Nothing could have prepared me for the purple and yellow fading paint of the large factory we had walked into.

"They're a b-bit... weird." He replied, reaching to tangle our fingers together.

"That's not very nice, Maxie." A sing-song voice said, causing the hairs on the back of my neck to stand on end. I could see the cringe on March's face at his mother's nickname for him but didn't have time to comment on it before another voice said. "We've known you almost as long as Hayden, and you would call us weird?"

"Well, I think Hayden is a different case." The sing-song voice said, with a giggle.

"A very different case, indeed." The other voice echoed, before adding. "I wonder how he would feel about our dear Maxton holding hands with the Resistance's leader?"

I rolled my eyes, and said, "Cut the shit. Do you want to help us put an end to the Red Party?"

"I like her." The first voice said, before lights flooded the warehouse. "Directly to the point."

"It's nice to finally meet you, Alice Young." A small red headed woman, said, approaching.

"I'm Idalia, and this is my sister, Ilaria." A second, small red head introduced, before adding. "Though I wonder if you would prefer our monikers? Tweedledee." She introduced, "And Tweedledum." She finished, motioning to her twin.

"I don't care for code names." I declared.

"Interesting." Idalia said, inspecting me carefully. I found that I was on edge as the two women watched me, but I didn't move an inch, hoping there was some point to this charade.

"Your mother is the White Queen." One said, in the midst of them walking around me, I had forgotten which one was which.

I nodded in response, trying to identify the differences between the women. I looked to March wondering if he'd shared that information with them. He shook his head slightly, as he turned back toward them. "Ilaria is a bit shorter and has a higher pitched voice. Otherwise, we are identical." Idalia explained, reading me carefully.

"Magick user?" I asked, keeping my mind quiet.

"Psychology degree, and years of practice." She offered, and I found that I was finally at ease. Idalia and Ilaria clearly knew how to keep people on edge. It was nearly impossible to tell them apart even with the information they'd kindly provided. I could tell it was some kind of defense mechanism. I wondered about their past, but before I could begin to ask questions one spoke. "What is your plan, exactly?"

"I'll let you know when I figure that out." I replied, letting a dry laugh leave my throat.

"I like her." Ilaria said.

"We're in." Idalia declared, causing me to raise my eyebrows in surprise.

"That quickly?" I asked.

"You have the ability to the defeat the Red Party, we want that too, and we have the space you need." She replied, gesturing around the building.

"March hasn't told me about either of you. Care to share?" I asked.

"My father was Kingsley Tallant, adviser to the White King for ten years. Until he found out about the King of Hearts betrayal and was executed. After I finished my degree, I spent several years training as a commander to the Suits. Which is where Ilaria and I received our code names." Idalia explained, almost clinically.

I was shocked at the information she'd provided. Their experience within the Suits training was invaluable to the Resistance. I quickly realized that they were the best spies we could have, and March was their contact. I looked at him with a new appreciation. "I'm sorry the Red Party has caused so much pain in your lives." I said, sincerely.

"Everyone has a sob story, learning how to channel that pain is the key to success." She replied.

I nodded, understanding exactly what she meant. Pain either destroyed us or became our motivation. That was something the Red Queen didn't realize. All that she had done to me and to the citizens of Wonderland would be her downfall. If she could have let go of her grudge against my mother she could have kept everything she'd gained after taking over Wonderland. "Can you help me train the Resistance?" I asked.

"I will." Ilaria offered, stepping toward me, "But only if you teach me how to defend myself against magick."

"My mother is our magick specialist, but I will do everything I can." I offered, extending my hand.

"It's a deal. When do we start?" she asked, grinning at me.

"How does tonight sound?" I asked, returning her grin.

"Perfect." And just like that I had a plan. I had my phone in my hand in seconds, we would move tonight as soon as the sun went down.

"If we can avoid killing people, we have to try." I declared, standing at the front of Idalia and Ilaria's training room.

It had been easy to pack our things and move them into the warehouse the twins were so willing to provide for us. Cheshire had grumbled when I'd asked him to reach out to Tillie, asking her and her husbands to join us. We hadn't heard anything from them yet. I had hope we could gather more people before we moved to take down the Red Party.

"And if they're trying to kill us?" Caterpillar challenged.

"We are not the Red Party. We are not going to run around slicing throats and shooting people, because they have different beliefs than us." I argued, and then added, "However, I don't want anyone to die, so defend yourself as you must."

"What are you going to do with the members of the Red Party who do not want to convert?" Idalia asked.

I glanced at my mother, and she nodded. I took a deep breath before explaining my plan. "We have discussed exiling them." I could hear some dissent, so I held up my hand. "However, we do not want them to be able to plot against us, away from watchful eyes. So our plan is to use the mental institution as a prison, until another can be built, somewhere in the warehouse district."

"And if that doesn't work?" Griffin chimed in, surprising me.

I took a moment to look at the faces of my friends and family, trying to find the words to answer that question. A lifetime of fear and exhaustion stared back at me, I could see their desperation to be free. We had faced so much already, and I knew there was only more to come. I couldn't bear to imagine anyone losing their life to our cause, but I knew death was possible. "We will work it out, but if worse comes to worse." I paused unsure how everyone would take what I had decided. "If we cannot win this fight, we leave Wonderland, permanently." No one knew what lay beyond the city borders, but I was willing to risk what was out there if it meant we had a chance at a life free of the Red Party's tyranny.

"We aren't going to lose." Caterpillar said, coming to stand beside me. "I want my future children to grow up in a Wonderland that is no longer controlled by the Red Party." I stared at him, taking in his words, and the comfort he was offering me. I smiled, soaking in his optimism. It was a first from him, I needed to talk to him alone, to make sure we were on the same page. If I went down, he would have to save them.

"Everyone pair up, based on height and weight. For now, you'll be facing off against someone who is built similarly to you. Soon you will have to face someone is more powerful than you, so don't get used to it." I ordered Ilaria coming to join me. "We will start tallest to shortest."

I watched as Rab and Caterpillar faced off first, listening to their quiet conversation. "Be easy on an old man?" Rab said, grinning.

"Yeah, right." Cater replied, a smirk curling up his lip.

"Begin." Ilaria said, circling them.

Their fight was longer than I expected, but ultimately, Caterpillar put Rab on his back. Their skill was matched but it was clear that Rab hadn't been involved in any physical encounters in many years. "Next." I yelled, watching with interest as March and Hatter walked onto the mat.

Hatter immediately pinned March against the wall, but I could tell March allowed it to happen. I cocked my head, trying to figure out his strategy. "Hatter, you're hurting me." I heard March whisper, and I nearly laughed at the way Hatter stumbled back.

"Whoa," Ilaria said, stopping them, and waving for me to come onto the mat. "Magick?" She asked.

I nodded, raising an eyebrow at March who turned red. He'd come far if he could already manage that much control, I couldn't help but be impressed. His ability to manipulate could come in handy if he could use it against our enemies as well as he used it against Hatter. "This is your field." She said, stepping off the mat.

"I think we should make this fair." I said, pulling my hoodie off. I faced off with March, keeping my arms loose at my sides. "Mom's been helping you control it." I stated, glancing at the way our group had formed a circle around us.

He nodded, standing completely still. I knew he was waiting for me to make a move, but I knew it would only feed his magick if I did. March took a few steps toward me, keeping his arms up. I still didn't move. He tried to kick my legs out from under me, but I lunged toward him, causing him to back up. I had hoped he would lose his balance, but I had no such luck.

"You're f-fast," he said.

"Only because I'm smaller than you." I replied. I'd never considered how skilled March might be in hand-to-hand combat. My father had trained me himself, ensuring I could easily defend myself against anyone. However, I knew March needed a taste of his own medicine. I conjured an illusion, who stayed where I was, and creeped up behind him.

"Alice, you shouldn't cheat." Cheshire said.

March swung around when my double disappeared. "All's fair in love and war, Cheshire," I said, rethinking my plan. I leapt at March, but he caught me, and immediately had me pinned to the ground. His face was hovering directly in front my mine, and I noticed him glance toward my lips. I smiled, wrapping my arms around his neck, and pressing my lips against his. It took him a second to realize what was happening, but soon his arms wrapped around my back, as he bit my lip. I heard him groan and knew that I had the upper hand. In one swift motion, I flipped him on to his back, stood, and placed my bare boot on his chest. I hated that this was my first intimate moment with March, but I knew there would be plenty of opportunities in the future.

"I think I win." I said, grinning.

I saw Cheshire raise his hand, so I motioned for him to speak. "So, I should make out with the Suits? Because that's all I learned from this demonstration."

I rolled my eyes, and explained, "The point is, you have to use whatever tools are at your disposal when fighting someone. March is larger than me, and could have easily manipulated me using his magick, but I had one card he didn't." I grinned, "My womanly wiles."

"Oh my god." Lily said, before she started laughing hysterically. Everyone soon joined in, while I leaned to help March to his feet.

"Okay, well. That was...something. Next." Ilaria said.

Griffin and Dina appeared, facing off. Hatter joined me, distracting me from the fight. "Why doesn't his magick work on you?" He asked, leaning against the wall next to me.

"It does. I'm just more aware of it now," I explained. "He's getting better control over it." I added, as an afterthought.

"I know, he's been spending two hours every night with your mother." Hatter said, shocking me.

"He's dedicated." I said.

"He told me he didn't want there to be any question as to why we were friends." He said, looking at the ground.

"I think it's more than that." I said, watching March from across the room. He was standing chatting happily with Lily, who laughed at something he said.

"He's the happiest I've ever seen him." Hatter admitted.

I turned to face him fully, "You want to talk." I noted, feeling my chest tighten.

"I do." He replied.

"Ilaria should be fine without me today." I said, before making my way toward the stairs that led up into the kitchen.

Once we were settled at the table, Hatter said, "After you were arrested, March asked me if we were... going to do stuff."

"I mean, you already do stuff." I said, trying to lighten the conversation.

"That's what I said." He smiled, reaching for my hand. "I... I told him it wasn't exactly the time for that conversation, but I didn't say no." He explained, watching my face carefully.

I smiled, knowing where he was going, "Hatter, do whatever you're comfortable with. If that means dating March exclusively, I understand."

"No, that's not what I meant. It's just... damn, this shouldn't be difficult." He trailed off for a moment, staring at our interlocked hands. "I love him, Ali. I think I've loved him since we were kids. It just didn't seem right after everything he went through, but now... I don't know. We're with you, and I finally feel like it could work. This whole relationship, maybe even kids and a white picket fence someday." I opened my mouth, but he stopped me, "I know, I know it's a little too soon for all that, but I already know what I want."

"Hatter, I would love to have a whole house full of kids sometime in the future, white picket fence, and the four of you at my side. Maybe I'm crazy, falling in love with four men, during this war, but I don't care. If I die, at least I've been with the people I care the most about." I added. "Caterpillar was right that we need to work on some boundaries, but you being with March in any way you want isn't wrong."

"God, I think I'm in love with you. How is it that you can say exactly what I need to hear?" He asked.

"I'm just special that way." I laughed.

"We should probably rejoin the rest of the group." He said.

"Yeah..." I trailed off. We stared at each other, I could feel his body heat through the yoga pants and sports bar I had put on. I stepped in closer, turning my face up toward his, hoping he'd meet me halfway. Our one night together hadn't been enough.

"Jesus, you two, just go fuck already, and spare the rest of us." I jumped at Cheshire's sudden appearance.

"Can you please stop sneaking up on me." Hatter shouted, chasing Ches around the kitchen. I laughed, as Ches stuck his tongue out, and jogged back downstairs. I kissed Hatter on the cheek and followed Cheshire back into the training room. I was surprised to find Lily facing off with Idalia.

"Bring it on, pretty girl." Idalia said, hopping from foot to foot.

Lily tried to land a punch, but Idalia jumped out of the way. "Not as fast as your little sister." Idalia taunted.

"I'm going to make you suffer, little woman." Lily threatened,

"In your wildest dreams." Idalia shot back.

I watched as Idalia landed a punch on Lily, who didn't seem to notice. I furrowed my eyebrows, until I realized she was using her magick. No glow lit her skin as it had the night the Red Queen had attacked us, I wondered if she was able to control it. I filed the question away for later. Lily and Idalia fought blow for blow, dancing around each other. I was surprised to find that they were equally matched. Lily was far more talented in hand-to-hand combat than I was. I decided immediately I'd ask her to work with Idalia to train everyone. Ten more minutes passed, and they were both panting heavily.

"Give up?" Idalia asked, straightening.

"Never." Lily replied, holding her hands loosely in front of her. In a move too fast for me to follow, Lily pinned Idalia, knee to chest. I saw the look of awe on Idalia's face, and smiled, glad to see that Lily was having a good time. I watched as something passed between them, making note of the clear attraction they shared. I could only hope that Lily would find the same love I was slowly finding with the guys.

Several more hours passed, as Ilaria and I gave instructions, and gathered more information. It turned out that Mary Anne was a fantastic fighter, but she could not beat my mother, who was highly trained. I wondered momentarily who was watching Lewis, when I noticed him sitting on Rab's shoulders. I glanced around the room, looking at the tired faces of our small Resistance. The determination in their face filled my chest with more hope than I had had in longer than I wanted to admit. I no longer doubted that we had a real chance at winning the fight with the Red Queen.

"I think that's enough for tonight. We will meet each night for the next month, after which, we will re-evaluate our skills." Ilaria declared.

"Those of you with magick, will also be meeting with my mother and I, three days a week to train separately." I added, eyeing Cheshire and March specifically.

"Hydrate, get some food, and rest." Caterpillar said, dismissing everyone from the training room. Everyone filed from the room, chatting quietly. I stood in the center of the room, thinking over training plans. "Alice, you need to rest more than everyone else. You're still hurt." Caterpillar demanded, interrupting my thoughts.

"I'm okay. Mary Anne said I should be completely back to normal in a few days. Mom did enough healing after the Caucus that I feel back to normal," I tried to ease his worry. I was careful not to mention that my mother had very little magick to draw from. It was almost as if the Red Queen had drained her ability to wield her magick.

Caterpillar didn't respond as he walked to the wall, and sat, draping his muscular arms over his knees. He stared at me for a few moments, before patting the ground next to him. I sat next to him, waiting quietly for him to speak. "I can't tell anyone else this," His stormy eyes stared into mine, as if he was debating whether he could even tell me. "Have we ever told you about Hatter's dad?"

I shook my head, my eyebrows furrowing in confusion, "I assumed he had passed."

"We assume that, but the truth is, he went on an exploration mission outside of Wonderland. We held out hope for a long time that he would return with news of a safe place for us to move to."

I took a moment to process the information, not sure why he was telling me this. "After my parents died, all I wanted to do was escape this hellhole, but I knew I had a responsibility to the Resistance, with your parents and mine gone."

"I'm glad you didn't leave." I whispered, lacing my fingers through his.

"I would have never fallen in love with you if I had." His confession stirred something in me. I moved in between his legs, his arms wrapped around my back, careful not to hurt me. "If something happens to you, I don't know if I can keep doing this,"

"Nothing is going to happen to me," I said, I slid my fingers into his dark hair, pulling his mouth to mine.

"You don't know what it was like to wake up, and only remember you hovering over me, trying to protect me from her." He growled into my mouth, "Don't ever chose my life over yours again."

"I won't make that promise," I snapped back, starting to pull away.

He gripped my hips, pulling my body into his, crushing me into his chest. His breaths coming out rough. "Princess, if something happens to you, they aren't enough for me to keep doing this. You've wormed your way too deep into my heart, you'll be taking me with you if you die."

Tears pricked my eyes, as love filled my heart. "I'll fight until my very last breath, Roman."

I don't know how long we sat there, holding each other, whispering our secrets to each other.

Hours later, I crawled out of bed, careful not to wake March or Hatter. I was unable to sleep with the thoughts running through my head. Caterpillar and I had parted ways, closer than I'd ever been to anyone. I'd held so few parts of myself back as we'd talked for hours. I considered going to his room but knew that dark circles under his eyes meant he was getting far too little sleep. So instead, I crept down the stairs, listening to the quiet sounds of the warehouse. Mary Anne and Rab had returned to their home with Lewis after training was over, but everyone else had claimed a room, and fallen fast asleep.

"Here." I heard Griffin's voice, as I approached the kitchen. I paused, something stopping me from entering the room.

"Thanks, Griff. I don't know what I would do without you." Dina replied.

"I think we should leave." Griffin declared, causing my eyes to widen.

"We are not having this conversation again." She sighed.

"We aren't powerful like they are, Di." He sighed.

"I didn't betray Alice, while the Red Party held me hostage, I won't do it now." Dina demanded.

"It's not betrayal, it's the reasonable thing to do." Griff said, after a beat of silence, he added, "Have you told her yet?"

"No, and I'm not going to distract her." She replied.

"It's not a distraction, Dina!" He raised his voice, surprising me. Griffin had always been the calmest of the three of us. "This is our child's life, you're playing with."

Tears pricked my eyes, and I slammed open the kitchen door. "You're pregnant?" I asked. Dina stared at me for a moment, before nodding, "Then Griffin is right, you can't fight."

"Finally, someone is making sense." Griff said.

"I'm not leaving my home, Ali." Di demanded.

"I don't want you to." I replied, Griffin threw his hands in the air, "I want you both to go stay with Mary Anne. She will be protecting Lewis, so she won't be fighting. It would help her to have a couple more adults on hand," I said.

"But—" Dina started.

"No, keeping you and your unborn child safe, is my priority." I said.

I watched her struggle in her eyes. I knew she wanted to help; Dina had always hated the Red Party. She watched her mother kill herself trying to scrap together enough money to survive. I stared at her, willing her to make this easy and go to safety. "Okay, if you're sure you don't need us." She replied.

"I need you to keep my godchild safe." I said, smiling, and then I realized, "You were pregnant while the Red Queen had you." Tears began to fall down my face, unchecked.

"It's okay. I'm fine, my baby's fine, and you kept Griffin safe," she said, wrapping her arms around me.

"Speaking of which. How long have you two been together?" I asked, wiping away tears.

"A few months, it was just casual at first," She admitted.

"I can't believe you didn't tell me." I said, pouting. I wanted to be hurt by the secret, but I had plenty of my own. If the two of them were happy then that was the only thing that truly mattered to me.

"I was going to." She. said, sweeping her straight black hair away from her face.

"So, what are you naming my goddaughter." I asked, trying to keep the mood light.

"It could be a boy." Griffin said, wrapping an arm around her shoulders.

I hadn't ever considered it, but they complemented each other very well. Griffin had bright red hair, hazel eyes, and pale skin. Dina was his opposite with her beautiful dark skin, shiny, black hair falling down her back. Her onyx eyes were currently shining with unshed tears.

"It's going to be a girl." I said, shaking my head to clear my thoughts.

"It could be both, twins run in my family." Dina chimed in. I laughed as Griffin's eyes widened. "I'm kidding, honey," she said, patting his cheek. I had always known that Dina had a crush on Griffin, finally seeing them together was amazing. My best friends deserved the very best. I would do everything in my power to help them bring their child into a safe world.

"Ali, come b-back to bed." March said, appearing in the doorway. I watched as he rubbed a hand across his naked chest but didn't move.

"Dina's pregnant." I exclaimed, bouncing in my seat.

"Congratulations." He smiled, before walking over to me. "Bed." He said, trying to tug me out of my seat.

"Okay, okay." I said, waving to Dina and Griffin.

I let March pull me back to our room, when he opened the door, I was surprised to find Hatter sitting up in bed. "Why's everyone up?" Hatter asked, rubbing sleep from his eyes.

"Dina's pr-pregnant." March replied, climbing back into bed.

"Oh, that's.... not really great cause of the Red Party and all." Hatter said, glancing my way.

"I'm sending her and Griffin to stay with Mary Anne, Rab, and Lewis." I said, climbing in between them.

"That is for the b-best," March said as we settled back into bed.

"Is Griffin the dad?" Hatter asked, brushing fingers through my hair.

I nodded, and then closed my eyes, finally tired. "G'Night, Ali." March whispered, wrapping an arm around my middle.

I enjoyed the warmth of the men wrapped around me. I allowed myself to slowly drift to sleep. Nothing mattered so long as at the end of the day I ended up sandwiched between them.

Chapter 21

September 30th, 2157

A month passed quickly, I'd barely seen Caterpillar and Cheshire. Hatter, March, and I crawled into bed together at night completely exhausted from training and planning. Tillie and her husbands had joined us at the warehouse, helping where they could. The Resistance was now seventeen people strong. I was careful not to cringe when we were all gathered. Idalia had confirmed that the Suits were well over two hundred strong. We had managed a few decent ideas for taking the Red Queen out, but gaining full control of the city was still an issue. Today, we were back in the training room, waiting for the rest of our group to join us. Ilaria and I had grown close over the last few weeks. Since we were forced to work closely, doing our best to prepare everyone to fight for their lives. She and I had spent hours in the training room after everyone else was sleeping training with daggers. I hadn't met anyone else who preferred blades over guns. "Do you think they're ready?" she asked, flipping a dagger between her fingers.

"As any of us will ever be." I said, taking aim. I cheered when my knife sank into the center of the target.

"Your aim has seriously improved." She offered, as she aimed at the same target.

"Thanks to your help." I said, watching as her knife landed directly above mine.

"We're ready." Lory said, interrupting Ilaria and I. I turned, looking over Lory, Rab, Griffin, and Dina. Di was sitting in a chair, playing with her phone, looking a bit green from all the throwing up she'd been doing. She had spent most of her time at Rab's house but was here to watch training today. Mary Anne had given Dina a few self-defense tips, but I knew it wouldn't be enough if she was actually attacked.

"Lory face off with Rab." I said, moving off the mat.

"Alice, I'm not sure she's ready." Ilaria whispered into my ear, as we watched Lory and Rab circle each other.

"If she isn't now, she never will be." I replied.

We watched in rapt silence, as Rab pinned Lory to the mat. She hooked a leg around his thigh, helping her flip him onto his back, as she stood in a single fluid motion. Griffin let out cheer. "You're getting better." Rab said, watching her.

"I know." She said, and I rolled my eyes.

I laughed when Rab lunged toward Lory, and she rolled between his legs. He was grinning as he turned to her, catching her in a headlock. She struggled for a moment before becoming completely still, lifting her legs off the ground, making Rab take on her full weight. I heard him grunt, and watched as he dropped her. "Time." Rab said, rubbing his back.

"Tired you out old man?" Lory asked, hands on her hips. Rab didn't respond, instead he made his way off the mat, nodding to me as he went to sit next to Dina. Ilaria took over, leading Lory through a few more exercises.

I heard footsteps coming down the stairs and turned to meet Hatter. "How is everything going?" I asked, meeting him halfway.

"I think we need your help. Cheshire has been staring at the computer screen for days, nothing I've done so far has convinced him to get up." He explained, wrapping his arms around me.

I silently cursed myself for not noticing his absence sooner. I had been neglecting all of my men even more over the last few days, focused on getting everyone prepared to fight. I sighed, and looked to Ilaria, "Go deal with your boy drama, I can get everyone started." She said, a knee to Lory's stomach.

Hatter started to follow me, but I said, "Stay here, you need to be here for training." He nodded, but I could see his hesitation. Hatter was definitely well versed in hand-to-hand combat, but I knew I needed to handle Cheshire alone.

I jogged up the stairs, greeting Idalia and Lily on the way. They were both dressed in work out gear, holding green smoothies, and chatting away. I smiled, glad that Lily had found a friend. They'd become very close since we'd started training. I was fairly certain I'd seen Lily sneaking out of Idalia's room one night, but so far, I had chosen not to pry.

When I finally made it to Cheshire's room, I ran directly into Caterpillar who was leaving. "I've never seen him this bad before." He said, adding, "I hope he'll listen to you."

"Me too." I muttered, opening the door. I walked into the room, and squinted, because it was so dark. I could only see Cheshire because the computer screen lit up his face. "Ches, you doing okay, babe? Hatter and Caterpillar are worried about you."

"I'm fine." He snapped, although it sounded strained.

I found the light switch, and flipped it, allowing light to flood the room. He groaned, covering his eyes, "Turn it off."

"No, you don't need to sit around in the dark, staring at the computer. Nothing has changed, and if it does, I'm sure you will get a notification." I said, walking over to him. "Come on, go take a shower, and then I'll make you a sandwich."

"I'm busy, Al. You wanted me to monitor the Red Queen, that's what I'm doing." He said.

"You've been stressing about this for a week, take a break. For me?" I asked, standing behind him. I leaned down and ran my hands over his chest. "Shower, food, sleep." I said, trying to tempt him.

"Will you stay with me?" he asked, holding my forearms.

"Sure." I said, reaching to hit the power button on the computer. I noticed him twitch as I did it, but he didn't try to stop me. I pulled him up and started dragging him toward the shower.

He was silent as I turned the water on, but when I turned to leave the room, he asked, "Join me?" I didn't respond, simply pulling my shirt and sports bra off, before kicking my leggings off. He looked me up and down for a minute, before ripping his clothes off. I watched in rapt attention as his naked form climbed into the shower, my mouth a bit dry. "You coming?" he asked, a small smile on his face.

"I wouldn't miss this for the world." I said, stepping in after him.

As soon as the hot water hit me, I groaned, relaxing. Cheshire wrapped his wet arms, around me, letting his head fall to my collar bone. I tangled my fingers into his wet hair, surprised that none of the dye was washing out. "I'm so tired, Al." He whispered.

"I know, Ches, I'm sorry. I shouldn't have expected you to do all of the surveillance on your own." I replied, grabbing my shampoo. "Wash my hair?" I asked, turning my back to him.

He ran his fingers over the scars that littered my back now, and said, "I should have helped you." The scars had faded a lot in the last month, but they were still a bright pink, standing out against my skin. Last time Mary Anne looked at them she said some of them would disappear in the next few months.

I was suddenly a bit self-conscious, but said, "You're helping me now." He didn't respond, simply massaging the lavender scented shampoo into my hair. Once he was finished, he pulled me under the stream of hot water, letting the soap rinse out.

"God, I want you." He said, running his hands down my sides.

"You've got me." I said, wrapping my arms around his neck.

His lips crashed into mine hungrily, hands roving over my wet body, finally settling on my breasts. I moaned into his mouth as he gently tugged on my nipple. Suddenly he pulled away, panting, a feral grin painted on his face. "I've been wanting to do this for months." he said, just before sinking to his knees. He lifted one of my legs over his shoulders as he hungrily took me into his mouth.

I moaned, grinding my hips, I could feel his tongue ring lap against my clit, driving me closer and closer to orgasm. "Chesss," I hissed.

"Cum for me Al," His husky voice pushed me over the edge. My chest heaved, and my legs shook, he took on all of my weight as the waves of pleasure rolled through my core. He stood, "I always knew you would taste like candy," I blushed at the comment.

"It's my turn," I said.

I woke up curled around Cheshire who snored quietly. I glanced down at my arm to see if I was still glowing, luckily it had mostly faded. I leaned over his sleeping form, and grabbed my phone to see what time it was. I cursed quietly when I realized I had completely missed training. I climbed out of bed, keeping the sheet wrapped around my naked body, and left the room. "Walk of shame?" Caterpillar's deep voice said, causing me to turn red.

"Shame would indicate I was doing something wrong." I shot back, making my way to my room.

"You missed training." He replied.

"I know." I said, opening the door to my room. Caterpillar and I still hadn't slept together, and I'd started to feel a bit insecure about his rejection. I knew I didn't have to time to focus on my feelings, but anytime we were alone together my mind raced with possibilities.

"Is he doing better?" Caterpillar asked, as I dropped the sheet to pull on jeans and a hoodie.

"Sleeping like a baby." I replied, turning around.

"Do you want to go somewhere with me?" he asked.

"Like where?" I asked, raising my eyebrows.

"It's a surprise," he replied, smirking.

"Is this where you reveal to me that you like to cut people's faces off?" I deadpanned.

"Smart ass." Cater said, rolling his eyes. "Let's go." I tucked my phone and wallet into my pockets and followed him out of the warehouse. He opened the Hummer door for me, and I said, "I've always wanted to ask this, but why yellow?"

"Hatter picked the color; he claimed it was reverse psychology. The more obvious you are, the less likely people will pay attention. Personally, I thought that was a load of bullshit, but I let him keep the yellow." He explained, pulling out of the warehouse. "Actually, Hatter does pretty much anything he wants, a bit like someone else I know."

I grinned, "Well at least you know you have to give us our way."

"Put this on." He said, handing me a blindfold.

"Kinky." I said but didn't argue. I didn't even have to see him to know he was rolling his eyes. "Where are we going?" I asked.

"Why would I tell you after I had you cover your eyes?" He shot back.

We fell into a comfortable silence for the rest of the drive. I always felt safe with Caterpillar now, instinctually I knew he wouldn't let anything happen to me. When the car stopped, I reached for the blindfold, but he stopped me. "Sit right here for just a minute, I'll be right back."

I sighed, impatiently, but did as he asked. Several minutes passed before my car door opened, and he helped me down.

"Okay you can open your eyes now." Cater said, I gently pulled the blindfold off, and gasped.

We were in the same field of yellow flowers that I had come to right after Lily and Dina had been taken. The same one where we had our fight, and I left. He had laid out a large red and white blanket, and a picnic basket. The headlights of the Hummer were on so we could see in the dark. "Roman...thank you so much." I said, leaping into his arms.

"I knew this place had to mean a lot to you if you come here when you need to think. I thought I would make some happy memories here too." He said, holding me, so my feet dangled off the ground.

"I love it." I squealed, dropping back to the ground, and sitting down on the blanket.

Caterpillar took a seat next to me, and handed me a wine glass, before carefully pouring a sparkling liquid into it. I took a sip, surprised at the sweetness that met my tongue, a gentle warmth spreading in my chest. "I realized today that we've never even been on a date. In fact, I don't think you've gone a date with any of us, so I decided tonight was as good a night as any." He said, and I could tell he was nervous.

"I love it." I said, leaning my head against his shoulder. We had spent so much time focused on taking down the Red Party. We didn't have a lot of time for dating, even though I felt completely at peace with that I knew it bothered Caterpillar most of all.

My stomach growled, causing both of us to laugh. "I guess I better feed you." Caterpillar said, pulling out some fancy cheese and grapes. We ate in comfortable silence, and I enjoyed the quiet peace of the night so far away from the city. The stars twinkled above us, and I laid back on the blanket, my head in Cater's lap.

"I would love to build a house, right in the middle of this field, but that would ruin the view." I said.

"Maybe a small cabin, so we could visit sometimes, but not disrupt nature too much." He offered.

"I like that idea." I whispered, locking eyes with him.

He leaned closer to me, my breath hitching as he pressed his lips to mine, his hand coming to rest against my cheek. I sat up quickly when he pulled away, not second guessing myself. I pulled my hoodie over my head, leaving myself bare as I crawled further into his lap. He was too still, and I nearly begged, "Please touch me,"

As if the words set him on fire, he had me on my back, lips on my neck, hands exploring my body. He didn't hesitate to unbutton my jeans but paused before pushing them down. "Princess, are you sure about this?"

"Are you?" I shot back, extremely frustrated, "You're the one who seems unsure about it."

I was shocked when Caterpillar growled and sunk his teeth into my neck. I whimpered, digging nails into his back when he gently bit my nipple, "If we do this, you belong to me. I will never let you go."

My core was flooded at his words, I whispered, "Please."

I gasped as he flipped me over, pulling me to my knees in one smooth move. His hand wrapped around my throat; he used the other to push my jeans down to my knees. "I always wonder if you have panties on, the answer is usually no, isn't it?" I couldn't answer as he slipped a finger into my wetness, "You're already ready for me, Princess. What a good girl." I felt his cock at my entrance, teasing me slowly. I tried to push back, desperately wanting him inside me, "Ah ah, you're not in control right now." My eyes watered, I'd never been more turned on in my life, when he finally entered me, I saw stars. "I want you to think about this moment every time you come here."

Without any further pretense he drilled into me, hand never leaving my throat. I could tell he was close when his other hand came forward circling my swollen clit. "You're going to cum for me, I want the Red Queen to hear it all the way from here." His pace quickened, and within moments I gave him exactly what he wanted. My throat was raw when I heard him groan, the feeling of him spilling into me nearly made me cum again. After a few moments, he pulled me down to his chest, stretching out on the blanket. We soaked in the afterglow, staring up at the stars.

"Could we just stay here forever?" I broke the silence.

"Wonderland still needs us." His voice was grim, "Alice, there's something I need to tell you," He was cut off by my phone ringing loudly.

"Fucking ruining the mood." I muttered, checking to see who was calling.

"Alice Evangeline Young, you have a few things to explain." Hatter barked, causing me to pull the phone away from my ear.

"What the hell are you talking about?" I asked, glancing at Caterpillar.

"Half the fucking boonies just showed up at our door, asking for you. Any idea why that might be?" Hatter asked, sarcasm dripping from his voice.

"Damn, they were supposed to contact me first, so this wouldn't happen. I'll be right there." I said, hanging up.

"What did you do?" Caterpillar sighed, as he packed everything back into the picnic basket.

"You remember when I left Wonderland, and you came to 'rescue' me from the boondocks?" I asked, rubbing the back of my neck, nervously.

"Yes." He said, raising an eyebrow.

"Well, I might have misled you as to what I was doing during that week." I said, taking the keys from his hand.

"Okay, why did you do that?" he asked, his tone carefully neutral.

"Because, after I left, I realized I needed more people on our side. So I went to the boondocks, and started spreading the word that I was the leader of the Resistance. That I was going to take down the Red Party." I explained, wincing that the angry look on his face.

"Why didn't you tell me?" He asked, as I started the car.

"I needed to keep everything quiet. I didn't know if the warehouse could be bugged, or what. I did know that if I was the only one who knew exactly how much help we had, I could keep it quiet." I replied, praying that he would understand.

He sighed, "I can't even be angry, I would have done the same thing."

"I'm sorry to keep another secret, but this was important. The fact they've shown up now, means that Sammy and Patrick are ready." I said.

"Ready for what?" He asked.

"To put an end to the Red Party for good." I replied.

The warehouse was in total chaos when Caterpillar opened the door. Hatter was standing on the coffee table, trying to talk over the loud chatter of voices. March was sitting on the couch between a man and woman who looked to be flirting with him. Cheshire was arguing with Tillie. They seemed to argue a lot, I still hadn't had a chance to ask why they seemed to hate each other. I certainly didn't have time to now. I marched over to Hatter, who was getting increasingly frustrated, as people continued to talk over him. I put my fingers in my mouth and let out a loud whistle causing everyone to look my way. "If everyone will please take a seat and be quiet for a moment I think I have some explaining to do." Everyone shuffled around, but soon fell quiet, expectant eyes fell on me. I took a deep breath, and began to explain, "I left the city, after having a fight with....my boyfriends. I was feeling defeated; I couldn't figure out how was I supposed to end the Red Party and save my best friend and my sister. After all, I'm only one woman. So, I made my way to the boonies, with no plan and no hope." I locked eyes with Lily who was standing stoically in the corner. She inclined her head, giving me the confidence, I needed to continue. I had kept this secret for weeks. I couldn't be certain that Sammy would be able to convince people to try to take the Red Party down. People started to talk again, and I waited for several seconds, hands on my hips, for the noise to die down. "Any way, as I was riding down the road, my bike ran out of gas. Luckily a nice old man stopped to help me," I glanced toward Sammy who looked solemn. "He offered me a place to stay, and a shoulder to cry on." I smiled at the memories, and then added, "And lots of vodka."

Everyone laughed. "I woke up the next day with a hangover and a plan. I can't defeat the Red Party on my own, but I knew I wasn't the only one who wanted to see them gone. Sammy, Tillie, and I devised a plan," I glanced toward Tillie, who grinned, she had been the only person in on my plan. "We gathered people to the Resistance's aid, and I left her and her husbands in charge of training. The Suits only visit the boondocks once a week, so everyone there was safe from scrutiny. They could move through Wonderland in silence because no one wants to acknowledge anyone poor or different." I finished, stepping down from the table, with Hatter's help.

"I'm honestly ashamed I didn't think of it first." Caterpillar said, watching me with a look of awe.

"We don't have enough room to accommodate everyone." Idalia said, glancing around the room.

"We don't need places to sleep, we only came because it's time to topple the cards." Sammy said, coming to stand next to me.

I took a moment to appreciate the changes he had made. His long gray hair was tied back at the nape, he had shaved his beard into a stylish shape, and he was obviously sober. He looked twenty years younger than the first time I had met him. A meaningful purpose could change anyone. "What did you find out?" I asked.

"Patrick can share." Sammy said, waving over his son. The young man couldn't be a day over sixteen, he had short brown hair, and shared his father's jovial look.

"The Red Queen rarely leaves their base, and security is tight, except for Sunday's. For some reason, every Sunday at exactly three o'clock, most of the Suits are sent home." Pat explained. "I don't know much about the blueprint of the building, but I know we have to end this on a Sunday."

"I have blueprints." Ches said, speaking up for the first time. "I'd noticed the Suits movements were different on Sunday, but I didn't know that." He gave me a look that I didn't have time to decipher, before walking toward Patrick. I thought a saw a hint of shame on his face, and I knew I'd have to talk to him soon.

"You two get together, figure out where we need people. Share your plans with Mom and Caterpillar. Ilaria, I want you to get with Tillie. Put everyone into groups based on their strengths and weaknesses." I commanded, everyone nodded breaking off to begin their tasks.

"What is your plan?" Idalia asked, once everyone else had cleared out.

"While everyone else puts an end to the Red Party, I'm going to confront my aunt." I said, grimly.

"Are you sure you're ready?" She asked, crossing her arms.

"It isn't a matter of preparedness. I either win, or we all die." I said, leaving the room.

Chapter 22

October 2nd, 2157

Only a couple days had passed, but Sammy's late-night appearance had stopped any sleep I might have gotten. Organizing over a hundred people had been a far larger task than I'd realized. I stared into the cup of tea I'd made myself hoping it would give me enough energy to make it through the rest of my day. "It's okay to rest," My mother's voice penetrated my foggy thoughts. "In fact, it's even more necessary now than it has been before.

"I know, I just...." I trailed off, studying her. She had put some weight back on, her skin taking on a healthier color, some of the stress lines in her face had lightened. She had her curly golden hair pulled out of her face and was still dressed in training clothes.

"All the problems will still be here when you wake up,"

I nodded before changing the subject, "How are March and Cheshire doing in training?"

She sighed, "March is gaining control, but I am worried for his mental well-being. His power has done a lot to make coping with his trauma easier, having to face it without the magick could..." She gasped. "Alice, what if March and Penthea have similar gifts?"

My eyes widened, "You think that she was traumatized so her magick developed as a coping mechanism?"

"It would make sense, her father died shortly after my mother left him."
I was surprised at the information but didn't dig any deeper. "Does that
change your strategy?"

"I don't know. Even if her magick manifested because of trauma, it isn't
an excuse for the evil she's done." I stared down at my nails, unable to meet
her eyes.

"I agree," I could see the sadness in her eyes, "I trust you will make the
right decision."

"I hope so," I said as she left the room. I knew she had to think through
what she'd just discovered. I couldn't stop my worry for March. I knew he
could never turn into my aunt, but dealing with the amount of trauma he's
been through wouldn't be easy. I left the kitchen, abandoning my cup of
tea, as I wandered toward the training room. Tillie and Ilaria were running
drills, ensuring they were on the same page as they worked with the entire
Resistance. Tillie made Ilaria seem large, though she only stood at maybe
five foot three. It was shocking what Tillie was capable of. I watched in awe
as she flipped the bigger woman over her shoulder, ending the move with
Ilaria's stomach on the ground and her hands behind her back. I clapped,
drawing their attention toward me.

"Alice, I assumed you'd be sleeping," Tillie said with a smile.

"I probably should be, but here I am," I sat down, doing a few stretches
to take my racing mind off everything we needed to do.

They both watched me for a moment, before speaking quietly. Ilaria
quickly departed, and Tillie came to sit next to me mirroring my exercises.
"Ali, we've noticed you're on edge." She chewed her bottom lip before
continuing. "It's completely understandable, but I'm worried for you.
You're not getting enough sleep; you don't need to shoulder the burden
alone. The rest of us have been a part of the Resistance a long time, we can
handle a lot of this."

I sat absorbing her words, I knew she was right. I closed my eyes,
desperately wanting to go back to the field with Caterpillar. It was the first

time in what felt like forever that I'd had just a little peace, and I hadn't been able to fully enjoy it. I chose my next words carefully, "I appreciate you guys being supportive. I will get some rest; I just need some time to process everything that's happened. Honestly since July."

"There's nothing wrong with needing to process. I just want you to know you aren't alone," She pulled me into hug, though the position was awkward I really appreciated it.

"What happened between you and Cheshire?" I blurted out. I couldn't contain my curiosity any longer.

Tillie turned bright red, "I-I, no one has ever asked." She sputtered. "We used to date." I kept my face blank; I didn't want her to stop speaking, "It was a long time ago, I was freshly eighteen. We met working on a mission together. The King of Hearts disappeared for a couple of weeks, even our people closest to him had no idea where he'd gone."

"Did you ever find out?" I interrupted her, information could be useful to me.

"No, we didn't, it's still a mystery to this day. Wonderland is a big city, a certain amount of anonymity is possible, but it was still very strange." She explained, "Anyway, we grew close in those months. I asked him out, we dated for about six months before it became obvious, we weren't well matched."

"In what way?" I asked. I probably shouldn't have pushed her, but I wanted the whole story.

If it was possible, she turned redder, "Alice... Okay fine, he was great in bed, but we couldn't get along unless we were fucking. We argued as much while we were dating as we do now. We just aren't compatible. I think he's an arrogant asshole." I couldn't contain my laughter, "No offense, you seem wonderful for him."

"None taken, thank you for telling me,"

"I'm glad for the experience, if I hadn't worked with Cheshire on that mission. I would never have met Jackson and Cahir," she said, the love she had for her husbands shown in her eyes.

We continued to chat for a while before I started to fall asleep sitting up and Tillie insisted, I needed to lay down. I trudged toward my bedroom. There was still sunlight streaming through the window as I entered, but I threw myself into bed. I tossed and turned for a while unable to settle my body or mind. My thoughts swirled, wondering what would happen if I couldn't take down my aunt. I had to protect my family, but I couldn't be certain I was stronger than her.

I heard the door open; I sat up watching as Hatter made his way toward me. Dark circles under his bright green eyes reflected my own exhaustion. "Tillie said you'd come up here to sleep, so I thought I'd join you," He smiled though it didn't reach his eyes.

I patted the bed beside me, "You look as exhausted as I feel."

"Gee thanks sweetheart." He responded. "I thought I was regaining my ego after the beatdown Caterpillar gave me yesterday."

"Well, we can't let that happen," Once Hatter had settled, I curled against him, listening to the beat of his heart. Slowly the sound of his heart and the warmth he radiated lulled me into a dreamless sleep.

October 3rd, 2157

I sat crossed- legged in my bed looking over the plans to attack the Red Party's base. Some part of me felt like this was too fast. Even with another month of planning and training we couldn't be certain we'd accounted for every factor. The warehouse was quiet for the first time in a few days. Tillie and Ilaria had been running all sorts of training exercises, coordinating who would work together. I had stepped back, sleeping as much as I could stand to. I needed to be at full power, the Red Queen was stronger than I was, more practiced in her abilities. The confidence I had faded as the time to act grew closer. My back tingled, a physical reminder of how she had already defeated me before.

"You should take a break," Hatter said, leaning on the door frame, watching me. His shoulder length hair was pulled back in a bun at the crown of his head. Black sweatpants were slung low on his waist, the grey tank he wore for training hiked up just enough to show the trail of hair leading below his waistline.

"Hypocrite," I shot back, "When have you taken a break lately?"

"I will if you will. March has been begging to get out of the warehouse all day." He said, offering me his hand.

I glanced down at the plans on my lap, choosing to push them away to grab his hand. It took less than twenty minutes before we had gathered March and Cheshire, waiting for Caterpillar to join us outside. I chose to stay in the comfortable workout clothes I was wearing. Though I regretted the decision when I saw that Cheshire was wearing the deep purple shirt, I had convinced him to get. It wasn't his usual style, he had paired it nicely with simple light washed jeans, keep the button up casual. "I should change," I said, turning back toward my room.

"Don't, you look p-perfect the way you are," March spoke up, a grin on his face.

I hesitated, but nodded, wrapping an arm around his waist, waiting for Caterpillar to show up. "We're borrowing Rab's truck," Caterpillar said, as he entered the room. He tossed Hatter the keys, before leading us to the back door of the warehouse. A couple unfamiliar faces were milling around, one woman looked at us in awe. I hadn't had much time to introduce myself to everyone Sammy had brought with him, and a shred of guilt ate at me. In just a few days some of these people could be dead, and I hadn't taken the time to learn all their names.

"Where are we going anyway? We can't go into the city." Cheshire asked, as we piled into the truck.

I wondered the same thing; we couldn't risk being captured by the Red Party. "We're going to my apartment." Hatter explained, "We shouldn't be in any danger there, very few Suits spend time in the twelfth district." I looked at Caterpillar, wondering what his thoughts on Hatter's plan were. He nodded, easing some of my anxiety about going into the city. We sped away from the base as if we could outrun the fear, I knew was chasing us all. What if this was our last night together? Worry filled me, I wasn't certain our plan would work, who would I lose? But I knew we couldn't wait any longer, the people of Wonderland didn't deserve to continue suffering. I shook the thought away and focused on the present. I was cuddled between March and Cheshire. Quiet conversations took place, the ease we all had warmed my heart. Even though we hadn't known each other long, we had found quiet comfort together.

"Alice, if you could do anything after this, what would you choose?" Hatter asked, meeting my eyes in the rearview mirror.

I bit my lip, pondering my answer for a moment, "I like baking, I haven't made anything in months, but I think I'd like to go back to it. The smell of freshly baked bread is one of my favorite things."

"Why didn't you mention that sooner?" March asked, his eyes lighting up.

"It didn't seem important," I whispered, staring at our interlocked fingers. There was so much they didn't know about me, that I didn't know about them. I could only hope we would have years to learn everything about each other in peace.

As we entered the city, the streetlights flickered eerily; a chill ran down my spine. The tension in the car thickened. I could tell Caterpillar desperately wanted to object, but I don't think he had a better idea. We all needed to feel close and blow off a little steam.

"Do we have an escape plan?" Cheshire asked as Hatter parked the truck in a spot right behind the apartment building.

"It's under my dad's name, no one would make the connection," Hatter responded, a bite in his voice. I watched as March laid a careful hand on Hatter's shoulder. I wondered for a moment if they had had time to discuss their relationship more, if they had taken the next step. We were silent as we made our way up the stairs. Hatter unlocked the door quietly. I ran my hand over chipped paint, as Caterpillar and Hatter made sure the apartment was safe. "We're all clear," Hatter said, motioning us inside. Memories of the first night we met flooded me as I looked around the small place. My blue dress was draped over the back of a kitchen chair, I walked over fingering the silky fabric. "You looked so beautiful that night," Hatter said, as he wrapped his arm around my waist, resting his head on top of mine.

"It seems like it was so long ago," I breathed, turning in his arms.

"It's only been about two months."

"I know," I stepped out of his arms, "So much has changed."

"For the better," March said, as he handed me a cup full of clear liquid.

I sniffed it, quickly realizing it wasn't water. "Is this a good idea?" I quirked an eyebrow. He didn't answer as he chugged from his own cup. I shrugged and shot back the burning liquid myself. I watched as Caterpillar pulled a bottle of Scotch from a cabinet, twisting the lid off, and chugging down a quarter of the bottle in one breath.

"So, here's a question," I started, setting my empty cup down, "When are we going to quit using codenames? Shouldn't I be calling my boyfriends by their given names?"

Caterpillar grunted, "I don't care what you call me," I could see hunger in his eyes as they roved over me. He was a sight; he had unbuttoned the first few buttons of his shirt. His long legs were widely spread as he sat in a dark leather chair, the bottle of scotch still in his right hand. I walked over, and he pulled me quickly down into his lap. I took the bottle from him, taking a swig for myself.

"Hatter or Hayden works for me," Hatter spoke next.

Ches spoke next, "I prefer Cheshire," I could hear the grimace in his voice. I wasn't surprised by his response.

I glanced at March who had taken a seat next to Hatter, his feet kicked up onto the coffee table. He smiled at me, "Just please don't call me Maxie."

"Some part of me will always think of you all as your codenames, you won't be offended if I switch back and forth?" I asked.

A chorus of no's answered my question. I settled further into Caterpillar's lap, enjoying the quiet of the moment. After all of us got sufficiently drunk. Hatter found a deck of cards, and we began playing various strip games. Only Caterpillar had managed to keep his pants on, all of us in varying degrees of our underwear. Hatter, March, and I watched as Caterpillar and Cheshire faced off. "Full house, beat that buddy," Cheshire grinned as he slammed his cards on the table.

Caterpillar glared at him, but stood pushing his pants down, revealing that he did not wear anything underneath. Standing in his naked glory, I nearly drooled at the sight of his manhood, standing erect just a few inches from my face. Memories of our night in my meadow flooded me. Cheshire coughed, ending my hyper fixation on Caterpillar's sinful body.

"Well, I guess Caterpillar loses," Hatter said, yawning.

"And I win," I said, taking another shot.

"I think we should lay off the drinking, Al. It's getting late, we should get some sleep so we can head back to the base in the morning."

"It already is m-m-m," March grunted, unable to get the word out. "Morning."

"You know what I mean," Hatter said, sternly.

I stuck my tongue out at him, going for another drink. Caterpillar snatched the bottle from me, "Come with me,"

I crossed my arms over my chest, stubbornly. "I'm not done."

"Yes, you are." He growled as he pulled his clothes back on. I pouted as my men dressed and began to clean the mess we'd made. Caterpillar stood over me, arms crossed, waiting. I ignored him, staring at my nails. I didn't want this night to be over. Without a word, he picked me up and threw me over his shoulder.

"I'm coming too." Hatter said.

I smack Caterpillar's butt, trying to get him to put me down, a hard slap on my own bottom rang in my ears. "Hey!" I slurred, as he threw me down in bed.

"Hush, I'm drunk and tired," he said, crawling in beside me. Hatter stripped his shirt off and climbed in on the other side. Pressed between two warm, hard bodies the exhaustion I had been fighting started to take me.

"What 'bout March?" I asked, turning to face Hatter.

"He's with Cheshire, if anything happens, they're in the next room," he said, pressing a kiss to my forehead.

"Goodnight, Alice," Caterpillar said, throwing an arm over me.

"I love you guys," I said, "I don't want to lose any of you." Tears pricked my eyes as the thought left my mouth.

"We aren't going anywhere," Caterpillar tried to comfort me.

"How can you be so sure?" I asked, turning to stare at him.

"I just do, princess," He responded, pulling me to his chest. "Sleep, it's only a couple more days until this will all be over."

"I love you too sweetheart," Hatter whispered, pressing a kiss to my head before he turned over to sleep. I stared at Caterpillar's chest as his breaths evened out. Once I was sure he was asleep, I finally forced myself to close my eyes. I knew the people I loved were safe for now, I would keep them that way.

Chapter 23

October 6th, 2157

I stood alone, staring up at the Red Party's base. The grey stone building blocked the sun from view. I wished I could feel the warmth of the sun on my face before this started. All my friends were in place, waiting for Cheshire's signal. I had spent the final hours before coming here talking to the people I loved. Dina was safely hidden with Mary Anne, watching over Lewis. Griffin had chosen to guard the house. Our final conversation had been a goodbye I wasn't prepared for, but all that mattered was Dina bringing their baby into a world that was safe. If everything went the way, it should we would all meet back at the base soon enough. "It's time." I heard through my earpiece.

My phone vibrated, and I pulled it out. "Hello." I whispered, watching as the first team of people went into the building.

"Ali, it's me." Mom said, I could hear all the emotions in her voice. "Please..." She trailed off. "You know what to do."

I had asked her to stay behind and oversee everyone's movements. "I love you." I said, before hanging up. I couldn't let my feelings distract me from my mission. We hadn't had enough time to reconnect, all I could do was hope that we would have the chance to after I defeated Penthea.

Shouting and gunfire came from the building, I rooted my feet to the ground. I couldn't go in too soon. I had to wait for Sammy's people to clear the Suits out, there wouldn't be many if what we knew about Sunday's was correct. If we stuck to the plan, we might succeed. Time crept by slowly, things had quieted down, but the signal hadn't been given yet. Caterpillar, Hatter, and Rab had gone to the Suits barracks in the ninth district of the city to stop any assistance as the rest of teams took control of the city. Penthea was my only responsibility, the longer I waited the less confident I became in my plan. Finally, I watched as Patrick stepped out, waving to me. I nearly leapt with joy when I saw his youthful face unharmed. Sammy didn't deserve to lose his son. I took several deep breaths and began making my way into the building. A few people nodded my way, as they escorted elite members of Red Party out. I grimaced at one of the men who had blood running from his nose, but I continued without comment. Jabberwocky's appearance threw me off. I could see the recognition in his eyes, two of Sammy's men held him as I walked by, he bared his teeth at me, and said, "I know you. You'll never win, remember even if today goes your way Wonderland will always belong to us."

"It was never yours to begin with," I snapped, a bit of my electricity jumping from my skin. Jabberwocky didn't respond as the men pulled him away from me, but the smirk on his face would haunt me for a long time.

The Red Party's base was torn apart from the hostile takeover. I'd argued that with Penthea in the building I should go in first, but it seemed Mom and Cheshire had been correct that she would wait to show herself. I slowly made my way up the stairs, my magick buzzed angrily as I approached the end of the hallway. "I was wondering when you would show up." A voice said to my left, causing the hairs on the back of my neck to stand on end.

"Penthea." I said, straightening my spine. My aunt stepped out of the shadows. Her hair was falling out of her tight bun, her skin was translucent, causing the red of her eyes to stand out harshly.

"You will not address me by that name," She snarled, stepping forward. "You think you've won, don't you? Attack the Queen at her weakest, and the rest of the government will fall." She ranted.

"You are not a monarch. Don't fool yourself." I snapped, not interested in her brand of insanity. What did she mean her weakest? I didn't have time to focus on the comment as she flew at me, nails scraping down my face. I hissed, kicking her away from me.

"Has your mother told you about your grandmother?" she asked, chuckling.

I rolled my eyes, but replied, "No."

"Mother was an idiot; even with magick she couldn't protect herself." I desperately wanted to know what kind of magick my grandmother might have had, but I didn't want to interrupt her tirade, at least it kept her distracted. "I loved my father, he worshipped me, as everyone should. Of course, I knew he was a cruel man, but he was intelligent. When she fell pregnant with Alcinda, my home was destroyed. Mother left Father, taking me to live with her lover, your grandfather. He was the mayor of Wonderland at the time. The public had taken to calling him the White King." She trailed off, her eyes glossing over. "Of course, I killed him once I was old enough to realize it was the only way for me to have the power I deserved. Mother was weak, I was the only person who could rule the government." she added, grinning at my look of horror. Her hands glowed red, and I had to jump away from her. She was slower than I would have expected so it wasn't that hard to escape her. The building was shaking hard, as she stalked my movements. I put small tendrils of magick out, letting them electrify the air, knowing she would walk right into the traps. When she hit one, her body stiffened, and she nearly dropped to the ground. I breathed a sigh of relief, pulling my daggers from the belt wrapped around my waist. "You know, you remind me of your grandfather. Such a sense of doing the right thing," She stood, shaking off the electricity, "Even when it will destroy you." She laughed hysterically. "He did this to me." She held her hands up, I could tell they were shaking uncontrollably, "Cursed me with his dying breath."

I furrowed my eyebrows, confused. "I killed him on a Sunday, while Mother and Alcinda were out, helping the poor," She sneered. "He said, I would feel all the pain I inflicted on others, every week for the rest of my life. I laughed in his face when he whispered that to me as he drew his last breath." A hand suddenly wrapped around my bicep, and I dropped my knees as agonizing pain shot through my body. I yanked my arm free and struggled to my feet. I slammed my back against the closest wall, taking several deep breaths. Hot, slick blood ran down my back, as if every wound she'd inflicted on me had reopened. I ignored it, grabbing her as she came at me again, pushing electricity into her. "Until a week later, when I found myself writhing on the ground, but that didn't stop me. Nothing will. His curse pushed me forward. Wonderland will always be mine." She screamed in my face, spit flying as if I had done nothing to her. "Your little shocks can't hurt me. I'm the Red Queen." Penthea ranted, I watched as she pulled more magick into her hands, making them glow a fiery red.

Fear caused my heart to beat faster. I ran up the hallway to avoid her. I knew she didn't need her hands on me to inflict pain, so I couldn't figure out why she wasn't attacking more. I raced down the stairs, luring her out into the open. I heard a sudden crash and a scream, before eerie silence reigned. I stood still for several moments expecting her to appear. When she didn't, I walked back up the stairs carefully, concerned she was waiting to attack. What I found shocked me, she was crumpled to the ground, convulsing. Her back bowed unnaturally, her mouth open in a silent scream, I could see tears leaking from her eyes. Even if she deserved every moment of this it was horrific to watch. Surprisingly the fit ended, and she was on her feet coming toward me before I could prepare myself. She grabbed my hand, but her power was weaker and while I felt the pain, I could push through it. I put my hand to her chest and sent electricity into her, before breaking away from her quickly.

She laughed, "I already told you, your little magick can't hurt me."

"But this can." I said, yanking my gun out of my pants, and firing two shots in her direction. I watched as she dropped to the ground, before slowly making my way over to her prone body. One shot had hit just below her ribcage, the other must have missed. I couldn't believe my plan to shoot her had worked, but I trusted my mother's instincts. She had only told me about the night before that I shouldn't rely on my magick to defeat her.

She giggled quietly, as I cuffed her hands. "I can't believe you didn't use magick," She whispered, staring up at me. "Your mother would have if she had your power."

"I'm not my mother." I replied, pulling her to her feet. Any magick she had left after her curse had drained away when I shot her. I walked out of the Red Party's base with her under my arm, a trail of blood behind us. She was unconscious when I handed her off to Patrick and his friends, "Have Lily and Idalia arrived yet?"

"They're coming in, probably five minutes out," He responded, before looking down at the prone body of my aunt. I didn't believe her injuries were actually life threatening. "You did it."

"I did," Allowing myself space to breathe for the first time in almost three months. It wasn't over yet though. I felt my phone ring and rushed to answer it.

"Alice." The voice was weak, but I could tell it was Cheshire.

"Ches what's wrong?" I asked, panicked.

"Did you get her?" he asked, ignoring my question.

"I did." I heard his sigh, "Cheshire you're scaring me, what's wrong?"

"I'm fine, Al. Finish this." he said.

"I'm going to send Hatter to you, babe." I said, knowing something was wrong. He didn't respond and I began to panic. "Cheshire, Ches. Come on, love." I yelled.

With no response I glanced toward Patrick panicked. "Have Lily and Idalia take her to the square; I have to find Cheshire." I didn't give them a chance to reply, before running out of the building. "Who was the last person to have eyes on Cheshire?" I asked, dialing Hatter.

Static filled my ear before I heard a male voice say, "Sammy."

"Ches has been hurt; I want everyone looking for him." I commanded.

Hatter answered, voice gruff, "Ello."

"Cheshire, we've gotta find him." I said.

"Stay calm Ali, we will find him." He replied, but I ignored him as I spotted Sammy, who was running toward me covered in blood.

"I... I left him. Suits came out of nowhere." He panted, hands on his knees.

"Where?" I demanded, gripping his shoulders.

"About a mile into the woods." He said, pointing down the path.

I left without a word, running. I knew I was close when I saw a Suit slinking through the woods. I grabbed him from behind, sending a series of shocks through him. I let his body drop the ground, I didn't care if I had killed him or not. I pushed through some bushes and found the clearing where Cheshire and Sammy had set up to monitor everyone's moments. Bodies littered on the ground. I could see a few men and women who were part of Sammy's crew, along with more Suits. Blood coated the ground and I panicked, not sure that I would be able to find Cheshire. "Cheshire, Ches... I'm here, baby, but I need you to do something so I can find you." I said, stepping carefully toward the center.

The clearing was silent for several seconds before I heard a quiet cough off to the right. As soon as I turned, I noticed his bright pink and purple head. I rushed over, dropping to my knees at his side. "Hey, you're going to be okay. Hatter should be here soon, he'll take you to Mary Anne, and everything will be fine." I said, tears filling my eyes.

"Al... I don't think I'm gonna make it." He whispered, his eyes dropping.

"You have to, I still haven't taken you out on that date." I said, trying to keep the pain of seeing him like this out of my voice.

"Where are we going to go?" he asked, as I pressed my hands over the wound in his chest.

"I think we should go see that newly released movie about the talking cat." I said, letting magick flow into my hands. I didn't have healing magick, but I had energy that I could share.

"I like that idea." he said weakly, closing his eyes.

"Wake up, Ches. You have to stay awake until Hatter gets here." I begged, pushing more energy into him.

He took a shallow breath and opened his eyes to look at me. The blue was slightly dimmer, and his skin was paling quickly from blood loss. I felt the moment his heart stopped, my tears dripped on his face, and I sobbed. "No, no, no, no," I knew the voice was mine, but all I could think of was bringing him back. I calmed myself enough to summon my magick. I carefully concentrated on just a small amount of electricity and pushed it into his chest right over his heart. If I could get his heart beating again there was a chance, we could save his life.

"Alice!" I heard Hatter shouting.

"Over here." I yelled back. Hatter appeared, followed immediately by Ilaria, March, and Sammy. Ilaria and Sammy had March in the middle of them, helping him walk. I continued to push magick into his chest, begging the Creator to let his heart beat again. Everyone stopped gathering around us.

"Alice..." The sound of Hatter's voice nearly broke me, but I didn't stop, I knew I could do this, "He's gone, sweetheart." I ignored him, willing Cheshire's heart to fill with blood, to hear him laugh again. My eyes blurred with more tears. I felt hands on my shoulders, looking up to see Hatter kneeling behind me. I tried once last time, unable to find my voice. When nothing immediately changed, I sat back, staring at the blood covering the ground.

"You did every—" Hatter stopped staring at Cheshire's body, "Oh my god. Alice look,"

I lifted my eyes to see Cheshire's chest rise once. Twice. Joy filled me, "It worked." I kneeled over him again, "Ches, you're not healed, Hatter is here, we're going to get you help." His eyes fluttered but he remained unconscious. I held his wrist feeling his pulse, it wasn't strong, but at least it was there.

"We'll stay with him, until Caterpillar can get the Hummer over here. Go, Lily and Idalia need your help. People are already gathering." Hatter ordered.

"I need to stay with him." I said, tears rolling down my face.

"We won't let anything happen to him, A-Ali." March spoke up, trying to limp to my side. I noticed the bandage wrapped around his thigh; blood had already started to soak through.

"You're hurt." I stated dumbly, as Sammy took my place.

"I'm fine, g-go it's time to be the leader of the Resistance." March replied.

"We shouldn't have done this." I said, glancing between March and Cheshire.

"No, we had to do this. You knew it was possible someone would get hurt. Ending the Red Party is worth a little pain." Hatter said, pulling me to my feet.

"Pain..." I trailed off, staring as Sammy pressed his hands into Cheshire's chest. I glanced down at my own hands covered in his blood. I knew exactly what I had to do. Pain was what had started all of this. "Please, don't let him die, Hayden." I begged, gripping his hands. I realized this was one of the first times I'd ever used his real name, but I didn't have time to dwell on it. We had already discussed the codenames.

"I'll do everything I can." He vowed, shooing me away.

I grabbed Ilaria, and whispered, "Keep them safe, this all means nothing if I lose them."

She nodded but didn't say anything as I left.

I jogged back toward the base and found my motorcycle. I jumped on and sped toward the town square. I had to swerve around crowds of people, who were gathering in the streets, making their way to the commotion in the center. I parked the bike behind an old-world statue. I had forgotten the name of the woman, but if I remembered correctly, she was the founder of Wonderland. My steps stopped, staring up at the woman. Something about her face sent tingles down my spine, but the sounds of a large murmuring crowd drew my attention away. I spotted Lily and Idalia standing up on the large fountain that sat in the middle of town. The Red Queen and the King of Hearts were bound at their feet. Someone had wrapped bandages around Penthea's midsection, and I was thankful. I didn't want to kill her. I made my way over, pushing past men, women, and children to get to them.

"Alice, is Cheshire, okay?" Lily asked, concern lighting up her eyes. I just shook my head at her, unable to keep my calm if she continued to stare at me with pity. Idalia handed me a megaphone, as I stepped up to stand beside them.

"Hello everyone. My name is Alice, I am the leader of the Resistance." I was surprised that the crowd was deadly silent as I made this announcement. "I am here to expose the corruption inside the Red Party," the crowd muttered, but no words stood out.

I took a deep breath, handing Lily the megaphone so she could continue as I laid my hands on the Red Queen. "My sister and I are magick users, taught by our mother. Alice has a special gift, one she's never used before, but today she would like to demonstrate it for you." Lily announced, looking at me. She was the only one who I had even mentioned this possibility to. I had sent her a text as I drove here, letting her know what I was going to do.

I pulled every ounce of magick I had into my hands, eyes widening as they glowed silver so brightly, I was forced to squint. I let the energy slither into my aunt whose eyes widened in horror as my magick touched her magickal core. I gripped it, imaging sinking my nails deep into the twisting, red ball of light, and yanked it out. Penthea bellowed as every ounce of her magick was ripped from her body. My own voice joined hers as her pain magick filtered into my own. Sharp indescribable agony shot through my entire body. My knees hit the cobblestone so hard it shook my teeth. I don't know how much time passed before I could open my eyes, but a gasp left me when I did. In my palms, a twisting ball of red and silver battled. I stared at it in awe, it was pure magick, fighting for dominance. I had no doubt mine would win, though I'd never used this gift in this way before. I could hear gasps from the crowd, as I turned to them, "Allow me to show you, her memories." I yelled, pushing the red and silver ball into the air. I watched as it expanded and morphed, showing scene after scene of horror. I saw the young face of my mother, twisted in pain. More images followed, full of people I didn't know, when Dina face filled the cloudy display, I flinched. All of these people had suffered at the hands of my aunt. I saw a few people puking, and I flinched as my own face appeared with the magickal bubble, twisted in pain.

The scenes ended, and the twisting ball floated back down toward me. I wrapped hands around it, surprised to find that it was cool to the touch. I watched as it absorbed into my skin, my silver finally purging the red. I felt peace as my magick settled back into its rightful place, no sign of Penthea's magick was left. I glanced down at her, tears fell from her eyes, and I wondered what it felt like to have all your magick stolen. I gulped knowing I shouldn't use this power often. "I only want to end all the suffering in our city. For those of you who can barely feed your families or find jobs, for those unjustly convicted to be released. For those who have lost everything to find happiness once again. I do not wish for power or anything from you, but peace." I said, feeling weak. The influx of power had drained me of energy, but I still had things to do. "I know these things will take time, but I hope you will give me that." I turned away from the crowd but added. "Your voices will be heard."

"Thank you." I heard a quiet voice say, as I walked toward my bike. I turned to find an elderly woman watching me.

"Do I know you?" I asked, looking into her face. An odd sense of recognition filling me.

"No, dear." She said, before disappearing. I stood in silence watching the spot she had disappeared from, wondering who she could have been. I could not pinpoint why she had been familiar, but there was no question in my mind that I knew her well.

"Alice watch out." I heard a voice scream; I turned just in time to see the knife that was meant for me plunge into Mary Anne's heart. Idalia and Lily ran toward us, as I caught Mary Anne before she could fall to the ground. Lily helped me ease her onto the ground. I grabbed the gun that was situated on Idalia's waist and turned to catch the masked man. My vision was red as I stalked him down the street, people clearing out of my way. I caught him, slamming his head into the concrete of the road, my booted foot keeping him on the ground.

I ripped the mask off the man, finding the Knave of Hearts snarling back at me. "We're coming for you Alice." He spat, right before I shot three rounds right into his chest. I felt nothing as I watched the light leave his eyes. I heard screams and gasps from the crowd, but I didn't care, only grief fueled me. I heard his final, dreadful words as I turned to check on Mary Anne, "You will never know peace."

"What are you doing here?" I asked Mary Anne whose breathing was too shallow.

"I came to help, Rab called to tell me Cheshire was hurt." She whispered, placing a hand on my cheek. "Take care of Roman. You are everything to them." It was only a moment before she took her final breaths, I sobbed, holding her head close to my chest. I hadn't known her for long, but she had become as dear to me as my own mother. Seeing her blood mixed with Cheshire's on my hands was more than my mind could take. A guttural scream left me, my skin burned, the ground shook slightly. I didn't have enough magick to try to restart her heart but some part of me knew it wouldn't work on her.

"Alice," Lily snapped me out of my horror, "We need to call Jonah, and get her body out of the street." Lily said, wrapping her arm around my shoulder. I stood and started to lift her body. Idalia and Lily immediately came to my aid. The three of us made our way to Idalia's car, laying Mary Anne gently in the back seat.

"Take her to the warehouse, we will all meet back there. I'm going to make some calls." I said, emotionless.

I dialed Caterpillar first "Hey, princess." He said, relief coating his voice.

"Mary Anne is dead." I said, tears filling my eyes once again.

"No, she's safe with Dina, Griffin, and Lewis." He denied.

"She saved my life." I replied, "Idalia and Lily are taking her to the warehouse, get to Rab he will need someone with him right now." I added, before hanging up.

"Alice are you okay?" My mother's panicked voice said, when she answered the phone.

"Mary Anne is dead; Cheshire and March are hurt. They're headed your way, take care of them. I'll be back later…I need time." I said, hanging up before she could respond.

I turned my phone off, and jumped onto my bike, heading to the one place I knew no one would disturb me. I couldn't face anyone right now, especially not Caterpillar and his uncle. I knew I would have to pay for all that I had done today. Even with the my aunt neutralized, it wasn't truly over. It may never be. Regret filled me, but I lost myself in the wind blowing through my hair, carrying my tears with it.

I sat with my knees pressed against the wall. A bottle of vodka rested between my legs, my eyes had run out of tears hours ago, but I couldn't bring myself to leave this room. The first rays of dawn were peeking into the bathroom. When I heard a series of noises, I knew that they had come to find me.

"Alice?" Hatter's voice floated through my grief-stricken haze.

"In here." I called back, in a voice I barely recognized.

The door creaked open, and I felt Hatter sit down behind me, wrapping arms around my middle. "Caterpillar is waiting in the car, sweetheart, he's been a wreck since you disappeared." He finally said.

"How is Rab?" I croaked.

"Doing as well as can be expected since he just lost his wife. Lewis and your mom haven't left his side, which I think has helped." Hatter replied.

"Cheshire?" I asked.

"Your Mom sedated him, but he's stable. He's lucky, the bullet only missed his heart by fraction of an inch." He explained. "Whatever you did worked, he's going to live."

I nodded along to his explanation, glad that Cheshire was okay, "And March?"

"He's fine, one of the Suits stabbed the femoral artery in his leg." Hatter said. We sat in silence for several more minutes before I finally decided it was time to leave. Hatter helped me to my feet, keeping a grip on my hand as we exited my old house. I turned taking on final look, knowing it was unlikely I would ever be back here.

Caterpillar jumped out of the car, as we came into view. He grabbed me, lifting my feet off the ground, holding me close. "You aren't allowed to leave like that again." he said, thickly. I felt wetness hit my shoulder, and realized he was crying, "Do you understand me? Never again. I needed you."

I started sobbing, my body shaking, and my breaths coming out in pants. "I'm so sorry, Roman, I'm so sorry I couldn't save her." I cried, grabbing handfuls of his grey shirt.

"It's not your fault." he muttered, cradling my head to his chest. Hatter soon joined our hug, sandwiching me between their larger bodies. I could feel his tears mixing with mine. I knew losing Mary Anne was like losing his mother all over again, guilt and sorrow warred inside of me. Even their warm bodies couldn't entirely take away the coldness I felt. We stood like that for what felt like an eternity, until rain started to pelt down on us.

"Let's go home." Hatter said, tiredly.

Chapter 24

October 14th, 2157

A week had passed since the raid on the Red Party. In that time, we had buried Mary Anne and several of the people who had joined us from the boonies. Sammy and Patrick had taken those deaths hard, I offered to pay for their funerals, and while they had accepted, we all knew it wasn't enough. Cheshire was still on bed rest, and sleeping for the most part, and March was on crutches. Dina was suffering from morning sickness, spending most of her time locked in her room with Griffin. I had spent a few days sleeping and crying, but I couldn't take much time to grieve or rest. We had started to have meetings on how to keep the city from falling into chaos. We were still having to hunt down higher members of the Red Party, as a few had escaped. I was trying not to worry, but now that the Resistance was in charge, we were stretched thin. Trying to help the citizens of Wonderland was far harder than the battle with the Red Queen had been. We hadn't found a new location to live in yet, thankfully Idalia and Ilaria didn't mind us staying at their warehouse for the time being. We needed to move into the city to be more accessible to everyone, but we all needed more time to recover and grieve.

I was in the midst of popping some popcorn for a movie night with my men, when the front door of the warehouse slammed open. I sighed, knowing that more than likely this was some new form of drama I would have to deal with.

"Alice, we found her trying to escape Wonderland." A burly, blonde man said, yanking Duchess forward.

I tried to remember his name, but eventually gave up, instead looking to Duchess.

"Um... Bring her upstairs with me." I said, padding toward the bedroom. My bare feet slapping the ground was the only sound that could be heard in the building, as most everyone was out trying to relax today.

I opened the door, smiling when I saw Hatter and March cuddled on the floor. My eyes drifted to Cheshire who had the bed to himself, propped up with six pillows, and throwing jellybeans into Caterpillar's mouth. It was a picture I wish I could capture forever, so I whipped out my phone and snapped the photo.

I coughed, drawing their attention, "We have company." I announced.

Caterpillar straightened trying to look serious, but it was impossible when the last jellybean Ches threw smacked into his cheek.

"Ma'am, what would you like us to do with. I can lock her up in the same facility as her parents." The man spoke up, looking uncomfortable.

Duchess looked terrified for a moment, before quickly covering it up. I felt pity well in my heart and knew I couldn't ignore my feelings.

"Stay outside for a moment, I need to discuss this with my boyfriends." I ordered, closing the door.

"Alice there's something you should know. Duchess is the one who called to give me the intel about the Caucus." Cheshire said, not meeting my eyes. "I know that was a trap, but I don't think she realized it was."

"Do you think she was on our side?" I asked, unperturbed by this new information. I couldn't dwell on the past if I wanted to enjoy the present.

"I think she was confused; I think her parents were abusive, but I also think any decisions made in this scenario are up to you." He said, locking eyes with me.

I turned to Caterpillar and raised a brow, silently asking his opinion.

"It's up to you. I don't have anything against her, but I can see where she might be a problem." he said, shrugging his shoulders.

Hatter spoke up, "Of all of us, I've spent the most time with her. I don't think she's a threat to anyone here."

I ignored the jealousy I felt at Hatter's statement, he might care for Duchess, but I knew it was innocent.

"I'm going to go talk to her. Keep the bed warm." I said, winking as I left the room.

"Come with me." I said, motioning for the guards to follow me with Duchess.

I entered the training area downstairs, knowing it was the safest place to speak with her.

"Leave us." I ordered the men away.

"We'll be right outside." One spoke. I nodded but waved him away.

I took in my cousin's appearance for a moment, from her short, tangled hair, to the dirty sweatpants she was wearing.

"If you're going to lock me up, you might as well get it over with." She snapped, but I could see the tiredness behind it.

"Are you a threat to me?" I asked, taking a seat on the bright blue mat, crossing my legs.

"What?" She asked, looking confused.

"Are you a threat to me?" I repeated.

"Why would I be? You have magick, and four men who barely leave your side." She said, and I could hear envy in her words, and I suddenly felt bad for her.

"I'm sorry if you feel like I stole Hatter from you." I said.

"You didn't, he's hot, but we would never have worked out." she said, mysteriously.

"Can you be trusted to be a part of our Wonderland society?" I asked.

"I've never hurt anyone." Duchess said.

"What's your real name?" I asked, standing.

"Vivica Rose." She answered, freely.

"Well, Vivica, I don't see any reason to treat you any differently than any other member of the former Red Party." Her eyes widened, and I thought I could detect some hope within their depths, "However, I would like you to stay here with us, at least until we can set you up with a job and a home." I added.

I started walking away, praying that I would make the right decision. "Thank you, Alice." I heard her whisper.

I smiled as I jogged back to my room, a weight lifting off my shoulders. I had thought about Duchess a lot, I couldn't imagine how she was treated by her own mother. Maybe we could become friends.

"Let's do this." I said, slamming the door open, and dropping into the bed beside Ches.

"I don't see why you want to watch this old show so much." Caterpillar said, rolling his eyes.

"Werewolves don't exist." Hatter chimed in.

"And none of us are teens." March added.

"I like it, especially the hot hunter girl." Cheshire said, grinning down at me.

I rolled my eyes at their banter, content to stay this way forever.

"I don't like the broody dude." Caterpillar said, leaning his back against my legs.

I made eye contact with Cheshire, right before we both started cracking up.

"What?" Caterpillar asked.

"Nothing, honey." I said, patting the top of his head.

Cheshire winked at me, before we all fell into a comfortable silence.

Hours passed as we devoured the snack food, and the entire first two seasons of the show.

"That's enough." Caterpillar said, yawning. "This old man needs to sleep." He added, stretching.

"Should I give you a sponge bath and tuck you in?" I asked, moving my legs so he could get up.

"Maybe later." he said, smirking.

"Well, there went my night." I said, standing to stretch.

"I'm sure we can find some way to save it." Caterpillar said, wrapping arms around me.

"None of that, you need to get to bed... old man." I said, ducking out of his arms.

"If it wasn't two o'clock in the morning, I would get you back for that," He said.

"Oh, I'm shaking in my boots," I said.

Arms wrapped around my back, trapping me, as Caterpillar made his way toward me, eyes lit with glee. I stomped on Hatter's foot, trying to have him release me, but he just flexed his arms.

"Let me go." I said, no heat in my voice.

"Hm. I don't think so." Hatter replied, as Caterpillar unbuttoned my jeans.

"This so isn't fair." Cheshire said, from the bed.

"Alcinda said restricted activity." Caterpillar said, before returning his attention to me.

"I like the view." March said. I turned my head toward him, as he sat in Cheshire's desk chair, with his leg propped up.

"You would." Cheshire shot back.

"How about you both shut up." I breathed out.

"So bossy." Caterpillar muttered.

"You of all people shouldn't—" My sentence was cut off, as he grabbed my face, wrapping fingers into my hair, before kissing me.

I wrapped a leg around his waist, letting Hatter and Caterpillar take more of my weight. When Caterpillar pulled away, I was breathless.

"Not so old after all." I said.

"I think that's all you, princess." Caterpillar said.

Hatter's hands moved down, gripping the bottom of my hoodie, and for the first time I noticed the slight silver glow already lighting up my skin.

"Back to the fun." Hatter said.

For the first time in a very long time, I was completely relaxed.

Caterpillar and Hatter had dragged another queen-sized bed into Cheshire's room, so we could all stay together. I found myself cuddled between Hatter and March, which was now a common occurrence when we slept together.

"I think we should all get married." Hatter said, breaking the silence.

I stared at his face in shock.

"What? We aren't going to live forever, we all love Alice, I don't see the issue." He defended.

"As often as I've said she's my wife," Caterpillar added, thoughtfully.

I thought for a moment, I wasn't ready to get married, but there was no question in my mind that the four men surrounding me, were the ones for me.

"Ask me again in a year." I said, ruffling his hair.

"I will." He said, grinning up at me.

Epilogue

One year later

September 20th, 2158

It hadn't taken quite a year for me to agree to marry the loves of my life. A lot had happened in that time. We had managed to find a comfortable apartment near the town square of Wonderland. Dina and Griffin had moved in down the hall from us. The rest of the Resistance had settled into peaceful and quiet lives, though they helped where they could. The citizens of Wonderland had a city-wide vote, electing me and Caterpillar to lead the city. I had tried to convince my mother to run, but she had refused. It hadn't been easy to adapt to leading instead of fighting, but in some ways, it was much the same. Unfortunately, Jabberwocky and a few other Suits had escaped from us in the chaos. We kept eyes out for any problems but so far none had occurred.

"I can't believe my little sister is getting married." Lily said, repeating herself for the tenth time today.

"I can. They've been talking about it for months." Idalia said, rolling her eyes. Ignoring them both, I fluffed the short, white dress I was wearing, twirling slightly. It was the same silk material as the dress I had been wearing the first time I met Hatter, even a similar cut.

Dina burst into the room; baby carrier strapped to her chest. "I'm here, bitches."

"Di, Elsie can hear you." Griffin chastised, putting a hand on their daughter's head.

"Have you met her godmother and godfathers; she'll be saying fuck by the time she's a year old." She shot back. When Dina had given birth, her daughter had quickly become the most spoiled child in all of Wonderland. At just over four months old, she already knew she had everyone around her, wrapped around her tiny fingers.

"Are you ready for this, Ali?" Griff asked, "Because you can always run away with me." He said, mirth filling his eyes.

"Griffin Earl Alexander." Dina said, her voice shrill. "Why would she want you, when she has the four hunks who are waiting for her at the altar?"

"Gee thanks, Dina. At least I know you married me, because I knocked you up." He shot back. I loved to watch the banter between them, ecstatic to see them so happy with their little family. They'd made a perfect couple, my best friends getting married was still one of the happiest days of my life. Not counting today, I'd grown even closer to my men in the year we'd worked together to erase the Red Party's influence from Wonderland. There was no doubt in my mind that marrying them would be the best day of my life. "Jonah is coming to walk you down the aisle. I've got to get out of here since I'm supposed to be with your soon to be husbands right now." Griff said, before quickly exiting the room. Jonah had struggled a lot since losing Mary Anne, but my mother had stayed with him. Lewis needing someone had been a good distraction from his grief. I had asked him to walk me down the aisle the day after Roman, Hayden, March, and Cheshire had proposed.

"We probably need to get in our places." Lily said, dragging Dina and Idalia out of the room.

I took several deep breaths, I wasn't nervous about marrying them, but something felt wrong. Almost as if it was wrong for me to be so happy so soon after we had lost so much. March still had to use a cane if he was walking very far. I don't think Jonah would ever be his jovial self again. "Alice, are you ready?" Jonah asked, distracting me from my thoughts. I nodded, looping my hand through his arm. "You look beautiful." He said, leaning to place a small kiss on my cheek.

"Thank you, Rab." I said, smiling. I wrapped my fingers tighter around the boutique of lilies, my sister had brought me to carry down the aisle.

"I'm honored you're letting me walk you down the aisle. I knew your father well, he would be so proud of the woman you've become," he said, bringing tears to my eyes.

"I'm so glad to be part of your family," I dabbed my tears away carefully careful to not mess the makeup I wore up.

I heard the wedding march begin to play, and we took the first steps into the chapel. It was filled with people who had come to wish us well. I spotted Tillie, sitting between Jackson and Cahir, smiling brightly at me. Her sister, Lacie was sitting with her five husbands, her twin boys waving at me frantically. Lacie had been a huge help when we had started to rebuild and had given me helpful tips for dealing with multiple partners. Duchess was sitting in the middle row, and nodded at me politely as I made eye contact with her. I wouldn't say we were friends, but things were getting better. We'd set her up to help organize supplies and ensure everyone in Wonderland had safe housing. She'd done a fantastic job, and I had hope that with more time we would become close. Mom was sitting in the front row, grinning back at me, tears brimming in her eyes. I stepped up onto the dais and had to hold back a laugh when Dina sent me a thumbs up. The officiant smiled and began his speech.

"Dearly beloved. We are gathered here today to witness the marriage of Alice Evangeline Young to Roman Cade Ainsworth, Hayden Matthew O'Hare, Maxton Brady Danara, and Sinclair Elijah Malone." At the sound of his name, Cheshire flinched slightly, and I smiled at him. "If anyone has any objections—" The officiant was caught off by a loud banging noise.

I saw Caterpillar and Cheshire reach for their weapons. I reached down, pulling my daggers out of my thigh holster. Even with a year of semi- peace none of us went anywhere without a weapon, not even our own wedding. Multiple armed men appeared, stationing themselves at the exits. Silence reigned until a woman with long, red hair appeared walking down the aisle toward me. Her rosy, round cheeks gave her a deceptively innocent appearance. The intelligence and arrogance shining on her face told another story.

Duchess was the first one to speak, "You old cunt, I was sure you were long dead. How dare you show your face in Wonderland."

"Now is that anyway to talk to your aunt, Vivie?" The woman responded; her voice raspy.

"Fuck you." Duchess responded, pulling her twin axes out from the sheath at her back. After that all hell broke loose, almost every person at the wedding pulled out their weapons moving to protect the children or their loved ones.

"Who are you?" I snarled, anger winning out as I stomped toward her.

"Why, Alice, dear. I'm the Queen of Hearts. I'm sure my sister-in-law must have mentioned me." The woman said, clapping her hands together.

"You've got to be fucking kidding me, right?" I said, rolling my eyes. Of all the times for a new enemy to show up, it just had to be my wedding.

"I assure you; I am not playing a prank." Her glossy red lips pursed as she took us all in, "Let's do this quickly. You have one chance to leave Wonderland, relinquishing it to me. If you do not, I will kill everyone in this room." The Queen of Hearts said, a cheery tone to her voice.

"Can I see what's behind door number two." I asked. I heard Hatter chuckle quietly but ignored it. I motioned to my mother behind my back, praying she would notice.

"Well, I guess we can do this the hard way." she said, walking away from me. Once she made it to the exit, she added, "Kill them all."

A flurry of things happened. Several gunshots went off, and I watched as a couple of the armed men dropped to the ground. I saw Lily grabbing the kids, and wrapping her golden shield around them, so she could get them out. I sent up a silent thanks to whatever Creator was out there, as I slung one of my daggers into the throat of a man who was running toward me.

I saw Jonah and Roman back-to-back fighting off four men. I noticed that Hatter was being overwhelmed, and I ran over shocking two of the men that were attacking him. "Thanks, sweetheart." He said.

"Anytime, love." I said, kissing his cheek. As I glanced around again, I didn't see any more armed men. I went to the dais, helping the officiant to his feet. "I think we'll have to reschedule. I'm very sorry." I offered him a sympathetic smile.

"Of course." He replied, but I could see how scared he was, if the shaking in his fingers was any indication.

I turned to see March making his way toward me, "Hey, baby, you doing okay?" I asked, wrapping my arms around his neck.

"My leg just h-hurts a bit. One of them stabbed me in the exact same spot again, but it's shallow." He said. I helped him into a chair and tore the leg of his pants open a bit, enough to see the blood flowing from his thigh freely. I took one of my daggers and cut the bottom of my dress off, tying it around his thigh to staunch the flow of blood.

"Why do they keep going for this spot?" I asked, wiping some blood away from his knee.

"Because I have a bit of a limp on that s-side now, it's an effective way to disable someone." He reasoned, kissing the top of my head. "Love you."

"Love you too."

I suddenly felt a hot feeling rush through my abdomen, followed by pain. "Ali, what's wrong?" March asked.

I couldn't answer so I stood, only for March to gasp and yell for Hatter. I glanced down, and found that my white dress was stained red with my blood. "I got shot." I said, swaying on my feet. Shock masking the pain I should have been feeling.

"I kn-kn-know," March said, helping me to lay back on the floor.

"Oh my god." I heard Cheshire say, right before he fell to his knees beside me. "Listen, Al. I know weddings are supposed to be exciting, but not like this."

"You're always so sassy when you're nervous." I said, patting his cheek.

"Alice." Caterpillar said, rushing to my side. "Princess?" He asked, I couldn't form words, around the pain blossoming.

"Sweetheart?" Hatter said. I felt him pull my head into his lap, and I blinked up at him. His green eyes were shiny with unshed tears, and I wanted to sit up to make him feel better.

"I'm…. fine" I muttered, reaching to touch my men. "I want you all to know I love you. You've stood by me even when you knew it could mean the end of any one of our lives…" I trailed off pain shooting through me. "I have never loved anyone any more than I love the four of you." I saw tears run down each of their faces, and I wished I could heal myself, so I didn't have to watch them cry. A giggle escaped as I realized that after all of my hard work I was going to die before I could enjoy a peaceful Wonderland. I felt hands on my arm and midsection trying desperately to staunch the bleeding. I was too weak to speak as I saw my mother approach.

"You can save her," Hatter begged.

"No," Lily said, grabbing my mother's shoulder, "She'll die, and there's no guarantee it'll save Alice. Healing magick requires balance."

"That's bullshit," He responded, I turned my head toward him, my eyes going wide as I saw a white glow cover him.

"Hatter…" Cheshire followed my line of sight.

Everyone stared for a moment, my mother was the next to speak. "Hayden, place your hands over Alice's heart, and picture energy flowing into her body."

White hot fire burned through my body; I arched my back to relieve some of the pain. "Sit still." Caterpillar commanded.

"Go to hell." I ground out, glad to have found my voice again.

"There's my girl." Cheshire said.

Hayden's hands slid away as my pain subsided. Caterpillar ripped open my dress revealing a bright pink scar, as if I had been shot weeks ago. I sat up, finding Hatter half conscious, his hair looked as if someone had bleached part of the color from it. White and silver threaded through his long, dark tresses.

"You're hurt." Cheshire said, as I reached toward Hayden.

"No, I'm not." I said, pushing him out of my way.

"He drained himself completely," Mom said, her hands over his heart.

"Is he alive?" I asked, panicked.

"I've never seen anything like this, he's alive, but we need to get him somewhere I can look him over better."

"You're, okay?" Hayden wheezed out as I took his hand.

"I'm fine, but I'm so furious with you right now I could spit fire." I replied.

"I'll be fine." He coughed out.

"Please don't ever do it again, I'm not ready to lose you again." I whispered, hugging him, "How can we get married if you die."

Jonah and Roman lifted Hayden between them. "We need to get to the safe house. I imagine they've hit the base and city building as well." Roman said.

"We will get married, Alice." Hayden whispered to me as I helped him into the Hummer.

I was worried that getting married wasn't going to be our biggest problem anymore. We had a new enemy to fight, and we knew nothing about them. I spent a moment watching the four men I had fallen in love within the midst of this war. I knew the bad feeling I had felt earlier was a warning of what was to come. The war had only just begun.

Acknowledgements

First, I must acknowledge the people who brought me into this world. My family has supported me in every way they could, and I cannot thank them enough for everything they have done throughout my life. Thanks Dad, Papaw, Whitneigh, Ashley, and even little Teagan.

I want to thank Tyler, my wonderful fiancé, who while not a reader himself has supported my reading and writing so much. You pushed me forward when I was certain I would give up.

I also want to mention Jacob and Aleena, you were there for almost every version of Code Red, without your support I would never have made this a book worth reading. So many more people read, supported, listened, and helped me along this journey. Without all of you, I would never have reached my dreams. I also want to thank Leah, my cover artist, who had so much patience with me while I learned how to navigate self-publishing.

Last, as any ego-driven person would, I'd like to thank myself. I still cannot believe I've gotten all the way here, it was a long journey, and while I did not do it even nearly by myself, I have to acknowledge my own hard work.

About the Author

Taila has always had an obsession with stories, cultivated by a loving grandmother. She always had her nose in some book or another, but at fourteen she began writing her own stories. Code Red may be the first to publication, but you can expect many, many more to come. Taila lives in the hills of East Tennessee. Where she can often be found cuddling naughty kittens, reading, or working her day job. Occasionally, her family or partner will convince her to leave her cave to see the outside world.

If you want to chat with Taila or stalk the socials for book updates:

Facebook Page: Taila Cantrell Author

Facebook Group: Taila's Writing Wonderland

Twitter (X): @tailatalks

Instagram: tcantrellauthor

TikTok: @tailatalks

Coming Soon

Blue Dreams (Reclaiming Wonderland #2) Coming 2025